ALSO BY KATHERINE KOVACIC

Kill Yours, Kill Mine

Ms. Fisher's Modern Murder Mysteries

Just Murdered

True Crime

The Schoolgirl Strangler

The Alex Clayton Art Mysteries

The Shifting Landscape

Painting in the Shadows

The Portrait of Molly Dean

PRAISE FOR KATHERINE KOVACIC

Seven Sisters (Australian title for *Kill Yours, Kill Mine*)

SHORTLISTED FOR BEST CRIME FICTION IN
THE 2023 NED KELLY AWARDS

"[This] taut, morally ambiguous thriller measures out a precise cocktail of parable and revenge fantasy."

—*Sydney Morning Herald*

"A love letter to Hitchcock and Highsmith, fueled by women's rage. Once you start, you won't be able to stop."

—Hayley Scrivenor, bestselling author

"An intense, page-turning psychological thriller that grips the reader with two-handed fury. Perfect for fans of Patricia Highsmith, Candice Fox, and Jacqueline Bublitz, *Seven Sisters* will have you questioning your idea of justice and how far you would go to help others—including taking an eye for an eye."

—*Books+Publishing*

"A cracking thriller that I could not put down for a second... This is a chilling, compelling, and completely addictive descent down the rabbit hole."

—Dinuka McKenzie, author of the Detective Kate Miles crime fiction series

"Compelling reading! *Seven Sisters* is the ultimate fight-back novel."
—Vikki Petraitis, award-winning true crime author

Just Murdered **(A Ms. Fisher's Modern Murder Mystery)**

"A sprightly pace, amusing characters, and a vividly rendered Melbourne bode well for the sequel. Fans of Kerry Greenwood's Phryne Fisher series will want to check out this one."

—*Publishers Weekly*

"A splendid read with an authentic '60s flavour. I recommend it unreservedly."

—Kerry Greenwood, award-winning, international bestselling author

"Based on the hit TV sequel, this has all the pizzazz of the Phryne Fisher novels updated for a younger generation."

—*Kirkus Reviews*

"A fun, fast-paced read, *Just Murdered* also has a great heroine. Peregrine is intelligent and independent, and her jack-of-all-trades background allows her to cleverly unspool the threads of the mystery."

—*BookPage*

NO GOOD DEED

NO GOOD DEED

KATHERINE KOVACIC

Cover design by Danielle Christopher
Cover image © Ian Hitchcock/Shutterstock

Published by Poisoned Pen Press, an imprint of Sourcebooks
1935 Brookdale RD, Naperville, IL 60563-2773
(630) 961-3900
sourcebooks.com

Cataloging-in-Publication Data is on file with the Library of Congress.

Printed and bound in the United States of America.
PAH 10 9 8 7 6 5 4 3 2 1

This one's for you, Papa.

'No pressure, no diamonds.'

—THOMAS CARLYLE (1795–1881)

ONE

The afternoon sun was in Rena's eyes as she blasted down the Great Northern Highway. Halls Creek was a memory in the rearview mirror, Fitzroy Crossing—her destination for tonight—still a good hour and a bit away. Either side of the road was red earth, yellow grass, and scattered low trees and shrubs, a magnificent expanse as potentially hostile as it was beguiling. She passed a bus stop in the middle of nowhere, no sign of a building save for the shelter itself. No place for people to come from to catch a bus that was maybe no more than a phantom, a dream of travelling somewhere, to a place with other life, other voices to break the silence.

The vastness of the cloud-flecked azure sky stretched above her, a reminder of her own insignificance, of the infinite cosmos. On this straight stretch of road, the highway simply carried on until it reached the horizon's vanishing point, tipping into nothingness.

At least, that was how it felt until she saw the black smudge ballooning up from the earth, blurring the line between terrestrial and celestial. It was slightly to the left of the road, and it seemed to get thicker and darker as she approached, rolling forward to meet her like a malevolent host.

Rena eased her foot off the accelerator slightly, letting the Ford Ranger drop back a bit from the 110-kilometre-an-hour limit, but she was still travelling at speed when she flashed past and saw the source of the dense smoke: fire, orange flames shooting into the air from a point a couple of hundred metres off the side of the road. Then she spotted the track. Rena hit the brakes without thinking, only checking the rearview when it was too late. Luckily, there was no one on her tail; hers was the only vehicle on the road right now. Rena's relief at not being rear-ended immediately turned to disquiet: she was also a long way from help.

Another mirror check and she slammed the camper into reverse, backing up until the mouth of the track appeared, barely more than a break in the spinifex. She swung the wheel and pulled off the highway, following a line that meandered around termite mounds and woollybutts—the dominant eucalypt—while roughly following the bank of a dried-out creek. Now she could see the fire directly ahead. Whatever it was, it was burning strongly, and Rena felt a surge of adrenaline.

Maybe it was just louts. They'd found some tyres or piled up some rubbish, set it ablaze and were probably long gone now. That is, if they weren't sitting around with a slab of cold beer, enjoying the pyrotechnics.

Then the smoke cleared briefly, and Rena saw it: a four-wheel drive, being consumed by fire. It was skewed diagonally, rear wheels still on the track in front of her, nose buried in the creek bed. She registered blistered royal-blue paint and the shape of a blackened number plate, but the flames billowing behind cracked windows obscured her view of the interior.

Rena brought her own vehicle to a stop at a safe distance, but even so, she could feel the intensity of the blaze the moment she stepped from the cab and held up an arm, shielding her face.

'Hello?' she yelled above the crackle and pop of the fire, the groan of metal under stress.

No response. Rena ducked around to the passenger side of her Ford Ranger, retrieved the small fire extinguisher from beneath the front seat, then advanced on the flames.

This close, her nostrils were assaulted by the smell, a pungent mix of rubber, chemicals, and an assortment of unidentified odours that stuck in the back of her nose and throat. Had the fuel tank already ruptured? She knew that if there had been propane or some other compressed gas, the whole thing would have gone up by now, but in the absence of those accelerants, the fuel tank might be intact. But even if there was still a risk of a petrol fireball, it didn't matter; there was no chance Rena would just walk away. At the very least, she had to stop the fire from spreading.

She scrambled down into the creek bed and walked a wide arc around the front of the four-wheel drive. The vehicle had come to rest in a way that meant the grille was visible and Rena could make out the Toyota logo, devil's horns glowing white with heat. By contrast, the cab's interior was an unknown, its depths entirely obscured behind the blackened glass of the windshield. A burst of flames drove her back a few steps, and she turned her head from the heat and light. When she looked back, she noticed the driver's side door for the first time.

It was hanging open.

'Hey!' She shouted as loudly as she could. 'Anyone here? Hello?'

Rena moved around the open door of the Toyota, one eye on the fire, the other scanning the surrounding landscape, hoping to see the driver. She looked back in the direction of the highway, just visible between billows of smoke, but if there had been any other vehicles, they'd kept on driving. Pulling the pin from the extinguisher, she swung back to the Toyota, covered the last few metres in quick strides and blasted foam into the cab, beating back the flames. Steam and white smoke billowed.

'Shit!' Rena's stomach heaved and she swallowed heavily, forcing herself forward another step, emptying the meagre contents of the extinguisher into the belly of the fire.

A new smell had hit her, from the fire but not of it. Meat. Barbecue.

And with the flames in slight abeyance, she could see its source.

The driver, still behind the wheel, head turned towards her, blackened mouth open in a silent scream.

TWO

Rena half-ran, half-stumbled back to her Ranger, wrenched the door open, and slid into the seat. Snatching up the UHF radio's mic, she tuned the unit to channel 5, the emergency frequency.

'Urgent, urgent. Medical assistance required. National Highway west of Halls Creek, over.' Medical was a massive stretch at this point, but she didn't know what else to say. She thought of the phone. A direct call to triple zero would be better, but there was no signal for her regular mobile and the satellite Wi-Fi hot spot device—the only way to get a signal out here—was powered off and stowed away. The UHF would be faster. She made a mental note to keep the satellite connector somewhere more accessible in the future.

Rena waited, leaning into the UHF radio, listening to the hiss and crackle of empty air. Then she repeated the message. Still nothing. Rena keyed the mic again, ready to transmit a third time before changing frequencies, when she got a response. A volunteer from Radio Rescue Emergency Communications had heard her call. Rena gave her coordinates and clarified the situation, then abandoned the radio, relying on the anonymous operator to get things moving.

It felt like an eternity, but in reality, less than an hour passed before Rena saw the approaching red-and-blue flashers of a police car, closely followed by a fire engine. Out here in the Kimberley, that was the equivalent of ten minutes in the city. With her meagre extinguisher, Rena had no chance of putting the fire out by herself, but she'd kept an eye on the perimeter, dousing flare-ups with water from her supplies or stomping on anything that looked like it might get away into the grass and trees.

She'd already moved her Ranger to give better access to whoever turned up, and now Rena stood at a distance, watching the fireys do their thing, while two cops hovered, waiting like vultures for their chance at the Toyota and its occupant. They'd called some information in to their station not long after arriving, then spent a bit of time pacing up and down the track, crouching in the red dirt once or twice, gesticulating, pointing, nodding. Rena couldn't hear what they were saying, but the conversation was easy to subtitle, their conclusions obvious even from afar. Just where the ruined Toyota lay, the creek bed and the track beside it took a sharp turn, veering off almost at right angles. It seemed the driver had missed the corner and then something—a fuel leak, an electrical fault, even a dropped cigarette—had turned bad luck into tragedy. It wasn't the first time Rena had dealt with an accident in the remote outback, but those had been manageable: broken bones, lacerations, even a snakebite. Nothing like this.

She took a swig of water, trying to wash the taste of smoke from her mouth and throat, but it was all-pervasive—nose, clothes, hair...not to mention the image of the charred corpse seared into her mind. She closed her eyes, feeling the smoky sting. When she opened them again, one of the cops was walking towards her.

'So you're sure you don't know who that is?' The officer hooked a thumb back at the blackened shell of what had once been a Toyota.

'I'm sure.' Rena had already told the coppers her story, from the moment she'd spotted the smoke to calling for help. 'Don't you just run the rego? The plates looked…almost legible.' She gestured towards the smouldering wreck.

'Yeah, but…' The officer hesitated, scratched behind one ear, then sighed. 'Suppose it doesn't matter if I tell you. It's come back registered as a company car. Gunna take us a bit longer to get an ID.'

Rena thought about the person in the driver's seat. She hoped he—was it even a he?—was already dead or unconscious when the Toyota went up. She remembered the open car door and shuddered.

'So what, you just pulled off the road and there it was?'

Rena snapped her attention back to the cop and gave him a proper once-over. Clean shaven, sun-bleached blond hair cut close, lean and whippety: the physique that comes from playing footy rather than lifting weights. His blue eyes were hidden behind large sunglasses now, but Rena had seen them earlier, wide with shock as he stumbled away to vomit in a bush. The kid was just doing his job.

'I didn't just pull off the road. Like I said, I saw the smoke and came to check.'

'Why?'

'Because that's what civilised humans do. They check to make sure others are okay. And if they're in country like this and they see smoke, they also do their best to make sure whatever it is doesn't turn into a bloody great grassfire.' Rena spoke as calmly as she could, but it had been a shit of a day, and she couldn't keep the sting from her tone.

But, surprisingly, the baby copper seemed to respond to the mild rebuke. His mouth turned down at the corners in a way that said, *Makes sense*, and he let out a small *humph* of acknowledgement.

That was the thing about grey-haired women. People either assumed you were senile or, very occasionally, they realised you might actually know what you were about. Rena had no time for bullshit generally, but being dismissed because she was sixty-something really pissed her off. She'd spent half her professional life proving herself in a masculine industry and she had no intention of going soft in retirement. Rena took a steadying breath, letting go of the mild aggro that'd been brewing.

'You've got my details,' she said. 'Can I go now?'

'You said you'd be in the district for a few days?'

Rena shrugged. 'I hadn't planned to be around longer than a day, but I can be.'

'Thank you, Mrs Novak. In that case...we'll be in touch.' He raised a finger to the brim of his police baseball cap and started to turn away.

'Hang on. You've still got my driver's licence.'

'Oh, sorry.' The cop fiddled around with his notebook and retrieved the laminated card, glancing at it again as he handed it over. 'You're a long way from Melbourne.'

'Yeah, well. You retire, you've got time to take a bit of a trip.'

'Drive like that is more than a bit of a trip.'

Rena stowed her licence back in its wallet slot. 'I guess it's *the* trip. Trip of a lifetime.' Before the conversation could go places she didn't want it to go, Rena nodded a sombre farewell and made for the Ford, feeling the baby-faced cop's eyes on her the whole way.

Minutes later she was driving back along the red-soil track. At the point where track met highway, she waited while a couple of camper vans and a double trailer thundered past before pulling out and heading for Fitzroy Crossing.

'Poor bastard,' she said.

It was a shit of a way to go, but as Rena knew very well, sometimes in life—and death—you couldn't avoid the shit.

THREE

Rena's Ford Ranger was not your average ute. Sure, it had the high and low four-wheel drive, upgraded suspension, and all-terrain tyres, but more importantly, it had been customised—completely fitted out for camping. Years ago, when travelling around Australia was nothing but an idea for the time when retirement became reality, Rena had envisaged a motor home, or at the very least, towing a flash caravan. But as the plan evolved, the limitations of that sort of equipment became clear. There'd be no Canning Stock Route, Gibb River Road or Tanami Track in a motor home, no spontaneous turns onto paths less travelled with a caravan bumping along behind. No deep silence of a night in the desert, blanketed only by star-filled sky above.

Hence the Ranger. From the solar panel and hardshell rooftop tent to the built-in kitchen with fridge, eighty-litre water tank, fold-down table, and LED lighting, it had everything needed for complete, remote camping. Basically, she had the freedom to drive just about anywhere and set up in a matter of minutes. But tonight she wanted a decent shower, and the best chance of that was one of the caravan parks at Fitzroy Crossing.

She scored a spot at the first place she tried, the Fitzroy River Lodge. A member of staff directed her past the heavily occupied powered sites to a spot that was blissfully quiet, and in less time than the paperwork had taken, she'd unpacked and arranged a basic camp; the awning could wait until tomorrow. With a towel over her shoulder, thongs on her feet, and sponge bag in hand, Rena made for the amenities block.

There was only one other woman in the disinfectant-scented showers, and she was just leaving. Rena stepped into a cubicle and undressed, sighing with relief as she unhooked her bra and cast it aside. Then she undid her thick hair from its customary plait. She had worn it the same way for years and wasn't about to change just because it had turned grey. The water pressure wasn't great, but at least it was hot, and luckily for Rena, there was no line of impatient people waiting for a shower. It took a while and a lot of soap and shampoo before she'd managed to scrub the smell of fire from her skin and hair.

Finally feeling somewhat more human, Rena started back to her ute, aware of the fatigue in her limbs, weighing up whether she could be bothered cooking or if she should go to the bistro for dinner and a chilled wine. She was walking along a fully occupied row of powered sites when a kid whipped past on a bicycle, coming from behind, a deliberate close shave designed to startle. The little bastard kept going but turned his head back, looking for Rena's reaction at the same moment a man emerged from a motor home. Dressed in running gear, he was looking over his shoulder, talking to someone back inside the RV as he stepped onto the path.

'Watch out!' Rena shouted.

The man leapt backwards, tripped over a neighbouring tent's guy rope and fell arse-first in the dirt while the kid swerved, nearly lost control, then managed to recover before disappearing around the corner.

'Shit,' the man said as he sat up.

Rena hurried forward. 'Are you okay?' She offered a hand and helped him to his feet. Close-cropped blond hair, freckled skin, runner's toned physique, and a strong grip. Not young, but not as old as her.

'I think... Ow!' The man stumbled slightly. 'My ankle. Not to mention my dignity.'

'Given you managed not to scream swear words at that kid, your dignity is doing fine. Come on.'

With the man leaning on her arm, Rena helped him hobble back to the RV, a late-model Tiffin Allegro Breeze, the last word in luxury.

'Babe!' He called out.

'Adam?' Another man appeared in the doorway. Shaggy, grey-streaked brown hair framed a broad face, and smile lines radiated from the corners of his dark eyes. Rena placed him a few years younger than her own sixty-five. 'My God, Adam! What happened?' He bounded down the stairs.

'I'm okay, I think.' Adam let go of Rena's arm and took a step, then let out a hiss of pain.

The other man hurried forward, wrapping a protective arm around Adam, casting a questioning look at Rena.

'Kid on a bike,' she said. 'Hope it's nothing a bit of ice and rest won't fix. Do you have a first aid kit?'

'Yes, we've got all that. Or we could head in to the emergency department?'

Adam shook his head. 'No. I don't think it's that serious.'

'In that case, I'll leave you to it.' Rena smiled and started to turn away.

'Wait! What's your name?' Adam asked.

'Rena. Novak.'

'Thanks for the warning shout and for picking me up out of the dirt, Rena. I'm Adam, and this is my husband, Michael. Mike.'

'Pleasure to meet you both. Circumstances aside.'

'The least we can do is offer you a drink,' said Mike. He tilted his head towards the RV's door.

Rena hesitated, a combination of unwillingness to intrude and dislike of superficial chat. But she didn't want to be rude, and it solved her wine dilemma.

'Thanks,' she said, and followed them inside. 'Holy—' she gasped, surveying the RV's interior.

'Yeah, she's pretty plush.' Adam hobbled to the sofa and dropped with a sigh of relief.

'You're not kidding.' Rena stared unashamedly, taking in everything from the dining area fitted with bespoke wood-finish cabinetry through to the bedroom, and what looked like a queen-size bed.

Mike was rummaging in the fridge. 'Ice for you.' He gently tossed a frosty blue pack to Adam, who had already taken off his shoes and was probing his puffy right ankle. 'And alcohol all round. Are you okay with a white, Rena? Margaret River sav blanc?' he said, holding out a bottle.

'Perfect.' Rena sat on the edge of one of the banquettes.

Mike set them all up with wine, then returned to the fridge. In a matter of minutes, he'd assembled a plate of assorted nibbles, which he set on the table in front of Rena. 'You'll stay for dinner?' It was less a question than a statement of fact.

'Mike, don't be so bossy. Rena's probably got someone waiting for her.' Adam rolled his eyes. 'He's a doctor, used to having everyone do as he says.'

'Retired doctor now.' Mike sat next to Adam, took his partner's foot into his lap, and began examining the injury. 'Sorry, Rena.'

Rena shook her head. 'Don't be sorry. And there's no one waiting.'

'You're travelling alone?'

'Yes, I am.' Rena took a sip of wine.

The two men exchanged a swift glance.

'In a non-threatening, non-Wolf-Creek-psycho-killer, just-retired see-the-world-solo traveller kind of way.'

'Oh, God! I never thought that! It's more a woman alone out here and...' Adam reddened.

'Yeah, I'm just a feeble old lady, waiting for someone to come along and scam me or murder me in my sleep. Don't worry, I'm pretty good at looking after myself.'

There was a moment's silence, then Rena grinned.

'Well, cheers to smashing stereotypes!' Adam tilted his wine-glass towards her.

'What about the two of you?' Rena asked.

'Both also recently retired. We sunk our savings into this baby,' Adam patted the wall behind him. 'Rented out the house in Sydney, and here we are.'

'What did you do before you retired?'

'Defence Force.' Adam turned to Mike. 'I'm starving. We'd better start cooking something or I'll eat too much of this cheese.'

Rena recognised the conversational diversion; it was something she was quite good at herself. She offered the only neutral topic she could think of. 'I came across a car fire today, just off the highway.'

'What? Engine fault, that sort of thing? Everyone okay?' Mike stood up again, moving across to the kitchenette.

'Actually, no. Some sort of accident or fuel leak, I guess.' Rena frowned as she said it, a memory of the scene she couldn't quite recapture. She shook her head, chasing away the errant thought. 'The police are investigating.'

'Police?' Mike turned, a Tupperware container in his hand. 'So someone was hurt?'

Rena winced.

'Oh.' He leaned back against the kitchen bench.

'As far as they could tell, only the driver was in the car.'

'As far as they could tell,' Mike echoed bleakly. 'So it was that bad.'

'Sorry. I shouldn't have said anything. I'm not much good when it comes to small talk anymore. Too much time in my own company.' Rena took another mouthful of wine then set her glass down. 'Perhaps I should go.'

'Don't be ridiculous; stay where you are. After today, you definitely need company, and of course it came up—it must be preying on your mind. Finish your drink while I make pasta.' Mike smiled warmly at her.

'Just do what he says, Rena; it'll save time,' said Adam 'And we're a pretty unshockable pair. More likely to make a bad taste comment than take offence.'

Rena stood. 'Okay, but if I'm staying, at least put me to work.'

After that, the conversation turned to the usual grey nomads subjects: what are you driving, where have you been, where are you going, highlights, places to avoid, funny stories. It took them through to coffee and fruit cake, becoming more convivial as the evening wore on and they found common ground. Rena was regaling her hosts with a story about how she'd stopped a pub brawl in Broken Hill, and as Adam and Mike cried tears of laughter, she made a misstep.

'My son had a fit when I told him. Scolded me like I was one of his kids.' She sighed, leaning back in the very comfortable chair.

'You have a son? Grandkids?' Adam asked, cradling his coffee mug.

'One son, three grandchildren.'

Music and voices filtered in from outside as the campground wound down for the night. Inside the motor home, it was quiet.

'You're wondering about my husband.' Rena said quietly.

'Not our business.' Mike shook his head.

'It's okay.' Rena never talked about it—not to people she barely knew—but she felt comfortable here. She felt...able to speak.

'My husband's name is Tom. Married forty years.'

Mike and Adam murmured their appreciation, but she knew they were waiting for the rest.

'The round-Australia thing was our retirement dream. Tom had the route all mapped. I pushed work out for an extra year so we'd have a bit more money, splash out when we wanted.' She stopped, picked up her mug and found it empty, stared into its depths and returned it to the floor by her chair. 'But he died.'

Someone sucked in a harsh breath, but Rena didn't know who.

'There one week, and then the next... It was doubly awful—and ironic in a way—because we were close to hitting the road, so he literally spent the last month of his life saying goodbye to everyone we knew. Didn't know it really was the last goodbye, until it was too late.' She dashed away the tears that had sprung to her eyes.

'Oh, Rena.' Adam leaned forward, reducing the space between them but not pushing.

'The last thing he did'—Rena's voice caught but she had to finish now—'was make me promise to do the trip we'd planned. And to enjoy every minute. Not sure how I'm doing with that part.'

She looked at their faces, seeing the pity there, and for once, not resenting it quite so much.

'Well. Sorry to bring the mood down with a crash after such a lovely evening. Thanks for dinner and the conversation, but I'd better go.'

'You don't have to. Stay. Have another coffee,' said Mike.

'No. Thank you, but it's late anyway.' She nodded at Adam. 'Hope that ankle is better soon.'

'It's feeling a bit better already.' Adam stood, testing his weight on it.

Rena moved to the door, open except for the screen, which she now unlatched. 'Thanks again. Might see you if you're staying here a couple of nights.'

'We'll be here at least one more night.' Mike stretched his arms out in front of him then got to his feet, putting an arm around the other man.

'Might depend on this ankle. I want to be able to do my share of the driving,' said Adam.

Rena nodded. 'Well, I hope I can cook you a meal sometime. If not here, then maybe somewhere else on the road. Good night.'

She stepped out, feeling the slight coolness creeping into the evening air, and turned towards her own campsite. Why had she told them about Tom? The thought occupied her as she walked slowly down the row of motor homes and caravans. Had she drunk too much, or was this a new part of the grieving process? She knew about Kübler-Ross and the stages of grief, but Rena thought she was still too full of anger to be at the acceptance stage of things. Maybe today's death had shaken things up more than she cared to admit. She stopped walking as the scene inside the Toyota's cab flooded back: the blackened corpse, the smell and… Again, something snagged in her memory. The open door bothered her, but there was something else.

'Blast.'

She was tired, slightly tipsy, and a bit emotional. There was no point chasing the errant thought. Rubbing the back of her neck, Rena stepped forward again, quickly covering the short distance back to her camper.

Fifteen minutes later she climbed the ladder into the rooftop bunk and zipped the fly screens. Ten more minutes and she was out like a light.

Several hours passed, and somewhere in the strange in-between time when yesterday has faded but today is merely a suggestion, Rena sat bolt upright.

The gearstick.

The Toyota's cab had been a wreck, the dash warped and melted, and the horrifying sight of the driver had filled Rena's vision and her thoughts. But beyond the corpse, the gearstick.

It was fixed in neutral.

FOUR

Rena twisted the vision in her mind's eye, assessing her own responses. Was it real? Something she'd actually seen, or just a random notion tossed to the troubled surface of her conscious brain? She felt the rightness of the memory in her gut.

It was the sort of feeling she used to get when she was working in the field, and the geological structures and rock types all began to sing the same tune. That was the point when she started taking soil samples, when she knew with a high degree of certainty that this was the place she would find what she was looking for, whether that was gold, coal, minerals, or something else.

She wasn't imagining it about the gearstick.

From her bed atop the Ranger, Rena looked out at the night, nothing more than a paler shade of ink beyond the flyscreen. The police would know about it; they must've noticed. But just in case, she'd talk to them first thing.

'You'd make me go to the cops, wouldn't you, Tom?' She smiled, picturing her handsome, dark-haired husband. He had been instrumental in shaping her moral compass, because for the forty years they'd been married, Rena had always tried to be at least half the person he was, and there was no one like Tom. Even now, she still felt surprised that she'd been lucky enough to be married to him. Tom always teased her, saying it was her figure—five feet eight inches tall and curvy hips—that he'd first noticed, but the dark eyes and wide grin that made him look again. For Rena's part, the moment Tom first said her name, *Serena*, she was gone.

Rena's smile twisted, mirroring the wrenching of her heart. She pressed the light on her watch, checked the time, and even though it was only just gone four thirty, decided to get up anyway. There was a pool here at the lodge, and some hard laps in cold water would do her good.

A few hours later, Rena spruced herself up—clean blue shirt, beige shorts, a straw hat instead of her regular baseball cap—and drove the couple of kilometres into Fitzroy Crossing proper. The short trip from the campground took her across the Martuwarra Fitzroy River, currently just a series of waterholes in a broad tract of sand. She rolled the Ranger past the edge of town then followed the signs for the police station, weaving through back streets already heating up in the morning sun. When she got there, the cop shop was a surprise. She'd been expecting an old house, inefficiently retro-fitted, too small, and generally care-worn, not the modern, angular structure before her.

Despite the relatively early hour, there were people coming and going, both uniformed officers and regular citizens, making the place seem more like a community centre than an outpost of the law. She stood outside for a few minutes, inhaling the clean scent of eucalyptus and trying to figure out exactly what to say without sounding like she was giving the locals a lesson in how to run their investigation. In the end she decided it didn't matter. They could take offence or not, but they needed to hear what she had to say. Rena strode across the forecourt, paused as long as it took the automatic doors to part and fronted up to the counter of the Fitzroy Crossing police station, whipping off her hat at the last moment.

'Good morning, my name's Rena Novak, and I have some information about the car fire yesterday.' She told the young officer behind the desk.

The man gave her a quick once-over, eyes flicking from her grey hair down to her sun-weathered hands resting on the counter.

'The one out on the highway?' he asked, looking down and reading something on the computer screen in front of him. His light brown hair was parted to one side, exposing a razor-sharp line of skin.

Rena was tempted to ask how many car fires they had each day, but all she said was, 'That's right. Up towards Halls Creek.'

'Hang on Mrs…Novak, was it?'

She nodded as the young man reached for the phone, punched two buttons, and murmured something to whomever picked up the internal line. 'Someone will be out shortly.' He tilted sideways, looking around Rena, his attention already on the person she could sense behind her, standing too close.

'Morning, Joanne.' He smiled. 'What can I do for you?'

Rena stepped aside and turned, allowing a small woman with short purple hair to take her place. Her face was mapped with contour lines of a life full of peaks and depressions, but she was fit: her wiry, toned physique evident beneath black shorts and a green singlet.

'Morning, Nic. Need a chat with your boss before the community meeting tonight. He in?'

The rest of the exchange was lost as Rena moved away. She drifted across to the notice board, filled mostly with Crime Stoppers flyers asking for information about a variety of offences, a few community announcements, calls for volunteers, and a couple of wanted posters illustrated with blank-eyed mugshots of the persons of interest. Rena sighed.

A few minutes later an internal door opened and another uniformed officer stepped through, and waved her over. Rena had been expecting yesterday's baby-faced cop, but this man was closer to her own age, the beginnings of a paunch riding the top of a utility belt, grey-flecked hair cut close, brown skin, crow's-feet.

'Mrs Novak? Senior Constable Halloran.'

They exchanged a handshake, then Halloran ushered her into the inner sanctum. When they were seated on either side of a paper-strewn desk, he arched an enquiring eyebrow.

'So, you have some information for us?'

'It's probably nothing you don't already know, but…' Rena explained the reason for her visit.

Halloran nodded and took notes, his expression of polite interest never faltering throughout Rena's brief monologue. From where she was sitting, it looked genuine, but Rena still felt mildly embarrassed, like she was wasting the man's time. The only reason she didn't shut up, apologise, and leave, was that it would bother her more if she hadn't said something. She finished speaking and sat back with relief.

Halloran clicked his pen. 'Well, thanks for coming in, Mrs Novak. I haven't read the responding officers' report in detail, but it's always good to have as much information as we can, and we appreciate it when citizens come forward.' He stood, the chair scraping across the linoleum. 'We've got your details?'

Rena wasn't sure if it was a question or a statement, but she nodded anyway and got to her feet. She was about to say something generic, but Halloran had moved back around the desk and was already halfway to the exit before Rena had a chance to push in her chair and put on her hat. Halloran had been polite, but Rena recognised the old lady brush-off.

'Do you have any new information?' She asked, raising her voice above the background noise of the room, forcing the man to stop.

'I mean, do you know who it was or. . .anything?' Rena didn't quite know why she'd asked for a name, except perhaps that after Tom, she'd felt a need to whisper a few words whenever someone died, to acknowledge a life that had touched hers in any way. And given what she'd seen yesterday, Rena wanted to put a name to the person behind the wheel of the burnt-out Toyota.

Halloran turned and scratched at one thick earlobe. 'Investigations are ongoing, and in any case, we—'

Rena waved away the rest of his words. 'Of course.'

'Thanks again.' He extended a hand, shepherding her towards the door.

'But regarding the investigation. . .' said Rena. She saw Halloran's lips press together, his mouth becoming a tight line, and she held up a reassuring hand. 'I'm not asking for details; I just want to know if I can get back on the road. The officers yesterday asked me to hang around in Fitzroy Crossing, but is that necessary?'

Halloran's face relaxed into a smile, and he shook his head. 'Nah, you're good to go—much as I've always wanted to utter the immortal words, don't leave town! We can find you if we have to.'

'Great, thanks.' Rena had planned to stay another day or so anyway—there were several local rock formations she wanted to see—but liked to operate on her own terms. She might have wanted to stay, but once someone told her she *had* to. . . Tom called her contrary, but he'd also figured out early in their marriage that it was harder to make Rena do something when she didn't want to than to simply claim it was her idea in the first place and therefore a highly desirable plan. The fact that Rena was wise to how he played her was beside the point.

She crossed through reception and out the automatic doors. The heat enveloped her, and Rena stopped, giving her eyes a moment to adjust, mentally planning the rest of her day. She'd buy something for lunch, then head out of town. The broader geology of the region would have to take a back seat, because she wanted to investigate one particular aspect of the landscape. Specifically, a dry creek bed next to a red-dirt track, about an hour out of town.

Rena still couldn't decide if Halloran had believed her about the car not being in gear or even if it was something they already knew. Presumably, Halloran would have to pass her information on, but would he preface it with something along the lines of, *An old lady came in with a crazy story about the gearstick in the burnt-out Toyota*? Rena had spent her career as a field geologist in the male-dominated mining industry, so she had a lifetime's experience of both being dismissed and of trying to get men to take her seriously. But since she'd gotten older—since she'd retired—Rena had discovered it was even easier for people to underestimate and patronise her.

The fire and death were really nothing to do with her, but Rena decided to take another quick look. Not to confirm what she'd seen—she knew she was right about that—but because she wanted to see if there was anything else off-key, something she might not have noticed amid the chaos of yesterday. Besides, it felt as though she had a vested interest. Or maybe she just needed to whisper those few words where it mattered most. Either way, Rena had no demands on her time and no one to tell her to pull her head in.

Not that it was her style. Rena usually led with her chin.

FIVE

The bakery was doing a brisk trade when Rena brushed through the multi-coloured fly strips. From the signs out front—not to mention the postings on travel forums—Rena already knew the award-winning croc pies were a big drawcard. But something in her recoiled at the thought of eating one of nature's living fossils, a creature whose earliest recognisable archosaur ancestor appeared around two hundred million years ago in the Late Triassic period. You didn't survive all that time to end up in a pie.

She eyed the display cabinet of cakes and pastries, waited while a mini-bus worth of tourists cleared out of the shop, then moved in front of the register. A staff member was crouched down on the other side, adding a fresh tray of coffee scrolls to the cabinet, and when she straightened up, Rena found herself face-to-face with the purple-haired woman from the police station, now wearing an apron over her singlet and shorts.

'What'll it be, love?'

Rena ordered a ham and salad roll and a doorstop-sized coconut slice, handed over fifteen dollars, then transferred the handful of change to a plastic charity box next to the register. This earned her a beaming smile from Joanne. 'Ta, that's very kind. The local youth outreach program is doing fantastic things. Won't be a tick with your roll; if you want to wait outside, I'll bring it out.'

Outside Rena tugged at the brim of her hat, sliding it down over her brow, shading her face from the morning sun. Part of the front of the bakery was given over to a notice board, and right in the middle, adorned with a red border and an army of exclamation points, was a notice advertising a community meeting about the Synastria proposal.

'Here you go, love. Ham and salad roll and a coconut slice.' Joanne was standing next to her, holding out a pair of brown paper bags. Out here in the brighter light, Rena could see she was younger than she seemed. The strong arms made sense now—kneading dough every day would work wonders—but the weathered complexion and general don't-give-a-damn aura had added decades to what was probably only forty-something years.

'Thank you.' Rena took the food from her. 'What's this about?' She tapped the notice.

Joanne's eyes narrowed slightly. 'Just local stuff.'

'What's the Synastria proposal? Sounds intriguing.'

'Why, who are you? A reporter? A plant? I saw you in the cop shop.' She folded her arms and scowled.

Rena frowned and shook her head. 'Whoa, relax! I'm just an old broad who's travelling through town and *thought* she was asking a reasonable question.'

Joanne gave her the face to feet once-over, then puffed out a heavy sigh. 'Sorry. Lot of BS flying about at the moment because of that.' She jerked her head towards the notice board. 'Hence tonight's meeting.'

'So, what is it?' Rena asked.

Joanne licked her lips and looked away, staring out at the sunblasted street. Then she shrugged. 'Depends on who you're talking to. Could be the answer to everything or the coming of the devil incarnate.'

Rena's interest deepened.

'Rumour is there's a bunch of city greenies on their way, ready to tie themselves to shit and scream obscenities while they live stream to a global audience.' She snorted. 'Guess no one's told them about the Wi-Fi out there. Or rather, the complete lack of it. I'm hoping they don't crash the meeting tonight, because we've got enough to contend with. The way local feelings are running right now, tonight's meeting could go off, and not in a good way. But—'

She was interrupted by a young man who stuck his head through the bakery's doorway. 'Oi, Jo! Could use a hand.'

'Sorry, Jase. Coming.' She half turned then swung back to Rena. 'Synastria is a mining company. Finger in a lot of international pies, but word is after the close of Argyle, they're looking at starting up operations. Means jobs and income for the town, but also a bloody great blight on the land. And that's before you even start talking to the Traditional Owners about the importance of Country.'

'You're saying diamonds?'

Joanne nodded. 'Billions of dollars' worth, apparently. Synastria says it's only in the exploration phase and a long way from making any commitments but...' She shrugged.

'Jo!' The shout came from inside the bakery.

'Gotta go. Enjoy the roll. Skip the meeting.' Joanne trotted out the sentences with the same dry inflection, but they were more than just empty words: She did want Rena to enjoy the roll she'd prepared, and she really was expecting that the community meeting would go to shit.

Rena stood there as the woman hurried back inside. Diamonds. Why was it that the thought of diamonds made pulses quicken? Personal feelings aside, it was hardly surprising a mining company like Synastria was looking at getting in the game, given what had been pulled out of the Argyle mine over its twenty-plus years of operation. An average of eight million carats per year, and even if only a small percentage of the stones were gem quality, the presence of rare pinks and reds made Kimberley diamonds the stuff of legends. And fortunes.

SIX

Rena slowly made her way back to the car, mind fully occupied with diamond geology and gemology, specifically the unique distortions in the crystal lattice that created fancy pinks.

Other than her husband and family, geology had been—was—Rena's life. As the only child of migrants, money had been tight when she was growing up. Her parents worked hard to build a good life in Australia and give her a decent education, but in the early days, there was little room for luxuries. That made it more thrilling when, on her tenth birthday, Rena had received something incredible. To this day she remembered the air of expectation in their tiny kitchen as her father pushed a flat wooden box across the green Formica table. Rena had run her fingers over the polished mahogany and fingered the brass hook that fastened it closed before, with an encouraging nod from her mother, she carefully raised the lid. The box was sectioned into forty compartments, each one containing a different labelled mineral specimen, and with a corresponding list tucked into the lid, full of scientific information about the rocks. Rena would later find out her father had bought it at the pawn shop for next to nothing, but that was an irrelevant detail: Here was the history and makeup of the very earth laid out for her. She still marvelled at the astuteness of her parents—how had they known that an old box of rocks would ignite a life-long passion for geology and mineralogy? Rena still got excited about land formations and her own collection of Australian minerals and fossils. And she still treasured the set her parents had given her on her tenth birthday. Of course, none of those original specimens was valuable, but the Kimberley was an entirely different treasure box. Gold, iron, zinc, uranium, and heavy rare earth elements like terbium and dysprosium—vital elements in renewable energy technology—were just some of the things hidden deep within the ancient rock formations of the Kimberley. And then of course, there were diamonds.

Someone cleared their throat, and Rena pulled up with a start, turning towards the source. She'd just walked straight past Mike and Adam.

'Good morning,' she said.

The two men were sitting on a bench in a small patch of dusty park, the thick trunk of a boab tree providing a strip of shade. Both were wearing variations of the standard extended driving holiday ensemble: big hats, sunglasses, sneakers (Mike) or thongs (Adam) and shorts, Adam's topped off with a red and white Hawaiian shirt, while Mike had on a loose T-shirt emblazoned with the logo of the LA Lakers.

'You were miles away,' said Mike, holding up an arm to shade his eyes.

'Yeah, sorry.' Rena moved a bit so the sun wasn't directly behind her.

'Hardly surprising given the day you had yesterday.'

Rena nodded. 'How's the ankle?'

Adam grimaced. 'I can weight-bear, but it ain't pretty, which is why we're taking a moment to regroup here.' He waved an arm, his gesture taking in the tree behind them and the surrounding dusty ground.

'I'm heading out of town for a bit now, but might see you around later.' She took a step backwards, started to turn away. They'd shared a pleasant dinner last night, but Rena was wary of people thinking they had to include the poor solo traveller in whatever they were doing, or worse—invite themselves along on her planned excursion to 'keep her company.' She didn't need charity, and she bloody well didn't like finding herself hamstrung by other people's slow pace, desire for long lunches, or inability to get organised and be on time. On the other hand, she didn't want to offend anybody, especially when there was a reasonable chance of meeting them again somewhere down the track. So the easiest thing was to not get involved in the first place.

'What are you up to?' asked Mike.

'I'm keen to do the gorge cruise, but that'll be tomorrow if I can get a ticket. Today's just a drive, bit of a nose around, have a better look at the countryside.' Rena kept her tone casual, but she could feel Mike scrutinising her, even though his eyes were hidden by the sunglasses.

'That sounds like a great plan; both Danggu Geikie Gorge and puttering around the land,' he said, shifting his weight forward as though preparing to stand.

Rena tensed, bracing for a self-invitation, but it never came. Then she noticed the smile teasing at the edges of Mike's lips. He was wise to her. She gave him a wry grin.

'I should get going before it gets too hot,' she said.

'Good idea,' said Adam. He pushed himself to his feet. 'Babe, maybe we should head back. I think this is going to be a day by the pool. See you, Rena.'

Mike stood and offered Adam his arm, which was waved away. He turned to Rena. 'I don't need to tell you to stay hydrated, do I? But stay safe. Sorry if I'm overstepping; Adam always says I go overboard trying to take care of everyone.'

'No problem.'

Now he reached out and placed a hand on her forearm. 'I know an unquiet mind when I see it. Are you sure you don't actually need company today?'

Rena shook her head, part in admiration at Mike's perceptiveness. 'Nope, I'm good. Something I need to get out of my system, but I'll be right.'

'Good.' He stepped past her, striding out to catch up with Adam, who—despite the gammy leg—had made good ground.

'Hey, Mike?' Rena called at his retreating figure.

He turned.

'Thanks.'

Mike flashed her a smile, and then she was alone.

Rena covered the remaining distance to her vehicle, which remarkably was still in part-shade. She stowed her lunch in the fridge, settled behind the wheel, then pointed the bull bar in the direction of Halls Creek. Back to the accident site.

As she pulled onto the road, the swing of the steering wheel moved her left hand up and Rena's wedding band flashed in the sunlight. She hadn't taken it off since the day they were married, and at this stage she doubted she ever would. Looking at the ring now made her think of Tom, and she wondered what he would've had to say about this venture. She wished she could hear his voice, hear him tell her in his words what she already knew: Rena wanted to see if there was anything else that didn't sit right, anything else someone might be trying to bury.

SEVEN

The Toyota was gone.

She hadn't really stopped to consider that the authorities would remove the burnt-out wreck, but if she had, Rena would've bet good money they wouldn't manage it for a day or two at least. Not out here, where the remoteness meant anything outside the ordinary scope of business generally took far longer and cost a lot more to achieve.

The temperature had fallen to about 10°C overnight, so things would have cooled down enough for an investigator to gain access, and for a truck to collect the destroyed vehicle, but, even so, it was barely past midday, just one day after the event.

Rena parked her Ranger a short distance from what was now nothing more than a large patch of blackened earth and bush, with a few strips of blue-and-white police tape tied to nearby trees and shrubs. It wasn't so much an attempt to cordon off the scene as to mark its extremities, or possibly make the site more visible from a distance. The smell lingered in the still air, pungent top-notes of rubber and plastic trickling through the pervading charcoal aroma, overpowering the cleaner scents of earth and eucalyptus. Rena walked down the track, noting broken and bent branches to either side and a set of deep, wide, wheel marks in the red dirt—evidence that a large truck, presumably designed for off-road recovery, had passed this way. Closer to where the Toyota had burned, a muddle of footprints joined the tyre marks, some of them probably her own.

Rena stood for a moment, hands on hips, surveying the scene. To a casual passer-by, the only indication that anything noteworthy had occurred were those forlorn bits of police tape, hanging limp, a cruel reminder that the emergency had passed, hope was gone. Settling her hat more firmly on her head, Rena half-jumped, half-slithered down the bank of the dry creek. It had seemed easier yesterday, a trick of adrenaline and intense focus that had propelled her to the creek bed without consideration.

Now Rena moved towards the black patch of earth, casting her gaze left and right. She didn't stop to ask herself what she was doing or why. She was simply going with her gut, and her gut was telling her there was something very wrong about the whole situation.

After ten minutes of fruitless poking around, she scrambled back up the bank and turned her attention to the track on which the four-wheel drive had been travelling. She started walking deeper into the scrub, red dust rising around her feet, eyes scanning the ground. There was nothing—no washouts, rocks, or fallen trees—nothing at all to indicate why the driver had failed to make the turn and ended up in the creek bed, but Rena hadn't really expected to find anything here. Tyres blew, medical crises happened, and sometimes inattentiveness, the sun in your eyes, or plain old speed and stupidity brought people undone. She got less than one hundred metres along the track before turning back. It was too bloody hot for this. The sun was riding high, mirages shimmered in every direction, and shade was virtually nonexistent. She could feel sweat under her boobs and on her forehead, dampening the band of her hat and sending a rivulet of moisture running down the side of her face. Even her plaited hair felt heavy and hot between her shoulder blades.

'Stupid old broad,' she muttered to herself, stomping back over the same ground. At the point where the Toyota had left the track, she took one last look, first at the scorched patch of ground, then back in the direction the four-wheel drive had travelled. A narrow lane of earth, stretching away to a lateritic-capped mesa, a dark red beacon in the otherwise uninterrupted flatness. She swivelled her head, gauging the distance back to the highway. It wasn't far but with no traffic in sight, she was alone; in the vastness of this landscape, she may as well have been the only person within a thousand kilometres. Not a bad place to die if you liked the outback, but getting incinerated was a shit of a way to go.

She'd done her bit yesterday. Regardless of whether the cops knew what they were doing or not, regardless of whether they cared, it was none of her business. Besides, she was too old for this shit and too young to be classified as a nosy old lady with nothing better to do than stick her beak where it didn't belong. Rena got back in the Ranger, started it up and pulled away. She'd see Danggu Geikie Gorge then get out of town, back on the road to Derby, Broome, and then who knew where.

She reached the highway and spun the wheel in the direction of Fitzroy Crossing, resisting the temptation to watch the accident scene fade in her mirrors. Rena tried to distract herself with plans for the coming days, thoughts of a relaxing cruise on the gorge, but her mind kept circling around to the fire. She put some music on, but Fats Waller was too upbeat, Chopin too busy, Creedence too loud. The land here was flat, the sky overhead a cloudless, cerulean blue. And then Tom's voice was in her head.

I know what it means when you get like this, Reenie. Admit it.

'Dammit.' She smacked a palm onto the steering wheel.

Rena had spent her working life getting stuck in. She was bored in retirement, lonely without her husband of decades. Rena needed a project. And for better or worse, until something else caught her attention or the police officially told her to piss off back to where she'd come from, it seemed like digging into this stupid accident was it.

Well, at least her son would be pleased she had a new hobby. Or not.

EIGHT

Rena spent the rest of the afternoon doing all the inconsequential but necessary tasks that come with travelling long distances and camping in often-remote locations: filling the freshwater tank, buying fuel and full gas cylinders, and sourcing a new fire extinguisher. She also managed to get herself a place on tomorrow's cruise; usually solo travel meant expensive supplements and waiting on more people to book a tour, but every now and then it paid off when there was just enough room to squeeze in one last person.

Back at the campground, she unfolded a chair so she had somewhere to sit while she ate the ham roll and coconut slice, now qualifying as either a very late lunch or the sort of early dinner people attributed to the elderly. Rena had bought a coffee at the servo and regretted the decision on first sip, but she still downed the whole industrial-strength cup. On the plus side, she didn't have to worry that last night's lack of sleep was going to catch up with her any time soon.

With Danggu Geikie Gorge locked in for tomorrow, she would stay a few more days before getting back on the road. The Dampier Peninsula was next on her itinerary, but Rena hadn't decided whether to travel the long way—down to Broome then up the sealed Cape Leveque Road—or take the four-wheel drive shortcut up the Bedunburra Track. The scenery was reportedly better on the track, but she didn't know if she needed permission to travel that way. Rena made a mental note to check in with the local visitor centre. She'd prefer the isolation of Bedunburra, the demands of a route where driving required skill and attention, and left you physically spent at the end of the day, every bone in your body rattled, shoulders and arms sore from gripping the wheel.

Earlier, on the drive back into Fitzroy Crossing, she'd plunged deep into her own psyche—or as deep as she liked to go, attempting to analyse her reasons for caring so much about the car-fire victim. Other than the happenstance of discovering the body and the shock of what she'd seen, Rena had to admit to herself that the only reason she was poking around like some half-arsed Miss Marple was because she was tired. Not the physical exhaustion she craved, but a different sort of tired.

Tired of forcing herself to drive to places she'd always planned to see with Tom, tired of pretending she was coping with his death, tired of the guilt she felt when she chose not to tell a stranger that she was a widow. The word—even unuttered—left a bitter taste. If she didn't tell people, it was as though she was denying Tom had ever existed, denying all they'd had and all they'd lost. But if she confessed to her bereaved status, Rena then had to endure the empty platitudes of strangers or worse: the assumption that she was in the market for a new man. She'd promised Tom she'd do the trip, but Rena knew if she didn't shake her current despondency—or rather, desolation—she'd always regret tarnishing their dream. If she was going to do it, she needed to do it right.

So digging herself in at Fitzroy Crossing, pausing the travel while she regrouped, would allow Rena to regain her emotional strength. Then she could continue the holiday she and Tom had planned together.

That's what she told herself. But then the more prosaic part of her brain fired off a few neurons of its own. *Rena,* it told her, *you're full of it. Yes to all the emotional stuff, but this isn't about taking a break, this is about thinking about someone*—something—*else. If all your energy is directed towards the corpse, you don't have to think about your own misery.*

Both things made sense, and either way, Rena was already too invested in the fiery death of a stranger to let it go.

Having finally decided to do whatever the hell she wanted on this trip around the country, Rena felt immediately lighter. If she closed her eyes, she could almost feel Tom's cool hand, the way he had often rested it, briefly, on the back of her head, just at the hairline, when he wanted to soothe and reassure.

'A promise is a promise, sweetheart,' she murmured. Mind you, she'd never promised not to be a cranky old woman, but then, Tom didn't mind that; he'd always loved her cantankerousness.

As part of her new no misery-guts policy, Rena would not sit around by herself tonight. She was going to the town meeting. It wasn't exactly a night at the movies, but from what Jo had said, there could well be a show. Rena knew how divisive mines could be, but also the great benefits they could deliver. She wanted to know what Synastria Mining had found, the scale of their proposed operation; that alone would give her an idea how much potential wealth lay deep within the Kimberley's red earth.

She walked into town, relishing the feel of the heat fading from the air as dusk crept in. It was a subtle thing, but the intensity of the day's sunlight meant even the smallest change was noticeable and appreciated. The twilight sky reminded her of a stone she'd seen mined in Brazil, a combination of rich, royal-blue sodalite shot through with inclusions of orange feldspar. The new-agers called it sunset stone and now, with emerging stars adding lustre to the oncoming night, Rena could see why. She had no idea what miraculous properties were attributed to sunset stone, but she didn't believe in that rubbish anyway. If you asked Rena about sodalite, she'd tell you its crystalline structure was isometric, it had a hardness of about 5.5 on Mohs scale, and then probably rattle off a few localities for good measure. But hand her a crystal or gemstone and tell her it was for grief or IBS, and you could expect to be met with a face blank except for a tiny furrow between her brows: That was Rena attempting not to snort or roll her eyes so hard it hurt.

It took a good forty minutes to reach the rec centre where the meeting was being held, but with all the driving she'd been doing, Rena enjoyed the exercise. Once she'd gotten off the main road and into the town proper, more and more people had begun to appear, walking or driving, all drifting in the same general direction. There was almost a party atmosphere, delight in something out of the ordinary, but here and there Rena caught sight of a grim face or a stiffly set back, signs that not everyone was out for a good time.

The hall was packed. Every seat occupied, kids sitting in the aisles or on laps, and plenty more people on their feet, filling up the space around the walls, the whole lot murmuring like a swarm of bees. Not angry, just a hive with business to attend to. As she moved around the edge of the room, trying to find somewhere discreet to stand, Rena got more than her fair share of glances ranging from friendly through to curious, suspicious and openly hostile. And in a crowd that was fairly racially balanced, it didn't matter whether the person doing the staring was White or Black: Whatever feelings they were feeling were purely personal, and probably based on the assumption that a lone stranger, especially a White woman of her vintage, must be mixed up with the mining company. She met each look with a nod and a benign expression, letting her eyes slide away if there was too much heat lasering back at her. Rena had never shied away from confrontation, but that didn't mean she went looking for trouble when it could be avoided.

Bang on six thirty the dull, staccato thud of someone tapping a mic, followed by a screech of audio feedback cut through the air, instantly lowering the level of chatter by about 50 percent.

'Folks!' A baritone voice, gravelly in the way only a lifetime smoker's voice can be. 'Bit of shoosh, thanks. We're ready to start.'

Chairs scraped as people settled and the man with the mic came into view. Mid-fifties probably, grey beard, curly salt-and-pepper hair, mid-toned brown skin, and a wide smile.

'I reckon you all know me, Mal Lloyd, shire president,' He nodded to the crowd. 'I'm just going to introduce these good people here then step to one side, let you ask your questions. No need to remind you we all want what's best for the local community, the Crossing and the land. So keep it civil, and let's find out more about what these city fellas have in mind.'

Rena moved her focus away from the shire president. There were four other people up front—three men and a woman, all White—ranged behind a table, placed so they were facing the crowd. Mal Lloyd started naming them and giving their job titles: One was representing the WA government; the others were from Synastria Mining.

The man identified as the mine operation manager stood, the lights dimmed, and a screen lit up with a PowerPoint slide emblazoned with the red-and-blue Synastria Mining logo on one side and a picture of a multiracial group of smiling people in hard hats and orange safety vests on the other. The crowd shifted and whispered to itself; then the manager began to speak, launching straight into a glowing recital of core values, promises, and expectations.

Rena had attended a few of these meetings during her career, so she was mildly surprised when the mining execs managed to get through their entire presentation unchallenged, particularly because the whole thing was smoke and mirrors. It conveyed all the important information (so that in the future, the locals couldn't argue they'd been blindsided) but surrounded the vital bits with glitzy graphics, hard-to-read charts, and heavy emphasis on all the ways Synastria was going to be a gold-star corporate citizen and splash its largesse on the local community. Which, Rena conceded, may well be true. But no mining company she'd ever worked for was in it for the good of the locals.

Sifting through the window dressing, Rena learned that currently the enterprise was valued at nearly three hundred million dollars, mining options on the forty thousand-hectare site were already secured, engagement with Traditional Owners had begun, and now all they had to do was some bulk sampling to confirm what their initial tests had shown: fancy coloured diamonds, gem quality. A lot of them. Which would send the value of the company into the billions.

As the lights came up again, Rena could see the relief on the faces out front, but she also felt the atmosphere in the room, and something had shifted. The good citizens of Fitzroy Crossing and the greater region of Derby Shire had given the bigwigs a fair hearing, and now it was their turn. And if Synastria Mining thought it was dealing with a bunch of outback hicks, they'd seriously underestimated. As the questions began to fly, it was evident that these people knew the value of their country, both in real and mineral terms. They'd seen what had happened at Argyle and learned from it.

Things started off politely enough. Requests for clarity, more information, the usual questions posed in moderate tones. Then it was on.

'So you'll throw a few crumbs our way while you destroy the landscape, then screw us over, piss off with all the wealth, and leave us to pick up your shit. That it? Like a bastard husband.' A woman, anonymous in the group of people lining the far wall.

'Just another bunch of condescending pricks from the big smoke!' another woman chimed in from the seats near the back.

Heads turned and a few people tittered.

'Now, there's no call for that.' Mal Lloyd was on his feet, shaking his head, his benevolent, grizzled countenance turning from one place to the other. 'Nothing's final, we're just talking and there's plenty of consultation to come.'

'Bullshit!' a man shouted from somewhere over the other side of the hall. 'We talk and these bastards make all the right sounds; then they go and do whatever the hell they like.'

The crowd around the speaker shifted, nodding, muttering their agreement, one bloke reaching to grip the young Aboriginal man's shoulder and give it an affirming shake. He looked to be in his twenties or early thirties, but it was hard to tell because of the angry scowl twisting the features of his face. Now he stepped forward, pointing at the Synastria group, his finger jabbing the air as he moved towards them.

'You can dress it up as much as you like with pretty graphics and photos of playing footy with the locals and shaking hands, and fucking everybody fucking smiling, but the moment you get a whiff of serious money, you lot'll lob in dynamite, blow everything to kingdom come, then pretend it was a fucking accident!' The man was so angry spit was flying from his mouth, and as he advanced on the now even paler mining execs, half the crowd seemed to be moving too, rising up, surging towards the front of the room or the back, depending on their individual inclinations and regard for self-preservation. 'And if you think we're going to just sit back and take it, you're in for a nasty surprise. No mines, not here, not ever. Whatever it bloody well takes. We. Will. Stop. You.' He made a fist and shook it at the Synastria people, emphasising every word. They were leaning back, trying to create distance without actual retreat, while Mal Lloyd was holding up placating hands, moving to place himself between the city delegation and the rest of the room.

Just as an all-in brawl seemed inevitable, a piercing whistle cut through the air.

In the in-breath of quiet, a chair scraped in one of the front rows and a young woman got to her feet. Toned shoulders beneath a fitted white T-shirt gave power to her lean figure—clearly a woman used to physical work or working out. She turned slightly to better address the majority of the room, and Rena could see smooth brown skin, highlighted by the merest hint of blush on her strong cheekbones. Mid-twenties, but there was a maturity and assurance about her that Rena didn't usually associate with that age group.

The young woman stood, arms loose at her sides, and simply waited as the room around her resettled.

'Aitch? You wanna say something?' Mal asked, a slight tremor in his voice.

Aitch—the young woman—nodded. 'Yeah, Mal, thanks. Just my thoughts.' She cast her gaze around the room, meeting some eyes with a respectful nod, a few with a steady moment of acknowledgement or challenge. 'No good will come from acting like a bunch of yobs now. This is too important for us to stuff it up by getting all hot under the collar.' Aitch paused long enough to give the angry young man a wry look. 'It's right to be cautious. We know how it went for other towns—boom when the mine came in, bust when they left.'

The crowd responded with a swell of angry muttering, but it rolled over Aitch with no effect; she simply waited again before resuming. 'But this could be a game changer for the community. A change for the better. It would mean jobs, lots of 'em. Young folk wouldn't have to move off Country to get work and training. Money pumped into the town, not just tourist dollars, but money all year round. For schools and the hospital and all the places that are always short, always scratching to do the best they can with F-all. And if we get it right from the start, we can make sure we don't fall in a bloody great hole if and when they pack up and go. A mine could be a good thing; we just gotta make sure it's done right.' Aitch sat down. There was a smattering of applause, some enthusiastic, but to Rena's ear, some carried the slow, deliberate rhythm of irony.

A few more people stood up to speak. It became clear to Rena based on their words and the responses from the rest that the crowd was strongly divided between the for and against camps. She could understand why; the damage to the landscape would be significant and from what she was hearing there were several culturally significant sites within the land optioned by Synastria. The company had already given assurances, but everyone in the room knew the state government was a mining ally, and you only had to look at what Rio Tinto had done to the Juukan Gorge rock shelters to know that some people would stop at nothing when there was serious money to be made. And that was one thing every woman, man, and child in the room could smell. Money.

After another forty minutes of back-and-forth, the meeting came to an end. There had been moments where things threatened to boil over, and it was clear quite a few people wanted to launch themselves at the Synastria contingent. Fortunately, the shire president managed to settle the crowd every time; he had to work for it, though.

Rena joined the throng shuffling towards the doors, thinking about the potential of a diamond mine using the latest extraction techniques, and half listening to the snatches of conversation around her. She was crossing the car park, relishing the feel and smell of the cool night air, when she heard a smack, followed by a sharp inhalation. The noises had come from somewhere off to her right, beyond the pools of weak illumination cast by the scattered security lights, beyond a group of cars. Rena knew the sound; she'd broken up a few fights in her day, slapped a few faces too.

Without hesitation, she changed course, veering towards the source, pulling out her key fob as she went. Now she could hear a voice, a low, placatory tone, the words dropping into the darkness, too soft for Rena to hear.

She stepped around a Mitsubishi Pajero and emerged, steps away from where two people stood, one with a half-raised fist, the other with her arms loose by her sides. The first was the angry bloke from the meeting; the second was Aitch. Rena held up her keys, jangling them to draw attention.

'Hi there, sorry to interrupt. Can't remember where I parked my car. You didn't notice a grey Navara did you?' Rena chose a familiar car make at random and she craned her neck, making a show of looking around.

The two people stared at her for a beat, then glanced at each other. Rena could feel tension crackling in the air.

'It's not here.' The angry bloke was dressed in the ubiquitous uniform adopted by certain young men, regardless of their location: baggy basketball shorts, a singlet, and a back-to-front cap. He jerked his head in a clear piss-off gesture. As he did so, two more men appeared, stepping from the deeper shadows cast by the next car along and arranging themselves behind Baseball Cap, chests puffed, quiet menace in their eyes.

Rena made a quick assessment. She'd been wary when she thought this was something private between Aitch and the man, unsure who had slapped whom, but now she knew Baseball Cap had extra muscle backing him up. This wasn't a minor disagreement; this was three men against one woman. Well, against two, now. But things could still very easily go to shit.

She was aware of the space around her, the sound of people calling out goodbyes, cars starting up then moving away as the place gradually emptied out. Rena felt the evenness of the ground beneath her feet, inhaled the scents of the night: engine fumes, eucalyptus, dry earth. She was acutely conscious of the potential for violence, of the waves of hostility radiating from the three young men in front of her.

'What about you?' Keeping her voice light, Rena turned slightly to address the woman she recognised as Aitch. 'You seen a grey Navara?'

Aitch met her eye, shaking her head slowly, almost imperceptibly. A warning rather than a negation. 'No ma'am, sorry.'

The men shifted slightly, closing ranks, dismissing Rena. She took two firm steps forward, and they turned to her once more, dismay in Aitch's wide-open eyes. Before any of them could act, Rena was among them, forcing the group apart by her physical presence, catching Aitch's forearm in a firm grip.

'Help an old lady out, would you, please?' She turned her back on the aggressors, fixing Aitch with a look that she hoped conveyed *Trust me.* 'It was so busy when I arrived, and I didn't pay attention—just parked wherever. Now it's fully dark, my eyes aren't what they used to be, you know? I'm sure your grandma's are the same! And I've been wandering around, trying to find my damn car... I feel so silly, but could one of you young people help me?'

Rena kept her eyes fixed on Aitch's, trying to get her message across while also watching for any change in the woman's expression that might signal she was about to get grabbed or cop a fist to the back of her head.

Aitch rubbed her lips together, then slowly shifted her gaze over Rena's shoulder. 'Sure,' she said. 'We're done here. I can help you.'

'Thanks, love, appreciate it.' Rena started to move away, keeping a hand on Aitch's arm, pulling the other woman with her. 'Night, boys.' She glanced over her shoulder, smiling benevolently. 'Lucky to find some nice young people like you. Your mum must be proud.'

Together, Rena and Aitch walked slowly away. Rena continued her genial prattle, feeling all the while like she had a target on her back. Once she was sure they'd left the three men far behind them, Rena blew out a long breath. 'Bit touch-and-go there for a minute. You okay?' she asked, serious now.

Aitch closed her eyes for a brief moment, then flashed a smile and nodded. 'Yeah, I'm all right. And thanks. I mean really, thanks. I appreciate what you did.' Rena let go of Aitch's arm, and they picked up the pace.

'You're welcome. Who were they? Three men against one woman in the dark is not odds I like at any time, but you looked remarkably calm.'

Aitch shrugged. 'It was really only one I had to worry about. The other two are basically gutless wonders; they were probably just as glad when you turned up as I was. And if you thought I was calm, I wasn't. He was pretty worked up, but you grow up out here, you know what everyone's like: Who's decent, who's a dickhead, and who has a real mean streak and a taste for violence. That bloke, he's just a dickhead. He wouldn't have done anything like. . .you know, just thrown around a few more insults and threats and maybe punched me in the guts. Nothing too obvious, nothing worth reporting to anyone.'

Rena took a moment to digest Aitch's assessment of the situation and the local male population. It saddened her to realise it could be applied in almost any city, anywhere.

'Are you sure you're okay?' she asked. 'I heard someone getting smacked around. That's why I came over.'

'Oh. That was me. Slapping him, I mean. I don't let anyone talk to me like that. Not anymore.'

Rena slid her eyes sideways, studying the woman walking next to her. Fit, strong, Aitch looked as though she could inflict a bit of damage if she wanted to. In Rena's experience—a lifetime spent working in a male-dominated field—most women who'd just been cornered by three blokes in the dark would be distraught. She wanted to ask why this girl was so cool. She wanted to know what it was all about, but all she said was, 'You're Aitch, right? My name's Rena.' And stuck out her hand.

They shook.

'Good to meet you, Rena. Now where's this Navara of yours?'

Rena smiled. 'Don't have one. I was actually hoping you had a car, 'cause mine's back at the campground and, oddly enough, I don't feel like walking back all on my own. Not tonight, anyway.'

Aitch stopped mid-stride and turned, a look of wide-eyed incredulity on her face. 'Serious? Jesus!' Then she burst out laughing. 'I thought you were legit about the car when you first appeared, then you saw what was what and bluffed me out of there. But you knowingly walked into that to bail me out? That's pretty ballsy.'

'Nah, you would've done the same.'

'Yeah, but I'm... I mean, you're...'

'Old?'

'I didn't—' Aitch screwed up her face, clearly embarrassed.

'One of the benefits of being older, other than wisdom, is I find myself running out of fucks to give. Besides, I've dealt with plenty of men like that over the years, and if talking doesn't work, my nut-kicking score is one hundred percent. Anyway, as you just witnessed, even hotheads aren't always inclined to punch a sweet, grey-haired old lady. Looks bad.'

Aitch shook her head again. 'Bugger me. Come on, my ute's over here.'

Aitch's ride was an old red Falcon, the sort built back when people worked their utes to death. In the city, in pristine condition, it would be considered a classic car. Out here, with its faded paint and patched upholstery, it was no less distinctive, but from the look of it, appreciated more for its reliability and endurance than for any claims to icon status.

Rena waited as Aitch got behind the wheel and unlocked the passenger side door, then climbed in, pushing aside an Akubra hat and a couple of books as she slid onto the bench seat. She felt a flash of nostalgia as Aitch turned an actual key in the ignition and the V8 rumbled to life with a throatiness that indicated the engine, if not the body, was the subject of regular care and attention.

'Which campground?' Aitch asked, steering a course directly across the near-empty car park.

'The lodge.' Rena turned her head, checking first the wing mirror then over her right shoulder, looking for any sign of pursuit.

'Nah, mate. Moment's past. Doubt they'll bother now. Or if they do, it'll just be next time they see me. Besides, after that meeting, cops'll be out making sure everyone gets home nice and safe, no dramas.'

They drove through quiet streets, the sulphur glow of streetlights turning the dirt on the side of the road a richer shade of vermilion. Sure enough, as Aitch turned onto the highway, the ute's headlights panned over a parked police car, illuminating the watchful faces of two officers within.

Rena felt suddenly exhausted, a depletion of adrenaline after danger that left her right leg shaking. She clamped a firm hand on her thigh, forcing it into stillness. 'So what was that bloke's problem?' she asked.

Aitch shrugged. 'Nothing worth talking about.'

'Rubbish. You said you slapped him, and he looked like he was lining up to punch you. That's more than nothing. It's not because of what you said at the meeting, is it?'

Aitch sighed. 'Nah. Well, not really. Probably didn't help though. Then again, I've been called an uppity bitch and a coconut often enough that no one should be surprised if I can see the good that could come from a diamond mine hereabouts.'

'All right. You don't have to give me chapter and verse, but at least reassure me. Tell me that tomorrow, next week, next month, you'll be okay. That he won't be coming after you.'

Aitch shot a sideways glance at Rena but didn't answer. The silence lasted for a good few Ks of driving before finally, she cleared her throat. 'In town long?'

'Aitch—'

'I can look after myself.'

Rena opened her mouth to argue, but one look at the defiant tilt of Aitch's chin told her not to bother.

They crossed the Martuwarra Fitzroy River, moonlight glinting off shallow pools and a narrow ribbon of water flanked by vast swathes of sand, all that remained of the mighty tributary during the dry months.

'Just drop me at the entrance, thanks, Aitch.' Rena started to unbuckle her seatbelt.

'Sure?'

'Yeah. Best of luck with everything.'

Aitch eased the ute onto the verge, and they came to a smooth stop just shy of the lodge's sign. 'Thanks again for what you did, Rena. You saved my arse, but it was also…an education in diversion and de-escalation.'

'Bullshitting, you mean?'

Aitch smiled. 'Safe travel,' she said.

'Not going anywhere just yet.' Rena cracked the door open and swung a leg out. 'There's a Devonian reef to explore, plus a couple of other things I need to deal with.' She got out of the car and stepped away, letting the door fall closed with a heavy clunk. Rena pulled out her wallet and extracted a card, which she flicked through the open window. 'So…'

Aitch leaned across the seat and scooped up the card. She gave it a quick glance then looked up at Rena, waiting for the rest.

'Now you've got my number. Let me know if you need anything. Another lesson in how to throw bull dust like an old master, or if you want to have a drink. I know I prattle on, but I'm a good listener too.'

Aitch brandished the card then slid it into the top pocket of her shirt. 'I might just do that, Rena. I'd tell you to be careful if you're heading out bush, but I have a feeling I'd be preaching to the choir.'

Rena smiled. 'You're not the only one who can look after herself. Good night, Aitch.'

She turned and walked down the lodge's driveway, heading for her campsite, listening as the sound of Aitch's ute faded into the distance. Rena wondered what the young woman wasn't telling her about the diamond mine, and why she'd been prepared to stand her ground against three men intent on doing her harm.

NINE

Dawn broke in a cloudless sky, and as usual, Rena was up early. She swam in the lodge's pool, showered, did some laundry and by 7 a.m. was sitting beneath her camper's awning, enamel mug of tea in one hand and map in the other, planning the day ahead.

The gorge cruise didn't depart until four in the afternoon, and the empty hours stretched ahead of her. The Mimbi Caves beckoned, the chance to walk in a karst landscape, slip between towering cliffs into caves peppered with marine fossils and freshwater pools, and get up close to the rich ochres and sedimentary limestone layers, not to mention the ancient art and petroglyphs of the Gooniyandi people. Rena wanted to see it for its geology, but she also wanted to see it through the eyes of the Traditional Owners. Her fascination with the earth had remained constant throughout her life, and rocks, minerals, and geology still gave her a thrill, so she could never shake just a hint of envy at people whose connection to those things would always be far greater than anything she could ever have.

She made up her mind. It was only eight. She could be on the road in fifteen minutes and at the caves an hour later, plenty of time to tour the area with local guides and still be back by four.

Rena flicked the dregs of her tea onto the ground and was about to stand when she heard the crunch of tyres on gravel. A police car came into view, made its slow way down the line of campsites, and rolled to a stop in front of Rena's spot.

'Mrs Novak.' Senior Constable Halloran leaned an elbow out the open window, the insignia of the WA Police prominent on the short sleeve of his uniform shirt.

'Officer Halloran.' Rena nodded a greeting but stayed seated. Camp chairs didn't lend themselves to graceful egress, and she hated the thought of looking uncoordinated. Or worse. Old.

'Hoped I'd find you here. Got a minute?' He killed the engine then turned to reach for something on the passenger seat.

Rena used the moment to haul herself to her feet, dropping the map onto the chair. She waited as Halloran climbed from the dusty vehicle, settled a police baseball cap over his grey buzz cut, and took a moment to survey the immediate surrounds.

'Cuppa?' Rena offered, gesturing towards the kitchen area, open in the side of her camper.

'No thanks.' Halloran's dark eyes followed Rena's gesture. 'Nice setup you've got there.'

'The fit-out cost a bit, but worth it not to be towing a van.'

Halloran nodded, his gaze roving over the rest of the Ford Ranger, taking his time, letting a silence develop.

'What can I do for you, Senior Constable?'

Halloran pulled his attention back to her and flicked open a small notebook. 'We got an ID on...the driver of the vehicle you found.'

'That was quick.'

He raised a questioning eyebrow. 'You thought we'd have trouble with that?'

Rena frowned. 'To be honest, yes. I saw it...him, and—'

'What makes you say *him*?' asked Halloran, narrowing his eyes.

'Nothing. I just...' Rena shrugged. 'Look, I have no idea if it was a man or a woman, but, yes, I'm surprised you've identified them so quickly. I saw how bad it was. I don't know anything about forensics except what I've seen on *CSI*—'

Halloran snorted and muttered something that sounded like *fucking cop shows.*

'Anyway,' Rena continued, 'I assumed you'd need to check dental records or something like that, and it would take time.'

Over Halloran's shoulder, two kids on BMX bikes rode quietly to a stop. Rena thought she recognised one of the little buggers from the other night. She could see their heads swivelling between the police car with its open windows and the policeman's back. One of them dismounted, inching forward on quiet feet, a hand outstretched, his target something inside the car, out of Rena's sight.

Halloran must have noticed the direction of Rena's gaze, because he spun around. 'Oi!'

With a squeal they were away, one scrabbling for his discarded bike as his mate raced off in a cloud of dust, tyres skidding on gravel as he rounded the nearest corner. Definitely the same kid. Halloran took a half step forward, adding a spurt of energy to the straggler, and seconds later Rena and the cop were alone again.

When Halloran turned back, he was smiling. 'Little bastards,' he said, sounding avuncular rather than angry. 'I think some of the tourist kids are even more afraid of me 'cause I'm Black, but I don't mind putting the wind up 'em if they're that age and prepared to try their sticky fingers in my patrol car. Where were we?'

'Dental records, *CSI*,' said Rena. She realised she was still holding her mug and now moved to stow it and pack away the kitchen.

'Right. You going somewhere?'

Hearing the slight challenge in Halloran's voice, Rena stopped what she was doing and sighed. 'Depends on how long this takes, I guess. It's the one downside of a camping setup like this; you have to take everything with you, even when it's just a day trip.' Turning, she rested her shoulders against the Ford and folded her arms. Whatever game Halloran was playing, she'd had enough. Yesterday, she'd thought he was treating her like a dotty old fool; today Rena felt like she was on trial.

They stared at each other for a moment before Halloran relented. 'As it happens, you're right; usually it takes some time to identify a victim with...this degree of trauma. This is a presumptive ID only, based on who owns the vehicle and who was supposed to be behind the wheel. Anything solid comes from the forensic pathologist in Perth, and that's going to take weeks, if not months. But under the circumstances, we're pretty confident that the driver was an Adelaide man called Martin Kinnane. Does that name mean—'

'Kinnane? Marty Kinnane?' Rena gaped at the policeman.

'Are you saying you *know* the deceased?'

She ran a hand through her hair. 'Well, yes. I mean, I knew him. Haven't seen him for twenty or more years. My God!'

Rena could feel Halloran's scrutiny, aware that her admission had set off alarm bells, but heck! What were the odds?

'Mrs Novak, I suddenly find myself with a lot more questions, which means my colleagues—the detectives in charge of this case—will be very keen to have a chat, find out what you can tell us about our victim.'

'You're not doing the investigating?'

'Not my job. I'm here because...well, frankly, we thought this would draw a complete blank from you, just a box-ticking exercise. I was heading out this way, so I offered to save them a wasted trip. Now, however...'

'And how did you identify him so quickly? Oh, you said... So did you find anything in the car or out there somewhere that helped with the identification?'

Halloran winced, which Rena took as an acknowledgement that he was regretting yesterday's dismissive attitude; then he shook his head. 'I'm not at liberty to say, Mrs Novak. How about we continue this discussion back at the station?'

'Let me just...' Rena closed down the kitchen, going through the familiar motions while her thoughts bounced back and forth, an old-style pinball machine rattling her brain, shaking memories loose. Five minutes later she put a foot on the lowest rung of the ladder, ready to climb up and collapse the rooftop tent.

'No need for that, Mrs Novak. Just lock 'er up. I can run you into the station and bring you back later,' said Halloran.

Rena nodded, grabbed her wallet and keys, then climbed into the front passenger seat of Halloran's police car. She earned a few suspicious glances from other travellers as they drove slowly out of the camping ground, but Rena barely noticed. All she could think about was Marty Kinnane, the geologist she'd known and worked with decades ago in South Australia, turning up as a charred corpse in the Kimberley. And one question prevailed over all others.

How had Kinnane survived that long? Someone should have killed that slimy bastard twenty years ago.

TEN

This time, there was no informal chat at Senior Constable Halloran's desk. The officer guided Rena to a side room and left, shutting the door quietly. The room was blandly institutional, beige walls, darker brown linoleum, and furnished sparsely with what looked like an Ikea dining setting for four: a smallish table and four chairs that probably promised more comfort than they delivered. Rena stood for a bit, until it became obvious that Halloran wasn't coming straight back, then sat, confirming her initial impression about the chairs.

Fifteen minutes later, just when Rena was thinking about going looking for someone, the door opened again admitting two strangers, a man and a woman. They weren't in uniform, but both wore similar attire, and both carried themselves with authority. The woman was about forty, brown eyes, no makeup, a smile on her face; her white shirt and tan trousers looked expensively cool in both a thermal and aesthetic sense. The man had dark blond hair cut short and spiky, his take on the white and tan ensemble geared more to wash-and-wear. Rena pegged him as slightly older than his colleague.

'Mrs Novak?' The woman dealt out bottles of water to three points on the table as she spoke. 'I'm Detective Ito, this is Detective Fletcher. Thanks for coming in.'

'Sure. Constable Halloran thought you'd want to see me.' She half stood, reaching across the table to shake hands.

'When the senior constable told us about his conversation with you today, we were surprised, to say the least. So, yes, we're keen to have a chat with you ourselves. You don't mind if we record this, do you?' Detective Ito's tone made it a statement rather than a question. 'Helps us later.' She pulled out the chair next to her colleague and sat facing Rena.

Rena looked from one to the other, not bothering to hide her scrutiny. Their postures were relaxed, both leaning back, conveying a matey bonhomie. Ito was still smiling and her hands rested loosely on the table, while Fletcher was fiddling with a pen, tapping the end lightly against his lips. There was an expression of polite enquiry on his face as though he was about to ask after her health, but his hazel-green eyes were hard as flint.

Rena felt her senses sharpening. Once she'd told Halloran she knew the victim—knew Marty—of course the police would want more details. But Rena had attended enough meetings in her working life to recognise the signs of an ambush in play. Whether it was city suits who didn't understand the realities of geology and mining, men trying to claim her work as their own, or a couple of detectives who thought they were on to something, they all tripped Rena's bullshit detector.

She sat back, mirroring their body language, and waited.

They didn't mention Kinnane at first, instead getting her to repeat the story of finding the burning vehicle and what followed. Rena laid it out, answered questions that had already been asked, clarified points that were already clear, and generally danced through the minefield they were trying to lay. All in all, they did a reasonable job, but her respect for their interview technique wavered when Ito leaned forward abruptly, fixed her with a penetrating gaze and said, 'And you had no idea who the driver was?'

Rena couldn't help herself. She furrowed her brow and jerked her head back. 'Did you see the car? Did you see the driver? Or what was left of the poor bastard? There was nothing recognisable there, Detective Ito.'

The two detectives exchanged a quick, sliding glance.

'But when Senior Constable Halloran told you the victim was Martin Kinnane, you recognised the name, correct?' Fletcher's voice was smooth, all private school vowels and crisp enunciation.

'Yeah. I was floored.'

'Us too.' Ito smiled, this time without warmth. 'Tell us about your relationship with Martin Kinnane, Mrs Novak.'

'I don't have one. Haven't seen him since, oh, 2000 or 2001,' said Rena. On the drive over and while she'd been waiting, she'd had plenty of time to reflect on her dealings with Marty and also determine just how much she wanted to tell the cops. After all, it wasn't as though ancient history had any bearing on Marty's recent demise, and besides, maybe the arsehole had changed in that time. He might be a born-again Christian for all Rena knew, in which case, speaking ill of the dead would only confuse issues.

She gave the detectives an apologetic smile and reached for the nearest water bottle, twisting off the lid with an overly loud snap.

'Well, tell us about that then.' Fletcher stabbed the pen into the top of his notebook, a small crack in his facade.

So she did, explaining how she and Martin Kinnane had both been field geologists, how they had briefly worked for the same company back in the nineties, when Kinnane was fresh out of university and Rena was mid-career, a senior member of the team. And after Kinnane had left in pursuit of other opportunities, how the two of them subsequently crossed paths at a couple of conferences, exchanged a few minutes of polite conversation, then gone their separate ways again. In between those times, Rena would hear occasional snippets of news and gossip from others in the industry, but now she had no idea who Kinnane's current employer was or even if he was still in the industry.

'Once you retire,' Rena concluded, 'you lose touch.' She leaned back in her chair.

For a moment the only sounds in the room were the scratch of Fletcher's pen and the faint hum of the air conditioning.

'When was the last time you heard something about Kinnane?' asked Ito.

Rena didn't need to think, but she frowned and paused a moment anyway. 'About eighteen months ago, at my retirement party.'

'And what was it?'

Rena shook her head and waved the question away. 'Just rubbish. The sort of thing half-drunk people say about someone who isn't there. An ounce of truth laced liberally with a bucket of rumours and a dash of sour grapes.'

Ito leaned forward, eyes wide, asking an unspoken question.

Rena sighed. 'He'd apparently left a position with Verne Industries rather suddenly, and the stories were flying as to the reason. Everything from cuckolding the CFO to stealing stones to insider trading.'

'So he'd lost his job at...Verne Industries, did you say?'

'That's what the scuttlebutt was.'

'And this was eighteen months ago?'

'That was when I retired. Can't tell you when Marty had supposedly got the boot from Verne Industries, but if the rumour was true, it must've been a bit before that. You know how people are; they like fresh meat, and there was no tail to the story, no *and now he's...* So probably only a few months before that at the most.'

'And that's the last you heard?' Ito's tone was neutral, but she was watching Rena closely.

Rena nodded. 'Yep.'

Ito leaned back, her mouth twisting slightly in disappointment or anger; Rena couldn't be sure. The detectives exchanged a glance, and Fletcher's shoulders twitched, as if he was too impatient to shrug with any conviction. He gathered up his things.

'I think that's all for now.' Ito slid a business card across the table to Rena. 'But if you think of anything, no matter how insignificant it may seem, call me or Detective Fletcher, any time.'

Her partner nodded and, with a deft flick of the wrist, landed his own details on top of Ito's. He'd make a mean poker player.

'Can I ask a question?' Rena pocketed the cards.

'Go ahead,' said Ito, cutting across Fletcher's exasperated tsk.

'The way he was burned... What did you find to help you identify Marty so quickly?'

Ito's brow furrowed then cleared. 'I guess there's no harm in telling you. It was the car. It belongs to a mining company, Martin Kinnane is the assigned driver, and he's supposed to be out here in the West Kimberley. The coroner still has to deliver his findings, but that information's pretty conclusive.'

'Which mining company? Synastria?' Rena kept her tone light, as though they were chatting about the local bowls club over tea and scones.

'No, as it happens, Verne Industries.'

'Seriously? So, he must have been with them all along.' Rena shook her head. 'I told you that retirement party story was just a bunch of bull dust.'

'So you did.' Fletcher stood, his abrupt movement and clipped tone clear indicators that he was done.

'And one more thing.' Rena also stood.

Fletcher opened his mouth, but Ito shot him a quick look and he subsided. 'Yes, Mrs Novak?'

'The fact that I'm here, this conversation we've just had.' Rena looked from one face to the other. 'Marty's death wasn't an accident, was it?'

ELEVEN

Rena left the police station with mixed emotions. The detectives had dissembled, but it was clear things had changed in the last forty-eight hours and the death was being treated as suspicious. Which meant Martin Kinnane had been murdered.

Rena felt satisfied that she'd been right about the car fire being suss, but murder! And then there was the driver; she still hadn't sorted out her feelings about that, about...Marty.

It wasn't until she'd reached the near-empty street out the front of the cop shop that Rena remembered Constable Halloran had given her a ride to the station.

'Shit.'

There was no hope of hailing a passing cab out here, and the thought of a walk in the building heat had no appeal. She was just about to head back inside to organise a lift when a white taxi barrelled around the corner, two wheels dipping into the dirt at the side of the road, then jerked to a stop a few metres short of where Rena stood. She raised a hand and moved toward it slowly, taking her time so whoever was in the back seat could wrap up their business, but no one emerged.

'You Mrs Novak?' the driver yelled. He was a big-looking bloke, a large head and thick neck atop a wide chest, the whole of him seeming to entirely fill half of the front cabin, his shoulders and torso far broader than the driver's seat.

Surprised, Rena nodded.

The cabbie jerked his head towards the police station. 'Nic called. Said you needed my services. On their tab.'

Rena covered the remaining distance and slid into the unoccupied front seat. Since COVID far fewer people travelled in taxis the Aussie way, but Rena couldn't shake the habit; it felt too prissy and entitled to ride in the back.

'Thanks,' she said, buckling her seatbelt.

'The lodge, yes?'

'Yes.'

Rena studied the driver as he executed a careful U-turn. He was large without being obese; wide, clean-shaven chin, no visible tattoos on his exposed neck or forearms, and a shock of unruly blond hair fading to silver.

Once they were on the way, he took his right hand from the wheel and reached across. 'I'm Wojciech—Wally. You need a taxi in Fitzroy Crossing, you call me.'

Rena shook. 'Nice to meet you. Slavic?'

'Poland. Long time ago.'

'How'd you end up here?'

Wally flashed her a wide smile, punctuated by a gold tooth. 'Came to make my fortune. Made only a little bit—not a fortune but enough—then I met my wife and had to make more so...taxi!'

Rena felt herself instantly warming to the bear-like man behind the wheel; there was something about his openness and enthusiasm that struck a chord. 'So, no more prospecting?'

Wally laughed and pinched his thumb and index finger together. 'Always a little bit. My wife, she comes too. Up near Halls Creek, you know? Sometimes down to Marble Bar. Because how can I stop? Every time might be the time. Every ping of the metal detector might be thumbnail or big nugget.' He shrugged.

'Yes, I know what you mean. I've got a detector myself, not that I've used it for a while.'

'So you know! Is hobby or obsession, but also something to do when business is slow; I keep detector in the boot of cab, just in case. Because as well as gold, sometimes I do jobs for people, you know? They lose something like a wedding ring, radioactive capsule that fall off truck—you hear about that?' He turned to look at Rena and the cab swerved.

'Yeah, I did. Cesium-137, wasn't it? From one of the Rio Tinto mines? You found that?'

'Not me, but I look. And sometimes people hide things and forget where. Then they call Wally and his metal detector.'

'Hide things? Like what?'

Wally shrugged, a massive gesture that carried his chest skyward with his shoulders. 'That I don't ask. But no banks out here, no steel vault, so sometimes you need to hide things, keep them safe. I've done this maybe half a dozen times. Sometimes they tell me, *Wally, it's this* or *Wally, it's that,* but sometimes I have no idea. And once—recent, actually—not only big secret, but such a big secret they don't want Wally at all. They tell me something hidden in tin can.' He took a hand off the wheel shaping it to cup an invisible tin, indicating the size. 'Then they say not you, just want to rent or maybe buy Wally's metal detector!'

'And did you rent the detector? Did they find whatever it was?' It would drive Rena nuts not knowing what she'd found. Drugs? A wad of cash? Family heirlooms?

'Pfft.' Wally puffed out a derisive breath. 'No. Wally and detector are package deal. Plus, I don't want to sell. At least not for the few zloty—dollars—offered.' He tipped his head from side to side.

'But I think my client maybe think again. Decide to pay Wojciech for his time.'

'So they didn't find the tin?'

'Don't know. Haven't seen for a while, but will hear something soon. Small town.' Wally flipped on the indicator and turned into the lodge's driveway, coming to a stop in front of the main reception. He fished a business card from a holder on the dashboard and passed it to Rena. 'You need taxi, you call.'

'Thanks, I will.' Rena accepted the card and stepped out of the cab. She gave the roof a pat, then watched as Wally drove off, raising a hand in farewell.

It was too late to visit the caves today, but now Rena had a call to make. Despite what she'd told the detectives, retirement hadn't meant losing touch with everybody, not the people who mattered. She wanted to find the truth behind the story about Marty leaving Verne Industries and, if he had, how his reinstatement had come about. Just as importantly, she wanted to find out why Verne Industries had a field geologist sniffing around by himself, way out here in the Kimberley.

TWELVE

Rena waited for the call to connect, picturing the room at the other end where an old landline phone would be trilling. Les had been retired for nearly a decade now, his wife, Margot, a little less than that. But they were active in all the professional societies, regulars at gem and mineral club shows, and most importantly, they had one of the best mineral collections in the country. What that meant was that anyone who called themselves a rock hound at least knew of them and had probably spoken to them, sold them something or bought a specimen from them at some point. As pioneering geologists back in the days when it seemed as though every bit of Australian ground was a potential mine—whether iron ore, uranium, gold, or something else—Margot and Les were legends. They knew everyone, they knew the country, and if anything, retirement had only given them more time to keep tabs on everything going on in the industry.

If they didn't know what Marty Kinnane had been doing the last year or so, they'd know who to ask.

There was a click on the line, a hiss, and then the answering machine kicked in, Les's voice, telling her they were unavailable and to please leave a message.

'Blast.' Rena had been prepared for a few minutes of pleasantries and scrambled to come up with an innocuous message before the beep sounded.

'Les, Margot darling. It's Rena. Just wondering if you can give me a bell when you have the chance. Hoping you can shed some light on Verne and a certain past and apparently current employee of theirs.' She cut the call. That should do it. There was a fair chance they'd know who she was referring to, and if not, they'd either dig up dirt from as many people as they could until they uncovered Marty's name and got the whole story, or they'd hurry to call Rena back. Either way worked.

With her plans for the day torpedoed, Rena decided to make use of the local library's aircon and decent Wi-Fi to do a bit of her own research. She had a broad idea of what had previously been mined in the area and what potentially might still be untapped, but as far as she knew, there were still no Aboriginal people sitting on the boards of big mining companies. Rena wanted to understand exactly what was at stake for the locals and what consideration would be given to Traditional Owners if Synastria got the green light.

She still hadn't heard from Les and Margot by the time she stepped onto the boat at Danggu Geikie Gorge, but Rena wasn't fazed; they'd call when they had something. She settled herself into a forward seat and, for the next hour and a bit, gave her attention entirely to the guide, the magnificent Devonian limestone, the crocs, and all the other flora and fauna of the Martuwarra Fitzroy River.

Back at her campsite, tired of the company of others but not of the landscape or of crocodile sightings, Rena made up her mind. She'd been kicking around here for the last couple of days, waiting for God-knows-what. Now she knew the police were investigating Marty Kinnane's death—murder—there was nothing for her to do except congratulate herself on her instincts and powers of observation and leave it up to them. One more night here then she'd be off, head for the Dampier Peninsula then maybe down to Karratha, get herself a miner's permit and head into proper gold country. The metal detector was stowed in the Ranger, and she'd not even bothered to use it yet.

The only thing left was to say goodbye to Adam and Mike, but when she wandered over, instead of their RV, she found a family-sized caravan, complete with harried mother, excitable kids, and barbecuing-with-stubby-in-hand father. Rena pivoted smartly and returned to her own vehicle, thinking about friendship and the fleeting interactions that were part of being a grey nomad.

She stayed up long after the campground had fallen silent around her, then slept, dreaming a geologist's dream of orogens and sinistral strike-slip faulting, and of lamproite and kimberlite volcanic pipes, thrusting diamonds upwards from deep in the earth's core.

When she woke in the pre-dawn, Rena had a different plan, one that took on a more solid shape as she showered, ate, and folded the camper back in on itself. The moment reception opened, she checked out, pocketed a message that was waiting for her without a glance, and had the Ford pointed down the Great Northern Highway within minutes.

There was a buzzing in her head and a tightness in her gut that was both familiar and strange at the same time. It took Rena a while to identify what the feelings meant.

For the first time since she retired, since her husband died, Rena had a purpose.

THIRTEEN

Once again, Rena drove back to the scene of the fire, easily finding the turn from the highway onto the dirt track. She didn't stop near the patch of scorched earth—now marked only by a small tab of police tape caught among the yellow flowers of a nearby kapok bush—but slowly steered around the site, bumping over uneven ground until she could regain the track.

The burnt-out car had been facing away from the highway, which meant—assuming it wasn't a random dump site—that whatever had drawn Marty here lay somewhere in the outback beyond. There was probably nothing to find, and maybe the cops had already been out there; didn't they do that—look for secondary crime scenes? Then again, even if they had come this way, how far would they go? In this country, the parameters of distance and time seemed to become less tangible, the vastness somehow imparting an illusory quality, as though millennia could pass in a heartbeat, and a few steps could take you beyond the horizon. It would be possible for police to drive for hours, days even, and see nothing of relevance to the life and death of Martin Kinnane. Which is not to say there was nothing to find, just that they hadn't quite travelled far enough, or had veered a hundred—or maybe just ten—metres to one side of...whatever.

But unlike the police, Rena had nothing else to do and was prepared for a few nights camping, so she could keep searching. And Rena had another advantage: She knew what to look for. Not discarded beer cans or a convenient shred of clothing or even an ominous trail of blood. If Marty was out here working for Verne Industries, it meant he was looking for something. And whether it was lead and zinc deposits or something even more valuable, Rena, like Marty, could read the earth, its colours and folds and protrusions. She wasn't seeking signs of Marty's presence; instead Rena would look for indicators of minerals. Because that's where Marty would have been—where the earth held something special, something precious. If nothing else, it would be an interesting exercise for Rena, a check of the skills she'd honed over decades but recently mothballed.

The track continued to weave its way through the scrub, skirting trees and termite mounds, switching back on itself, but always continuing in a rough, northerly direction. Ahead lay marginal uplands that formed part of the Wunaamin Miliwundi Ranges, a nearly six-hundred-kilometre-long crescent of quartz sandstone intruded by dolerite, separating the Fitzroy plains from the main Kimberley plateau. Rena knew once she reached that country—if she reached that country—there would be flat-floored valleys where the terrain would make for good driving, but those valleys would be flanked by rocky strike ridges, some up to three or four hundred metres high, with few if any passes. There would be no cutting across open ground if she made a wrong turn. On the plus side, it was distinctly possible that spring-fed waterholes existed in this sort of landscape, although Rena wasn't stupid enough to rely on finding those without prior knowledge.

Rena had supplies for several days, a UHF radio, a GPS beacon, and an iridium satellite adaptor for her smartphone if things went to shit. She was also in possession of a reasonable degree of bushcraft, and no one to either please or give a stuff about what she did. Basically, everything an inquisitive retiree with time on her hands, no fucks to give, and a thing for rocks needed to head for the hills. Well, that and a pick and metal detector, but she had those too.

The conditions required slow driving, but Rena took it even slower than necessary, scanning the surrounding scrub for anything that might indicate someone had camped there, watching the edges of the track for signs a vehicle had turned onto rougher ground and, after a while, casting her gaze a bit wider, assessing the land, looking for variations that might suggest a pleasant camping spot. And always heading for the uplands, knowing that if there was mineral wealth to be had, that was where it would lie.

About forty minutes after she drove past the accident site, the faint track petered out to nothing. Rena brought the Ford to a stop in a small clearing. There was spinifex, a few woolly butts here and there, and a profusion of overlaid tyre tracks, jagging back and forth in the soft earth, suggesting at least one vehicle had turned around here. Not so much a three-point turn as eight or ten points.

Killing the engine, Rena grabbed her hat and exited the cab, the heat hitting from all directions, rising up from the red dirt, beating down from the sky. She slammed the door, and silence rushed to fill the place where sound had been, not even an insect daring to break across it.

She needed to pee, and even though she was alone in the middle of nowhere, Rena moved behind the nearest shrub. As she did her business, she contemplated the country beyond, where a couple of rocky outcrops broke the horizon. That had to be it. Unless she'd missed some secondary trail, there was no way Marty had come here and turned around. Despite indications to the contrary, he must have driven beyond this point, and the fact that there was no obvious sign of his passing made Rena's antennae go up. In geology and mining, secrecy meant money. If Rena was right, all those back-and-forth tyre marks were a bluff, designed to make anyone who came this way think they'd reached the end of the road, or at least cast doubt on which direction they should take from here. It was a clever idea, but no one who had driven this far off-road could possibly be that bad at turning their vehicle around; anyone with half a brain who knew Marty had been out here wouldn't be deterred.

Rena finished what she was doing then began a slow circuit of the clearing's perimeter.

Nothing.

Then she took five steps into the scrub and repeated the process. You could hide the start of a trail, but you couldn't hide it all.

Still no sign of anything, let alone that a four-wheel drive had passed through and kept going.

She widened the circle another five steps, stomping her booted feet and keeping alert for snakes. An encounter with a death adder was more likely at night, and they were known to often give dry warning bites, but Rena had no desire to test either hypothesis. Besides, there were always taipans, a few varieties of brown snake, and an assortment of other venomous things to consider.

Rena's focus was on the ground ahead when she saw it on a short stretch of bare, sandy earth between the grasses: the imprint of a tyre, cutting across her path and heading northwest.

'Gotcha,' she muttered, adjusting her trajectory.

It was less than a metre of ground, but now that she'd seen that tyre mark, other signs became obvious, pointing the way: a couple of broken branches, a flattened tussock, and, on a knee-high termite mound, a scrape of royal-blue paint. Rena scouted out about fifty metres or so, until she was confident she knew which way Marty had headed, then she went back to get her vehicle.

No one ever said travelling around Australia meant sticking to the highways, and if personal development was all about taking the road less travelled, surely Rena was on a path to enlightenment with this caper.

Either that or she'd die out here. It was six of one, half a dozen of the other, really.

She put the car in gear and nosed it into the spinifex, marking a point on the horizon to lead her forward on the all-but-invisible trail, confident that any obstacles would also show signs of being overcome. Or at least, detoured around.

As she leaned forward over the steering wheel, she could almost hear Tom's sardonic voice, *Having fun yet, Reenie?*

Alone in the Ford, and possibly in the surrounding hundred kilometres, Rena smiled.

FOURTEEN

It wasn't what she expected to find, but then again, she didn't know what she'd been expecting.

A camp. An honest-to-God, tent-pitched, firepit-dug, equipment-laid-out camp.

Rena had pushed the Ford Ranger overland for another hour, watching the ridges slowly grow larger up ahead, knowing that if she found anything, it would be there, in the shadow of those uplifts. She'd had to curb her impatience, keen to forge ahead but not game to nudge the speed above forty. And even that felt like a gamble at times. The country she was crossing looked featureless, and it would be easy to think that if you dodged the trees and anthills, you were good, but the whole area was one vast floodplain, crisscrossed by myriad shallow washes and dried creek beds. Nothing she couldn't navigate in four-wheel drive, but not the sort of thing you wanted to hit at speed. On the other hand, creek beds meant sandy soil or dried mud, where the dual tracks of a vehicle's passing stood out like a blowfly on a wedding cake. They reassured Rena, kept her going, and now here she was.

Exactly where here *was,* was another matter. Rena had the GPS coordinates, and the scree slope and laterite breakaway rising immediately in front of her was only the first of many such formations, so there was still nothing to distinguish this location from anywhere else. Rena was surprised by the camp's location; she'd thought whatever Marty had been doing, he'd have been doing it in deeper back country, someplace where the rock types or land formations whispered a different geological story.

Rena rolled the Ford to a stop about one hundred metres out, cut the engine, and surveyed the area. The tent had been pitched on the last flat patch before the ground began its gentle rise toward the escarpment towering above. The canvas was a dull, rusty brown colour, not exactly camouflage, but certainly nothing that would stand out in this country. And it was big—far too big for a single person, but about right if it was also a mobile workspace—with an awning extended out the front providing shade for a folding table and chair. The tent's door and window vents were zipped up tight.

For the first time, Rena felt uneasy. Perhaps it was knowing Marty had left this setup, obviously intending to come back. Or perhaps it was the realisation that if Marty had been murdered, the reason might be right here. Despite the fact Marty was—had been—a consummate arsehole who could nominate *how to be an utter bastard and piss people off* as his special subject on a quiz show, he might not have been killed over someone's wife, an argument in the pub, or an escalation of a road rage incident.

Rena got out of the Ford, but remained behind the open door, scanning the sloping ground behind the camp, looking for anything out of place, trying to expand her hearing beyond the tick of cooling metal and the crescendo-decrescendo of a sandfly making sorties on her head.

'Hello?' Even as she called, she knew it was stupid. There was no one here; if there was, the noise and dust of her vehicle would have announced Rena's impending arrival some time ago.

'Get a grip,' she muttered to herself. There was no one hiding in the tent, behind the tent, or up the slope. Everything was tidy. No one had been here rifling through Marty's things, looking for... what? Rena was utterly alone.

She stepped away from the Ford, slamming the door loudly. Rena knew she should call the police, but figured it was better to have some idea of what to tell them before she bothered.

Using a hanky from her pocket, Rena grabbed the tent flap's zipper, ripped the door open and flung it aside. Stifling heat wafted out to greet her, and she stood, waiting for her eyes to adjust to the dimness within.

There wasn't a lot to see: a rolled sleeping bag in the corner next to a pile of clothes, a sturdy-looking backpack, sunken sides proclaiming its emptiness, a camp cupboard stocked with non-perishable food, and a large metal chest set against the back wall. Rena glanced over her shoulder, taking in the red landscape where not a single leaf stirred, then crossed the canvas threshold, entering the tent.

She should call the cops.

Rena prodded the clothes with the toe of her boot then crouched down and checked through everything, right down to the groundsheet beneath. Next, she inverted the backpack, gave it a good shake, and felt in each pocket. It yielded no secrets, only confirmation of its owner, the name *Kinnane* written on the top flap in permanent ink.

She couldn't use the UHF radio to contact police—wouldn't want to broadcast the location over an open channel where anyone could hear—but she could use her smartphone with the satellite adaptor. Rena had the detectives' business cards somewhere, but it was too late for anyone to drive out here before darkness fell. She could probably wait until morning to phone.

Rena unrolled the sleeping bag, patting down every inch. There was nothing in the cupboard other than food, and she stopped short of emptying out open packets.

Finally, Rena turned to the metal chest. She had deliberately left it till last, feeling its looming presence all the while.

It was the sort of chest she'd used throughout her career, a lockable place to store charts and sensitive company documents, equipment like laser range finders and hand lenses, even the iPad. And somewhere secure to keep samples: a lump of gold-bearing quartz or garnets embedded in a piece of chloritic schist. If there was anything Marty had wanted to keep safe—assuming it hadn't been stolen already, or he wasn't carrying it with him when his car became a fireball—this is where it would be.

Rena squatted down in front of the chest, hearing her knees pop. A large combination padlock dangled from the hasp.

She spun each of the three wheels to zero and gave it a tug, but it remained locked.

'Damn.'

She stood and hurried from the tent. Hands to her head, Rena strode around the campsite. The sun had fallen closer to the horizon, and with the lengthening shadows came a small dip in the temperature, a welcome change after the stuffy confines of the tent.

There were tools in the Ford that could break the lock—it would be a matter of minutes. But it would also be guaranteed to piss off the police and probably ratchet up their suspicion of her a few notches. It was definitely the wrong thing to do, but there was another party to consider in all of this: Verne Industries.

If Marty had been out here sampling for the company, they were looking for mineable quantities of something. Potentially, there could be millions, even billions of dollars in returns, depending on what Marty had or hadn't found. Rena knew Verne had diverse interests. Along with various international operations, they had a lithium mine near Kalgoorlie and held licence over a uranium deposit near a place called Oobagooma; Rena had no idea where that was, but assumed it was somewhere remote. Rare earth minerals were an emerging and lucrative market, but if they were setting their sights on diamonds... Since the closure of the Argyle mine in 2020, no new sources of fancy pink diamonds had been found. A new deposit would be incredible, but it would also hit the rapidly rising value of Argyle pinks; someone holding a cache of stones could lose a fortune. And then there was Synastria. They clearly intended to become the next major source of coloured diamonds and wouldn't welcome competition. Not to mention the hard pushback there would be from environmentalists and Traditional Owners if two mining companies wanted to break ground relatively close to each other. Basically, that meant a whole lot of people who had good reasons to stop Marty Kinnane and Verne Industries.

Marty's chest might hold commercial-in-confidence material, the files that showed the what and where of any potential mineral wealth. Once the police went through everything, it'd be a matter of hours before everyone and their dog knew all there was to know about Verne Industries' business.

Rena walked slowly back to her Ranger, thinking about the potential fallout.

She set up her own camp, unfurling things and snapping catches into place, working from muscle memory, hands going through the motions without her thinking about any of it.

It was getting darker now, and as Rena flicked on the LED lights illuminating the kitchen unit, something concrete was thrown to the surface of her jumbled thoughts. Grabbing a torch, she hurried back to Marty's tent. The flap was still open; Rena entered and dropped to her knees in front of the chest. It took a moment to find a spot for the torch so it would point in the right direction, then Rena grabbed the lock again. It was probably a dumb idea—Marty had probably set the combination to his birthday or some random pattern—but what did Rena have to lose? She spun the tiny dials, 6, 1, 2. The atomic number of carbon, and its atomic mass. Diamonds.

The lock clicked open in her hand.

FIFTEEN

Rena raised the lid and pointed her torch into the chest. The beam first fell on some pieces of equipment, snug in a padded compartment. She panned the torch slowly, lighting up a microfibre dust cloth, a pile of documents, then a laptop, sitting up so high there had to be another layer beneath.

Rena hesitated: She'd already overstepped by a long way. Besides, it was too dark to examine this stuff properly, and she didn't want to take everything back to her camp. So a quick glance at a few papers now, then she'd know a bit more and be able to give police a clearer picture of the situation when she called. Tonight.

She slid a hand between the documents and the side of the chest, reaching for the bottom of the pile, the place where *she'd* stash the most important thing. Rena teased paper with her fingertips, tugging gently, the object of her attention moving slowly, finally sliding free of the weight above it. An exercise book, missing its cover.

A quick glance at the topmost page showed lines of cramped text, interspersed with a couple of field sketches. Even with digital cameras, nothing beat the detail of a labelled drawing when it came time to write up your findings. No doubt Marty's laptop was packed with geological software, but programs need input, accurate input. Rena thought about taking the computer as well, but instead, she grabbed the dust cloth and used it to shift the laptop to one side, exposing a plastic box underneath. She knew her caution was stupid—she'd pawed through a lot of Marty's things without a second thought—but at least she might bluff the cops into believing she'd never had this chest open. Still using the cloth, she opened the box and grunted, surprised at what she was looking at: a collection of medium-sized sacks, each one securely tied and carrying a tag inscribed with a GPS point. Rena picked one up, feeling the weight and looseness of its contents. Soil samples, probably about eight kilos per bag.

Just to be sure, she set the sack on the ground, undid the fastening and stuck her hand in, dragging her fingers through the soil, testing its consistency. It was fine earth, small grains, a sign that Marty had sifted the sample, as Rena would expect. But it was just a soil sample, and all she pulled out was a dirty hand. Frowning, Rena retied the bag and put it back with the others.

'What the fuck, Marty?' she whispered.

If Marty's soil samples were about finding diamondiferous ground, it wasn't as though he'd just be hoping to stumble on a patch of earth peppered with sparkling gems. Even if you were standing on the right sort of land, the chances of seeing anything with the naked eye were small; there wouldn't be any obvious diamonds, just signs, possibilities. If the geological auguries were encouraging, you mapped out a grid and started sampling dirt, and those samples would get refined and microscopically assessed in a lab, probably in Perth. Then if the results were positive—if minute traces of diamonds or indicator stones were found—Verne Industries would set up a plant somewhere out here to process large quantities of gravel and determine if the promise of diamonds was borne out.

Something wasn't right. It *looked* okay, if you were a casual observer who didn't know the ins and outs of this stuff, but…

The small size of the samples suggested Verne Industries—assuming they were after diamonds—was only in the early stages of exploration. If they'd already had some positive indicators, if they thought they were onto a pipe, they'd be running check samples by now, digging out big chunks of earth about thirty kilos or so each, packing them in large crates that would be retrieved from collection sites by chopper. Not these sackfuls—and there were only six of them. If exploration was in its infancy, there should be more bags, not to mention other Verne geologists out here, collecting dozens of samples at different sites across thousands of square kilometres, not just one man. Not just Marty Kinnane.

Yet the cops had been able to ID Marty quickly based on the fact he was driving Verne's vehicle, which meant it was the only one out here. No other Verne four-wheel drives meant no other geologists, at least not in this particular corner of the Kimberley. Even if Verne was after something else like rare earth elements instead of diamonds, they should have had more people in the field. People who could have swooped in, secured this camp, and cleared it of anything important. Unless of course, they were still on their way.

'Idiot,' Rena muttered. She'd been distracted by the competition, thinking of Synastria's interests, not the bigger picture. Just because one company had located a deposit didn't mean others had been so fortunate. And diamonds weren't necessarily the only game in town. Mining wealth came in a variety forms, and the Kimberley was rich with many of them.

On impulse, Rena pulled her phone from her back pocket, powered it up, and snapped a picture of each tag, making sure the details were legible in the low light. Regardless of what the bags were supposed to contain, the GPS details should be legit. Given that right now Rena had no idea what was what, she figured it was best to gather as much information as possible.

Rena replaced the laptop, tucked the microfibre back in its spot and picked up the notebook. If anything Marty was seeing or finding mineral-wise had gotten him genuinely excited, he would have noted it in here. And even if he'd kept things general, or used code words to hide his real purpose, there should be enough for someone with Rena's expertise to figure out what Marty was looking for. The police wouldn't understand geological notes, let alone realise if Marty had used some sort of code.

It sounded crazy, but there was a precedent for using code. No one in the Argyle joint venture ever talked about diamonds when the hunt was still on; it was all baryte: large quantities of baryte, traces of baryte, baryte this and baryte that. How would the cops know if they were reading about baryte—which was a useful mineral but also very low value and unlikely to make anyone ridiculously wealthy—that things didn't make sense? Whereas Rena would pick it immediately. And if she came across something relevant in the notebook, Rena would tell the police, wouldn't she? As long as she could come up with a plausible excuse for having the notebook. Or act like a doddery old lady who absent-mindedly put it in her pocket. Whatever she did, Rena sure as hell wouldn't mention where she'd found it. Tucking the notebook under her chin, Rena closed and relocked the chest. She'd go over Marty's field notes and the police could deal with the rest.

She re-zipped the tent and let the lights of her own camp guide her. The sun was nothing more than a memory, a faint afterglow on the horizon, and the crescent moon offered little in the way of illumination, too low and small in the sky. But despite the darkness and isolation, or perhaps because of it, Rena felt quite serene. In fact, she was surprised to realise how at peace she was, given the location and circumstances.

Back at the Ranger, she had another flick through the notebook under the kitchen LEDs. The handwriting was cramped, the notes often in pencil; even with her reading glasses in this decent light, it would take time to decipher. It wasn't as if Marty's life depended on Rena reading the notebook and, besides, she was having second thoughts about taking it. Maybe she'd put it back, let the police find it, then offer her assistance. That was what Tom would tell her to do. But after all her effort, it seemed a shame to just hand it over. She fingered the pages again, then sighed. The off-road driving had taken more out of her than she'd expected, and she could feel the fog at the edge of her brain. Rena wanted a clear head when she applied herself to the pages of scrawl—*if* she did—and once she'd started, there was no way a quick glance would suffice; she'd still be hunched over the notebook when the sun came up.

Instead, Rena stowed it in the back of one of the kitchen's lockable drawers then powered up the satellite adaptor and connected her phone. It took her a few minutes to find the business cards, tucked into the holder on the sun visor, but by then her phone had two satellites in range and was ready for service. She thumbed through the options, made a note of her GPS coordinates; then despite the hour, she called the police, trying the number at the station first. It went straight to a robotic message that told her which number she'd dialled and suggested she call triple-O if it was an emergency, so she disconnected and tried the mobile. Different message, same result. This time, Rena left a brief voicemail, stating what she'd found and giving her location in latitude and longitude. There was no need to request a return call—she assumed Ito would be on the phone the moment she heard what Rena had to say.

After a scratch meal, Rena switched off all but one of the lights, moved her chair a bit farther away from the Ranger, and turned her face to the star-strewn sky. All her working life, it had been Rena's habit to end days in the field like this. When she was younger—*much* younger—she'd throw her swag down on the ground and sleep there, fatigue and fitness enough to counteract the hardness of her bed, any resulting aches a cheap price to pay for the luxury of having the universe spread out above her.

Meteor showers and shooting stars were a thrill, her geologist's mind excited by the possibilities. Did something fall to earth? Where? What minerals were in its makeup? Was it a simple iron meteorite, or did it perhaps contain olivine crystals, or—most exciting of all—could it be a carbonaceous chondrite, consisting of some of the oldest material in the solar system, including amino acids, the building blocks of life? Could it contain something entirely alien to earth? Some people counted sheep; Rena pictured rocks, crystals, and the mineralogy of the universe.

Tonight when she looked up, a chain of Starlink satellites were ripping across the sky, an intrusion that made her briefly, unaccountably angry.

'Bloody Elon Musk,' she muttered, shifting in her seat so all she could see were unadulterated stars. Then she opened her mind to the geology of the country around her, mentally scanning the topography, inviting thoughts on the what and precise where of Marty's survey, or whatever the hell it was. The Kimberley was such old, rich earth, the possibilities were boundless, but Rena was still thinking diamonds. Unless a whole lot of equipment was stashed somewhere else or had gone up in flames with Marty, the man hadn't been digging deep. He was looking at geomorphology and then for tracer minerals and perhaps even diamonds themselves; he had to be.

Except...why here? Up near Ellendale, or the Northern Territory's Merlin Mine, yes. Even at Leopold Downs Station, about an hour north of Fitzroy Crossing, there were known lamproite pipes; the whole region had been extensively explored by the Ashton Joint Venture in the mid-1970s before they found the

Argyle deposit. That early data might show smaller deposits, useless decades ago, but now—with developments in technology like vertical pit mining—potentially viable. There was no legal way Verne could have that information, but if they did, Marty might have been out here on a scoping study, reassessing a previously rejected deposit. It still didn't explain the low number of samples. Even if he'd only been working this area for a week, there should be a lot more.

Not long after Rena first saw those bags, she'd wondered if they were window dressing, designed to fool a lay person. But now another thought occurred to her. What if Marty was somehow double-crossing Verne Industries? Or if he had stolen that old data and was acting alone? It wouldn't explain everything, but if a fortune in diamonds was involved, either scenario was a motive for murder.

Rena pulled out her phone and swiped through the pictures she'd taken of the bag labels, noting the similarity of the coordinates, a tight group. That made sense. Marty was pinpointing a locality, homing in. But Rena could also see that wherever that locality was, it wasn't here. She'd looked up the latitude and longitude to direct police to this campsite, and those coordinates didn't match the labels in her photos. So why was Marty here? Rena groaned. She was going around in circles.

At some point before midnight, Rena rose from her chair and ascended into the camper's rooftop tent, crawling into her sleeping bag, hoping the change would enable her to switch her brain off and allow her exhausted body to rest. She closed her eyes, feeling the heaviness in her limbs, willing herself to sleep, trying to send her thoughts in other directions. But if she wasn't thinking about diamonds and Marty, all she could think about was that her husband should be here, lying beside her, sharing this trip. If Tom were here, Rena would not be using a murder to distract herself from the aching abyss in her soul. For the first time in weeks, Rena let herself cry.

She was awake at 1 a.m., when her phone—still connected to the satellite adaptor—buzzed and lit up with an incoming call. She keyed the green button.

'Just where the hell are you, and what on earth do you think you're doing?'

Hours later, she stood in the shade of her own vehicle, watching the growing dust cloud that heralded the imminent arrival of the police. Rena had been surprised to hear Fletcher's voice on the other end of the phone, and his aggressive opener had almost been enough to make her feign a bad connection, the satellite just vanishing over the horizon. Instead, she played the old-lady card, completely ignoring his attitude, greeting him affably, thanking him for getting back to her so promptly, and being generally calm and polite until she heard the subtle yield in his voice, a grudging change of tone that signalled an apology even if he didn't actually say it.

At the time she'd thought his anger somewhat justified; after all, she was in the wrong. Then she remembered he didn't know she'd been snooping through Marty's things; for all the police knew, Rena had just stumbled across the camp. Maybe it was the late hour that made Fletcher tetchy. Or the fact he was having to return Rena's call while Ito was presumably off doing something more interesting. Rena had definitely left her message on Ito's phone. It was Ito's voice on the outgoing voicemail message, plus Rena had thrown Fletcher's card away the day she'd got it, knowing she'd never want to call him. Anyhow, whatever Fletcher's problem was, Rena intended to keep out of his way as much as possible. She squinted at the horizon, gauging how long she had, then grabbed a roll of toilet paper and went to find a bit of privacy.

Fifteen minutes later, she was standing in the shade of the awning when two police four-wheel drives pulled up behind her camper and cut their engines. The occupants sat for a moment, waiting for the dust to settle before opening their doors and putting boots on the ground. Ito and Fletcher emerged from the first vehicle and headed in her direction, while a trio of uniforms bailed out of the second unit and stood in a loose group, awaiting instructions. Rena glanced between Ito and Fletcher, but both were wearing sunglasses; she couldn't tell if they were looking at her or assessing the scene over her shoulder. Rena could see Fletcher looked pale beneath his tan, and when he pulled off his sunglasses to fix her with a hard stare, there were circles beneath his eyes.

'Detectives.' She nodded a greeting. 'You got here fast, considering the lack of road.'

Fletcher shrugged. 'It may surprise you to know that we drive off-road quite regularly. Besides, you gave us the coordinates.'

'All we had to do was follow our noses and not hit anything.' Ito stuck out a hand for Rena to shake.

'But tell us exactly how you…stumbled across this campsite.' Fletcher replaced his sunglasses and Rena had to stifle a laugh. He reminded her of a TV cop.

'I wondered what Marty Kinnane was doing out here, so I decided to see for myself.' Rena shifted her position slightly so she wasn't staring straight into the sun.

'Seriously? In all this'—Fletcher spread his arms wide and turned a slow circle—'you trundled out for a look and got lucky?'

'Course not. I considered what might interest a geologist, added that to places that might stand out as a good spot for a base camp, then headed in the general direction while keeping an eye out for signs anyone else had passed that way.'

Ito coughed sharply and brought a hand up to her mouth, but not fast enough to hide a smile.

Fletcher shook his head. 'Did you go into the tent?'

'Yep. Checked to confirm it was Marty's, but that was it. Oh, no. Sorry. I touched the lock on the chest.' Rena dropped her gaze, trying to look contrite.

Fletcher sucked in a breath.

'But I guess if Marty was working for Verne Industries, whatever is in the chest is their property, which means you'd need a warrant, wouldn't you? And for that you'd need to have a good reason to believe whatever was inside was pertinent to your investigation?'

'Shit,' Fletcher muttered.

'You realise you're not doing yourself any favours here, Mrs Novak?' Ito's tone was mild, her expression unreadable.

'Sorry, Detective. I spent most of my working life dealing with commercial secrets and no one schools you on the legal aspects of confidential stuff like a company that stands to lose or gain billions.'

'And you think that's what we're dealing with here?'

Rena shrugged. 'All I know is what Marty did for a living and the sort of country he was poking around in. You don't mess about out here for no reason. So maybe someone wanted to stop Marty finding stuff. I mean putting aside his...colourful past, that could give you a few suspects, right?'

'You think so, Mrs Novak?' Fletcher snapped.

'For starters there's the anti-mine contingent. There were some very angry people at that town meeting the other night, and if Synastria's enough to make them spit, the thought of a second mine wouldn't go down well at all. Plus there's Synastria itself and God-knows-what other mining companies might be sniffing around out here.'

Rena could feel the detectives' scrutiny, despite those impenetrable sunnies. 'Sorry. Didn't mean to tell you how to suck eggs.'

Ito and Fletcher continued to stare at her in silence.

'How about I go for a walk?' She gestured to the left of Marty's camp. 'Let you and your people do your thing?'

'How about you go back to your vehicle and wait there?' said Ito. Her tone was pleasant, but it still didn't invite argument.

Fletcher abruptly turned away, his boots scratching in the dirt, and stalked off in the direction of Marty's tent.

'I give him the shits, don't I?' asked Rena.

'All I'll say on that score is I've been working with Detective Fletcher for a while now and he's fantastic. However, something has been bothering him these past few days, and the only variable I'm aware of...'

'Is me, right?' Rena held up her hands in surrender. 'I'll be over there if you want me.' She went back to the Ford and fixed herself a drink, making a show of poking about in the kitchen in case she was being observed. But once a surreptitious glance confirmed everyone was busy, Rena pulled her chair around, faced it towards the action, and settled in to watch. She wasn't expecting much drama, except for when Fletcher spotted her taking in the show.

As it turned out, Fletcher's stink eye was nothing compared to the fireworks that erupted several hours later when Rena told the detectives she would not be following them back to Fitzroy Crossing.

Probably best not to mention the purloined field notes.

SIXTEEN

In the end there was nothing they could do to force her to return to Fitzroy Crossing, especially when Rena made a show of striking her current camp and driving about two hundred metres farther away. It hardly mattered. The cops had first documented, then packed every last scrap of Marty's stuff up to take back to town, although from what Rena had seen, they'd only found a couple of things deemed worthy of evidence bags.

She was at war with her feelings, a mixture of regret and Catholic guilt: sorry she hadn't taken one of the soil samples, but also sorry she'd taken the field notes, a stupid, impulsive decision that couldn't be reversed now. Maybe when she got back to civilisation, Rena could anonymously post them to Verne Industries. Of course, the problem with that was not everyone in the company might be in on this particular bit of field exploration. Things got compartmentalised when the stakes were high and the fewer people who knew, the less chance there was of a leak. She'd have to think about it.

For now, Rena decided she'd leave the notebook where it was and resist the urge to look; it was either a case of overcompensating for pinching—*borrowing*—it, or creating a sense of anticipation for when she finally cracked the pages.

Despite the discrepancy with the GPS coordinates, Marty had been in this spot for a reason, and Rena figured that instead of reading his notes and doing things the easy way, she'd have the sort of holiday she probably should have taken in the first place: a rock hound's fossicking trip, messing around in the dirt with a pick and shovel. She wanted to see if she could figure out what attracted a field geologist to this stretch of country. Just thinking about it made her the happiest she'd been since Tom died. Still shit, but marginally less so.

Even if she had swiped a soil sample, Rena didn't have the means to analyse it. Maybe Marty had sent other samples back to a lab where, even now, they were being screened, concentrated, and examined microscopically. Rena was still banking on diamonds being the target. In which case, if Marty was on the money with any of his locations, there might be some minuscule flecks of honey-coloured zircon or black ilmenite, maybe even some red garnet or yellowy-green olivine. Any of those or other indicator minerals would do. Far more common than diamonds, they could be found in rocks that occur with diamonds in lamproite and kimberlite pipes. That's why they were called indicator minerals: Find them in the gravel and it's a strong possibility there are diamond-bearing pipes in the area. Rena didn't have a lab, but she had an instinct, a good eye for landforms, and decades of experience she was keen to use again.

Once the police had left, Rena moved straight back to the site of Marty's tent, where nothing remained except a patch of flattened earth. She wasn't being bloody-minded; it just happened to be the best spot to make camp, ready-made firepit notwithstanding. It was mid-afternoon now, too hot to stay in the full sun for long, so Rena settled in the shade of the camper's awning to plan her next move. Marty had been up to something out here. Whether it really was exploration and sampling or something else entirely, Rena figured the site of activity wouldn't be far away, but it wouldn't be right on the doorstep either. There was no dirt bike at Marty's camp, and no drone. That could've been incinerated in the Toyota, but Rena figured if Marty was doing an aerial survey, the drone—or at least some spare tech for it—would've been in the locked chest. Put all that together and whatever made this part of the Kimberley interesting had to be within walking distance.

She could see no tracks in the immediate area other than footprints left by police, but it didn't take a bloodhound to figure out two points of the compass were irrelevant: There was nothing to find back towards the highway, and directly behind the camp was the escarpment. Which meant first thing tomorrow Rena would start walking north, looking at the geology and for any sign of Marty's movement across the land. If that didn't yield anything, she'd try the opposite direction, skirting along in front of the ridge. That felt less likely to Rena, but then she didn't know what she was looking for: Anything was possible.

Rena was aware the police thought her behaviour fell somewhere along a spectrum that started at slightly odd and ranged all the way up to criminal guilt. She had no real reason to stay out here, no reason to trace Marty's movements, even if she was pretty certain he'd been looking for diamonds. It was a field Kinnane had worked in before, which might explain why Verne Industries had kept him on or rehired him after whatever stink he'd caused. If you spent a lot of time looking for diamonds, you didn't just get to know what diamond country looked like; you started to feel it on a visceral level. Marty Kinnane knew diamond country. And if that wasn't enough to convince Rena, the combination he'd chosen for the chest's padlock had been the clincher.

So why was Rena bothering when she knew? What was she hoping to achieve by pinpointing the site where Marty had been messing around? Was she hoping to find a diamond of her own?

Hardly likely, although you never knew; there were legendary stories of field geologists catching sight of a single stone winking in the sun.

Part of it was Rena's antipathy towards retirement. She'd only stopped work so she and Tom could travel, and without him, all she had left of her identity was Rena the Geologist. Out here, on the hunt, she felt like she was recovering from a stroke, a paralysis that had overtaken her soul, draining it of strength, sapping her will to live.

The other part was murder. Maybe Marty Kinnane had been killed because of something from the past, or maybe it was recent. But why? If you were going to find a bloke in the middle of the Kimberley and light him up like Guy Fawkes, the reason had to be pretty bloody compelling.

Rena reckoned that meant big money. Diamonds.

Which meant the answer to Marty's murder was out here somewhere. And if Rena didn't find it, chances were it would find her.

Shit might get interesting. And Rena thrived on that kind of interesting.

The next morning, Rena was out as soon as there was enough light to see properly, wanting to do as much as possible before it got too hot. She was working under the assumption that Verne Industries had a valid exploration licence for the area, something she'd check via the Department of Mines website when she could get an internet connection. If the area was considered an unknown mineralisation zone, Verne could be exploring across hundreds of kilometres of land; this might simply be the latest sample site of dozens, and it might be crap. Maybe Marty found the best stuff months ago and this trip was an extra test, seeing how far a deposit extended. Or if Verne—and by association, Marty—had already found something worth digging up, this whole thing could be a sham, designed to suggest they were still looking. Rena had tossed that idea around in her head a lot; it made sense. Marty was out here, in a place that had zero relevance to anything, making a show of exploring, letting the competition think there was nothing to get excited about. In the meantime, his bosses in the city would be scrambling to get financial backing, and more importantly, to stitch up the mining rights before someone else jumped their intended claim. The only thing that scenario didn't explain was why Marty wound up dead.

The walk to the end of the ridge was a pleasant stroll in deep shadows, no sound but Rena's own footsteps and the occasional dry skitter of small creatures fleeing her advance. Rena kept an eye out for any irregularities in her surroundings, but her gut was telling her there was nothing to see here.

She stopped where the ridge gave way to open country, surveying the horizon before turning to follow the edge of the rising ground. She immediately felt the full bite of the sun and knew this would be a short-lived enterprise. Despite her broad-brimmed hat, sunglasses, water bottle and a thick layer of sunscreen, spending too much time in this was not an option, no matter how fit she was. For now, Rena kept walking, alternatively scanning the ground in front of her and the slope to her side.

In the end, it was the trees rather than the earth that pointed her in the right direction, a subtle deepening of green, a line of thickened foliage—things that indicated a water course, tracing a path through the dry, a path leading somewhere into or behind the rocky elevation she was skirting. Obviously, it would only flow in the wet season, but wet or dry, a creek bed was the perfect trap site for indicator minerals washed down from their source, caught up, and deposited in an area of slower flow. And so far, that line of green was the only feature in sight.

Rena picked up the pace a little now she had a clear objective, no longer bothering to eyeball the ground she was crossing. She reached the line of trees. They offered minimal shade but took the edge off the blasting sun and cut the glare, making it easier to see the creek bed: an unbroken crisscrossed lattice of dried mud. No one had dug here.

She studied the land, her gaze following the shallow arroyo as it traced its way further into open country. She wasn't going that way. Even if Marty had found indicator minerals somewhere out there, that direction was not only part of the floodplain, where such things were dispersed in all directions, it was also downstream. Anything of interest would be found... Rena turned away from the flat country, towards what looked like an impenetrable, almost sheer rock face, the monolith whose foot she'd been hugging. She ran her eyes up the side but could see no evidence that a wet-season cascade was responsible for the creek. It had seemed most likely, and she could picture monsoonal rains turning this rock into a wedding cake of rivulets and rills, myriad waterfalls big and small plunging from the plateau above to cover the ground where she stood. But nothing stood out.

Rena pushed forward, finding the undergrowth more tangled with every step, acutely aware of the risk of snakes.

She felt it before she saw it. A cool breath, a kiss from Tom when he was eating gelato. A hint of moisture in the relentless dry.

A cleft in the rock.

The way the rock was formed, almost folded, the narrow slot was invisible until she was almost in front of it. Only then could it be seen, extending up the full face of the mesa, a glimpse of sunlight raking through, high above.

She scrambled closer, heart beating faster from exertion and anticipation. It would account for the creek bed, an internal waterfall that then funnelled out, but it looked impassable, too tight a squeeze for an adult or at least a woman with Rena's curves. A tumble of rocks and gravel blocked her path, some fallen from above, some deposited when the water was running. As Rena edged past, one foot slipped on some loose stones and she instinctively shot out a hand, grabbing the nearest branch. She stumbled slightly then regained her balance, feeling the rough bark pressing into her palm. Releasing her grip, Rena held up her hand to check for cuts, but then she saw the tree itself. Two branches stuck out towards her at slightly different heights—the one she'd grabbed, and a second, just a bit lower and bent. Or rather, broken enough so that the last third of it hung down, exposing the fresh white splinters of its interior.

'Well, look at that,' Rena whispered.

Someone had been this way.

Using her hands for extra support, Rena crab-walked her way around the natural cairn. It looked impossible until suddenly she was past the obstruction: One side of the slot widened out at its base, the force of the water over millennia carving out a generous scoop from the stone. She took a moment to scan the recess for snakes and other hazards before ducking down and shuffling forward.

The change in light and temperature was immediate, and she paused to pull her shirt away from her sweaty skin, giving it an extra couple of flaps. Up ahead, Rena could see the slot seemed to taper in again. She didn't think of giving up. Going back wasn't even a question at this point.

She was enjoying herself far too much to even think of turning around now.

The ancient landscape, the isolation, and untouched rawness of her surrounds were like a tonic, nature reminding her of where she belonged. She'd hoped to share at least a tiny part of this sort of thing with Tom, to show him why the remote country beckoned her back time and time again, to explain what it was that she saw and how she understood the shapes of the land. And now, somewhat to her surprise, in this most remote corner of the Kimberley, she felt Tom's presence, close, as though he was leaning over her shoulder, looking at the world through her eyes.

She didn't think she was going to find anything extraordinary. In fact, she was starting to wonder again exactly what Marty was doing out here. Because nothing looked like diamond-producing ground. Not here. She could be wrong, but she'd be bloody surprised if she were.

Still, right now, it didn't matter. Rena just wanted to see what lay within this narrow cleft.

She stepped forward, straightening up as the slope of the rock face allowed it, then stopped. Cultural sensitivity wasn't something she'd learned at university. And in the first decades of her career as a field geologist, working for companies riding high in the mining boom, desperate for new finds, it was secondary at very best. But Rena had always tried to be respectful, to talk to and understand the concerns of Traditional Owners and to be as honest as she could be without giving away company secrets. It had created some professional friction for her. Suggestions she wasn't doing her job properly if she heeded a request to avoid a certain area because of its cultural importance. Another sign women were too soft, not cut out for the world of mining, the rigours of field geology. A man's world. She had ignored it all, working harder, better, longer than the men around her. Proving herself time and again. Once or twice she had found herself in a corner, permission refused but knowing she needed to sample earth from a sensitive place, forced to ask again with the caveat, *rather me than some bloke who won't give a damn what you think is important.* Rena earned a reputation as a person locals could deal with. She earned respect.

Now, standing in this fissure, Rena wondered if she'd stumbled into just such a place. She craned her neck, looking up at the rock, unwilling to abandon her quest, reluctant to step forward if she shouldn't. Then she did something Tom had taught her. She took a deep breath, settled her mind, and thought about how the immediate environment felt. In her youth she would have laughed, dismissed it as new-age rubbish, but she'd spent decades deep in the outback, long enough to learn that her science didn't have answers for everything. Call it what you liked—gut instinct, prescience, situational awareness, disruptions in the earth's magnetic field, or simple empathy—places had energy. Whether somewhere remote like here, or a house or building in the city, there were spaces that welcomed you, spaces that made the hair on the back of your neck stand up and everything in between. Sometimes it was about the people occupying the spaces, but ghost stories didn't spring from nothing. Even Stephen King had experienced a terrifying nightmare when he'd stayed in the hotel that inspired *The Shining*. The energy of place was also what dowsers relied on, although Rena had never tried to find minerals with a couple of bent rods.

Now all she needed was some sort of permission to proceed. She felt nothing negative, no reason to stay away; Rena began to move again.

She didn't get very far.

Another recess appeared on her right, larger than the first, deeper, almost her own height. Its back wall was invisible, an impenetrable blackness. Without a headlamp and gaiters, Rena was reluctant to venture more than a pace or two into the gloom. There would be snakes, and if she got bitten by anything serious out here, she was as good as dead. It occurred to her that perhaps Marty's death was as simple as that. Perhaps he'd been nailed by a snake and was trying to get to help. Although, if it had been Rena, secret location be damned. She would've called someone, told them where she was and hoped they could get to her, or at least intercepted her on the highway, start treatment.

'Shit.'

It was entirely plausible. If Marty had been fighting the effects of envenomation, he could've passed out at the wheel, knocked the car into neutral and run off the track. Then a fault in the car caused the fire. The fact that police were investigating didn't necessarily mean anything. They were simply making sure what looked like an accident was an accident.

Rena sighed. Real life was never as interesting as movies and books. She pulled out her key chain with its mini Maglite, pointed the torch towards the back of the cave and pressed it on. The small beam was strong, but not strong enough to show anything more than the rock wall disappearing into black. Then Rena pointed the torch down, playing the light over the sandy earth.

She sucked in a breath.

The sunlight spilling from behind her had shown light and shade, nothing more than the depressions and ripples you'd expect in a space worn by water over centuries. But now, illuminated by the torch, she could see that the pockmarks in the dirt weren't natural. Someone had been digging. Not deep, but with no seeming plan: There were shallow holes and scratches all across the cavern. One or two, close to the centre of the space went down ten or so centimetres, but most were about five centimetres deep, and a few were bare scrapes, a removal of the top layer.

'What the hell were you doing, Marty?'

All she got back was a faint echo, calling her from the darkness.

SEVENTEEN

Rena left the cave thinking about pushing farther into the slot, but quickly changed her mind. The space between the cliffs was narrow, and judging by the vegetation and undisturbed soil, no one had gone that way, at least not recently. She had convinced herself Marty was out here looking for diamonds, but nothing made sense: The geology was completely wrong, and the pockmarks and holes in the floor of the cave were about as far from best-practice soil sampling as you could get. Maybe Marty had gone deeper into the cave, but crawling into an unknown space when you were alone in the middle of nowhere was dangerous; caution held Rena back. Not that she considered herself overly sensible, but the thought of Detective Fletcher's reaction if he had to come out here and rescue her was enough to make Rena start back to camp.

She emerged from the rock and was enveloped by heat, already at least thirty-two Celsius, even though it wasn't yet noon. Around her, the buzz of unseen insects provided a soundscape oddly in tune with the hot shimmer visible out over the plain, a combined distortion of reality that heightened Rena's sense of unease.

Tracking the path of Marty's vehicle across open country to his base camp had been diverting and exciting and, yes, a way to thumb her nose at Fletcher and his aggro. Rena had thought Marty was chasing diamonds, but there was no way diamonds were Marty's reason for being in this part of the Kimberley. But as that had become more apparent, everything else had become increasingly confused; Marty's actions made no sense at all.

Rena forced herself to shift mental gears, putting aside the problem that was Marty Kinnane. An arsehole when he was alive, it turned out Marty was an even bigger prick in death, although maybe, Rena conceded, that wasn't his fault.

No longer looking for signs of human presence, Rena ambled along, taking time to appreciate the land, inhale the scent of the dry earth. She tipped the brim of her hat a bit lower, shielding her face from the worst of the glare, and let her thoughts turn to future travel destinations. She had to keep going because although the road felt lonely, it was not as lonely as an empty house, where Tom no longer waited for her return.

A clattering sound broke into her reverie.

Rena stopped walking and looked for the source of the noise—rock on rock, a small sound, nothing to cause alarm. Probably a few pebbles dislodged by a bird or wallaby. That's what her rational, science-based brain said. But the primitive, instinctual part was reading the situation differently, making the hairs on her arms stand up.

Rena's mouth felt dry, and she forced a couple of swallows, unsticking her tongue. The scree slope rose beside her, sparsely covered with scrub, but still enough to conceal someone. She studied it through narrowed eyes. A person climbing would create much more noise—footsteps on loose rocks, dislodging other stones. Which meant if the sound had been caused by a person, they were still, silent, concealed somewhere near the top of the mesa. It seemed highly unlikely, but Rena picked up the pace, casting a couple of uneasy glances towards the line where rock face met sky as she retraced the path she'd taken earlier.

Even when she'd reached the reassuring familiarity of her camp, Rena still couldn't shake the feeling that someone else was out here, watching her.

The sensation only intensified when she stepped into the shade of the camper's awning. She'd locked the Ranger's cab and the various storage compartments but left out a few bits and pieces: a chair, her towel hung over a guy rope, the small mat she'd unrolled at the bottom of the ladder that led to the rooftop tent. It all looked fine, and yet...

Her nerves were jangling, and she could feel a pulse thumping in her jugular. The towel. Hadn't she sort of spread it out more than that? And the mat. It seemed dustier than it should be, given she'd shaken it out this morning. Rena took a slow tour of her camp, feeling more than seeing something was off-kilter. She ended up standing, her back to the side of the Ford, staring out at the empty landscape. She drew in a deep breath through her nose, but there was nothing she could detect, no scent that shouldn't be there. No exhaust fumes lingering in the still air or anything that would suggest the presence of another human being.

Except from where she stood, she could see four small impressions in the earth, mere millimetres away from where the legs of her chair now sat. There were no scuff marks, such as she would have caused herself standing up from the chair and sending it slightly backwards. It was more as though someone had picked up the chair then carefully put it down again, aiming for but not quite hitting the same spot.

Of course there were footprints all over the place, but it was impossible to tell which were her own, which had been left by police yesterday and which—if any—were new and unknown.

'Shit.'

Rena turned to the Ranger. It wasn't unknown for people to steal fuel, car batteries, or even parts from remote camping places, leaving the driver stranded. She checked all the handles, caps, and hatches, but everything was just as she'd left it. Leaning against the bonnet, she gazed out across the open country, looking for a telltale puff of stirred-up earth, a flicker of movement in the stillness, the flash of light reflected from a man-made surface...basically anything that would confirm what she already knew.

Someone had been here.

While she was messing about, trying to prove to the police or herself that she was still in possession of all her faculties and not some irrelevant, invisible pensioner, someone had been poking around her camp.

She scanned the horizon again. Nothing except a wedge-tailed eagle, wings outstretched as it rose, ascending higher and higher into the cloudless blue on a thermal current.

This posed a couple of possibilities. The steep slope behind the campsite would be a good vantage point but left nowhere to go. Which meant either the intruder had made off around the base of the mesa, heading away from Rena's approach, or they'd come from the highway and were long gone before she returned.

Unless they'd never left.

The place felt empty, but Rena had no clue what the hell was going on, and was therefore disinclined to take anything for granted, least of all the vibe.

Putting aside the uneasy thought that maybe someone *had* gone part-way up the mesa—was even now watching her—Rena knew the only other places to hide were in the tent or under the car. She dropped to her haunches to look between the wheels. No one there, nothing but a different perspective on the Kimberley.

Rena straightened up and circled around the Ranger. She'd check the rooftop tent to confirm her own stupidity then get something to eat and decide whether to stay out here another night or head back to the Crossing. She'd left the tent with the main flaps rolled down, keeping the dust out, knowing it would cool quickly when night fell. No shadows lurked behind the fabric; the only way someone could be up there and unseen was if they were lying down, pressing themselves into the camp mattress.

Rena went up the ladder's six rungs as fast as she could, visions of coming face-to-face with a gun or a fist playing in her mind. She tore the zipper open, confirmed the vacant status, and had the zipper halfway closed again when she caught a faint whiff of something.

BO. The unmistakable, musky fug of someone else. Of a man. Not a pleasant, crisp aftershave scent overlying a hint of sweat. No, the aroma that was now prickling her olfactory senses was rank: layers of unwashed with an unmistakable top note of onions.

'Bloody hell.'

Rena leaned into the stiflingly hot tent and inhaled but couldn't recapture the illusive smell. She left the tent flap open and returned to the ground. Any thoughts of remaining here overnight had dissipated with the hint of body odour. The fact that her visitor had been so furtive was more unsettling than if they'd stolen the Ford's battery or left a bullet in her bed. At least then she'd know something about their intentions. But this was clear evidence that whatever had gotten Marty killed, it wasn't over. Someone was still out here, playing a long game.

She took the time to have a cold drink, making a point of standing out in the open as she sipped, just in case anyone was watching. Then Rena folded and packed the awning, collapsed the rooftop tent, and stowed all the bits and pieces, making an unhurried production of it. Yes, she was leaving, but Rena didn't want anyone thinking she'd been scared off.

Every now and then as she worked, she let her gaze wander over the stands of scrub and the changing shadows playing across the mesa. Not staring, just surveying. But there was never a flash of bright fabric or the sudden glint of sunlight off a pair of binoculars, just the pressing weight of the place, as though it too was willing her to leave.

Half an hour later she was driving slowly back towards the highway. There was no need to consult the sat nav: The tracks left by the two police vehicles were like strips of neon light in the landscape. It took Rena less than a quarter of the time of her journey out, and before long, the emptiness of the landscape ahead was broken by the movement of a truck, tracking right to left across the horizon, marking the Great Northern Highway. Ten minutes later she passed the section of charred earth, barely tapping the brakes but feeling just the tiniest frisson of guilt.

That sparked a mental argument. She couldn't do anything more: This wasn't her problem, and police were on the job. Rena's best option would be to leave Fitzroy Crossing, gather the frayed strands of her plans and try to weave them back into a semblance of a pattern. Her only involvement in this was to come across the burning car. It was a coincidence that Marty was the victim, not some cosmic call to arms.

Rena turned onto the highway and pressed the accelerator, watching the needle climb until she was at the speed limit, relaxing her grip on the wheel, enjoying the smooth ride after so long bumping around in the dirt. There was nothing for her here.

She checked the fuel gauge. Half a tank. She wasn't hungry, and Ito and Fletcher had her details, so there was no need to stop in Fitzroy Crossing. She thought about Derby, weighed up her desire to see the largest tides in the country, pondered looping through the outback town before heading back east on the storied Gibb River Road, then decided to stick to her earlier plan and tackle the Dampier Peninsula. She'd stop for the night at the Willare Bridge Roadhouse, a place recommended by other travellers for its campground and barista coffee, but more interesting for its links to the Blue Streak rocket project in the 1950s and '60s.

Rena settled her shoulders again the backrest and flipped down the visor. Ito's business card was still there, staring her in the face. Rena plucked it free and threw it aside, not caring where it landed.

There was no one to please but herself.

EIGHTEEN

It would have all gone smoothly, and Rena would've passed a pleasant evening at Willare Bridge talking to other four-wheel drivers about the back road up the Dampier Peninsula, if she hadn't pulled into the rest area at Ellendale.

She blamed her bladder. If she hadn't needed to go, Rena would've swept past at 110 kilometres an hour, registering the blue of the amenities sign without noting the details. And even after she'd seen the name *Ellendale* and stopped, Rena could've laughed at the irony of the universe and carried on her merry way.

But instead she'd let it get under her skin. Because Ellendale meant diamonds. North of this rest stop was an area explored in years past and dismissed as not profitable enough. But now, new mining techniques meant new interest, and companies desperate to tap a market deprived of its Argyle pinks.

This was diamond country, potentially the next big source of fancy colours. This was the sort of land Marty should have been exploring.

Rena may have physically retired, but mentally she'd always be a field geologist, always want to have an Estwing pick swinging from her belt and feel the excitement when her assessment of the land delivered results, when she knew—even when the dirt was fresh on her hands—that she was standing on riches.

When she got back in the Ranger, Rena called up the GPS coordinates of her location and saved them. She stopped short of comparing them to the numbers on Marty's tagged bags of dirt, but what she was looking at now didn't ring any bells; Marty hadn't been out this way. At least that made sense. This part of the Kimberley—the diamond-yielding section, anyway—was already under a mining lease. No point sampling here.

Rena resumed her trip to Willare Bridge, diamonds dancing through her mind, the puzzle of Marty's location refusing to unravel. Ten minutes away from her destination, Rena gave in to the twist in her gut and acknowledged she wasn't ready to let things go.

She considered Marty's field notes, safely locked in the back of the kitchen drawer. Rena would, of course, forward them to Verne Industries as soon as she knew precisely to whom they should be sent. But after today's events, she thought a little bedtime reading was in order. A fairy tale of hidden treasure, with a grim ending. Except maybe it wasn't the ending, just the first twist in a bigger story.

The campground at the Willare Bridge Roadhouse was small, but the pool was clean and cold, there was a licensed restaurant, and surprisingly few guests. In other words, a perfect stop for the night. Throughout her life, Rena had often found it hard returning to civilisation after extended periods in the field, and even though this time she'd only been alone for a short time, she experienced the same discomfort. Conversation was an effort; the words felt strange in her mouth. Noises seemed twice as loud, and the glare of the shop's fluorescent lights—so much harsher than natural light—made her blink, then put her sunglasses back on. There was something about the stillness of the outback, her connection with the dirt and rocks beneath her feet, that made Rena's spirit expand in a way that the structure of the modern world felt oppressive.

Tom had always been her anchor, a reason to return and a calm presence to ease her back into everyday life. His steadying hand on her arm, his ability to quickly intervene and speak for her when her speech dried up and all she could manage was a grunt or a sigh, soothed Rena's discomfort and made her feel safe.

Tonight she had no one. Sitting out beside her camper would invite overtures from other travellers, so she decided to spring for a solitary, civilised meal in the roadhouse's restaurant. Besides, she really did need better light if she was going to read Marty's scrawled writing. Rena swiped on some lipstick, the only concession to makeup she was prepared to make, and grabbed the notebook.

She managed to score a table in a comparatively dim corner of the restaurant—enough light to comfortably read but not so much she felt like her retinas were burning. Five minutes later, she'd ordered a chicken schnitzel with chips and salad plus a glass of red without having to exchange more than routine pleasantries with the young waitress. Once the girl had delivered the wine and a couple of bread rolls, Rena put on her glasses and spread the notebook open on the table to the right of her knife, signalling her preferred engagement level with other people was set to go-the-hell-away.

It took her half a page to adjust to Marty's scribble, but once she had her eye in, it was easy to interpret the diagrams, shorthand, and occasional heavy underlining. She was so engrossed that the waitress had to clear her throat loudly before Rena realised she was there.

'Sorry, thanks.' Rena pushed the bread plate aside and the girl deftly slid the plate in front of her. Her stomach growled, and she grabbed a couple of the thick chips, relishing their hot saltiness, before cutting into the chicken and portioning off half a dozen mouthfuls. Now she could give most of her attention to the notebook, forking up food without looking at her plate or interrupting her reading too often.

It was a great schnitzel, but even a five-star meal wouldn't have interested her more than the contents of Marty's notes. At one point, Rena pulled out her phone to cross-check the GPS points recorded on the pages with those on the bags of dirt. They all matched, although there were a number of locations detailed in Marty's notes that didn't figure among the soil samples.

By the time Rena ate the last piece of iceberg, she was about halfway through the notebook. She turned the next page and stopped. Blank. She flipped back, checking the last date Marty had recorded.

And groaned.

It was five days before the car fire.

Rena banged a fist on the table, making the cutlery jump. Across the room, the waitress gave her a wide-eyed stare, then hurried over, weaving between the now fully occupied tables.

'Is everything okay, ma'am?' Her voice was timid, as though she was expecting Rena to unleash a tirade.

'Yes. Sorry again. The meal was excellent. Just some other issues causing me a bit of grief.'

The waitress smiled uncertainly, and Rena felt a wave of guilt.

'But while you're here, could I order coffee and dessert, please?' She didn't really want dessert, but it would give her a chance to linger.

'Ice cream, apple pie, chocolate cake, or sticky date pudding?' The girl scooped up Rena's plate as she spoke.

'Vanilla ice cream, thanks. And just black coffee, an espresso if possible.'

She nodded and bustled away, collecting a couple more empty plates as she made her way to the bar.

The coffee and ice cream came at the same time, which would have been irritating if Rena hadn't already planned to turn it into one of Tom's favourite desserts, an affogato al caffè.

She tipped the espresso over the ice cream, grabbed her spoon, and considered what she had read.

If Marty's notebook was genuine, Verne Industries was definitely after fancy diamonds. This was a second survey, and the ground he had been on was extremely promising. But Marty had also mentioned a couple of run-ins with the locals—both Traditional Owners and more recent blow-ins—sightings of what he thought might be other geology teams out in the same country, and a developing concern that his every move was being watched. He'd noted it for purely professional purposes; the language was plain—time and place plus a few details about each event. As far as Rena could tell, Marty hadn't been the tiniest bit worried about any of it; at least, not as far as his personal safety was concerned. All those incidents had been recorded so he could inform the powers that be at Verne Industries, to let them know they might have problems with rival companies or local resistance to the establishment of a mining lease. The sort of information that would be valuable when it came time to actually talk to the stakeholders and get them onside. It was great to finally get a handle on Marty's work, even if there was nothing in the notebook to explain what he'd been doing just before he died. Reading the notes, it was clear to Rena that the diamond-rich ground was not in the same area as Marty's final location. So where was it?

Rena was keen to map out the list of GPS points, but when she pulled out her phone and tried the Wi-Fi, it was slow to connect and quick to drop out; at this time of the evening, every traveller in the place was trying to get online.

She signalled to the waitress for the bill and gathered up her bits and pieces, excited by the diamonds, still completely baffled about

Marty. Everything about the field notes—about diamondiferous earth—seemed on the up and up. In which case, maybe that really was why he'd spent days in the wrong location, doing God-knows-what: an elaborate ruse, designed to throw watchers off the scent of the real diamond deposit.

Rena paid cash, leaving a generous tip, then made her way out of the restaurant and around to reception. The man behind the counter was on the phone but nodded a greeting, raising a finger on his free hand to signal he wouldn't be long. Rena hated people hovering, so she nodded back then moved to the other side of the room, where a detailed map of the region dominated half the wall. She stuck her hands in the pockets of her cargo pants and studied the map, finding her location then moving northeast across to the Ellendale Diamond Field, which was marked with a tiny crossed pick and shovel. She glanced across at the Argyle mine site then back, the geology of the region filling her mind. The Ellendale field was significant because back in the 1970s, it led to the recognition of a new host rock for diamonds. The company that made the find was excited back then, but they abandoned the area in 1979 to focus on a new prospect at Smoke Creek: That deposit became the Argyle mine. Then, more recently, another company identified areas of eluvial diamond enrichment—soil just below the surface with a higher concentration of diamonds. Over the next few years, some diamonds were mined, but the company went broke and operations were abandoned. Rena thought about the Kimberley and all the places within it, known and unknown, that might hold diamonds. She really needed to map those GPS points.

'Sorry 'bout that.'

Rena turned. The man behind the reception desk had finished his call and was now looking at her with an expression of polite enquiry.

'Can I help you?'

Rena cast a final glance at the map then crossed the room, folding her hands on the counter. The bloke looked tired. Or ill. Thin face, receding hair, a short-sleeve work shirt that hung too loose on his frame.

'Is there a decent spot around here for the Wi-Fi, please? Somewhere to get a more reliable signal?'

The man ran a hand across the top of his shiny head, lingering at the back where the last follicles of his pattern baldness were making a heroic stand.

'It's better when most people are asleep, but...' He glanced from side to side then leaned forward. 'There's a place—don't tell anyone—that the employees use.' His volume had dropped about thirty decibels.

Rena nodded and leaned in, ready to receive secrets.

'Did you see the couple of boab trees in the campground, down the back corner? If you stand at the base of the big one, you get strong Wi-Fi.'

Rena rolled her eyes, ready with a smart retort, but his expression was deadly serious.

'No. Really?'

Jack—the name was embroidered on his shirt—nodded emphatically. 'No idea why, but yeah. Keep it to yourself, ay?'

'Sure. And thanks.' Rena started to leave then stopped. 'One other thing.'

Jack raised his eyebrows.

'What's going on with diamond mining and exploration around here? Any rumours?'

It was as though she'd flipped a switch. Rena saw the shutters come down over Jack's eyes and the previously open face set into hard lines.

'Nup.' He looked away, straightening a pile of maps that was already straight.

'Nothing at all?'

'Why? Who are you?'

Rena held up both hands, palms forward. 'No one, mate. Just an old retired lady who likes diamonds. I'm honestly nothing to anyone.'

'Right. Good night.' Jack spun around and disappeared through a door marked *Employees Only*.

Rena waited a moment, wondering what had just happened, then sighed. At least she could connect to the internet. She'd taken two steps away from the desk when she saw a light on the phone start glowing red, and from behind the closed door came the unintelligible muttering of a single voice. Jack had called someone.

No point hanging around. Clearly she wasn't going learn anything from Jack, tonight or ever.

Rena pushed through the exit and out into the night, her footsteps soft in the loose dirt as she made her way back to the camping area. Lights glimmered from within a smattering of caravans and tents, augmenting the sulphurous glow emanating from sparsely placed lampposts, marking out the different rows of the campground and spotlighting the amenities block. As she walked past some of the occupied sites, Rena could hear snatches of conversation, the sounds running counterpoint to the natural rhythms of the night: the trills and ticks of insects, the dry rattle of eucalyptus leaves, and somewhere, a sudden, short burst of maniacal laughter from a blue-winged kookaburra, roused into action by a disturbance in its environment.

She walked past her own setup and continued down the dirt path. Rena intended to head to the Wi-Fi tree—the boab that was somehow a hot spot—but hearing the activity around her, she decided to wait until the majority of people had given up for the night. Maybe there'd be a free washing machine; it was worth a look. She made an abrupt 180-degree turn, and as she did, a man—West Coast Eagles singlet straining slightly over a small paunch, knee-length shorts, long, sinewy arms—who had apparently been walking not far behind, dropped his head and veered away, ducking between two tents and out of sight.

Rena frowned. It seemed...off. Or maybe she was jumping at shadows. She retraced her steps, checking between the two tents for any sign of the man, chastising herself for reading something into the presence of one person in a campground full of people. There wasn't even really anything remarkable about him. Change the club or code of the football team on his singlet and you'd find someone like him in just about every town and city in the country. Still, back at the Ranger, Rena avoided turning on the LEDs, conscious of the way they both spotlit her and made it impossible to see much beyond the field of their illumination. She put Marty's notebook back in the same safe place, at the very back of the kitchen drawer, tucked beneath the fry pan.

Filling a couple of supermarket bags with dirty clothes, she headed for the amenities block. It was after ten now, and while there were still dim lights in a couple of caravans, most were in darkness, the occasional snore emanating from behind a flywire door.

The laundry room was harshly lit by half a dozen fluorescent tubes; there was even the obligatory one on the fritz, blinking in random morse code before dimming, only to burst to life again seconds later. Moths and other insects were having a ceiling party, some flying, most simply crawling on and around the lights. In the corner, a blue bug zapper snapped with depressing regularity. Rena was the only one there, and she surveyed the bank of washing machines. Three were mid-cycle, flashes of colour visible through the portholes, drowning in oceans of suds.

Tom hated communal laundries, always did as much as he could—at least their smalls—in a little hand-churn washer. These machines, he claimed, were unhygienic; who knew what someone had put in them before? It didn't matter when Rena pointed out that hot water and detergent were involved or told him about the laundry facilities she encountered in the field. Tom was a medical biologist, and was almost as obsessive about germs and microorganisms as Rena was about rocks.

She stood there, a bag of dirty washing in each hand, and felt a wave of grief so strong her knees almost buckled.

'Goddammit, Tom.'

Of all things she was going to lose it over dirty knickers in a Besser block wasteland that smelled of bacteria, mildew, cheap soap, and exhaustion. She swallowed, hard, then opened her mouth, letting loose a sound that was halfway between groan and primal scream, feeling the pressure of its passing run through her chest.

'You right there, love?'

Rena swung around, the bags of laundry like a cheerleader's pompoms, forcing her emotions back down, flipping back to a facsimile of normal with practised ease.

It was the man from before, football singlet. His voice was light, his vowels rounded, incongruous coming from this weather-beaten man in sports merch, as though a British aristocrat had been used to dub a show about outback truckers. And now Rena could see his face. Yellowy-grey hair sprouted in erratic tufts from his head, a counterpoint to the clean-shaven chin. His mouth was disproportionately large but appeared to contain a full set of even, white teeth. Above that, a fine, patrician nose, and one blue eye, the other just a sunken socket, the skin around it shiny and mottled pink, while the rest of his face was weathered and lined. Impossible to tell his age, but anywhere between sixty and Methuselah.

'Yeah, thanks, I…thought I was alone.' Rena shuffled over to a machine and set her washing down, acutely aware that this man was blocking the only exit.

'You're sure? Because you sounded like you were having some sort of turn. If you need a doctor—' The blue eye appraised her, scanning back and forth across her face.

'No. It's just been a rough couple of days. I don't need a doctor.' Rena forced a note of confidence into her voice.

'Well, thank Christ for that. Out here there's a bit of a wait this time of night. In fact, any time.' He stuck out his hand. 'I'm Stu Rothwell but most people call me Chuck.'

'Chuck?'

'Because I sound like King Charles.'

'Ah. Right. Nice to meet you, Chuck. I'm Rena.' She stepped forward, trying not to let her wariness show, and gripped Chuck's calloused hand, feeling her own palm dwarfed.

Intelligence glinted in Chuck's one good eye. Rena forced her shoulders to relax; didn't mean she was going to turn her back in a hurry.

'Mind if I...?' she gestured at her abandoned washing.

'Go ahead. And if you're not in danger of measuring your length on the floor, I'll leave you to it.'

'Thanks. For checking, I mean.' Rena stood side on to the machine, shovelling clothes in while facing Chuck, making sure her underwear was bundled invisibly with the rest.

'Of course. Have a pleasant evening!'

'Hang on. Are you a local or passing through? If you don't mind me asking?'

'Hard to say. Define *local*. Out here it's a relative concept. So much space and so many people who are from *somewhere else*.' Chuck's voice dropped insinuatingly on the last two words. 'Local to the Kimberley in that I live here? Yes. Local in the sense that I'm from here? No.' His right hand sketched a wavy line through the air, highlighting the everywhere-nowhere dichotomy of the outback.

'Yeah, I kind of figured out that part.' Rena wanted to ask about diamonds, but not as much as she wanted him to go away. 'Might see you round then.'

'Quite possible!' Chuck took several backward steps until he was out the door, then faded away like an actor leaving the stage. Rena stared at the rectangle of night for a moment, half-expecting him to reappear, before slamming the washing machine closed on her dirty laundry.

NINETEEN

Once Rena had fed the machine with coins and the wash cycle was underway, she figured she had at least forty-five minutes to kill, so she abandoned the amenities block and went in search of Wi-Fi.

There were two people under the boab, faces illuminated by the glow from their phones' screens. She recognised the waitress from earlier, who was sitting with her back against the tree. Close beside her was a young man whom Rena assumed must also work at the roadhouse, given the logo just visible on his polo shirt. Rena nodded politely—not that either of them paid her any attention—then turned her back and checked the signal on her phone.

She could've used her satellite gizmo to connect to the internet, but she'd bought it for emergencies, not so she could always be in contact with the whole damn world. Besides, the plan was bloody expensive. Mess around too long and you'd be like one of those millennials who whined when they ran up a grand's worth of global roaming without realising. But it didn't matter because just as the reception guy had said, the Wi-Fi at this spot was strong, and in addition to the Telstra signal, Rena's old iPhone offered her three arcs of connectivity.

It also told her Les and Margot had left a voicemail message. A couple of taps and a brief pause while the automated voice told her stuff she already knew, then Les's voice, loud in the way only the vain and recently hard of hearing can be.

Rena! Where are you? A voice in the background, Les shushing and mumbling an aside. *Margot sends her love. You're interested in Verne Industries? And I'm guessing the employee you mention is Marty bloody Kinnane, ay? Look, call me when you can, because there's a lot of dark waters swirling here, but the short version is, they supposedly gave him the heave-ho because he was behaving inappropriately with some of the women in the office. Same old Kinnane; well, you'd know better than I! Sorry, Rena, Sorry. I shouldn't have said… Anyway, I have it on good authority that was a bluff. He was never fired; they just didn't want anyone to know that he's out woop-woop on their behalf, looking for diamonds. Finding them too, from what I hear. Except that's not the end. Since Argyle closed, there's a few more rumours about Kinnane that have folks pricking up their ears; beyond his usual lechery, lies, treachery and backstabbing, I mean. Give us a call. Hoo-roo.*

'Shit. Tell me the stuff I don't know, Les.' Rena sighed and saved the message. It was way too late on the East Coast to call back now. Still, at least it confirmed that not only was there dirt on Kinnane, but Les and Margot knew what it was and were happy to share. She turned her attention to the GPS points. Finding a website was easy; then it was just a matter of flicking between it and the photos she'd taken of the sample bags and their labels. The first point lit up east of the Ellendale mine site, the next, north and a bit further east.

A sudden burst of laughter from behind her reminded Rena the young couple was still there. She cast a quick look over her shoulder, but they were engrossed, arms around each other as they watched something on the screen of a single phone.

Slowly, as she entered point after point, it became clear where Marty had been focussing his search. A scattering of dots, following a loose line that sat south of the Gibb River Road, and also happened to chart a rough course between the Argyle mine and Ellendale. It petered out hundreds of kilometres before each mine site, but still. Most interesting of all was the area where the scattered points became more concentrated, darts aiming for the bullseye.

Rena took a screenshot, then shut the website down. Another nod to the couple, which she doubted they'd seen, and she moved away, noting as she did that within a dozen steps, the Wi-Fi had dropped down to almost nothing again. She shook her head. What made a boab tree a Wi-Fi beacon?

Back in the laundry, she transferred her ball of wet washing to a dryer. Usually, she'd hang stuff up to dry, but no one needed to see her bras, and besides, she wanted to be up early tomorrow. She wanted to get back to Fitzroy Crossing.

Because the most noticeable thing about all the points Marty had apparently sampled, was that the nearest one was at least three hundred kilometres away from where he'd died. And on the opposite side of the Great Northern Highway.

By quarter past seven the next morning Rena was on the road. The sun hadn't long crested the horizon, and it was in her face, forcing her to half-squint against the glare, even from behind sunglasses. There was no heat in the day yet, and she drove with the windows down, right arm propped on the sill, elbow out, fingers hooked lightly around the wheel. She didn't bother with the radio or any music, didn't want anything except the rush of air and the sound of rubber on the road.

And Rena felt…not exactly happy, but at peace.

She'd stopped kidding herself about heading up the Dampier Peninsula and didn't care if she didn't make it to Broome in time to see the Staircase to the Moon this season. Those things would still be there next year. Last night, she'd realised—or rather, acknowledged—that she was bored and heartbroken, so she had decided to throw all her energy at the mystery of Martin Kinnane and the diamonds. It wouldn't matter if things got dicey or she stuffed up when she was alone in the outback; there were worse things than dying while chasing rocks in the Kimberley.

Like loneliness.

Losing your independence. Or your marbles.

Being a burden.

Growing decrepit.

Spending your final days in a room somewhere, being talked to like you were a baby. No chance to feel the sun on your face or the dirt under your fingernails.

Rena had never thought about growing old until Tom up and died on her. Or if she had, it had always been along the lines of what would Tom do if she left him a widower. After all, her job had much more inherent risk, didn't it? Then when he got sick, the cancer had filled their lives, beating it, stifling it, cursing it. There was no time to think about growing old because their collective focus narrowed down to today and tomorrow.

Then she was alone. Oh, her son was there, cramming single meals into the freezer and coming over to do pointless odd jobs at her place, stuff that didn't need to be done, or that Rena was quite capable of handling herself. Busy work now, an excuse, a distraction.

Next minute she was on the road, fulfilling her promise to Tom, setting out on the trip—*their* trip—putting miles between the present and the life she had known.

Never did she acknowledge that the thing she'd been running from all this time was herself.

Until now.

Rena had finally woken up, and she'd decided.

Stuff that.

She didn't plan to hassle the police or try to figure out why Marty was murdered. She'd thought from the start it was a wonder he'd survived this long; the possibilities for who killed him and why were endless. Besides, Rena wasn't bloody Miss Marple. What she was, though, was a damn good field geologist, which a company like Verne Industries could use about now.

Someone who already knew what they were after.

Someone on the spot.

Rena planned to get herself back in the game. Except she didn't plan to offer herself to Verne or any other mining company. Forget about experience and skill; given her age they'd probably turn her down. But to hell with them; she'd do it anyway.

She was going rock hunting. And when she found diamonds—if she found them—there was Aitch. She'd been impressed by the young woman's commitment to the people and the land, but also by her calmness in a dangerous situation. Rena figured if she located the diamond deposit, she'd pass the details on to Aitch and walk away. Then the real owners would have the upper hand.

And if she found nothing, there was a fair chance Rena might turn into one of those weird old bush people, the sort who only came to town every few months, stocked up, then disappeared again, locked in a never-ending quest to uncover the riches of the earth. She'd let her hair grow wild, even as stories about her did the same.

Rena had met plenty of people like that over the years—mostly men, but a few women—people for whom the lure of opal or gold or even something like crocoite or sapphires saw them spend increasing amounts of time prospecting, moving dirt, or digging in a remote mine shaft, sure that a big find was close. Ultimately, most let go of the last shackles of society and surrendered to the dream of striking it rich, and from that moment to the end, their eyes never lost the fever-glint of the obsessed.

She had a few things to do in the Crossing, and number one was call her son and tell him she was going bush and that he shouldn't expect to hear from her for a while. He'd be worried, but also relieved his mother was doing something that was, for her, normal. He'd see it as a sign of her emotional recovery, and whatever happened, he'd believe Rena was doing something she loved. Rena wanted that for him, a good memory of his mum.

She guided the Ranger around a sweeping bend and past a sign advising of local liquor restrictions, even though she still couldn't see Fitzroy Crossing itself. Two more signs warning that the road was subject to flooding, one scored with depth marks stained to an almost incomprehensible height. It was hard to imagine this dry, flat land submerged beneath more than a metre of water. The speed limit dropped to eighty, then sixty. A scattering of trees flanked the road. Nothing tall, and their numbers were still few, but after the emptiness of the floodplain, even that was a noticeable difference in the landscape. Rena drove around a final curve and the town rose up to greet her, sunlight bouncing off the corrugated iron roofs, like the flare of a dozen matches. She adjusted the sun visor but the angle had already changed and she'd arrived—lampposts, tourist information, people. She turned left off the highway, heading for the town centre and the bakery.

Parking wasn't a problem, but as Rena walked towards the bakery's door, she could see the breakfast rush was on; the fly strips were never still; a constant stream of people pushed through, going in empty, reappearing with coffees and paper bags in hand. Jo, the bakery owner, seemed to be a good barometer of the town and the Synastria Mining project, and Rena wanted to see if she knew anything about Verne Industries or had maybe spoken to Marty. But now clearly wasn't the moment.

Checking her watch, she calculated it was the perfect time to phone her son on the East Coast and tell him her plans. Ben would be at work, but it was close to the hour, which meant theoretically he should be in the small window between two of his physio patients. He'd pick up Rena's call; they'd have a few minutes for Rena to say she was well but going to be out of contact; Ben would fuss briefly then have to go. As she brought her phone to life and tapped his name, Rena was reminded of her teenage years, the times she'd try to slip news of detention or lower-than-expected test scores past her parents when they were busy with other things. She wondered when her life had redefined itself like this, her age passing a peak and descending through the Gaussian curve of maturity.

But sneaking unwelcome news past family hadn't worked then, and it didn't work now.

'Mum, what's wrong?'

'Not even a *Hello, Mum, how are you?* Nothing's wrong. I'm just calling to say hi, let you know I'm fine—that sort of thing.' Rena tried to sound light and breezy without overdoing it.

'Uh-huh.'

'And to tell you I'll be out of mobile range for a bit so not to worry.'

'There it is! I knew it.'

'Ben love, you knew this would happen occasionally; it's the nature of travel! I'm letting you know so you *don't* worry, not so you can get a head start on catastrophising.' Rena was walking as she talked, but now she stopped and hunched slightly over her phone, the faux privacy of the modern era where people assumed others were listening in but conducted their business in public nonetheless.

'Mum, I'm always going to worry. Love you, but I've got to go. Are there rocks involved?'

'When is your old mum not involved with rocks?' Rena laughed now, relieved her son wasn't getting too worked up. Tom had said that even as a baby, Ben had the soul of an old Italian woman, some-one like Tom's mother whose most uttered word was *Madonna!*

while her favourite phrase was, *Vecchi peccati hanno le ombre lunghe: Old sins have long shadows.* Ben would fret, but if he thought she was just alone in the outback looking at rocks, at least his fears would be familiar, not the angst of worrying about his mother's profound grief.

'Take care and call when you can, okay?'

'Bye, sweetheart, love you,' said Rena.

She disconnected the call then scrolled down to another contact. Les and Margot. Rena listened to it ring, willing them to be home and not out at some medical appointment or other. There was a click and a short silence, enough to make Rena think the answering machine was about to kick in, but instead she was greeted with a barrage of loud, phlegmy coughs. She pulled the phone away from her ear, wincing as the noise went on and on until finally, it descended into a croak.

'You right there, Les?'

'Argh.' An inarticulate sound somewhere between a word and throat-clearing.

'Les?'

'Christ! That you Rena? Sorry, felt like I was bringing up a lung with that one.'

'I thought the next thing I'd hear was Marg doing CPR. Sure you're okay?'

'Yeah. Doctor reckons too much dust down mines over the years. Nothing that'll cause the big C, but enough to make every little chest infection crank the phlegm production into overdrive. Anyway, you didn't call to talk to me about my health. Verne Industries, ay? And was I right? We're talking about Marty Kinnane, the little shit?'

Rena checked her surroundings, sure that Les's over-loud mention of Kinnane would have attracted attention, but there was no one within earshot, and just a single car crawling past.

'Yep. But I have to tell you, he's gone and got himself killed.'

'Fair dinkum? Accident?'

'Police don't think so.' Rena decided not to go into detail.

'Bugger me! Margot always said he'd come to a sticky end.'

'Listen, Les. In your message you said he was definitely on the Verne Industries payroll, but there were some other things you had to tell me.' Rena had been standing in the shade of a scraggly coolabah tree, but now she began to slowly make her way towards the library, wishing she'd stuck on a hat before leaving the car.

'Strewth yes! First of all, rumour is fact—but you didn't hear it from me—that Verne aren't just going after any diamonds; they've been zeroing in on what looks like it could be a small but rich deposit of… Are you ready?'

'Les!'

'Violets!' Les spoke the word with dramatic flair.

Rena stopped moving as her brain processed the information. 'Violets? Seriously? As the main colour in the deposit?'

'S'right!' Les crowed. 'And not just babies either. Stuff going over a carat.'

'And not a variation on blues?'

'No, darl. Just like the few they pulled out of Argyle. Not a trace of boron in there to cause the colour, and they're true violet. They could be the next big thing, rarer than a pink.'

'Hell! If this is legit, they're sitting on a fortune.' Rena started walking again, the news adding length to her stride.

'Oh, it's legit, all right. Totally hush-hush, but you know me; I have my sources. And you're the only person I've told, seeing you specifically asked about Verne Industries and Marty. Bloody hell, he's really cashed in his cheque?'

'Yep. You don't think it could be anything to do with the diamonds, do you?'

'Geez, hadn't thought of that. Assumed it'd be someone's husband or someone he'd screwed over in the more figurative sense who'd do him in. But now that you mention it…there's a lot of money in this thing. A lot. Blokes have killed for less.'

'Listen, Les. I can't thank you enough for telling me about the violets, and rest assured it won't go any further.'

'Never doubted it, Rena. You and I go way back, and you've always been straight as a die. I know you wouldn't be asking if you didn't have a good reason, and I also know you can keep your trap shut. Do you remember back in—what was it?—1979? '80? When they found the Hand of Faith nugget? And you—'

'Sure do!' Rena interrupted before Les could go off on one of his lengthy trips down memory lane. 'Listen, thanks again. I really have to be getting on, but in your message you mentioned something else about Marty. Something that surfaced after Argyle closed down?'

'Strewth! I forgot, what with the excitement about the violets. Plus the old memory's not what it used to be. Hope to Christ I cark it before I get Alzheimer's!'

It was the universal fear of growing old.

'So. Marty and the Argyle mine?' said Rena.

'See this is the sort of thing I thought would get him offed. He worked for Argyle a bit during the mine's last couple of years, and the story I've heard is that—' Les broke off, descending into a fit of harsh coughing.

'Les?'

More coughing, deep rattles interspersed by wheezing intakes of air. Rena waited but there seemed to be no letup. There was a clatter, which she assumed was Les putting the phone down, and the coughing grew fainter but no less intense. She heard Margot's voice, first far away, then in her ear.

'Hello?'

'Margot, it's Rena. Is Les okay?'

'Rena darling. It gets like this from time to time. Nothing we haven't dealt with before, but I need to go and help him with his medication. I'm sure Les'll call you back when he can, but it might be a while.'

'Right. Thanks, Margot. Give him my best.' Rena ended the call, feeling worry for Les tinged with frustration that she hadn't extracted the last piece of information.

The thing Les believed would be likely to get Marty killed.

'Ah, shit,' Rena muttered.

TWENTY

The small library had only just opened, but there were already at least half a dozen patrons inside. A couple of teenagers sat at a table, surrounded by the paraphernalia of schoolwork, heads bent together in whispered, giggle-laden conversation. Like libraries everywhere, this wasn't just about books; it was a climate-controlled haven, somewhere to sit comfortably and maybe page through a newspaper or simply doze, knowing you were safe.

Rena nodded to the librarian behind the front desk, then headed for the computers at the back, feeling the gaze of several people follow her until she passed between the first rows of books. Both computers were free, screens glowing with the Shire of Derby logo and an inviting *get started!* button.

She began by searching for anything on Verne Industries, but all she found was the company website and a few mentions in the *Australian Mining* newsletter, no mention of diamonds. Next she had another look at Synastria, this time dipping into message boards and hashtags, hunting for news that didn't make the news, rumours, lies, and innuendo with the potential to either send the stock market into a spin or blow away like topsoil after a drought. Plenty of stuff about the Ellendale prospect and the new techniques they'd be using, a number of stories about the Traditional Owners, either singing Synastria's praises for their approach or demonising the Synastria board. Rena wasn't surprised to see that while there was still considerable local disquiet about Synastria moving into the Kimberley; the most vitriolic rants came from anonymous keyboard warriors. And when she dug a bit on those—looking for posts on other topics and social media feeds—she got the distinct impression that the majority resided in bigger cities on Australia's East Coast. She had no objection to people protesting for a cause, but it pissed her off when the ill-informed took over the debate. Personally, she had only Aitch's taciturn assessment of the Synastria proposal to go on, but Rena would take that over online crap any day.

She checked the clock at the top of the screen, surprised to see she'd been at it for nearly two hours. Stretching both hands above her head, Rena took a moment to survey her immediate surrounds. The second computer remained unused, and the only person moving through the aisles was the librarian with a trolley of books. The soft, intermittent squeak of its wheels blasted through the closed door of memory, catapulting her back to Tom, the hospital, and those last days and nights, the sound of a gurney in the corridor. Time had seemed to pass so quickly, but for Tom, right at the end, it had not passed quickly enough.

Rena stood so abruptly her chair almost toppled and strode through the library, her breath coming in ragged gasps. She pushed between the automatic doors even while they were still parting, taking half a dozen more steps before bending, dropping her head, trying to stem the pain and nausea of grief, regret, and loss. Her chest hurt, her throat was tight, and she couldn't seem to draw in enough air to expand her lungs.

Suddenly she felt a hand on her back, pressing gently between her shoulder blades.

'Mate! Rena? Are you having a heart attack? Do you need an ambulance?'

The voice was familiar, but she couldn't place it, and from her position all she could see was denim-clad legs and dusty work boots. But it was enough to ground her, to pull her back from the precipice of despair.

Rena waved a hand without looking up. 'I'm okay,' she grunted.

'You're sure? Because you really look like a heart attack in progress.' Despite the wry comment, Rena could hear genuine concern in the woman's voice. She turned her head slightly.

Aitch. Worry driving a straight, horizontal line down between her brows, pinching the corners of her eyes. A large Akubra shaded her face, and she pushed back the brim with one finger, leaning in closer.

'Yeah, I'm sure.' Rena's voice was stronger, but still not quite her own. She straightened up, feeling the lightness in her head but knowing it wasn't going to get worse. Not now. 'Bit of a bad reaction. Just need some air, pull myself together. Thanks.'

'I saw you rush out and just about keel over. Your face... Now I know what a grey complexion looks like.' Aitch stared hard at her. 'Colour's coming back now though. How about some water? Or maybe something to eat. When did you last eat?'

Rena realised she was starving. 'Sort of forgot.'

'Right, come on.' Aitch's hand was still resting lightly on Rena's back, and now she gave Rena a soft double tap, presumably a gently-does-it version of a friendly slap.

Rena hesitated, thinking of the browser window she'd left open on the library computer, an opinion piece about Synastria's environmental record. Thinking also that she hadn't yet had the chance to more accurately map that cluster of GPS points she'd plotted last night. Her stomach growled.

No one would pay any attention to her search history, and she had all the time in the world to return to the library and chart a course into diamond country. Rena nodded at Aitch, and together they turned towards the street, crossing a wide swathe of patchy grass before Aitch jerked her head in the direction of the bakery.

'My shout,' was all she said, holding up a hand when Rena opened her mouth to protest.

Rena subsided. Now that she was past the crisis, she was starting to feel embarrassed about her reaction. Hungry and sleep-deprived she may be, but it was only a squeaky wheel in a goddamn library. She told herself that, but knew in her heart it was really the enduring memory of Tom, ravaged by cancer, in pain, with no strength left to fight.

Aitch guided her to a bench in the shade. 'Wait here.'

Rena spent the few minutes redirecting her mind to happy memories of Tom, and by the time Aitch returned, the ache in her core had receded and her head was clear.

'Sorry about that,' she said, accepting the proffered bottle of water and paper bag.

Aitch shrugged and gave a dismissive grunt as she settled on the bench next to Rena. 'Got you a barra pie. Hope that's okay. Jo's famous for them and you looked like you needed something more substantial than a ham sanger.'

Rena had twisted the top from her water and paused in act of bringing it to her mouth. 'Thanks. Hadn't realised how hungry I was.' She took several big gulps of water.

Beside her, Aitch eased her own pie half-out of its bag and bit into it. A few flakes of golden pastry fell, dusting the front of her T-shirt. Aitch chewed, staring out at the town, glanced at Rena—who had set her water aside—then took another bite. Rena did the same. The big chunks of wild-caught barramundi were tender, and she savoured the almost buttery taste. The fish was complemented by a few veggies and just the right amount of mornay sauce, enough to lend a creamy texture to the filling but not so much that it oozed and got messy. Rena sighed; it was delicious. She was about to thank Aitch again when the other woman swallowed and lowered her pie slightly. 'Listen, Rena,' she said, looking at the pie. 'Don't want to stick my nose into another woman's business, but...' Aitch let the sentence hang.

'Health's fine; I'm fine. Well, physically. Just had...I guess it was a sort of flashback. Had some trouble with stress and anxiety and it kinda hit me.'

'PTSD?'

'I guess. It's only happened a couple of times before and not for a while. Thought I was done with it. Sorry.'

Aitch shook her head. 'Never apologise for that sort of shit, mate. Anyway, what are you doing in the Crossing? Thought you'd shot through days ago.'

Rena flashed a quick smile, acknowledging Aitch's not-so-subtle subject change.

'Well, my time's my own—nowhere I have to be—and a couple of things made me want to come back and spend more of it here.' She studied Aitch over the top of her half-eaten pie, considering.

Aitch nodded. 'Geology stuff? You mentioned the Devonian reef last time we talked.'

'Geology stuff is one way of putting it. Plus I still reckon I owe you a drink or a coffee. Could I tell you what's on my mind? Maybe get your opinion on some stuff?'

'My opinion? You're the rock lady.'

'Yeah. But you know more about diamond mining in this district—and I don't mean the geology of it. I mean the companies, what they want, where they want to do it, and what they're offering in return.'

Aitch swung her head around sharply when Rena mentioned diamonds and now she favoured Rena with a long, unblinking stare, her face impassive. After a moment in which Rena did nothing but offer her own open countenance for scrutiny, Aitch drew in a long breath. 'Should I be talking to you? Who are you?'

'I'm a retired geologist with no skin in any game. Except I think I've stuck my nose into something big, and I'm not quite sure what it is. That's why I'm back here. Because for no particular reason, I want to figure out what's going on.'

'You—' Aitch began but Rena interrupted her.

'No wait, that's not strictly true. It's not for no particular reason. A man got killed, and there's stuff going on with the diamonds that doesn't make sense, except it was probably enough to get him killed. That's bad enough, but to me it also suggests that somewhere else along the line, people are going to get screwed over one way or the other.' Rena shrugged, picked up her water then put it down again. 'Maybe I'm just an interfering old woman, but I know minerals and I know mining companies and damn it, I've never walked away from a shitstorm and I'm not about to now.' She shook her head. 'So that's it, that's why I'm back. You can make up your own mind whether you should be talking to me or not, but at least let me buy you that drink and you can listen to what I have and then decide.'

Aitch snorted then bit into her pie again, chewed meditatively, swallowed. She took a breath and seemed about to say something but took another bite instead. After a moment, Rena did the same and they sat there, side by side, eating barra pies in the Kimberley heat, a wall of unspoken questions between them. The fly strips of the bakery swished repeatedly with the coming and going of customers, cars drove past, two Aboriginal women chatted away as they walked slowly by, giving Aitch a hint of side-eye but otherwise ignoring her. Overhead a light plane droned, coming in low, making for the airstrip.

Rena finished her meal first, crumpling the paper bag and tucking it next to her on the seat. She drank some more water and waited. Finally, Aitch swallowed the last of her pie, brushed the crumbs from her chest, and turned to face Rena.

'I don't want you to buy me a drink,' she said.

Rena sighed and nodded. 'I understand.'

'No, you don't understand. Because I don't want to stuff around waiting till beer o'clock and then have half the town listening in. What I want is for you to tell me everything *now*.' There was an intensity to her words that made Rena pause.

'Aitch? What is it?'

'Nup. You show me yours first.'

'Fair enough,' said Rena. She slapped her hands on her thighs. 'I guess I'd better start with a bit of background. About the man who was in that burned-out car.'

Aitch jerked back. 'Are you shitting me now?' But she didn't wait for an answer, clearly reading it in Rena's face. 'Not here. Come on, let's walk. If anyone asks, I'm giving you a cultural tour.' She stood, lobbed their rubbish into the nearest bin and adjusted her hat lower over her eyes, all in the time it took Rena to catch up with the developments and get to her feet.

'This way.' Aitch jerked her head. 'Down to the river.'

It was the thing that defined the town, that gave rise to its very existence and also the thing that wrought havoc during the big wet. And if you were to stand in the middle of the bridge, it was a bloody good place to talk without the slightest possibility of being overheard, and to look like you were discussing the landscape while you did so. The narrow bridge had a steel mesh walkway for pedestrians on its north side, protected from traffic by a thigh-high concrete and metal barrier, and from the river by much less substantial railing. Everything was thickly coated with red dust.

'It almost looks like it's a temporary barrier,' said Rena, patting the handrail.

'Smallest possible obstacle to floodwaters when the river's in full spate. If it rises this high, the idea is the road surface is protected while this'—Aitch stamped the open mesh beneath their feet—'lets a bit of water through. Mostly, though, we hope it doesn't get that high. People fuck up the land every which way then get upset when things go to shit.'

Rena looked at the dry sand of the riverbed, about twelve metres below, and tried to picture the river flowing, rising, breaking its banks and washing over the bridge deck. It seemed impossible.

They walked out to the centre of the span and stopped. It was hotter here, not only out in the full sun, but with heat radiating up from the metal beneath their feet, rising from the tarmac behind them and bouncing off the ground below. Rena's chest was sweaty, the nape of her neck tingled with the sun's bite, and she was doubly grateful for the bottle of water she'd just drunk.

They turned their backs to the road and stared northward, out at the land. The broad riverbed—all sand on its western side but with a few pools in the middle and a thread of water still trickling down near the eastern bank—curved gently to the left about five hundred metres further upstream before it disappeared from view. A wall of dusty eucalyptus marked its edge and above that, blue sky, traversed by a group of grey-white ombre clouds, a strange migration of otherworldly creatures.

During the walk, Rena had been thinking about how to tell Aitch everything in a coherent fashion, and now the story came freely.

'Best to begin with me finding the Toyota on fire,' she said.

'That was you?' Aitch's voice rose, and she twisted her torso to look at Rena. 'Heard it was a tourist. Somehow don't think of you as a tourist, but given your bloody boots and all approach to situations, I guess I shouldn't be surprised.' She shook her head. 'Bloody hell.'

'Anyway…'

After that Rena spoke without pause, laying everything out for Aitch: her connection to Marty, his work for Verne Industries, what she'd found at Marty's camp, and the fact that someone else had been out there, watching her and searching through her stuff. When she got to the part about cracking the combination on the locked chest and taking the notes, she shot Aitch a quick look, expecting condemnation or shock, but all she got was an impassive profile. She didn't bother to dress up her actions with bullshit justifications about commercial-in-confidence stuff. In the retelling, it was clear to Rena that her main motivation was curiosity.

Next, she told Aitch about last night's GPS mapping.

'The location and distribution of Marty Kinnane's sample sites makes sense, but what got me was the fact that they were nowhere near his camp or where he died. And now I've found out the diamonds in question might be something really special—violets. Think rarity of pink multiplied by thousands; that's a genuine violet diamond.' She was about to mention Marty's connection to the Argyle mine, when Aitch cut in.

'Hang on.'

Turning and leaning against the handrail, Aitch took off her hat, ran a hand over her head, replaced the hat and drew in a deep breath. 'Why are violet diamonds so rare?'

It wasn't the question Rena had expected, and it took her a moment to reorder her thoughts. Sweat beaded her forehead, and even the brief transit of a cloud across the sun did little to relieve the relentless glare. 'Aitch love, this part of the convo we could have in the lodge's bar, in air-conditioned comfort. What do you say?' She paused. 'Unless there's anything you want to share with me.'

'Maybe. But explain about the stones. With all the shit that's already swirling around the Synastria mine, probably best if it doesn't become general knowledge that there's a second mining operation in the mix and—if I'm picking up what you're putting down—an absolute crap-ton of money to be made.'

'Fine, but can we walk and talk?'

Aitch nodded and pushed herself off the handrail. 'Don't want you going to shit on me again. But just so you know where I'm coming from. Cops have someone in their sights for killing that Kinnane bloke. Someone I know. He's young, he can be a stupid fuck and he's done some stupid things, but torching someone?' Aitch shook her head and started walking. 'Not that. At least that's what I thought until you started talking about big money. So tell me about violet diamonds.'

Rena followed, their combined footsteps making the metal beneath their feet ring dully, the vibrations setting up an odd counter-tremor in her legs.

'Most stones, even most diamonds, get their colour from some sort of impurity. For example, rubies and sapphires are both corundum. Both crystalline aluminium oxide but rubies have chromium and sapphires—well it depends on their particular colour, but if we talk about blues, they have titanium and iron.'

'Yeah, yeah. Diamonds, Rena. There ain't no rubies in this country.'

'Actually farther south in Western Australia—'

'Shit. Forget the rubies; get to the diamonds.'

'Right, well. Impurities cause colour. For example, in yellow diamonds the colour is caused by the presence of nitrogen, but pink colour in diamonds is caused by...nothing.'

'Nothing? But you just said—'

'Yeah. Not only are pinks incredibly rare, they're incredibly special. Diamonds are just carbon, but the atoms are arranged in a rigid lattice. Pinks are caused by distortion of the lattice, which displaces a lot of the carbon atoms and that in turn alters the way the stone reflects light. And we see it as pink. You with me?'

Aitch stopped and shot Rena a look. 'Lattice distortion, reflection of light, pink.'

'Sorry. Sometimes I get carried away and forget that not everyone is as interested as I am in this stuff.'

'Nah, I'm interested, trust me. But you still haven't mentioned the violets.'

'Getting to it, but first I've got to tell you couple of things about Argyle pinks—it's relevant. See what I mean? When I'm talking rocks and minerals, I never use one word where ten will do.'

'For fuck's sake, mate. Get on with it!' Aitch threw up her hands, half in jest, half in genuine exasperation, and started walking again. 'For someone who wants a drink, you've got a pretty decent voice on you.'

Rena was tempted to protest, but decided it wasn't the moment. 'You get pinks in other places around the world, but Argyles have the best colour, the most intense saturation, because of another aspect of the structure which we don't need to go into.'

'Hall-e-bloody-lujah.'

'And I'm sure you know that for every million carats of diamonds that came out of Argyle, only one carat was high-quality pinks.'

'Mate, you're killing me here.'

'First the violets are even rarer. They got a few out of Argyle but mostly small stuff. The colour is most likely caused by nickel, and the thing about the Argyle violets is that besides the colour, they have a couple of properties that make them very different from every other stone that came out of that mine, pink, white, or whatever. The violet colour is very uniform—Argyle browns and pinks commonly show some patchiness or graininess—and violets have extremely high clarity, fewer inclusions. Now, you know how I said pinks get their colour through distortion?'

'Shit, mate.'

'I'll take that as a yes. Well, that deformation of the lattice is basically a characteristic of Argyle diamonds, and when you look at them—regardless of colour—under crossed polar filters, the birefringence pattern shows that strain.'

'Okay. I think.'

'But the violets don't.'

'So?'

'So! Stuff-all strain, nickel that doesn't occur in other diamonds from the Argyle mine, way less inclusions... It all points to a different growing environment. Possibly shallower, less pressure, but different. Now, if the Argyle pipe—the volcanic pipe that passed through the diamond stability field and carried all those pinks and other main colours toward the surface—if that only grazed the edge of the subterranean level where the violets formed, that would explain why there are only a few violets and they're different. But it also means that maybe there's an entirely different pipe that went straight through the middle of the violet-producing diamond stability field. Now, the main diamond-producing zone is about 150 kilometres below the surface, so depending on how dispersed that violet layer is, a pipe that hit its centre could break the surface quite some distance from the Argyle prospect. And if you found that pipe, found the place where it erupted...'

Aitch nodded slowly. 'You'd find the mother lode.'

'Exactly. So Verne Industries and their man Marty Kinnane aren't just throwing darts here, they're thinking about the geology and vulcanology and making some very calculated moves.'

'So, you reckon they found it? But where that bloke died—surely that was too far away?'

'Not only too far away, but nowhere near. And that's the problem. I do think Marty found it—or at least a bloody good indication of it—but if he did, why was he still out here at all, let alone hundreds of miles away from the hypothetical pipe? I'm starting to wonder if he was double-crossing his bosses, telling them he was still sampling and exploring while in reality he was… I dunno. Hiding out, afraid for his life? Looking for something else? Waiting for someone else to sell the data to?'

'And now he's dead.'

'Exactly.'

They turned down the drive of the Fitzroy River Lodge, climbed the stairs to the wide verandah and shouldered their way into the bar. Air conditioning immediately chilled the sweat on Rena's head and torso, and she pulled off her hat, relishing the cool. Aitch waited at a stand-up table while Rena bought the drinks: Cokes for both of them, the glasses piled high with ice.

'So, what are you going to do?' Aitch asked, after downing a third of her drink in one go.

'I'm going prospecting,' said Rena.

Aitch had been about to take another swig of Coke, the glass half-tipped to her mouth, but at Rena's pronouncement, she checked the movement, setting her glass down with a loud crack.

'You're what?'

'Listen, I've been told there's a story about Kinnane pulling something, some shit to do with the Argyle mine just before it closed. If we agree that there's a link between the Argyle violets and the current speculative prospect, maybe whatever Kinnane did back then is relevant.'

'What like stealing maps or sample data or something?'

'Who knows? I mean it can't have been a treasure map with a big red cross marked *Dig here for violet diamonds*, or the people at Argyle would have set up there. So I figured I'd have a look at the country around those GPS points. See if there's anything going on or if it looks promising from a diamond mine perspective.'

'But he wasn't killed there.'

'No, but we've established there was no reason to be where he was. Which means maybe the answer is where he wasn't.'

'You really crap on a lot, don't you, Rena mate? You can't just piss off into the outback for a gander.'

''Course I bloody can.' Rena downed the last of her drink, ice rattling in the glass. 'Want to join me?'

TWENTY-ONE

Although she'd asked the question on impulse, Rena immediately realised she wouldn't mind Aitch's company on a fossicking expedition. The younger woman's no-bullshit attitude and economy with words were an appealing combination in a travel companion. But even as she was seeing the merit of her own proposal, Aitch was shaking her head.

'I may be in a bar with you, during business hours on a weekday, but I do actually have a job. I can't just piss off.'

'Pity, but fair enough,' Rena sighed.

A sudden burst of noise caused both women to glance up. The bartender had just turned on a television mounted on the wall, and a random crowd somewhere in the world was cheering an unknown team in an undefined ball sport. Aitch leaned forward and made a gimme gesture with her right hand.

'Show me these GPS points.'

Rena fiddled with her phone for a moment, pulled up the screenshot and slid it across the table. She watched while Aitch studied the screen, swiping, splaying and pinching her fingers as she moved around the image, zooming in and out. Finally Aitch grunted and placed the phone on the table, turning it so the screen faced Rena.

'Well, first you're fucking nuts. That's bloody remote.'

'Most places out here are,' said Rena, swirling the ice around in her glass.

'Second, if that Kinnane fella was killed over whatever this is'—Aitch waved a hand over the phone—'you're *really* fucking nuts and setting yourself up for some serious shit.'

'Only if someone on the wrong side of this gets wind of where I'm going. Makes things more interesting, I guess.'

Aitch snorted. 'Why don't you just tell the cops or the mining company?'

'Because I don't know who to trust.'

'You trust me,' said Aitch, her voice quiet, almost inaudible against the background noise.

'I do,' said Rena, holding Aitch's stare.

'So trust me when I say handball this to someone else.'

'Yeah, no. I'll just have a bit of a poke around first. Once I have facts to back up my suppositions, *then* I can handball it to someone. Face it, right now I'd probably be filed under *irritatingly dotty old bird* and shown the door quick smart.'

Aitch's lips twitched.

'I'm right, aren't I?' Rena pressed her advantage. 'I've worked remotely my entire life; I can take care of myself. Look, now you know my plans. I've even got a head start on step one of going bush: Tell someone where you're going and when you'll be back. Give me a week, then you can call in the cavalry.'

Aitch let out a heavy sigh that incorporated the word *fuuuuck*. She tapped her index finger on the table next to Rena's phone. 'I don't think you'll be breaking any rules or travelling anywhere that needs permission from the owners, but if you see any signs or someone tells you to get out, you bloody get out, right?'

'I always respect the wishes of Traditional Owners.'

'I knew you would. I'm just saying.'

'Right then.'

'Right. And if you're not back in seven days, I can guarantee that not only will some pissed-off coppers be on your heels, but the media will be having a field day with *elderly lady driver gets lost in outback* stories. You'll be *that* fuckwit.'

'Duly noted. If that happens, I'd appreciate it if you didn't report to Detective Fletcher. He already thinks I'm that fuckwit.'

'Rena, mate...' Aitch pushed back from the table. 'Now that you've told me that, I can absolutely guarantee Fletcher will be the first person I tell.'

Outside, they stood in the shade of the pub's verandah, looking out over the surprisingly green lawn to the red dust of the road verge beyond.

'Thanks for sorting me out earlier, and for listening to me prattle on about diamond geology and murder conspiracies.'

'No worries. I should get to work.'

Rena knew there were things unsaid but had no idea what it was she should be saying, or which questions she should be asking. She nodded. 'I'm going to stock up and get back on the road today. What say you start counting my seven days from tomorrow?'

Aitch shook her head and sighed. 'Just don't fucking get yourself killed.'

They walked back to the town centre in companionable silence then parted company, peeling off in different directions. Aitch to get back to whatever she was doing before Rena had her wobbly in front of the library, and Rena to move her car down the road to the IGA supermarket. She eyed off the bakery, still hoping to catch up with Jo, but the breakfast rush had evolved into the lunch crowd and besides, most of her questions about local sentiment towards mining companies were probably superfluous, while others were the sort of things a wary local like Jo would be disinclined to answer. Things like: *So, Jo, is there anyone around here who'd be prepared to kill to stop a mine going ahead? What about if they could cash in?*

As she wrestled a recalcitrant trolley up and down the aisles, stocking up on non-perishables, Rena thought about Aitch. Specifically, what it was that had made the young woman want to know everything. She'd been so emphatic about hearing Rena's story immediately and away from listening ears, hinting that she had something of her own to share. Something relevant. Yet once Rena had spilled her guts, Aitch had been quick to play the work card, eager to get going.

Rena had noticed but decided not to push. She trusted her gut—her initial feeling that Aitch was a good person—and it hadn't changed. Aitch was a Kimberley woman, born and bred, and Rena was the blow-in with no business whatsoever sticking her oar in local matters, even if they did call to her skill set.

She shelved her disgruntlement, telling herself that if Aitch knew anything relevant to the Marty Kinnane situation, she would have shared.

Rena reached the end of an aisle and wrenched the trolley to the left, forced to take a wide turn because the thing was a piece of crap. She was looking down at one of the shonky wheels—currently pointed at right angles to the direction she was trying to travel—and smacked straight into a trolley coming the other way.

'Sorry. This bloody useless...' she began, then looked up. 'This is a surprise. What are the odds?'

'In these parts, perhaps less than you think, given the population and number of supermarkets.' Chuck stood, gripping the handle of the opposing trolley, his one eye flicking from Rena's face to her shopping. He jerked his chin towards the cans, bulk-buy water and packets of rice and noodles. 'Preparing for Armageddon?'

'Just heading out bush for a bit. Probably overstocking, but better dead sure than sure dead.'

Chuck tilted his head. 'What an odd expression. Very apposite, though. Where exactly are you going? Tackling the Tanami?'

'Nah. Keeping it local. Just fancy a bit of time away.' Rena shifted her weight and inched the trolley slightly to the left, wanting to edge past without seeming rude. But the aisle was too narrow, and Chuck showed no sign of moving.

'Where local? You're travelling alone, I gather?' Chuck's tone was conversational, and he leaned forward, bracing his arms on the trolley handle, a man with all the time in the world. But the intensity of that one-eyed gaze, and his last question put Rena on high alert. Maybe she was just jumpy.

'You said it yourself. Around here, *local* is a relative concept. Thought I'd head up the Leopold Downs Road, check out Tunnel Gorge then maybe make for the Wunaamin Miliwundi Ranges. But that might all change. The plan is to just follow my nose and not be held back by a lack of supplies.' Rena eased to the right. 'Anyway, must get going.' She pushed forward, gently, but enough to cause a metallic clatter as the trolleys clashed, enough to make her intentions crystal clear. 'Oops,' she said.

Chuck sidestepped, pulling his trolley with him. 'Did I see you talking to a young local girl? Aitch, I think her name is?'

Rena moved forward, drawing level with the man, their shoulders separated by less than a metre. She turned her head slowly. 'I don't know. Did you?'

Chuck smiled. It looked false, but perhaps that was just the scar tissue. 'It's just that if you need local knowledge, a guide perhaps, I can set you up with someone reliable.' The too-big teeth flashed as he forced the smile even wider.

'Thanks. I'll keep that in mind.' Rena resisted the urge to hurry away. 'Have a good one,' she said, hoping the 'good one' was a coronary.

Now she needed to ask Jo about this creep. Rena was confident Jo would know whatever there was to know and would willingly pass it on to a woman travelling solo. She made for the checkout, sure that Chuck was watching her from somewhere, determined not to look.

Emerging from the IGA's air-conditioned microclimate, Rena welcomed the Kimberley heat. Was it just age that made her feel the supermarket's chill deep in her bones, or was Chuck part of that sensation, the cold a manifestation of Rena's instincts, telling her to be on her guard?

She started to stow her shopping in the right places within the travelling kitchen, satisfying both her desire for organisation and her curiosity as to whether Chuck would appear.

Sure enough, Rena had only put away a couple of things when the IGA's automatic doors parted to reveal Chuck's lanky frame. Rena, watching from the corner of her eye, saw the man register her presence then make a show of snapping his fingers and stepping back inside, as though he'd just remembered a forgotten item. Except Rena could still see him, reduced to a looming shadow between two of the signs for weekly specials that adorned the supermarket's glassed facade. Watching.

Rena closed the metal cover, locking the kitchen and its contents away. She considered going back, confronting Chuck and asking him what the hell he was playing at, just to see what sort of a reaction she got. But maybe Rena was seeing threats where none existed; maybe Chuck did just want to set her up with a local guide and pocket a fat commission, or even act as a guide himself. That thought gave Rena the icks. But whatever Chuck's game was, it didn't matter. Rena would be out of range in a matter of hours, following a plan that bore little resemblance to what she'd outlined ten minutes earlier. And once Rena had left Fitzroy Crossing, good luck finding her again. In a town this size it wasn't hard to keep tabs on a person, but a few kilometres beyond, not long after the mobile signal dipped and died, there was no hope of following someone without being noticed, let alone tracking them down once they'd disappeared. For every marked road there was a score of dirt tracks vanishing into the Never Never, and those were the sorts of routes Rena planned to take.

Behind her, someone tooted their car's horn, a friendly double beep. Rena ignored it, assuming it wasn't meant for her, and opened the driver's door. The horn sounded again, more insistent.

'Rena! Mate!'

Rena turned and there was Wally, leaning out the window of his taxi, a hand raised in greeting, a wide smile bunching his cheeks into big red apples.

'G'day.' Rena half-closed the door and ambled across, bemused by the man's enthusiasm. Some people had a zest for life that shone through, no matter what.

'You are leaving?'

'About to, yeah.'

'Bah.' Wally's mouth turned down, a comical overexaggeration of disappointment. 'I heard your last name—Novak—and it made sense why you such a nice lady.'

Rena laughed. 'My husband was Croatian. I was born here.'

'Still, you understand. Anyway, I'm glad I find you. It's quiet time for taxi, so I thought a bit of gold prospecting, and then I thought, *Rena is free woman, she has a detector, maybe you like to join Wally and Mrs Wally!* I show you good places, and my wife love to meet you.'

'Thanks, Wally. I've got a bit of a project of my own on, so maybe another time? I reckon I'll be in WA for a while, so if you're serious, we can tee something up.'

Wally smiled again. 'Yes?'

'Yep, why not? I'd love to meet your wife too; we can talk about being married to mad Eastern European blokes.' As she said it, Rena realised she actually might enjoy a couple of days in the company of the taxi driver and his wife.

'Okay.' Wally pulled his mobile from the central console. 'You give me your number.'

Rena rattled off the digits as Wally's thumbs pecked the screen.

'And now I call you and you have my number!'

Her pocket buzzed and Rena fumbled for a moment before retrieving her own phone. She checked the screen. 'Got it, cheers. I'll probably be out of range for a week or so, but then I'll be in touch.'

'I wait two weeks, but then maybe I call you. And Mrs Wally and I will bring my slivovitz—best you ever try!'

'I want to look for gold, not pass out under a shrub.'

'Is good for cold mornings and toasting finds.'

'Speaking of finds, how'd you go with that bloke who wanted to buy your detector?'

Wally frowned. 'Gone. Never heard from him again. Nothing. I try to call but no answer. But I have idea, something I heard…' He shrugged, then his gaze flicked over Rena's shoulder. 'You need a taxi?' Wally called.

Rena glanced back in time to see Chuck disappear around the side of the IGA at a fast trot.

'He was coming over here slowly, slowly, circling round like maybe he wanted a ride. Maybe thought you were my fare. Nobody looks at dome light anymore,' said Wally, jerking a thumb towards the roof of his cab to emphasise the point.

Rena turned and studied the spot where Chuck had been, but if the man was still there, he was keeping well out of sight. With a shake of her head, she returned her attention to her new friend.

'Never know with some people.' Rena checked her watch. 'Right-o. I'd better hit the road. Good to see you and thanks for the invitation. It'd be lovely to meet your wife and go detecting with you, Wal.'

Rena patted the roof of the cab, exchanged final pleasantries, then returned to the Ranger, casting a sideways look at the IGA. She couldn't see anyone watching now, but you never knew.

She pulled into the road like she was the world's most conscientious driver, with not a single care in the world: slow, plenty of indicator use and cautious tapping of brakes. She turned in the opposite direction to that taken by Wally's taxi, rolled sedately back down the street, and managed to snare the parking spot directly in front of the bakery.

Out of the vehicle, she strode to the door, reaching out a hand to push aside the fly strips just as someone else hurried out. There was no contact, but a communal rearing back, as Rena and Detective Fletcher tried to avoid colliding. They succeeded, but Fletcher was carrying a takeaway coffee, lid off. Somehow, in the general flailing of arms, he managed to throw it directly at Rena's chest.

Rena froze, arms out to the sides, staring down at her polo shirt. Then a microsecond later she registered the heat on her skin and snatched at the fabric, pulling it and holding it away from her body.

'Shit,' said Fletcher, shaking a few stray drops of coffee from his hand.

'Detective Fletcher.' Rena looked from the officer to her shirt and back again. 'I believe OC spray is what most police forces are using these days.'

'Sorry.' He grimaced, staring at her chest then quickly looking away. 'Accident.'

'Of course it was an accident! What, did you think I'd be lodging a complaint about police harassment?' Rena let go of her shirt and the fabric slapped wetly against her, sticking to her skin. The smell of coffee wafted up, overpowering. From within her hip pocket, Rena's silenced phone vibrated, but she ignored it; there was no one she needed to talk to right now.

A woman came up behind her, shouldering past them both

and into the bakery, muttering something under her breath, the words unintelligible, the snarky tone clear. Rena moved back, and Fletcher followed her off to the side, clearing the path to the door.

'It's a good trick, though,' said Rena.

'Mrs Novak, I did not mean—'

'Relax, I'm kidding. You would have thrown it in my face if it were deliberate.' Rena saw his wide-eyed expression of horror. 'Seriously, Detective, we're fine. Well, my top isn't, but I know old folks who dress like this every single day, so...'

For the first time since Rena had met him, Detective Fletcher smiled. It was barely more than a twitch of the lips, but it was there.

'Thanks for being so nice about it,' he said. 'I can pay for your shirt.'

Rena waved off his offer. 'Don't be silly. But...' She hesitated.

'Go on.' He lobbed his empty takeaway cup into a nearby bin. A perfect shot.

'Can I ask how the investigation into Marty Kinnane's death is going?'

Fletcher frowned, and Rena could almost see him start to bristle again.

'Sorry. I don't want to risk our fledgling friendship.' She gestured to her shirt. 'So feel free to tell me to piss off—or whatever the official police-speak version of that is—but I thought it was worth asking. And I do have sort of a vested interest.'

Fletcher sighed. Crossing his arms, he drummed the fingers of one hand on his opposite elbow. Behind him, people passed in and out of the bakery, accompanied by the swish of fly strips and the occasional shouted greeting of farewell to those inside.

'We have several avenues of inquiry, and the investigation is ongoing,' he said, but with a rising inflection that Rena took as an invitation.

'Yeah, and?'

'Look, I'm only going to say this because you've already shown us you're going to be a pain in the—That is, you seem determined to insert yourself into proceedings.'

Rena grinned.

He pointed a finger at her. 'And we've checked up on you. I know you're not some doddery old duffer, so don't think you can play the vague pensioner.'

Rena bit her lip but the grin broke into a wide smile. 'So, you know I might be able to help you.'

'We—' Detective Fletcher snapped his lips shut on whatever response he'd been about to unleash. He threw up his hands in mock exasperation. 'No. Whatever you've seen on TV or read, it doesn't work that way. Ever. I will tell you—only because it's about to become public knowledge anyway—that we have confirmed the car was deliberately set on fire and that there will be a public appeal for dash cam footage and any other information.'

'So what? An accelerant was used to torch the car?'

Fletcher shook his head, mute.

'Suspects?'

He glowered at her, his eyebrows almost touching with the intensity of his frown.

'And the public appeal. That means you've basically got nothing, right?'

Fletcher opened his mouth, presumably to give Rena a serve, but at that moment his phone emitted an alert tone. He pulled it from the back pocket of his trousers, tapped at the screen a few times, then sucked in a breath.

'I have to go.' Fletcher stepped around her. 'Nice to see you, Mrs Novak. Sorry about your shirt. I'm sure you have to get on the road to somewhere other than my jurisdiction, so I won't take up any more of your time.'

'You know how to get in touch.' Rena turned to watch him, but

Fletcher was already moving farther away. 'Detective!' she called. 'One more question!'

'Nope!' He didn't turn.

'Now that we're on civil terms, you can call me Rena.'

He stopped, spun around. 'That's not a question.'

'It was the lead-in. Now that we're on civil terms and you can call me Rena, can I call you Robert? I saw the name on your business card.'

He took one step back towards her then leaned forward, his voice a low hiss. 'No, you may not call me Robert.' Spinning around he resumed his brisk walk. 'It's Bob.' He threw the words over his shoulder.

'See you again, Bob!' Rena called.

'Hope not!' He disappeared around the next corner and Rena stepped into the bakery.

Jo was alone in the shop, leaning on the top of the display cabinet, eyebrows raised in greeting. 'Making friends?' she drawled.

'Everywhere I go, it seems. And I do believe you're just the person to tell me about one of them.'

A group came in, a young woman with two children, and Rena stepped aside, gesturing for them to go ahead and order while she stared through the glass at the assorted cakes and pastries. Once they'd left, Rena asked for a loaf of sliced wholemeal, four jam tarts, and a half a dozen Anzac biscuits. Jo started picking and bagging, one eye on Rena.

'Well,' she said, 'get to it then.'

'First, what do you know about a mining company called Verne Industries?'

'The mob the barbecued bloke worked for?'

'I… Yes.'

'First I heard of them was when the cops started asking about the fire.' She slid another jam tart into the bag she was holding. 'All raspberry or did you want a lemon?'

'All raspberry, please.' On her side of the cabinet, Rena followed Jo, moving to her left when she moved to her right. 'So, you didn't know they're also looking for diamonds, same as Synastria?'

Jo stopped what she was doing and held her tongs aloft. 'Like I said, never heard of them before. But people and mining companies looking is nothing new in these parts.' She shrugged. 'Anyone can look.'

'But not everyone gets murdered for their trouble.'

Jo gave her a hard stare then crouched behind her display of cakes, disappearing from view. 'Some locals may be dead against mining, and we may be a remote community, but we're not bloody Dodge City. No one around here would do that.' Her voice had been slightly muffled, but now she abruptly stood, facing Rena over the glass countertop, loud, angry, in her face. 'People may be pissed off, but they're still good people.' She let the bag of biscuits fall. 'Besides, companies like that don't give a shit. Collateral damage, unfortunate. They'll just send someone else if they're serious.'

Rena nodded. 'You're right. About all of it. I wasn't accusing anyone.'

Jo snorted. 'Better than the cops then.'

'They got someone in their sights for the murder?'

'What they have is a young bloke who's known to police because he's done a few of the usual stupid things boys do when they're still figuring out how to be men. And he just happens to have gone missing from the local community.' She pointed to the wall next to her, where a homemade A4 notice queried, *Have you seen Tyse?*

Rena stepped over for a closer look. There was information about where the man was last seen, a physical description, and a couple of phone numbers to call. No reference to the police. The picture was in colour, but the reproduction was poor. Rena narrowed her eyes as she studied the face beneath a blue baseball cap worn backwards. Tyse had prominent cheekbones with a hint of fuzz dusted across his jaw. Dark, wide-open eyes stared straight at the photographer, and his generous mouth was slightly open, a face caught between two emotions. Rena thought the young bloke looked as though he'd hoped to aim for cool, but the person behind the camera or phone had been trying to make him laugh.

'And the police think this is the killer? Why?'

'Ask Aitch—I hear you've been talking—she knows Tyse and the family.'

'I just spoke to Aitch. Knew there was something up but didn't want to push.'

Jo laughed. 'Sure you didn't. In that case, not my place to tell you. Except to say last anyone saw Tyse was a day or so before your bloke got offed. He's not the sort of fella to just shoot through without saying anything, so the family's worried enough to tell the cops. But all the cops see is potential suspect, not a vulnerable missing person.'

'Vulnerable?' Rena leaned closer, but Jo shook her head.

'Uh-uh. That's all you get from me. Maybe try your pal Fletcher, if it's no go with Aitch.'

Rena shook her head. 'Don't fancy my chances with Fletcher; I may have cracked his facade, but he'd still rather see the back of me. Not that it'll stop me from mentioning Tyse if I get the chance. Okay, I get you won't talk about that, but can I ask you something else then? Because what I really wanted to know was what you thought about Synastria. You seem to know more about the company and what they're doing around here than just about anybody, so I thought you might have an opinion on how far they'd go if they thought someone else was stepping on their toes.'

Jo tipped her head to one side, considering. Then she picked up the bag she'd dropped and checked on Rena's Anzac biscuits. With a grunt, she replaced a broken one. 'Interesting idea,' she said, spinning the bag to twist the top closed. 'But from what I've seen, if they can't buy you off, those arseholes fight their battles with lawyers. Faceless, expensive. Wear you down, waste your time, hope you break first. And if that doesn't work, they call on their mates in parliament to squash their opponents and give them the edge they need.'

'Geez. Bit cynical, Jo.'

She shook her head. 'Just realistic. Seen it before.'

'So, with millions, maybe billions of dollars at stake, you don't think there's anyone at Synastria who's that ruthless? Who'd take the cheap and dirty way?'

'Oh, there's always someone like that.' She grabbed a loaf of wholemeal, lined it up on the slicer. 'Thing is, I didn't know that bloke was sniffing around for a mining company. For Verne Industries. I doubt Synastria even knew there was another player in the picture. If they had known, they would have been busy telling us locals why we should trust them and not the other guy. They would have been pushing the Traditional Owners to sign, spruiking their credentials, bad-mouthing Verne Industries. Synastria are keen and determined, but they're not rushing. I mean, even if this other mob had their eye on a different patch of dirt, there's no way two mines are going to get approval at the same time. Synastria would've been sweating bullets if they knew.'

Jo hit a switch and conversation paused as the slicer came to life, Rena's loaf shuddering through its blades. When the mechanical chatter died away, the silence felt almost unnerving, and Rena glanced over her shoulder, surprised to see they were still alone in the bakery.

'What about a bloke called Chuck? One eye. Pommy accent?' she asked.

Jo had just slid the sliced bread into a clear plastic bag and now she paused, hands still, shoulders suddenly stiff. She turned to look at Rena, her mouth a hard line.

'He's here? You been talking to him?' Her voice was flinty.

Rena pulled back slightly, frowning at Jo's reaction. 'He introduced himself to me last night. Saw him again today and something about the encounter felt…off.'

'*Off* is bloody right. Stay away from that one. Bad news.'

'Why? Who is he?'

'Piece of shit. That's all you need to know.'

'But…'

'Mate.' Jo's features had softened but her tone brooked no argument.

Rena held out her hands, imploring. 'Jo, c'mon. I know you don't know me very well, but you do know there's shit going down, and I've stepped in some of it. Give me an idea of what I have to watch out for, because I reckon he's followed me from Willare Bridge back here, and I have no idea why. I figured him for a creep, but I need to know what kind. The sort who'll piss off if I tell him to, or the sort I need a can of mace for?'

Jo fussed with her order, making a show of focussing on her hands, gathering the bags together, arranging them on the counter, ringing up Rena's total. Only when the numbers flashed on the screen of her cash register did she look up and meet her eye. She licked her lips, glanced at the door, where the rainbow fly strips hung limp, back at Rena.

She held Jo's gaze, saying nothing as she pulled out her wallet, waiting for the other woman to decide.

'Mace. But not for the reason you're thinking. Lost his eye in a pub brawl up in Kununurra couple of years ago. 'Bout a year before Argyle closed.'

Rena glanced at her wallet, pulled out a twenty, handed it over.

'Word was he stiffed someone on a diamond deal.' Jo took the money, her voice low, barely more than a mumble.

'But—' Rena frowned.

Jo cut her off with a swift shake of the head. 'On the sly. Workers smuggling stuff out of the mine. He was their contact, broker, fence. Whatever you call it.'

'So not really a brawl?' Rena pitched her voice at the same low volume.

Jo didn't answer, just arched an eyebrow in response.

'And I'm assuming no police involved after the incident?'

'Shit, no. Story was put about that in the melee, he tripped, fell on his own glass. But everyone knew who'd gone for him and why. 'Cept the cops, of course. Well, they knew, but they couldn't do anything about it, not when the CCTV camera outside the pub that would have captured everything was on the fritz.' Jo held out the change, but Rena waved towards the charity box.

'How unfortunate.'

'Wasn't it? Question is, now that Argyle's closed and Synastria hasn't broken ground, what's a crooked diamond dealer doing back in the district?' She pushed Rena's purchases across the counter.

The question hung in the air between them. None of the answers were good.

TWENTY-TWO

It was after two when Rena drove past the town limits and hit the 110-kilometre stretch of open highway. Her ultimate destination—Marty's cluster of GPS points—was actually in the opposite direction, but on the other side of the Wunaamin Miliwundi Ranges. With uncertain terrain and no mapped tracks, it made more sense to take the circuitous route, but it was still frustrating to be driving away from where she wanted to be.

Rena sniffed. Even though she'd had a wash, bought a clean T-shirt and stripped off her bra, she could still smell coffee. She turned on the radio and was greeted by a blast of static, but within seconds of pressing the scan button, ABC Kimberley was filling the cab with local news and sport. Rena let the voices wash over her, the varying tones and delivery enough to tell her when serious things were being presented, when the story was lighthearted, and when the anchor was wrapping different segments. The weather finished and was replaced by music, a few upbeat bars signalling the start of a show, abruptly cut off mid–theme song. There was a second of dead air, and Rena could picture a mad scramble in a control room somewhere, then the newsreader was back with a breaking story.

A man has been shot and killed in a brazen daylight attack. Police responding to reports of gunfire descended on the rodeo grounds, where the body of the man, believed to be in his late fifties, was found next to a vehicle. Local police are setting up a crime scene and…

Rena raised the volume, just as a different voice came on. Detective Fletcher.

From what we can see, the victim has a single wound to the chest. We have retrieved a weapon that will be sent for forensic analysis. There are no signs of a struggle and clearly we are treating this as a homicide, but at this stage I am unable to share further details.

The feed cut back to the newsreader, who quickly wound up and threw to the regular host. Rena snapped the radio off, a sense of dread twisting her gut. Fitzroy Crossing. They'd said a car, not a ute, and referred to a dead man in his fifties.

So definitely not Aitch. And Jo had referred to the missing man, Tyse, as a young bloke—he'd looked young in the grainy picture—so unlikely he was the victim, although as she'd gotten older, Rena had discovered youth was a relative concept; people in their thirties looked young to her now. Was the age a guess, or did police know the victim's identity? She thought of the men from Synastria, the seething anger at the town meeting, and then of Chuck, a man with a history of making enemies. But there were other men in their fifties in Fitzroy Crossing; not everything was about diamonds.

Rena had inadvertently eased up on the accelerator, and the Ranger's speed had dropped. She made no move to correct it, instead rolling her shoulders and tipping her head from side to side, trying to shake off the bad feeling. Shit happened sometimes, but it didn't all have to be linked. If this was a big town or city, she wouldn't think twice about another murder so close to that of Marty Kinnane. Except Fitzroy Crossing wasn't a big town, and while it might have its fair share of robberies and punch-ups, murder was presumably still a rare thing.

Her phone rang, the surprise of it causing Rena to jump, the car swerving slightly in response. She'd forgotten the phone was still on. Giving herself a mental shake, she accelerated as she keyed the call answer button on the steering wheel.

'Mrs Novak? It's—' The connection dropped briefly, but Rena recognised Fletcher's voice.

'Detective? I'm on the road. I might lose you.'

'Where...'

'Sorry, I didn't get that.'

'You...talk...questions...Crossing—'

'What? Can you hear me?' Rena raised her voice. 'I'll be back in Fitzroy Crossing in a few days, maybe a week. We can talk then. Is that okay? Hello? Hello?'

But the connection had gone, confirmed by the triple beep of her phone, and the message showing on the Ranger's information screen.

'Damn.'

She thought about turning around, driving back until she could at least pick up a decent phone signal again and find out what Bob Fletcher wanted, but she'd hate to waste half a day if it was just something simple, and odds were her phone would be able to connect somewhere along the way before she went bush. Maybe along the Fairfield Leopold Road, or up near Mount Barnett, if she went that far. She'd leave the mobile on, plugged in. That way if Fletcher left a message, the alert should ping as soon as she hit a patch of connectivity, and she'd call him back immediately. There was nothing she hadn't told him—well, nothing important anyway.

Feeling slightly guilty, Rena settled into her seat and let the speed edge up to 120. If the cops were investigating another murder, she doubted they'd be out enforcing speed limits. Less than thirty minutes later, she saw the signpost for Leopold Downs, Tunnel Creek, and Windjana Gorge, and turned off the highway onto a two-lane, unsealed road. It had obviously been some time since a grader passed this way; the corrugations were deep and Rena was forced to slow right down, steering the Ranger from one side of the road to the other, trying to pick the best path. Red earth kicked up behind her tyres, obscuring the past. After a while she noticed the road beginning an almost imperceptible climb, and what had been flat ground on either side of the track was developing features, low ridges of cross-bedded sandstone, outcrops of mudstone, siltstone, dolomite, and basalt with sills of grey dolerite, evidence of the ancient volcanic activity that helped shape the landscape.

Rena had hoped to push through and make it to the Gibb River Road by nightfall, but she hadn't factored in how bad this road would be. As the afternoon wore on, she started to think about finding somewhere to stop. She'd already passed one campground but had a feeling she should've made a booking with Parks and Wildlife for the main Bandilngan camping area. No harm in trying, though, and also no drama if she had to pitch camp off to the side of the road somewhere. It wasn't as though the traffic would keep her awake.

The sun was low in the sky, and she adjusted the visor, trying to cut a bit more of the glare. There was a mirror on the flip side of the visor, and as she fiddled with the angle, Rena caught a glimpse of the dust cloud she was leaving in her wake. It looked huge. She checked the main rearview mirror, its wider perspective showing her something the smaller mirror had not. A glint of sunlight on metal. There was another car on the road behind her, coming up so quickly that in the still afternoon air, its dust was merging with that of Rena's Ranger.

'Idiot,' Rena muttered. She didn't want a broken windscreen if the fool overtook her and threw up a stone, so she slowed down, pulled as far to the left as she could, and gently nosed the Ford's bonnet into some shrubs before coming to a stop. With the brakes on, Rena hoped the red flare of the tail lights would be enough to make the yahoo ease off a bit. She watched in her mirrors, waiting for the other vehicle to appear.

It came out of the dust like a bat out of hell: a black SUV, roaring straight down the middle of the two-lane like it was an expressway. The sun bounced off its windscreen as it approached, obscuring Rena's view of the driver or any other occupants, but whoever it was must've clocked the Ranger at the last second, because the black monster fishtailed, as though someone tapped the brakes too hard. It swung towards her, and Rena half-closed her eyes, bracing for the impact. Then the tyres regained their grip on the dirt and it flashed past. She registered a couple of aerials whipping overhead, a red-and-blue company logo on the passenger door. She couldn't be sure, but through the tinted side windows she thought she could see someone in the passenger seat—a face, a blurred pale circle—returning her stare.

The occupants may have been obscured, but there was no mistaking the Synastria Mining insignia. Haste like that was a rare thing out here, and Rena's thoughts went wild, imagining what disaster or emergency could be unfolding.

Then suddenly, she could picture Tom, in the seat beside her, shaking his head and smiling ruefully at her. *Rennie, come on. You're making yourself crazy.*

She leaned forward and rested her head on the steering wheel; Tom was right. Maybe they were anxious to get to their destination before dark and didn't have the luxury of pitching a tent wherever they chose. Or they were idiots; that was a possibility. Besides, driving a company vehicle was basically an open invitation to behave like an arsehole, particularly if you were showing off for the benefit of your passenger.

Rena straightened up, took a deep breath, and waited for the dust to settle a bit before reversing carefully back onto the road.

Perhaps it was a sign of her age that a shitty driver was instantly cause for suspicion, but she preferred to think Marty's death had given her ample reason to look askance at the actions of others, particularly people associated with the diamond business.

Thinking back to the community meeting, Rena tried to remember where exactly the Synastria prospect was; she'd forgotten to check the applications and permits when she was in the library. With the Ellendale mine to the west, and Argyle and Marty's GPS points to the northeast, the hopes of the Synastria board must lie somewhere out this way.

For a moment she considered planting her foot, trying to catch up and follow the black SUV. But what would that achieve? Nothing. It didn't matter where Synastria wanted to mine; that wasn't Rena's concern. She'd focus on Marty, check out those GPS points, then report to Aitch or the police, depending on what she discovered.

It was possible that when she reached her destination, Rena would find nothing more than kilometres of open country, maybe signs that some mineral exploration had taken place. But with luck—and assuming Marty's GPS points weren't another shifty diversion cooked up to throw rivals off the scent—Rena would see at least one peg marking Verne Industries' claim or better yet, a sign telling her she was trespassing on their patch. That would go some way to confirming Les's rumour about violets, and if Verne Industries really was sitting on a large deposit of rare diamonds, it might be worth killing for.

There was also something else. Old rock hound that she was, Rena was hoping to find a violet diamond. Nothing big or ostentatious—the only jewellery she wore was her wedding ring. Just a tiny stone, a curiosity that any mineral or gem person would want for its rarity and type locality. A thumbnail specimen for her collection.

Rena checked the time on the dashboard display, measuring it against the rapidly dropping sun. She had about another hour before she'd need to stop, before dusk meant wildlife would be on the move and driving became more perilous. Rena didn't want to kill or injure an animal, and out here there weren't just 'roos and wallabies to worry about. Cattle, camels, horses, donkeys, and pigs were all roaming across the Kimberley; even with a bull bar an encounter at speed could mean writing your vehicle off. Or worse.

Fifteen minutes later Rena saw something up ahead, an anomaly in the red, scrub-filled landscape. She was about half a K away, and it took her a few beats to realise what she was looking at. The Synastria SUV, half turned onto a side track. It wasn't quite blocking the road Rena was on, but it was definitely in the way. The morons must've blown a tyre or something. But then she thought of Marty's murder, another mining company car, another lonely stretch of road. She felt a jolt of apprehension.

As she drew closer, Rena spotted another vehicle through the straggly trees. Actually, two, and there were several people milling around. An accident? She pulled up close to the Synastria vehicle, mentally running through her first aid training, and even before she cut the engine, Rena could hear screaming. Someone must be seriously hurt. Then multiple voices began to chant. Cautiously, Rena got out of her Ranger and moved around the black SUV until she could see what was what.

An old Mitsubishi four-wheel-drive minivan covered in stickers relating to a dozen causes and an even more ancient Volkswagen Kombi that had no business driving out here were blocking the side track. Standing in front of the two vehicles were a ragtag bunch of people, and facing them were two men dressed in jeans and work shirts, presumably the erstwhile occupants of the Synastria SUV.

'No mines! No mines!' Several members of the group chanted, while one woman, neck taut, fists clenched, hurled a string of abuse at the Synastria men. What Rena had taken for screams of pain was just a shrill stream of profanities. No one had noticed Rena yet, and she surveyed the protesters: white, brown, black; Doc Martens on some, bare feet on others, plenty of piercings across the board—women and men—hairstyles ranging from dreadlocks to shaved to a nice ponytail, and all clad in an array of what Rena called activist-ware: slogan T-shirts, camo pants, jeans, or cut-off denim.

Rena couldn't see the faces of the mining men, only their backs. The bigger of the two had his arms open and low in a placating gesture, the other had a chunky satellite phone to one ear and his fingers pressed to the other. Just behind the group of protesters, a couple of metres beyond their vans, she caught a glimpse of a sign, not enough to read the text, but enough to see the Synastria logo and universal pictograms for *Danger* and *Keep Out*. No prizes for guessing where the track led. Rena wondered whether Synastria had any equipment out there, and if they did, if it was still intact.

The Synastria worker finished the call and brandished his phone at the protesters. 'Police are on their way!'

He was met with jeers and hoots of laughter. 'Oooh, should be hearing sirens any minute now!' someone shouted.

Rena smiled. The Synastria boys must be new to the game. Rena's first rule for engaging with the public on mine sites had always been: *They already think you're a fuckwit; don't prove them right*. But this wasn't her battle, so there was no need to delay.

She took a step backwards, beating a retreat, then caught sight of a face in the crowd. The bloke who had been menacing Aitch after the meeting. He noticed her at the same moment, and Rena saw recognition dawn on his face, his lips curling into a snarl.

'Shit.' Several possible courses of action flashed through Rena's mind, but none offered an easy escape. She stood her ground.

'I might have fucking known!' The man shouldered his way past a couple of the protesters, eyes fixed on Rena. 'You're one of them.'

The Synastria blokes did a double take, swinging round to see who the aggro bloke was looking at, surprise in their eyes, then quickly about-turning to face the potential threat. It would have been comical if Rena didn't have more important things to consider.

'I'm not one of anybody,' she said, keeping her volume low.

Whether it was her soft voice or the aura of an impending shit-storm washing over them, the chanting group fell silent, and the two Synastria men stepped apart like saloon doors swinging wide in a John Wayne Western, leaving Rena and the man facing each other, about twenty feet separating them.

'Bullshit, you're not!'

'Swear, it's true. I'm just a tourist, a grey nomad.'

'Do you think I'm stupid? An old woman driving around on her own happens to end up right here?'

'I'm interested to know if it's my age, the fact that I can drive a big car by myself, or my turning up here that's bothering you.' Rena knew she shouldn't stir, but it was worth it for the snort of laughter that came from somewhere over by the Kombi.

The bruiser's face turned red, and he rocked on his feet, a bull about to charge, and Rena subtly adjusted her balance. It had been a long time since she'd kneed anyone in the nuts. Then one of the protesters, a blond woman in short shorts and a singlet, a twist of braided fabric around her bicep, put a restraining hand on his arm.

'Pete,' was all she said, but there was both warning and plea in the way she uttered his name.

The rest of the mob—protesters and miners—seemed frozen in place, a weird tableau vivant, lit by the fiery glow of the setting sun.

Rena kept her eyes on the man, Pete, watching the bunch of his jaw, the clenching of his right fist, the narrowing of his eyes. Then she saw the shift, registered that the woman with her hand still on

Pete's arm had felt it too. The man's fist unclenched, fingers splayed as he forced the hand open. He jerked his chin at Rena.

'If you're just a tourist, what the fuck are you doing here? Middle of nowhere that happens to be the access road to some untouched country that scrotes from the city want to trash. And you just happen to fucking arrive right behind those two maggots?'

'Pete, son. Mind if I call you Pete? I'm Rena, by the way, and those maggots tore past me so fast on the bloody road I was lucky not to get a rock through the windscreen. Look at them and look at me; look at their SUV, for Chrissake. Do I look like one of them?' Rena wanted to shoot an apologetic glance at the Synastria boys but kept her eyes on Pete. She could see he was now calm enough to think things through, but he still wasn't convinced.

'If you're not one of them, or bloody spying for them, why were you at the meeting in the Crossing then?'

Rena shrugged, trying to make the gesture look loose and relaxed. 'Bored with my own company, interested in what's going on and finding out what people think. Always good when you can hear both sides of an argument without one point of view aggressively shouting down the other.' She nodded to the silent group standing behind Pete, and gestured toward the Kombi, which she could now see had South Australian number plates. 'You folks just arrived?'

No one answered, but the tension had dropped a couple of notches. The protesters and the Synastria workers were still eyeing each other off, but with resignation rather than aggression. Pete still looked as though he'd really like to punch someone, but it would probably only be one to the guts rather than a full-on attack. Or maybe he'd punch a tree or the Kombi; he looked like the type. The blond woman was leaning into him, murmuring softly, her eyes occasionally straying in Rena's direction. Rena caught the odd word—*careful*...*afford*...*again* and *old lady*—and saw the tiniest of nods from Pete. The old lady in question was clearly her, but what was it Pete couldn't afford to do again? He was clearly a hot-head, someone who liked to talk with his fists, and a few run-ins with the cops went with that sort of territory. So either Pete had a couple of relatively minor offences to his name and couldn't afford another strike against him, or he'd done something serious. Either that or the blond was worried if Pete menaced Rena or assaulted the mining people, it would not only mean cops, it would seriously damage the activists' PR and social media.

Rena squinted at the sky, then made a show of looking at her watch. 'I need to get moving,' she said, glancing sympathetically at the Synastria boys. There was just one more thing. Relatively sure of her own safety, she nodded at Pete. 'You're clearly very informed about the activity of mining companies in this part of the Kimberley.'

'Yeah, so? My backyard, my business to know when arseholes are trying to carve it up.' He puffed out his chest.

'So, I was wondering. You ever come across a man named Martin Kinnane?'

TWENTY-THREE

Pete's expression remained unchanged, but Rena caught the man's involuntary flinch and saw the blond woman's eyes widen before she ducked her head, letting her hair fall forward, guarding her expression. From the blank faces of the rest of Pete's crew, Rena guessed that none of them had any idea who she was talking about.

'Marty Kinnane? Geologist working out of the Crossing?' Rena raised her eyebrows. 'Just thought, your patch and all, you would've crossed paths at some point.'

High overhead, a plane cut across the sky, the noise of its passing a distant, ominous thunder.

Pete, his eyes boring into Rena's own, shook his head then spat a gob of phlegm into the dirt between them. 'Never heard of him.'

'What about you?' Rena jerked her chin at the blond woman. 'Marty Kinnane. Ring a bell?'

The woman's eyes flicked to Pete before she shook her head, a fast, tight movement that didn't convince Rena for a single second.

'I said we never fucking heard of him.' Pete took a step forward.

Rena nodded. 'Right, thanks. No harm asking. I'll be off then.'

She turned and walked away. Just as she was just rounding the back of the black SUV, someone spoke.

'Fucking Martin Kinnane.' A man's whisper, exasperation and anger in every syllable.

Rena risked a glance over her shoulder. The protesters had dispersed, busy resettling themselves in and around the two vans. But Pete was standing in the same spot, his arms wrapped around the blond, face turned to the clouds so he could rest his chin on her head. The blokes from Synastria Mining were standing as close to one another as they could get without being in each other's pockets, engaged in an intense conversation that seemed to consist of one man talking and the other nodding vigorously. No one noticed Rena leave, and she was not much wiser.

Someone knew something. The trouble was, Rena didn't know who it was or what it was they knew. Or if it really mattered.

She pushed the Ranger faster than she should, anxious to beat the fading light, glad to make it as far as the Gibb River Road before calling a halt for the night. Less than a kilometre after turning onto the better track, she came to the Lennard River Crossing and a small lay-by, blessedly free of other travellers. Rena parked and killed the engine, sighing with relief. Despite the relatively early hour, not quite 6 p.m., twilight was well advanced, and Rena was knackered.

Unsurprisingly, she hadn't seen any police racing to the aid of the Synastria men. The two had probably already left the mine site, trundling back to the nearest town, tails between their legs. Better to come back tomorrow with reinforcements than wake up to slashed tyres.

Rena set up the rooftop tent, then scratched around for something to eat, settling for a hot cup of tea, and a few of Jo's Anzac biscuits. She was too tired to think about anything except her plan for tomorrow, which was basically to follow the road until she either saw a likely track or got close enough to the GPS points to consider bush-bashing. The idea of looking for rocks and minerals gave her a sort of peace, so much so that she was beginning to think about reconfiguring the whole round-Australia thing to make it a rock hunter's tour. Opals in Coober Pedy; sapphires in Glen Innes; gold, silver, and copper specimens from dozens of locations, then all sorts of things in between from aquamarine to zebra stone. It wouldn't be the trip she and Tom had planned, but then, neither was this. Until recent events gave Rena something else to focus on, the whole grey nomad experience had been feeling like one long funeral procession, and when she got home—if she went home—Tom's death would become real.

She sat in the darkness, breathing in the eucalyptus tang of the surrounding trees and listening to the sound of frogs. Casting the dregs of her tea onto the ground, Rena pulled out her mobile to check the time and saw that she had a text message. She had no signal now, but at some point during the afternoon's drive the phone must've briefly connected to a scrap of network, the noise of driving on the rough dirt road enough to drown out both the sound of a call from an unknown number that looked vaguely familiar, and the chime of an incoming SMS. She swiped the message into prominence: It was from Les and Margot. Rena read it quickly, scrolling through the long missive, written with no abbreviations and full punctuation, as though it had been typed on letterhead in the 1950s.

When she got to the end, she swiped her finger down the screen, returned to the start and read it again, slowly this time, her heart rate increasing as what she was reading registered and coalesced with everything she already knew about the life and death of Marty Kinnane.

Dear Rena,

Apologies for the snafu when we were talking. Growing old is a rotten experience, never more so than when one's body packs it in at a crucial moment, as happened during our conversation yesterday. I am aware that you are anxiously awaiting details of the Marty Kinnane story, and also conscious of the precarious nature of communications in your current locale. Therefore, I thought it expedient to send you this dispatch and avoid further delay. Here it is: Rumour is highly probable fact that Kinnane was stealing diamonds from the Argyle mine during its final years. I've been told he was smuggling them past security in tubes of pink haemorrhoid cream, but can't confirm that detail (it may be an embellishment related to the widely held belief that Kinnane was an arsehole). Regardless, he got them out and amassed quite a haul over an extended period. Word is at least a million dollars' worth, possibly up to two million. Unlike others who filched the odd stone and were caught, he did not attempt to sell or move them at the time. (And, my, there were some creative export methods uncovered!) But back to Kinnane. He was questioned and investigated by mine security, but they had nothing solid to pin on him. Now, the more speculative part of the story. Kinnane stashed the lot somewhere out there in the Kimberley: not hidden in a house in Kununurra, but right out in the bush. Others know this tale, so if he was planning to retrieve his stolen pinks under the guise of carrying out work for Verne Industries—if he had already done so when he met his maker... Well, no honour among thieves. That's it. I've put out a few feelers and will advise immediately if I learn anything further. Margot reminds me to invite you for dinner when you pass our way.

Best, Les.

'Bloody hell,' said Rena, loud enough to cause the frogs to fall silent.

TWENTY-FOUR

The Gibb River Road wasn't exactly the M1, but unlike yesterday's route, the surface had been graded in recent memory and, with the tyre pressure down, it was generally good driving. Rena had all the windows lowered, relishing the feel of cool morning air blowing through the cab, the smell of the earth rising to greet her like an old friend. Travelling this road had been on the bucket list, but for the most part, Rena was oblivious to the experience. The bucket list had died with her husband.

She noted the rocky prominence known as Queen Victoria's Head as she powered past, registered the dirt shifting from red to a sandier colour as she travelled from flatlands into the limestone country of the Napier Range, but the thrill of tackling one of the great outback road trips was absent. Instead, her thoughts were completely occupied with the two faces of Marty Kinnane: One had apparently identified the location of what could be among the most lucrative deposits in the history of diamonds, and one had trousered millions of dollars' worth of fancy pinks and buried them in the Kimberley.

It explained what Marty had been doing at that location outside Fitzroy Crossing, and also the scrapes and digs in that cave within the karst outcrop. The more Rena thought about it, the more likely it seemed Marty had been killed for his stash of stolen diamonds. Not because of the prospects of any mining companies hoping to move into the area, or because someone hated his guts—either for what he represented, or for something he'd done to them in the past—but because someone found out about his stash and wanted it for themselves.

The trouble was, that didn't actually help much. It didn't throw any light on who the killer was, and there was no way of knowing if Marty had found the diamonds only to have them taken from him, or if the stones were still out there. The fact that so many holes had been dug in the cavern made Rena think something had gone wrong; the stash wasn't where it should be. Besides, if he'd found his diamonds, Marty would have struck camp and got the hell out of the district.

Unless whoever offed him decided they knew enough to continue the search alone.

Or maybe Marty did find the stones, only it was too late. He realised someone was onto him, so he abandoned his camp and tried to make a run for it.

Whatever happened, Marty was dead and the diamonds were in the wind. Rena tried to think about the geology of the land around her, to focus on the plants and the earth; anything but Marty bloody Kinnane. In the end, the best she could do was sing along to her playlist of '80s classics.

At the Mount Barnett Roadhouse, Rena stopped to top up with diesel. The spare tanks she carried were still full, but it wouldn't be long before she was really off-road. Inside, she grabbed two cans of Coke from the fridge and was halfway to the register before she realised there was no Tom to drink the second can. That hadn't happened for a while. She looked at the offending can, at the hand that held it, now shaking with emotion.

What was she doing? Why was she persisting with this stupid trip, this thing with Marty and the diamonds? All she really wanted was to close her eyes, curl up in a ball, and stop. All she wanted was Tom. She returned both cans, standing for a moment with the fridge door open, letting the chill wash over her, taking deep, shuddery breaths of the icy air.

Rena's phone pinged with an incoming message: Les again.

Rena, your man at Verne is Wilson Scott. You did not get his number from me 0224796382.

Without stopping to think, Rena slammed the fridge closed and called the number. She was done. She'd pass on what she had and then go, far, fast, away from here, away from—

'Wilson Scott.' He sounded urbane, designer suits and loafers without socks. City, young.

'Mr Scott. My name is Rena Novak. I have some information that you—'

'Novak? That name's familiar. Is your husband a geologist?'

'No, that's me. Well, technically I retired last year, but I'm up here in the Kimberley and wanted to talk to you about Marty—Martin—Kinnane.'

'Terrible tragedy.'

'Yes. But it's what he was working on that I wanted to discuss with you. As I said, I'm on the spot and there's something that I—'

'Mrs Novak,' Wilson Scott cut her off, 'it was good of you to call, and I appreciate you feel you want to do something constructive in light of the circumstances, but we have people, men in the field. As you said, you're retired.'

Rena could almost hear the unspoken *and a woman*, but she tried one more time. 'I'm telling you that I have Marty's—'

'No, I'm telling you, Mrs Novak. I'll pass on your condolences, but now I have a meeting to go to.' Wilson Scott's tone had changed from patronising to dismissive, and the next thing Rena was listening to dead air.

She checked the screen, confirming the call had terminated. 'Well, screw you.' Any thought of chucking it in had vanished. Now Rena had to find a violet diamond, even if only to send a photo of it to Wilson Scott, followed by a middle finger emoji. The cashier was surly but uncurious as Rena paid for her diesel, and she was relieved to escape without having to exchange banalities, fob off questions about being a solo female traveller, or blather about the next sight she supposedly planned to see.

Back on the forecourt, another vehicle was just pulling in, a massive black four-wheel drive towing an equally large caravan. Rena nodded in the way of strangers in remote destinations, then climbed back into the Ranger, moving it to a tiny patch of shade next to a dumpster. It only took her a few minutes to double check the GPS points and where she was in relation to them. She needed to follow the road for about another 170 kilometres, then bear right. Ideally, there'd be a track somewhere thereabouts that would take her more or less directly to the site, but if not, she'd forge her own path.

If Rena hadn't specifically been looking for a place to turn off the Gibb River Road, she would have missed the small scrap of orange tape flapping from a shrub. Any other driver who happened to notice it would assume it was just rubbish caught in the spiky embrace of a saltbush, but Rena pulled up and leaned out her window for a closer look. She could see the tape was tied in place, and when she studied the terrain beyond it, another flash of orange caught her eye. That, coupled with the fact that she'd travelled just on 165 Ks, was enough to tell her she was in the right place.

She checked to make sure there was no one else on the horizon, no one to observe her detour, then pulled off the road and bumped across the pitted earth, heading for the second marker. After that, Rena needed all her wits to focus on steering the Ranger across open ground. This was a rougher drive than the trip to Marty's camp, but Rena was pretty bloody happy about that; there had been far fewer visits to this location. No path had been established by the passage of many wheels, which meant Verne Industries hadn't yet thrown the kitchen sink at the site. Either the yield wasn't as high as hoped and they were backing off, or everything was still embryonic and wrapped in multiple layers of secrecy.

Rena didn't really expect to find anything out here, but that was the thing about being a geologist and a rock hunter. You never knew. Geology told you where to look, but it was still a spin of the wheel when you were out fossicking or noodling for the hell of it. It was part of the attraction. Each day, each hour, there was the chance of a find, the chance for riches. Whether Rena tripped over a rough diamond or not, this was turning into a bloody good holiday.

She and Tom had mounted a Garmin Overlander on the dash, a GPS navigation system for both on and off-road, and now Rena glanced at it occasionally, seeing the blue dot of her progress and the flicker of her coordinates, the changing numbers moving closer and closer to those of Marty's samples.

The land around her was changing. What had been a smudge on the horizon, a darker patch in the hazy, watery mirage of the heat-addled day, gradually became an irregular line of peaks and valleys, the toe of a range of low, conglomerate mountains. Rena knew without looking at the Garmin that her destination lay somewhere in there. Whether she could reach it was another thing; it was entirely possible that the site was deep within the range, and only accessible on foot or by helicopter. Rena gripped the steering wheel a bit tighter.

When she saw the distinct line of a creek on the screen, she knew she must be almost there. That was where she'd start the hunt for diamonds if she was running the show—a watercourse. A positive sample there and she'd move upstream, trying to zero in on the source through more samples and reading the landscape. Sometimes the eruption point of a volcanic pipe was visible from space, but it might have eroded away, its contours widened by shifting earth, no cone or crater remaining, not even a depression in the ground to hint at what might lie beneath. Rena was aware some of the Traditional Owners' stories included references to sparkling stones or something that hinted at diamonds. She knew the land, but a lifetime of knowledge didn't compare to millennia of living it. Rena wouldn't be surprised if a local could walk to the exact spot she was seeking.

Up ahead, Rena could see a slight change in the land and vegetation, confirming what the Garmin had already told her. As the Ranger drew closer, a flock of zebra finches circled up then resettled, a sure sign there was at least some water in the creek bed. Rena turned the wheel, angling the vehicle parallel to the creek—a narrow ribbon stretched between slightly wider pools—then applied the brakes, rolling to a gentle stop. Now she was in the general vicinity of the exploration sites, she plugged one set of Marty's coordinates into the navigator. It immediately offered her a route, basically a right angle, doglegging around a rocky hill that loomed up ahead.

Reality proved to be somewhat different. Loose rocks around the base of the hill made the terrain difficult, and after crawling along in low range 4x4 for a couple of hundred metres, Rena opted to take a much wider path, avoiding the slipping scree and the risk to her tyres. The creek was still to one side, also curving out and around the hill, creating the perfect conditions for trap sites, places where a person who knew what to look for might find traces, or even a diamond. Rena could understand why Marty's GPS points converged in this area. She passed the outer prominence of the hill and was immediately confronted by another hill, this one on the far side of the watercourse, and she swung the Ranger back, turning directly into the valley between the two outcrops. Rena smiled. She could almost feel the pull of the ground now. A small valley, the headwaters of a creek... It was perfect.

And then, just as the Garmin announced that her destination was on the left, she saw a deep gash in the dry creek bed, a place where a large amount of dirt had been removed, about twenty to thirty kilos by Rena's reckoning, enough dirt to constitute a major follow-up analysis of the site. The sort of sample you took when you knew you were in the right place but needed to see if the pay dirt would pay generously, if the potential yield of diamonds per tonne of earth was high enough—just 0.5 carats of pinks or violets would do—to make things worthwhile.

If samples that size had been taken from each of Marty's pinpointed locations, they must've been helicoptered out; someone would have noticed if they tried to do it by road. Rena spent a few minutes sitting in the air-conditioned cocoon of the Ranger's cab, tapping each set of points into the satnav and watching the screen shift slightly each time; nearly all were within a twenty-kilometre radius of her current position, but as far as Rena was concerned, they were no longer relevant. Now that she was here and could see the topography for herself, it was easy to imagine what those other sites were like and to visualise Marty's search. Those places must have come first, leading to this point. Whether he had been brought in by chopper or simply driven into this back country himself, Marty had approached Rena's current location via a series of promising spots, most of them downstream. He had chased the indicator minerals up the watercourse to this point, and then bunny-hopped beyond the headwater, to try to get a feel for how the pipe ran, to determine how far the claim should extend, and what should be its focus.

There was a chance that one of the locations beyond the valley was the real heart of the patch, but the fever that had pushed Rena to this point had abated. She'd planned to be out here for up to a week, but a couple of nights would do. Enough to have a fossick before she returned to Fitzroy Crossing and whatever questions Detective Bob Fletcher had for her.

It was early afternoon, and the broad valley felt airless when she stepped from her vehicle. Shadows were short, and it would be several hours before the sun dipped behind the hills. A stupid time to do much of anything out here, but Rena felt too close to stop now. An hour—two at the most—then she'd call it quits for the day. She slathered her arms and neck in sunscreen, turned down the broad brim of her hat, and grabbed two large bottles of water. Then she retrieved her pick and shovel from their place in the back, chucked everything into a daypack, and made her way down into the creek bed.

She gave the dig site a quick once-over, then turned and headed upstream, not focussing on anything in particular, opening her mind to the earth around her, waiting for something deep in her subconscious to suggest that *here* would be a good place to look. It was 95 percent science, 5 percent feel, but it had proven more successful with every year Rena had on the job.

She wandered along, jagging one way or the other when it seemed the right thing to do, occasionally scratching the surface with her pick a bit before another spot farther along seemed more promising. Forty minutes or so later she found an inviting rock, overshadowed by a small tree, and after crashing around for a moment to deter any snakes in the vicinity, she sat and opened a bottle of water. Removing her hat, Rena tipped most of the water over her head then the rest into the crown before nestling the hat on her grey hair again. The relief was immediate, and she revelled in the sensation as she cracked the second bottle and had a drink. The first few mouthfuls went down smoothly, then she took too big a gulp. She spluttered, held it for a moment, then started to cough, spitting out what she couldn't swallow.

Rena doubled over, still coughing, wishing Tom was there to thump her on the back. Finally it passed and she took a careful swallow of water, soothing and settling the last of the irritation. Her head was still hanging low, forearms on her thighs, and she stayed like that, waiting for her breathing to settle.

'Hell,' she croaked, eyes closed, feeling the blood pound through the vessels in her neck and temples.

Dragging her free hand across her face, Rena opened her eyes without sitting up. Her gaze fell on the loose dirt and gravel a few feet in front of her, now damp with the water she'd been choking on. And amongst the chunks of sandstone and granite, something tiny glistened. She stared at it. Most likely a piece of quartz or feldspar, the sort of thing you'd expect to find in granite, but Rena knew even as she thought of all the things she might be looking at, only one type of stone could be winking in the sun like that, only one that reflected light in such a way it had its own category of lustre.

A diamond.

Rena didn't move, except to let out a snort of laughter. It was the story of a rock hunter's life: She could've spent hours—days!—fossicking around this patch and never found a thing. *But have a rest and nearly choke, and there it is.*

It was minuscule, barely a chip really, but it had some colour to it. Not much, but enough.

Rena slid forward off the rock she'd been sitting on and into a squat, feeling her knees protest, not caring. Her daypack was on the ground next to her, but she didn't need the pick or shovel; she reached out a hand to pluck the stone from the loose earth.

A noise registered vaguely from somewhere behind her. Rena didn't look; even the quietest places had soundscapes of their own. All her attention was on the diamond.

Then Rena heard something which made her freeze, fingers outstretched. The unmistakable sound of a round being loaded into the chamber of a gun.

TWENTY-FIVE

'What's an old duck like you doin' out here?' The voice was deep, the broad twang clearly Australian.

'Travelling. I was just—' Rena pulled her hand back and started to turn her head, only to freeze again when the muzzle of a gun was pressed into the soft flesh behind her jaw.

'Nah. Don't do that.' The stranger spat at the ground. He was standing far enough away that the gun had to be a rifle or shotgun, something with a long barrel.

Rena's mouth was dry again, but the heat and seediness she had felt moments before had been replaced by a chill clarity. 'Look—'

'I am lookin', and I don't like what I'm seein'.'

'Listen. I'll go. No drama.' Rena lifted her shoulders, ready to stand, only to be quelled by the gun again, pressed below her ear with renewed intensity.

'Well, thing is, we've got ourselves a drama already, haven't we?'

'I'm just a lady who likes camping and rocks, having a bit of a fossick. I can walk away now, no harm done. I won't look back. I'll just get in my car and head off.'

Silence from behind her, but the gun was still there. Rena's joints weren't what they used to be, and staying in the same squat for this long was starting to get uncomfortable, which presented two problems. If she got hit by a cramp and moved suddenly or fell over, she'd probably get her head blown off. But what Rena was really worried about was not being able to move fast enough if an opportunity to save her arse presented itself.

'Do you mind if I sit back on the rock? Got dodgy knees and hips.' Rena tried to put a bit of a wheeze into her words, a bit of a quiver to make herself sound a bit more pathetic.

'Yeah, nah. Not my problem. But how's about you just lie on your front? Nice and slow.'

Rena did as she was told, easing onto her knees then stretching out full length in the dirt, small rocks jabbing her in various places. It was slightly more comfortable but her chances of leaping to her feet and making a run for it had seriously diminished. Was this the man who killed Marty?

'Hands under your forehead.'

As she shifted accordingly, Rena's right hand scraped across what she thought must be the diamond and she palmed it. 'You from Verne?' she said, hoping for distraction.

The kick to the ribs took Rena by surprise and she let out a scream.

'What the f—' she groaned.

Feet scuffled next to her head, and Rena flinched, expecting the next blow, or worse. Instead, what felt like a booted foot was pressed between her shoulder blades.

'I knew you weren't just some doddery old bitch. Verne, ay?'

Rena kept her mouth shut, mentally cursing herself for the misstep. Her forehead was against the ground and all she could see was red earth and flickering light and shadow to the side; she had no idea if the gun was still pointed at her, but she was acutely aware that it would be very easy to get rid of a body out here. Of all the ways she'd thought of dying, this was not one of them.

The pressure on her back increased. 'What do you know about Verne? Who sent you? Hmm? Who?'

Rena was having to work a bit harder to expand her lungs, but her brain was firing, analysing every bit of information and trying to piece shit together in a way that explained not only what was going on, but how the hell she could either talk this bloke down—unlikely—or somehow turn the tables. Also unlikely.

Based on his rather explosive response, Rena assumed the man with the gun wasn't working for Verne, but either way, employment status was something Rena could worry about another time. She considered her answer.

'All I know is Verne Industries have been looking for diamonds out here.' She sucked in a breath. 'No one sent me, I swear. I just wanted to nose about.'

'Bullshit.' The foot ground into her back, forcing a grunt from Rena. 'No one comes somewhere like this just for a look-see. If you're not working for Verne, you must be from the competition, some other mining mob. Who? Japanese? South African? Gina bloody Rinehart?'

'Okay, mate, okay.' Rena made her voice a whisper, her breathing a bit more ragged. 'I'll tell you everything, but you've gotta let me up. I can hardly breathe.' She gasped in air. 'And the sun. I think I'm gunna pass out.'

For a moment nothing happened, then she felt a tap—presumably the rifle muzzle—on the back of her skull. 'Try anything and I'll blow your fucking brains out.'

He lifted his foot, and she risked rolling her shoulders.

'Slow.'

Rena pushed herself onto her hands and knees, each movement measured and careful. 'I think I might be having a heart attack.' She lifted her right hand and pressed it against her chest.

'Tidy for me. But if you're about to cark it, you'd better spill your guts first.'

From the corner of her eye, Rena could see denim-covered legs and, rather incongruously, feet clad not in boots but in high-top sneakers. They were black with coloured stripes ranging from yellow to lavender, and despite a thick coating of dirt, a red Nike swoosh was visible on the side of the rubber midsole. She started to turn her head to get a better look, but the gun appeared in her field of vision.

'Don't.'

At least she knew where the man was.

'Can I stand up?'

The legs shifted, the gunman moving slightly behind Rena.

'Just don't fucking turn around. When you're up, I'll tell you where to go.'

Rena curled her hands into the earth then began to rise. The moment she had both feet under her, before she'd even straightened up, she spun around and threw two handfuls of dirt at her assailant.

Most of it missed, but enough hit the man's eyes to give Rena the opening she needed and she lunged for the gun.

'Argh! Motherfucker!'

Grappling together, both holding the rifle, Rena was inches from the man's face, and part of her brain not involved in the immediate battle took stock of her opponent, He was an older man. Maybe not as old as Rena, but certainly past the half century. Wild greyish hair, leathery skin. Shorter than Rena, but stocky, with a dirty chambray shirt stretched over a barrel chest and thick waist. Like a boxer gone to seed.

Strong. Not as strong as a young man, thank Christ, but definitely no lightweight. And stronger than her.

'You're gone, bitch,' he snarled in Rena's face.

Rena didn't waste her energy on words. It was taking everything to stay on her feet and keep her hands on the rifle, one high up the barrel, the other on the forestock, just in front of the trigger guard.

The man was on slightly higher ground, and he used it to his advantage, thrusting Rena backwards in erratic jerks, twisting the gun, trying to make her fall. And Rena had no doubt that if she ended up flat out in the dirt, her fall would be swiftly followed by a bullet or the barrel of the gun across her windpipe.

Each time the crazy fucker pushed Rena, he did so with his whole upper body, rocking forward with the force of his efforts. So when it happened again, Rena was ready. She met the looming face, hard, with her own forehead, aiming for just below the wide, bloodshot eyes.

There was a satisfying crunch and a howl of mingled fury and pain, then Rena was staggering backwards, the gun in her hands. She stumbled badly, feeling pain shoot through her left knee, but managed to keep upright. Rena stood there, sucking in air in ragged gasps, and swung the rifle up to point it at her assailant, nestling the butt into her shoulder. She wanted to say something smart and gritty, something Clint Eastwood or John Wayne would utter at a point like this, but all she could think was, *What the fuck do I do now?*

Rena became aware that her head was throbbing, a counterpoint pain to the knee, which felt like it might give way. It was a long time since she'd given anyone a Glasgow kiss, a long time really, since she'd resorted to physical violence as a means of defence, and Rena was surprised by how satisfied she felt.

The man had both hands to his face, blood pouring from between his fingers, and was making inarticulate grunting noises, the sort of sound a heifer with a heavy cold might make.

Fuck him, the fucking fucker.

'Happy now, arsehole?' It wasn't the snappy bon mot she'd wanted, but Rena worked with what she had. 'I'm going. You can leave how you got here, or you can go to hell, but keep the fuck away from me.'

Rena lifted the barrel of the gun, pointing it to the sky. She took a couple of backward steps, trying not to wince or limp when her bad leg hit the ground, trying for tough. She was still watching the bleeding man, so she saw the instant his head came up, saw the intent in the twist of his blood-flecked lips and wide eyes.

With a primal scream, he came at her, and without hesitation, Rena swung the gun down and fired at the ground between them. She was ready for the recoil but not the sound of the report, its volume intensified by the rocky outcrops around them, and it took her by surprise.

The man stopped. His raised hands—fingers like claws ready to grab at Rena—slowly fell to his sides. He let out a growl of frustration.

'I won't kill you, but it doesn't mean I'm not prepared to shoot some part of you,' Rena said. 'You want to tell me who you are? Or why you're here? Verne Industries? Martin Kinnane, anything to share?'

Silence was the only response she got; she hadn't expected anything else.

Rena took a moment to study the man properly, committing his battered face and general appearance to memory. She felt a flash of remorse for her actions, before reminding herself what the alternative would have been.

Keeping the gun between them, Rena edged around until she could pick up her daypack and sling it over her free shoulder.

'Right. This time, how about you just let me walk away and we can end this?' Rena waited until the man met her gaze, until she saw what she thought was tacit agreement, or at least resignation in those dark eyes, then she slowly backed away, keeping the rifle down but pointed in the man's general direction. Only when she was a good fifty metres away did she turn. She kept glancing back as the distance between them increased, but nothing changed until, after a minute or so, Rena looked to see the man had dropped to the ground and was sitting, head hanging between bent knees.

Once she was out of sight, Rena stopped to assess the damage. She had a thumping headache, and her left knee was starting to stiffen, but at least the leg was still working. All in all, she felt like shit and had no idea what had just happened, but she was alive and essentially unbroken.

She made it back to her camper and was pleasantly surprised to find there were no signs of damage and the tyres were intact. It was still the only vehicle in sight, but that wasn't surprising: If you were planning on sneaking up and attacking someone in the outback but didn't know exactly where they were, you didn't roll up and park next to them.

After lowering the windows to let the worst of the heat out of the Ranger's cab, Rena tossed back a couple of Panadol then grabbed a fresh bottle of water and the last of Jo's biscuits for the journey. She probably wouldn't make it back to the Gibb River Road before night, but the more distance she put between herself and here, the better.

All the while she kept looking back, expecting to see the lumbering shape of vengeance heading her way, but it—he—never materialised.

Rena propped the rifle against a shrub, placing it so it would be easily seen should its owner come to claim it, but then picked it up again. If that crazy fucker ever did actually shoot anyone, Rena didn't need her prints on a murder weapon. Much easier than convincing Detective Fletcher she'd touched the gun while wrestling and headbutting an unknown man who appeared from nowhere in the middle of hundreds of square kilometres of isolated outback.

She wiped down the gun with great care, even giving the trigger a gentle buff, then returned it to its place against the bush.

The shadows were lengthening, and Rena had a rough drive into the setting sun with a dodgy left leg for the clutch, but once she was behind the wheel, engine on and air conditioner pumping, she didn't immediately drive off. Instead, she reached into the breast pocket of her polo shirt and, after a moment of fumbling, extracted a tiny diamond.

TWENTY-SIX

It was one of Rena's least pleasant driving experiences, but she made it to within cooee of the Gibb River Road before reason and pain made her stop. There was no way she'd make it up the ladder to her bed tonight, so she threw out a groundsheet and unrolled her sleeping bag on top of it. From the back of one of the kitchen cupboards, she pulled out a small flask of Glenfiddich and did a bit of self-medicating before settling down. Between her now-swollen and stiff knee, worrying the bastard would come after her, and the hard ground beneath her back, Rena didn't expect to get much sleep, but she went out almost immediately.

Waking with the dawn, the moment she moved, Rena became acutely aware of every single painful spot in her body. Most were the niggles and twinges of protest you'd expect after sleeping on the ground, but her left knee was throbbing, and when she checked, twice the size of the right. She also needed a shower. Sweat from a day's work in the sun was one thing, but fear had a smell all its own.

Still, it wasn't the first time Rena had been dirty and whiffy, and her priority was getting back to civilisation; a proper wash could wait. No point radioing for assistance. She could manage as long as she took things slowly, besides, the thought of Fletcher being part of the rescue party was enough to make her grit her teeth, pack up, eat a bag of fruit and nut mix, and start driving again.

Things improved slightly once she was on the Gibb River Road, but it was still an unsealed surface, and Rena felt every hole and corrugation in her knee. At least the headache wasn't too bad. She'd developed a matching pair of shiners as a result of yesterday's head-butt, which Rena felt added a certain don't-fuck-with-me quality to her general appearance.

Wyndham was much closer, but Rena would survive without immediate medical attention, and besides, her business lay back in Fitzroy Crossing. She had to tell Fletcher and Ito about the gunman, which also meant telling them about the notebook she'd liberated from Marty's locked chest. There was no way to spin it that would make her come out looking anything other than a stupid, interfering old idiot, and Rena knew she'd have to take some heat for her actions.

But then the little diamond, sitting in the centre console, caught the light. Tom would've berated her for going out there in the first place, but in Rena's mind, the trip had—mostly—been a success. It had given her a possible lead on Marty's killer, and a tiny, hard-won chunk of carbon. That really gave her a thrill.

Rena had tucked it into her pocket when she'd feigned heart pain, hardly believing her sleight of hand went unnoticed. A bit of spit and a roll around in her mouth as she drove had removed a good deal of Kimberley dirt and now, even in rough form, she could see a hint of pinky-mauve in its depths. Cut, it might yield something around 0.2 carats, barely enough for the shoulder of a modest ring, but that wasn't the point. Rena had found a diamond, and she had a bloody good story to go with it!

With her bad leg, the trip back to Fitzroy Crossing seemed far longer than the trip out, and the sense of relief she felt when she passed the edge of town was enormous. She saw the sign for the hospital and slowed, then drove past the turn. She'd be fine after a couple of days rest, and the doctors and nurses had real sick people to help, they didn't need her taking up space.

The man who checked her back into the camping ground didn't even bat an eye at her appearance, his only concession being to emphasise the rules around drinking alcohol on the property. As she limped out of reception, Rena noticed him pull out a can of air freshener and wave it about with determination; she could hardly blame him for that.

A long hot shower—plus a clean cotton shirt and palazzo pants—made Rena feel more human, although the developing rainbow around her eyes made her glad her son wouldn't be expecting to hear from her for a few more days. The last thing she needed was a FaceTime call. She was shuffling back to her campsite, towel around her neck and sponge bag in hand, contemplating an early dinner, when someone tapped her on the shoulder.

'Rena!' Mike stepped around from behind her, a concerned frown on his face.

'Mike! I thought you were long gone. How's Adam's ankle?'

'Better. But what in hell's name happened to you? You're limping and you look like you've been wrestling a croc or whatever it is idiot tourists do to get themselves killed up here!'

'Long story.'

'Aren't they all? Well, come on. You can tell us both while I have a look at that leg and...' He moved his head from side to side, studying her face. 'Maybe shine a light in your eyes.'

'Really, I—'

'Nope, not listening. Let's go. Just as well we're still here.'

'I thought you'd left days ago.'

They began to walk, Mike shepherding her, Rena relinquishing responsibility.

'We did. Given Adam's ankle we'd planned to hole up in Broome for a while. But then we thought of all the magnificent country around here that we hadn't had a chance to see, the culture we'd skated past… So we turned around and came back.'

They rounded a corner and there was the motor home, dustier than when she'd seen it last, but no less snazzy for it.

'Adam!' Mike called.

He appeared in the doorway, blond hair wet from the shower or a swim. One look at her and he was down the stairs, hurrying to meet them.

'Jesus, Rena!'

'Nice to see you, too, Adam.'

She turned herself over to their care, letting them help her up the few steps and settle her on the built-in couch, her bad leg on a cushion. She rolled up her trouser leg. Adam moved into the kitchenette and started clattering, and a moment later Mike was kneeling next to her, unzipping his doctor's bag and frowning at her knee.

Several minutes of prodding and flexing of the joint followed. Rena tried to be stoic, only flinching once.

'Just as well nothing's broken or I'd have to give you a few slugs of hard liquor while I realigned the bones.' He shook his head at her. 'You are allowed to tell me it hurts, you know.'

'Well, it does but that's hardly a newsflash.' Rena smiled. It was nice to have someone fuss over her again, someone to look after her, even if it was just for a couple of minutes.

'Right. A bit of ice on it now, and we'll get you an elastic support or whatever they run to around here. Actually…' He looked at her knee again, compared it to the normal one. 'Adam, you still got that neoprene knee thing with your running gear?' Mike spoke over his shoulder then turned back to Rena. 'You actually have surprisingly toned legs.'

Rena laughed. 'For an old lady, you mean? My husband used to call them shapely; that was his polite way of saying muscly.'

Mike grinned. 'I like shapely—which they still are. With knobbly knees.'

'Here you go.' Adam had disappeared into the RV's bedroom and now returned, holding out a blue sleeve.

'Thank you,' said Rena. 'I'll replace it as soon as I can.'

'Pfft. Don't be ridiculous.' Mike pulled out a penlight. 'You can put that on your knee in a minute, but first I want to make sure you haven't got concussion.'

'Don't you need a CT or MRI for that?' Rena asked.

'Well, I can give cognitive function a tick.'

'Seriously, I'm okay; there's no need for all that. Bit of a headache, but I'm fine. I know I'm old, but I've got a skull like iron.' Rena knocked on her temple.

'I don't—'

'If I get blurred vision or feel nauseated, I'll go to the hospital, promise. But I've just driven a few hundred kilometres without issue, so I think I'm okay. Thank you for caring; I really mean that, but I'm okay.'

'Hmmm.' Mike dropped the torch back into his kit. 'I'm not thrilled, but all right. Must've been a hell of a fall.'

'Yeah, not exactly.'

Mike raised his eyebrows, inviting disclosure.

'Dinner!' Adam made the word both an invitation and a command.

Over sausages and salad, Rena told a modified version of the story, leaving out the location, the diamond, and the gun. She figured it covered all the bases without involving Mike and Adam in anything that had the potential to turn deadly, plus they were horrified enough by what she did reveal.

Later, as she prepared to leave, Mike stopped her with a hand on her arm.

'We're definitely leaving tomorrow, but I'm glad we caught up again.'

'Me too. Thanks for—' She gestured to her knee, now encased in neoprene and feeling a hell of a lot better. 'Well, thanks for everything.'

'Might see you again on the road somewhere.'

'Hope so.'

Adam stepped in for a hug, taking her by surprise.

'Good night, gents. Safe travel,' said Rena. She eased herself down the steps of the RV then turned to look back at the two men framed in the doorway. 'Meeting people like you is what makes being a grey nomad worthwhile.'

The following morning after a decent sleep and another proper meal, Rena was ready to tell her story to the police and face whatever music her rash actions brought on.

But first she phoned Aitch.

'Tell me you're okay and you're not phoning for me to rescue you from some shitshow,' Aitch greeted her.

'I'm okay and you don't have to bail me out of a shitshow.'

'Thank Christ for that.'

'I'm back in the Crossing. Had a bit of a funny experience.' Rena started to walk towards the campground's reception area so she could get a cab. Her knee was holding up, less swelling and only a bit of pain this morning.

'Funny ha-ha or funny peculiar?'

'The latter. With a hint of funny dodgy.'

'Do I want to know?'

'You probably should. And by the way, I saw your mate Pete.'

'Ah, shit! He didn't give you aggro, did he?'

'Well, yeah, but there were too many other people around for him to do anything. Besides, he was saving most of his aggro for a pair of Synastria Mining employees. It was out on the Leopold Downs Road, where I guess Synastria are planning to break earth.'

'Is that where—? When did you say this was?'

'I didn't. Bugger, hang on.' Rena had forgotten to call Wally and his taxi. She'd arrived out the front of reception, so she poked her head in the door and asked the young girl behind the desk to phone her a cab. Then she retreated outside and parked herself on the provided bench, stretching out her bad leg, enjoying the sun before it got too hot.

'So...'

'Day before yesterday—the day I left town. Why?'

'There was... Never mind, what's your story?'

'Are you at work? Am I holding you up?'

'Yes, and I've got a moment.'

'What is it you do, exactly?'

'I'm a youth worker, but stop changing the subject and tell me what happened.'

Rena rubbed a hand across her head, screwing her eyes shut at the memory. 'I'll cut to the salient point. I found the place Marty Kinnane and Verne are keen on, went to have a bit of a mosey around and scrape the dirt with my pick, and this man appears literally out of nowhere—I didn't see or hear a car or motorbike—points a rifle at me and basically threatens to kill me. Wanted to know who I was working for and got very upset when I asked him about Verne Industries.'

'So what did you do?'

'Eh, you know. Fought him for the gun, headbutted the bastard, and hurried back here.'

'Why do I sense there's a lot more to that story?' Aitch sighed.

'Well, because there is. But like I said, I've given you the salient points.'

A car was coming down the drive, and Rena leaned forward, hoping it was Wally in his cab, but it was just a regular car and it swept past, continuing on towards the lodge. She sat back, her shoulders against the warm wall.

'Tell me about this bloke who attacked you,' said Aitch, and Rena could hear speculation in her tone.

Rena described the stocky figure, the thickness of his torso, the wild hair, the face before Rena mashed that broad nose.

'Shit. Sounds like you ran into the Minister for Defence.'

'Very bloody funny.'

'Nah, mate, that's what we call old Eric. The Minister for Defence. He lives out there somewhere. Or out here somewhere. Moves around a lot. Old school. His mental health is not the best, but he's happy where he is, and as you've discovered, rather fired up about protecting the wilderness from any and all comers.'

'Hence the name.'

'Yep.'

'I thought at first maybe Verne Industries had hired someone to protect their patch. Then when he arced up at the mention of them, I thought maybe he was working for a rival, trying to jump their claim.'

'Nah. Eric's unbiased. He hates every company with equal passion. Any company prepared to destroy the environment, that is.'

'Now I'm starting to feel shit about headbutting him.'

'Don't. You're a stranger, and a smart-looking city woman to boot. Hundred percent he would've shot ya if he'd thought you were one of them. And being Eric, the deciding factor might bear no relationship to reality.'

Rena was silent.

'I know what you're thinking.' Aitch sighed.

'Can you blame me? After what happened and what you've just told me? *Is* there any chance the Minister for Defence topped Marty Kinnane? Shot him first then…'

The sun was starting to get too warm and there was still no sign of a taxi. Rena pushed herself up off the bench and moved into the shade of the verandah. The air around her was changing with the rising temperature, the scent of dirt brought forth by the morning dew now tinged with eucalyptus.

'Might've shot him,' Aitch conceded. 'But the car thing? Nup. Not old Eric's style. I mean, why go to that trouble when you could just bury a body out in the scrub?'

'Yeah, but what if he was in Marty's car? Hitching a lift and he found out—or already knew—who was behind the wheel, who Marty Kinnane worked for?'

'Shit.'

'Listen, I have to go. There's some things I need to talk to the police about, and apparently some things they want to ask me. Detective Fletcher tried to phone the other day but the signal kept dropping out. And I'm going to have to tell them about my run-in with Eric.'

Aitch sighed. 'Poor old bastard. Yeah, you'd better tell them. And don't worry, as soon as you mention the Minister for Defence, they'll know who you're talking about. In fact, they've probably already been looking for him.'

'Well, those crazy sneakers make him pretty hard to miss!'

'Come again?' Aitch fired the words out like bullets.

'Didn't I mention his sneakers?' Rena laughed.

'Rena, no.'

'I thought he'd be wearing boots like anybody out there. Sure as hell felt like it when he had his foot in my back! But when I got a look, the old coot was wearing high-top Nikes, striped, like you'd see a trendy teenager wearing.'

'Fuck!' There was a loud bang, as though Aitch had just punched or kicked something.

'Aitch? You think they were Marty Kinnane's sneakers? Marty wouldn't wear shoes like that. Not when he was working, or doing whatever. Not out here.'

For a moment, all Rena could hear was Aitch breathing, drawing in heavy, stressed gusts of air.

'Aitch?' Rena stood. There was nowhere for her to go, but she could hear distress, and it felt like some sort of action was required.

A taxi turned in off the highway. It wasn't Wally behind the wheel, but there were no passengers, so it was clearly Rena's ride. Rena moved to meet it as it swept up the last of the drive, then pulled open the passenger side door and manoeuvred herself into the seat. She'd just clicked her seatbelt on when Aitch finally spoke.

'The young fella who's missing. Tyse. He has sneakers like that.'

TWENTY-SEVEN

'Police station, please,' Rena murmured to the cabbie. He nodded politely then made a point of ignoring Rena and her phone conversation.

As the taxi pulled onto the highway, Rena tried to pump Aitch for more details, but Aitch had nothing to add. Instead, in halted sentences, she told Rena Tyse was still missing but the police were keen to talk to him in relation to certain recent events. Tyse had form for petty crimes and was therefore consistently on the radar of local law enforcement. And Tyse, who was twenty-one, a talented basketball player and, as Aitch put it, needed to sort his shit out, had recently spent a small fortune on a pair of Supreme x Nike Air Bakin' sneakers, which were apparently the very shoes Rena had described.

'If old Eric…' Aitch began. 'You tell the cops. Tell them what happened, and about the shoes. Maybe then they'll give a fuck.'

Less than ten minutes later, Rena was being ushered through to the working heart of the Fitzroy Crossing police station by an unidentified kid in a uniform. Obviously he wasn't actually a kid, but to Rena the officer looked as though he wasn't even shaving yet, and he carried himself with all the authority of a teenager home alone for the first time.

Ito and Fletcher were waiting for her, both looking sombre and tired. On Fletcher, tired was a serious five o'clock shadow, rumpled shirt, and less-than-immaculate hair, while Ito was pale and sported dark circles under puffy eyes.

Rena sat down and waited, aware of their scrutiny, the attention given to her own appearance.

'Thanks for coming in,' said Fletcher, somehow managing to make the word *finally* seep into the air, unspoken, between them.

'No problem.' Rena kept her voice mild. 'I got back to town late last night, so this was my first priority. Your message'—she nodded at Fletcher—'dropped in and out, so I'm not quite sure what you want from me, but as it happens, I've got a bit to tell you anyway.'

'How do you know Wojciech Bieliński?' He pronounced it *Woy-tek*.

Rena frowned and leaned back in her chair. Of all the things she'd expected, that wasn't one of them. Fletcher tilted his head, studying her.

'Wally, the taxi driver,' he said, in a way that implied he thought Rena was deliberately stalling.

'I know who you're talking about. I was just surprised, that's all. I assumed you'd wanted to talk to me about Marty Kinnane's murder, and I've…discovered a few things that might be pertinent.'

Fletcher and Ito exchanged a look.

'We'll get to that.' Ito picked up the top sheet from the open file in front of her, scrutinised it, then returned it, squaring the page with those beneath.

'If you could just answer the question?' Fletcher's mouth twitched, a false smile.

'He picked me up after my last visit here.'

'And after that?'

'Saw him in the car park at the IGA.' Rena looked from one grim face to the other. 'What's going on? Surely you don't think Marty Kinnane... Wally?'

Fletcher wrote something down. Rena could see from her side of the table that the page he was using was already covered in spidery handwriting, with heavy underlining and a couple of arrows chasing thoughts between the lines. He looked up suddenly, caught the direction of her gaze and adjusted the angle of his notepad.

'Where's your husband, Mrs Novak?' Ito was watching her closely.

'My husband?' The question was such a shock her voice cracked on the word *husband*.

Ito jerked her chin towards Rena's hands, resting on the table between them, her gold wedding band on display.

'You're travelling alone and yet...it doesn't look like something you just bought for window dressing. So where is your husband?'

Rena stared at her own fingers, twisting the ring back and forth. She wanted to cover it, to pull her hands into her lap and not drag Tom into this place, this discussion. But it was too late. She swallowed. Once, twice. She was about to tell them, but was it their business? Tom's life and death had no relevance to their investigation, but if Ito was trying to rattle her, or if she just felt like being an arsehole, well, mission accomplished.

'Why?' Rena stopped fiddling with the ring, splayed both hands out on the table and sat forward. 'Besides, the other day Detective Fletcher said you'd checked up on me, so don't you know?'

Fletcher shook his head. 'We can check if there are any police files on you, if you have any driving penalties. Other than that, we can Google you. So, no, we don't know.' He shot a quick side-eyed look at his partner, but Rena couldn't interpret the meaning behind it. Only a few days ago, they were moving to first names, and she thought Detective Bob Fletcher had changed his mind about her, but it seemed Ito had as well, and not for the better.

'Broad strokes, filling in the picture.' Ito held out a hand, palm up, inviting a response.

'My husband died. Last year. Prostate cancer.' Rena's voice was soft, overlaid with the thickness that comes from a tight throat and the threat of tears. She sat back.

For a moment she'd felt angry at the question, but now she just felt tired, exhausted in a bone-weary way that had nothing to do with fighting a gun-toting man in the middle of nowhere and a long drive on a rough road. What the hell did any of this matter? She thought she'd found a fragment of herself again when she'd gone looking for diamonds, a scrap of purpose when she'd turned her attention to Kinnane's death. But she'd been kidding herself. If forty years with Tom had been her diamond, life now was a cubic zirconia, a cheap stand-in for the real thing. Looked okay from afar, but ultimately worth nothing. If it wasn't for the massive bullbar on the Ranger, Rena would've driven out of town, found the next big boab and run into it at speed.

The scrape of a chair brought her attention back into the room. Fletcher was doubled over, reaching for something under the table. He sat up brandishing his pen, but when he looked at Rena, his intense frown had gone, and his face had softened. Rena could see sympathy in his eyes, which she neither wanted nor needed right now, but there was also something else, something she couldn't quite fathom.

'I'm sorry,' said Fletcher; it sounded sincere.

She grunted, looked up at the ceiling, blinking hard. 'Thanks. Can we get on with whatever this is?'

'Where were you three days ago? Nine a.m. to about midday?' Ito asked.

'I was talking to Detective Fletcher here outside the bakery around lunchtime, he chucked his coffee on me, and I have the ruined shirt to prove it.' It came out with more snap than Rena intended.

Ito half turned in her chair to look at Fletcher, who offered a weak smile and nod in response. 'That was at approximately quarter to one.' Fletcher directed his attention back to Rena, keeping the smile in place for her benefit. 'What about before that?'

'Library, catching up with Aitch, IGA. That was my morning.'

'Aitch?'

'Young First Nations woman. Met her at the community meeting and we hit it off. You know who I mean.'

'Hepzibah Davies.' Ito nodded.

'Hepzibah! Is that what Aitch stands for? I never asked. And while we're talking about Aitch, she asked me to…well, basically she asked me to put a rocket up whoever is looking into the missing kid, Tyse.'

'Hardly a kid, he's in his twenties.'

Rena waved away the answer. 'Barely. And he's a lot younger than me, so he's a kid.'

'Rest assured, we are actively looking for him,' said Ito.

'Well, I gather basically everybody thinks you're looking for the wrong reasons. Uh-uh!' Fletcher had opened his mouth to speak, but Rena held up a hand, forestalling whatever it was. 'Just let me say this, and then you can have the rest of the story.'

'Mrs Novak, we—' He tried anyway.

'These'—she cut across him, pointing to her black eyes—'were courtesy of a man I encountered in a location off the Gibb River Road, a place where Marty Kinnane had been working.'

'How did you—'

'I'll get to that. When I described the bloke, Aitch identified him straight away as someone called Eric, also known as the Minister for Defence because of the way he goes a bit gung-ho over protecting the land from certain people. Like miners.'

Rena paused, expecting one of the detectives to try to redirect her or get their two cent's worth in, but both were silent, Fletcher writing furiously.

'The thing is, when this Eric was threatening to shoot me, I couldn't help but notice the very flash pair of Nikes he was wearing. And if you have a description of Tyse, you'll know the shoes I mean.'

Ito hissed out a breath, not quite articulating the word *shit* but the sentiment was there in her face.

'Did you get a look at the gun he had?' Fletcher was leaning halfway across the table.

'Not only did I get a look at it, I grappled with him over it. Long single barrel, I think it was a rifle rather than a shotgun, because when I pulled the trigger there was only a single impact, not a scattering. So, I guess rifle.' She shrugged.

'You pulled the trigger.'

'I wasn't aiming at anyone. It was just a warning shot. Look, I can tell you where I left him, and he's definitely no friend of Verne Industries, 'cause mentioning Verne was about the point in the conversation where he lost his shit, so I can't help but wonder about Marty.'

'We're going to need the whole story, but before we get to that, I need to ask. Why would Wally the taxi driver be phoning you at twelve p.m. three days ago?'

'Did he? Like I said, I was in the library first thing, so my phone was on silent, and I forgot to turn it back on for hours. And I haven't checked my voicemail messages since, because I assumed it would just be Detective Fletcher from when I was on my way out of town, and then to be honest I sort of forgot about messages. You know once you've looked at the message that says you have a message, there's no longer a reminder that the message exists?'

Ito was rubbing her temples.

'Sorry, I'm talking too much. Well, why don't we phone Wally now and ask him what he wanted? Probably nothing. When I saw him in the IGA car park, we were just chatting about metal detecting and slivovitz.'

'You saw him that morning?'

'Yep, not long before our encounter at the bakery.' Rena pulled out her phone and tapped at the screen. 'You're right. Missed call three days ago at 12.02 p.m. No message left. Never mind, I'll phone now.'

'No.' It was one word, uttered quietly by Fletcher, but Rena registered the inflection, the weight of that single syllable. It was the way the doctors had spoken when Tom's cancer went to stage four.

'What?' Rena let her mobile fall on the table with a clatter.

'Three days ago, apparently not long after you saw him at the IGA, Wally got into an altercation with someone, out at the rodeo grounds. I'm sorry. He's dead.'

TWENTY-EIGHT

It didn't take long for Rena to tell the detectives what she'd been doing for the last couple of days. She was going to start with the Synastria mine site, but they already knew about the protest group, so she skipped forward to her encounter with the Minister for Defence. And before she'd finished the story, Ito stepped out to issue a be-on-the-lookout alert for Eric, surname unknown.

'We're getting someone to go out and check the place where you last saw him, but based on experience, we won't find old Eric unless he wants to be found,' said Ito as she resumed her seat.

'But he was wearing Tyse's sneakers and what with Marty and now Wally dead, surely you can—' Rena couldn't believe the lack of action.

'First of all, other than assaulting you, we don't know if he's actually done anything. Maybe Tyse gave him the sneakers for some reason.' Fletcher sounded like he was speaking to a fractious child.

Rena snorted in response, as a mature adult would.

'And second, Eric doesn't come home to one place at night. Out there is where he lives, and he knows it better than most. We'll check a couple of spots he frequents; of course we will. But for every place of his we know about, he's probably got twenty more that we haven't a hope in hell of finding. And last we heard, he was still using a dirt bike.'

'I definitely would have heard a motorbike out there.'

'Unless he was already there,' Ito clicked her retractable biro in and out, in and out, until Fletcher shot her a look.

'Do you think he shot Wally? Surely he couldn't travel that far that quickly, even with a motorbike. It took me the best part of a day's driving.'

Fletcher shrugged. 'We're considering everything. It's a pity Wally didn't leave you a message.'

'Do you know what he was shot with?'

'Not yet.'

'But I heard on the radio people reported gunshots. Can't you tell from that?'

Fletcher smiled. 'It's not as easy as that. Besides…' He hesitated, glanced at Ito. 'It's going to be in the media release—because we want everyone to keep an eye out for injured people—so we can tell you.'

'Tell me what?'

'Wally had his own gun, which we recovered. It was definitely fired.'

'You think he shot himself?' Rena was incredulous.

'No.' Fletcher shook his head. 'Our forensics people could see enough to tell that definitely wasn't the case. It's just that we didn't find a shell casing, so until the autopsy is complete we don't know what killed Wally.'

'What do you mean, *what* killed him? On the radio you said a single wound to the chest. I heard you say it.' Rena frowned at Fletcher.

'We can't really say anything more at this stage, but I mean—broadly speaking—the type of gun. The point is, did you see any sign of injury on Eric? Bandages, grazes even?'

Rena shook her head. 'Nothing. But he had on long sleeves and jeans so… He certainly wasn't moving like someone who had a serious injury.'

'Doesn't mean anything,' muttered Ito, making a note on the paper in front of her.

'And now'—she raised her voice and fixed Rena with a hard stare—'we need to talk about how you knew exactly where to go. How did you know where Marty Kinnane had been digging for diamonds?'

'Came across a notebook hidden out near his camp. After your people had been and gone.' Rena had the book in her daypack and now she pulled it out and slid it across the table.

'Really?' Ito's voice was rich with sarcasm as she snagged a corner of the battered cover and drew it towards her.

'Yep.'

'Right,' Fletcher sighed. 'Let's hear it then. Sounds like it's going to be a good story.'

Rena talked to Fletcher as Ito paged through the notes. She kept it vague about the notebook's location, apologised for not turning it in immediately, and played up her anxiety about Verne Industries' secrets and the fallout if they were leaked.

'It may surprise you to know that as police officers we do have some experience with maintaining confidentiality,' said Fletcher.

'I know you do. But I also know that in any organisation people talk. And when it's something exciting, people talk more. You might trust everyone here, but…' Rena spread her hands, palms up.

Fletcher grimaced, but didn't answer.

'I did try calling them, spoke to a man named Wilson Scott and got the complete brush-off.'

Ito blew out a breath then riffled the pages of the notebook, back to front, before slapping the cover closed. 'We'll go through it, but I can't see anything relevant to our investigation in here.'

'I didn't either,' Rena said, earning herself a black look from each of the detectives. 'It's exactly what I'd expect field notes to look like. And now you have the GPS coordinates, you can check the other site for yourself.' Rena didn't mention they were the same points recorded on the sample bags in Marty Kinnane's locked trunk. In her sanitised version of events, the trunk's contents were a mystery to her.

'Is there anything else you'd like to share? Or rather, anything else you haven't told us, however irrelevant or commercially sensitive you might believe it to be?' Fletcher threw his pen down on his notepad and leaned back.

'There was also Pete.'

'Pete?'

'Out at the Synastria site. Tall guy, very angry. Had plenty to say at the town meeting.'

'Peter King,' Fletcher nodded. 'What about him?'

'Well, I dropped Marty's name, and I'm pretty sure from the reaction I got that Pete knew who I was talking about. Then when I left, I heard someone say, "Marty effing Kinnane"; I think it was Pete.'

Fletcher sighed.

'Sorry. You already knew about the trouble out there, and that detail slipped my mind. But you might want to ask Pete about Marty Kinnane.'

'Thanks, we might just do that.'

Ito leaned close to Fletcher and the two had a short, whispered conversation. Then Fletcher turned to Rena and gave her a tight smile.

'Anything else? Got any other potential murder suspects up your sleeve?'

Rena winced. 'Not exactly, but there was something bothering me about Marty's camp, some digging he'd been doing in an odd spot. It wasn't right. Not from a geological point of view anyway. And then I found out something about Marty, something from his past that may be nothing more than a rumour, except it kinda fits and…' She closed her eyes. 'Damn.'

TWENTY-NINE

'Damn, what?' Fletcher leaned across the table.

'Do you want the short version or the long version?' Rena dragged a hand across her eyes.

'How about the concise version that contains all the facts?'

Rena nodded. 'Well, it's going to be facts, a rumour widely believed to be true, and my theory, but...'

'Mrs Novak, Rena. Seriously. Just tell us.'

'The place where Marty Kinnane had his last camp is not diamond country, and there was no reason—well, no reason to do with Verne Industries—that he should have been there.'

'We've already ascertained that.' Ito's tone invited Rena to keep going.

'I found a place back in the mesa where someone had been digging. Lots of shallow holes and I couldn't figure out why. Then I heard from an old contact that Marty used to work at the Argyle mine.' Rena looked at the detectives.

Fletcher sighed and rolled his hand.

'It was widely believed but never proved that, over time, Marty managed to smuggle out a large haul of Argyle pinks, close to two million dollars' worth or even a bit more. But unlike other Argyle staff working a fiddle, Marty was never caught, and the story goes that he hid them somewhere out there.' Rena waved her hand at the wall, at what lay beyond.

'So...' said Ito.

'So, either he found his diamonds and was killed for them. Or he didn't find them and was killed because someone else wants to keep looking.'

Ito started to speak, but Rena held up her index finger. 'Wait. Here's the extra wild part of my theory. The other day, Wally told me that sometimes he earned extra cash as a metal detectorist for hire—wedding rings, the radioactive capsule...like that. He said someone had wanted to look for something hidden in a tin can, but instead of hiring Wally, this person wanted to rent the detector. Wally said no—I think he was holding out for more cash—and that was the end of the story.'

The detectives exchanged a glance, and from the stillness in Fletcher's face, Rena knew she was onto something.

'I don't know who Wally's potential customer was, just that he'd dropped out of contact. And so I think—'

'You think Kinnane forgot precisely where he'd hidden his tin of diamonds and knew Wally had a metal detector, so he tried to buy it. Then—and we're not sure whether the diamonds were found or not—someone killed them both to get the stones and presumably keep Wally from talking or snooping. Once we released Marty's name as being the deceased, Wally thought there must be something worth looking for.'

'That's about the size of it. Sounds crazy when you say it out loud like that.'

'Yeah. But not as crazy as some of the stuff we've seen. If you're right about the Argyle diamonds, well, people kill for much less than that,' said Ito.

Fletcher picked up his pen and scribbled a quick note. 'Even if you're wrong. If someone else heard that rumour, it might be enough. Maybe it wasn't Marty digging out there at all. Maybe it was someone else who knew the story who went digging after Marty Kinnane was dead.'

'I didn't even think of that!' Rena slapped a hand against her temple then winced. She'd forgotten about the headbutting. 'I thought at the time I wasn't on my own out there.'

'Bloody hell, Rena! You might've mentioned that salient detail.' Fletcher looked as though he wanted to slap the other side of her head.

'I didn't actually see anyone, and I figured you were already pissed off with me, so...' She shrugged, a one-shouldered, *mea culpa* shrug.

'What do you mean *at the time* we were pissed off with you?' He dragged both hands across his scalp.

Ito had started clicking her pen again. 'You saw no one?'

'No, but I've just thought of something!'

'Again? Seriously?' Fletcher sounded defeated.

'Seriously. It just occurred to me as we've been talking, or rather, once you said maybe someone who already knew about the stolen diamonds murdered Marty then went looking for the cache. There's someone like that about. Someone who has a weird vibe and when I mentioned him to Jo—Jo from the bakery—she thought he was bad news. And he saw me talking to Wally outside the IGA.' Rena fell silent, seeing it in her head, piecing together the events around the deaths of Marty and Wally.

'Well?' said Ito.

'Chuck. That's what people call him, but Stu—Stewart, I guess—Rothwell. One eye. Jo told me he lost the other eye when he cheated the wrong person. Up in Kununurra, where he was working as a fence for diamonds nicked from Argyle. If he was handling stolen diamonds back then, it's odds on he'd know the rumour about Marty and his large stash of Argyle pinks.'

Ito looked at her colleague. 'I'm getting a bit of a vibe about this myself,' she said.

'Do you know this guy?' Fletcher asked, turning slightly in his chair to face his colleague.

'Back when I was a rookie, I did a stint up in Kununurra. I never actually met Chuck, but I know exactly who Mrs Novak is talking about because he was on my senior officer's radar. As far as I know he still had two eyes then, but he was as crooked as they come. We need to find him.' Ito started to push back her chair.

'What about the diamonds?' said Rena.

'We'll talk to Chuck about that. But to be honest, the stones are a secondary consideration right now.'

Rena nodded. 'Of course. Perhaps I could—'

Fletcher cut her off. 'Only finish that sentence if it ends with *stay out of things*.'

'I have to at least show you the place Marty was digging. And now that I know what he was looking for, I'll think about it differently.'

Fletcher was shaking his head, but it was Ito who spoke. 'We had really bad floods through here a couple of years ago. Record-breaking, took the bridge out. Nothing like it in living memory. Might explain why Kinnane was digging all over the place.'

Rena felt a surge of adrenaline. 'Of course! If the whole area was under water, it would change the floor of that cavern. Then depending on currents and the like, if the tin of stones was uncovered by the floodwater, it could've been washed right away. We should look for catch points.' She was half on her feet, her mind already sifting through memories of the cave and its surrounding terrain, picturing likely places.

'Rena. Mrs Novak!' Fletcher's sharp voice made her sit back down.

'Come on, Detectives! I can do this while you chase the bad guy. I know how this sort of thing works, and I even have a metal detector!'

'Like Wally?' Ito spoke softly. 'Look, maybe these diamonds exist, but even if they do, we have other avenues of enquiry. This could all be about mines and the environment, or a personal vendetta. Maybe the two deaths aren't even connected. But until we get a handle on things, I don't want you out there on your own. If—and it's still an if—this is about stolen Argyle diamonds, we don't know who's involved or how many people we're looking for. Which means you could find yourself in a lot of trouble out there.'

'I understand,' said Rena. 'But…'

Fletcher rolled his eyes. 'You never stop, do you?'

'I was just going to say you should go out there because what if that's where Chuck is right now? Looking for diamonds?'

'How about you leave the running of the investigation to us? This isn't a big city where we have infinite resources and can zip between locations in ten minutes. We will get out there when we can.'

'What if I take Aitch? Safety in numbers plus you don't have to worry that I'll do a runner if I find the stones.'

'Sure. Let's involve another civilian!' Fletcher threw up his hands. 'And why Aitch?'

Rena shrugged. 'Why not? She's a good honest woman. She knows the land, and if we have to do any digging, she looks like she could wield a shovel.'

Fletcher and Ito exchanged a look, and Rena pressed home her slim advantage. 'Plus, there's still Tyse to think about as well. I don't know if the two things have anything to do with each other, but either way, if Aitch is with me, she's not looking for Eric. I assume you don't want that to happen either.'

Fletcher jerked his head towards the door. 'Give us a minute, will you, Mrs Novak?'

Rena kept her mouth shut and her features composed as she hustled outside, but once in the hall, she had to shove her hands in her pockets to stop herself from drumming her fingers on the wall; she wanted to move, phone Aitch, get things underway. Do something. If Ito and Fletcher came out and told her to back the hell off, what then? They'd never believe it if she feigned compliance, but what could they do if she walked out. Arrest her? Surely not.

The door rattled and the detectives appeared. Ito nodded to her. 'Thanks for your help. No doubt we'll talk again very soon.' Then she brushed past, shouting for Halloran as she hurried down the hall.

Fletcher was standing propped against the doorframe of the interview room, arms folded, giving Rena a hard stare.

She returned it, eyebrows raised. 'You're letting me go out there? Really? You know I'll tell you what I find and obviously hand over anything?'

'I know you'll be straight with us. Now.'

Rena tried to look suitably chastened, but Fletcher wasn't buying it; he continued to glower.

'But, no, we're not letting you go out there. At least, not alone.'

'I'll call Aitch now and tee it up.'

'Sure, do that. And tell her to meet us here at five tomorrow morning.'

'Us?'

'Yup.'

'As in me, Aitch, and you?'

'I find the lack of enthusiasm in your voice offensive,' he said.

'Sorry. I didn't mean… I'm just surprised. You don't have to… But of course I'm delighted to have your company.'

Fletcher snorted then started laughing. 'Kidding. About taking offence, anyway. But, God, it was lovely watching you twist in the wind for a moment.' He pushed himself off the doorframe and stepped around her. 'Come on then. Find out if Aitch is in, because if not, it's just you and me. We need to get on this.'

'Dialling now.' Rena matched the words with actions, scrolling through the contacts on her phone.

'Oh, and one more thing.' Fletcher stopped walking and turned to face her, hands on his hips.

'What?' Rena was listening to the phone ring.

'I'm not coming with you. You're coming with me; you for geology, Aitch for local knowledge. This isn't the Wild West, you know. I'm in charge of this, whatever it is.'

Rena was about to reply, but the call connected, and she stuck a hand across her free ear, blocking out Fletcher and the noise of the police station as she tried to convince Aitch to get her arse down to the cop shop first thing tomorrow.

THIRTY

Rena sat in the front seat of Fletcher's police Land Cruiser. She'd arrived at the police station at 4.45 a.m., collected the metal detector and a few other bits and pieces from her own vehicle, and stowed them in the rear of the vehicle. Right behind Aitch.

It had taken some persuading to get Aitch to agree to join them, and in the end Rena had passed her phone to Fletcher. Where Rena's lure of possibly finding stolen diamonds had met with an assortment of expletives, incredulous laughter, the mention of work, then finally, threats to hang up, Fletcher got Aitch across the line with talk of solving crime and community safety. Rena considered it an exercise in knowing one's opponent, but more than that, she was pleased to have Aitch along.

Now, as they sped down the Great Northern Highway again, she turned in her seat and described the spot they were heading for, raising her voice to be heard above the engine and the wind whipping through Fletcher's half-open window. When Rena detailed the cleft in the rock, Aitch nodded.

'Yeah, I know the place,' she said.

'Been out there lately?' Fletcher spoke over his shoulder, and Rena could see him watching Aitch in the rearview mirror.

'Not for a couple of years, Detective.' Aitch's lips pressed together in a thin line, and she turned to look out at the landscape speeding past, its colour a burnished copper in the early light.

'You know I had to ask.'

'Did you?' Aitch didn't glance his way.

'What I want to know, is how you reckon the floodwaters would work out there. Have you seen it flood before the last time—what, three years ago? And if you have, what can you tell me about it?' Rena jumped in, anxious to dispel the tension that had filled the Land Cruiser's cab.

Aitch turned to look at her, a wry smile on her face. 'Mate, when it floods in the Kimberley, no one's heading out into that country.'

Rena shook her head. 'I'm not that obtuse. I meant after. After the water has gone.'

'After the water's gone, we're mostly too busy cleaning up and repairing shit and after that, while I do go bush from time to time, I haven't been there. Besides, when I'm out in all this somewhere, I'm not looking for tide marks or flow patterns or whatever. I'm not an environmental engineer or a hydrologist or whoever the hell you have to be to think about that stuff.'

'You know I had to ask.' Rena smiled and was rewarded with a soft snort of laughter from Aitch. 'The thing is, sometimes I assume everyone looks at land the way I do; I forget that usually I'm the only geology nut in the room, or on the schist, as the case may be.'

'You're certainly full of—'

'I said *schist*. Metamorphic rock that… Never mind.' Rena shut up. Both Aitch and Fletcher were smiling, and she didn't give a rat's if it was at her expense.

'I could ask,' said Aitch.

'Ask who, what?' Rena was looking forward, wanting to tell Fletcher they were nearly at the point where the track led off the highway, knowing he wouldn't appreciate the back seat driving.

'Ask one of the Aunties. They know this country far better than I do. They've seen plenty of floods and they've also heard the stories from their Aunties and Uncles. If there are stories of where floodwaters yield their trophies, it's the Aunties who would hold that knowledge.' Aitch pulled out her mobile and tapped the screen. 'But I don't have a signal.'

Without replying, Fletcher flipped on the indicator and slowed the Land Cruiser, easing onto the shoulder before bringing the vehicle to a stop. He raised his sunglasses, settling them just behind his hairline, and for a moment, he and Aitch regarded each other in the reflection of the rearview mirror. Then he reached through to the back seat and passed her his police-issue satellite phone. 'If you could ask, that would be really helpful, please.'

'No guarantees,' said Aitch, taking the proffered handset. She unclipped her seatbelt and got out of the Land Cruiser, slamming the door behind her.

Rena and Fletcher sat, cocooned in the vehicle, and watched as Aitch dialled then pressed the phone to her ear. She looked their way then turned her back, a slight squaring of her shoulders the only sign that somewhere, her call had been answered. Then she walked away from the patrol vehicle, a redundant quest for privacy given the engine was still idling. Fletcher hit a button, and his window buzzed closed.

'We sent someone out to talk to Pete King. Have to confirm but looks like he has an alibi for Kinnane's murder.' Fletcher stared straight ahead as he spoke.

Rena glanced at him, saw tension in the bunching of his jaw muscles, and looked away. 'But he knew Marty?' She focused on the horizon.

'Yeah, apparently. His story is Kinnane paid him to stir up a stink about Synastria. Pete was laughing all the way to the bank, because he planned to do that anyway and now some city boy was giving him cash in hand. Not so funny when Kinnane turned up dead though.'

Rena nodded. 'Makes sense. An extra distraction from what Verne Industries was up to.'

'S'what we thought.'

They lapsed into silence. Rena could tell there was something else the detective wanted to say. She fiddled with the angle of the air vents.

Fletcher cleared his throat. 'When did you—' He shook his head.

'When did I what?' Rena frowned, surprised by the detective's sudden hesitation.

'Sorry, never mind.' He angled his head to look in the wing mirror, presumably watching Aitch as she walked and talked.

'Don't pull that crap. You want to ask me something, ask. If I don't like the question or it's none of your damn business, I'll tell you.'

He glanced in the mirror again then pushed his head back into the seat, staring out at the endless red landscape, at the highway running all the way to infinity. 'When did you find out your husband was sick? Early or late?'

'Jesus.'

'Sorry, sorry. I know. Forget I said anything. Shit.'

'No. It's okay.' Rena had her back against the door, studying Bob; the tension in his body, the way his face was twisted, eyes almost closed, told her what asking the question had cost him, and how much an honest answer would mean.

'The thing is, it's subjective, isn't it?' she said. 'When you're talking about cancer, if it's aggressive, what's early and what's late? Things didn't look too bad. The stats were in our favour, the oncologist had a plan—surgery, radiation, chemo—and we figured, "Okay, this isn't good, but we'll face it head on. Tom will recover, we'll get on with our lives." Only the cancer didn't follow the plan.'

Fletcher nodded, swallowed.

'Bob? Someone in your family?'

He shook his head. 'Me. At least, got the gene mutation. You know the one? BRCA?

'Isn't that breast cancer?'

'Yes. But fun fact: Men can have the gene mutation too, and when that happens it increases the risk of prostate cancer up to as much as 50 percent. Plus, if you get it, the cancer can be much more aggressive, and you can get it at a much younger age.'

'And you?'

'Didn't have any inkling; my family is...' He waved a hand in the air, a substitute for a word like *gone, useless, estranged*. 'Found out a couple of weeks ago about the gene. Doc in Perth wants to test PSA levels and stuff. Need to decide what to do. Don't want to fuck my career though.'

For a moment, Rena couldn't fathom why he was telling her. Then she realised. No family to speak of, living in a small town. He probably didn't even want to tell the local doctors because while they'd keep his secrets, the very fact of him entering the clinic would start the rumour mill.

'Better than fucking your life,' she said. 'You're lucky. You're armed with this knowledge; cancer will never take you by surprise. Now you can have regular blood tests to keep an eye on things. Just a bit of blood every six months. These days, they don't even routinely stick a finger up your—'

Aitch opened the back door, startling them both, and slid back into her seat. 'Right.'

'Anything?' Rena asked, side-eyeing Bob Fletcher, who was scrubbing a hand across his eyes.

'Maybe. Dunno till we get out there and I can see what it's like.'

'So that's a no,' said Fletcher, his voice back to normal, sunglasses now returned from their perch on his head, covering his eyes.

'It's a maybe. It may surprise you to know that I did not receive precise instructions about walking fifty paces north by north-west and looking for the woolly butt with the branch shaped like a witch's hooked nose. But I did get some suggestions, and what with our resident geologist, we might have slightly more than a snowball's chance in hell of finding something. So, snap to it.' She pounded a fist on the back of the driver's seat for emphasis. 'Let's get out there.'

They drove past Marty's old campsite, and with Rena navigating, Bob Fletcher managed to get the police Land Cruiser to within a stone's throw of the narrow cleft in the mesa. Knowing it was there and approaching from a different angle, it was easy to see where the fissure began at the top of the rock. But from out here there was also plenty to indicate that finding Marty's tin of diamonds—assuming it hadn't already been recovered by someone—was not going to be easy. There was the creek bed that Rena had already looked at, but under the extreme flood conditions of three years ago, it would have been nothing more than a deeper part of one massive body of water.

Fletcher radioed in while Rena pulled her detector and other gear from the back of the four-wheel drive. Aitch, meanwhile, had stuck a torch in the waistband of her jeans then wandered a short distance away, whether to stretch after the rough ride, take in the barren beauty of the landscape, or survey the terrain with the benefit of knowledge, Rena had no idea.

She was just settling her hat more firmly on her head when Fletcher appeared and put a knee up on the tailgate, reaching deep into the Land Cruiser. He emerged with a small backpack.

'First aid, torch, and water,' he said, sliding his arm through one strap and swinging the pack into place.

'Got some water in here too,' Rena hefted her own bag. 'No bandages, though.'

'How about a bullet to bite on if we have to repair a burst appendix or cauterise a pumping artery?'

'Geez. Set the mood why don't you, Detective? But, nah. What you need for that is high-proof alcohol. Some for the wound, the rest for anaesthetic.' She slammed the tailgate shut.

'Duly noted. Listen. About...' He hesitated.

'Not going to say a word to anyone, if that's what you're asking.'

'Thanks. I didn't mean to dump on you.'

Rena picked up the metal detector, wriggled her shoulders to settle her daypack more comfortably, then nodded towards the rock, inviting Fletcher to walk. 'Yes, you did, and that's perfectly okay. We all need someone to dump on from time to time. Just don't think that's it. You want to talk more, we'll talk. And, actually, regardless of whether you want to or not, I think we should.'

'I don't—'

'I know you don't. So let's put that on the back burner and deal with this for now.' She gestured with the metal detector, raising the coil to point at the rock ahead. 'Better wait for Aitch to catch up.'

Rena stopped and turned away from Fletcher, leaving him to his own thoughts while she watched Aitch stride towards them.

'Well, I've got some ideas,' Aitch called. 'And they all begin with, it's un-fucking-likely, but...'

'Welcome to the club.'

Aitch covered the last few metres to join them in front of the entrance to the rock fissure. 'This is nuts.'

'Agree.' Fletcher put his hands on his hips.

'Of course it's nuts. That's how all great stories start! A First Nations woman, a frustrated cop, and a grumpy old broad walk off into the Kimberley. See?'

'That's how jokes start,' said Fletcher.

'Yep,' said Rena, moving forward to stand beside the mound of loose stones guarding the gap in the rock. 'But not all of them have a two million-dollar punchline.' She stopped. 'After you.'

'Fuck me.' Aitch gestured for Fletcher to precede her, but he demurred. With a shrug, she stepped past Rena and scrambled around the cairn. Aitch took a single step into the narrow cleft, placing a hand on the rock to her right. A steadying move, or a reverent touch. Then she pressed forward and was lost to view.

'Detective?' Rena hovered, keen to move, but not wanting to simply blaze ahead and leave Bob Fletcher to trail along behind.

Fletcher let Aitch get a few steps ahead then turned away and, despite his sunglasses, raised a hand to shield his eyes from the relentless glare of the morning sun. He scanned the landscape from left to right, and Rena, unsure what he was expecting to see, felt compelled to look as well. She saw nothing.

Finally, Fletcher sighed, spun around, and with a nod to Rena, made his way between the rock faces.

THIRTY-ONE

It was much cooler between the rocks with the sun still too low in the sky to breach the rim of the fissure. High above, the top few metres of the rock face were spotlit, deep red, streaks of black, dark green tips where tenacious plants clung, defying gravity, belying the harshness of the land. But where they walked, everything was in deep shade, colours muted, and it somehow made Rena feel as though time had slipped and the earth was younger by millennia, a place of prehistory.

'Shit!' Fletcher stumbled on a loose rock, arms flailing. He managed not to fall, but the moment was gone.

'You okay?' Rena's voice sounded loud, bouncing off the walls of stone.

He waved a hand in acknowledgement but didn't speak, pushing forward in Aitch's wake.

Rena let them get ahead, still nursing the knee a bit, studying the ground beneath her feet. Could Marty's stash have been swept from the cave and ended up somewhere out here or even on the plain beyond? Possible, but unlikely. If Marty Kinnane had hidden a tin can filled with diamonds in that cave, odds on they were still in there somewhere. The inrush of water pouring down the walls of the fissure and into the space would have first exposed the tin, then most likely pushed it farther back into the deeper recesses; how far was anyone's guess. Then there could be holes in the floor, natural shafts dropping away. Ten metres, fifty, or to the centre of the earth.

One way or another, whether by human intervention or force of nature, the diamonds were probably gone.

'This it?' Aitch was standing next to the cave's entrance, bent low, peering into the dim interior. Next to her, Fletcher braced his hands in the small of his back and stretched.

'Yep. That's the one I was talking about. Why, are there more?' Rena sped up to reach them.

'Rena mate'—Aitch turned and smiled—'place is full of them.'

'Good thing we only need to check this one then.'

Aitch pulled the torch from her jeans and switched it on, playing the strong beam around the cave's interior, letting it linger on the dark recess at the back. 'Depends how much we need to check. Also depends on where that goes.'

'You ladies realise this will go a lot faster if you stop talking and actually start looking, right?' Fletcher had his own torch out and was already moving into the cave.

'You're in charge, Detective,' said Aitch, flashing a wink at Rena.

'Damn right, I am. Now come on, let's get this done and get back. Although...' He stopped a metre or so inside the cave's mouth and ran his light across the floor. 'From the looks of this, we're not going to find anything. For fuck's sake, Rena! This is a waste of time!'

Rena peered over his shoulder. The floor of the cave looked like a demented wombat had gone to town. The holes and scrapes she'd seen last time had multiplied and deepened to the point that a good third of the dirt had been turned over.

'Hell,' she said. 'Wasn't like this. Someone has been here since.'

'You're sure?' Fletcher asked.

'I'm old, but I'm not woolly headed.'

'Chuck.'

'What about Tyse? Or Wally?' Rena stepped around him, scuffing a toe through the loose soil. 'Or someone else entirely?'

'Like who?'

'Someone you don't know about? Or someone you do. Like Eric.'

Bob Fletcher pointed his torch at her. Its beam threw Rena's shadow against the opposite side of the cave, her head massively enlarged atop an elongated torso, the whole a grotesque troglodyte.

Rena didn't look around. 'Don't tell me you hadn't considered the possibility.' She squatted, dropped her gear, and picked up a handful of sandy earth, watching as it trickled through her fingers. 'He could've followed Marty somehow. You said yourselves he knows the country and moves through it easily.'

Fletcher clicked his tongue and sighed. 'I could see Eric as Marty's killer, simply because Kinnane worked for a mining company. But why would Eric look for the stones? That's not in keeping with what we know about him.'

'Return them to where they came from? Or maybe you just don't know enough about Eric.' Rena shook her head. 'I honestly have no idea what's going on. All I can tell you is whoever was out here digging, it wasn't Wally.'

'How do you know?' Fletcher's voice had become soft, muffled by the acoustics of the cave.

'Because whoever it was didn't have a metal detector. There's no junk to give a false signal here. No Coke cans or nails from horseshoes. And if you only dig when you get a signal, you're not going to waste time and energy doing this.' She gestured to the cave around them. 'I mean, I suppose Wally could've come before or after the person who did all this. Except I don't think he knew about this place. But if Wally was ever out here, he must have another car—a four-wheel drive—because although he kept his metal detector handy in the taxi, there's no way anyone could drive out here in a regular car.'

'Wait a minute.' Fletcher strode forward, coming around in front of Rena and staring her in the face. This close, his eyes were nothing but reflective pools of black. 'What do you mean he had a metal detector in the taxi?'

Rena frowned, surprised by his sudden intensity. 'He told me he had his metal detector in the boot, ready to go if anyone called.'

'It wasn't there. When we found him.'

'Back at his home?'

He shook his head. 'Whoever shot him must've taken it. Which means they knew there was something worth finding.'

'That would make sense. If Marty didn't have the diamonds, his killer knew of or found this place, made a second, unsuccessful pass after I'd been here, then killed Wally for his detector—no witness and no competition for the stash.'

Fletcher moved to stand beside her, then slowly swung his torch from left to right across the sandy ground. 'Could he—and if I'm honest, I'm thinking Chuck—could he have already been back? With the metal detector?'

Rena shrugged. 'No way to tell. There's a very slim possibility Marty's tin can was washed out of here and it's gone forever or Chuck—or Tyse or Eric—found it in one of these holes. But I think we're in with a chance. Chuck or whoever would have to act fast to get out here after killing Wally, and we've seen no other signs of that. Besides, this corner of the Kimberley isn't the M1, so…'

'So fire up your detector and start looking,' he said.

Rena glanced across at Aitch. 'What do you reckon, Aitch? Any thoughts?'

'How big is this can likely to be? Two million or maybe more worth of diamonds? I mean how could you lose something like that? It must be a biscuit barrel or a massive, catering-sized tin of instant coffee.'

'If the colour of the stones is good, think more like a small tin of Milo or even that Coke can I mentioned.'

Rena had been surveying the ground and now, detector in hand, she advanced on the corner to one side of the entrance, the place that would act as a catch area if water was swirling in and around the cave. 'I'll start here then move back across the cave. If either of you have steel-capped boots, piss off.'

'I'm just gunna...' Aitch gestured with her torch toward the back of the cave and the solid blackness of the unknown.

Rena nodded then got to work. The coil she was using was sensitive, had good ground penetration, and Rena had adjusted the settings to reduce discrimination: If there was anything metal to find, her detector should ping on it.

It took her less than ten minutes to establish there was nothing in the cave. As she completed the final sweep, Fletcher swore and stomped outside.

'Fuck,' he yelled.

Rena decided to leave him to his own devices and went to find Aitch, somewhere in the darkness beyond the main cave.

'Aitch?' Rena fumbled for her Maglite, wishing she had a head-lamp instead.

The only thing she heard was an echo of her own voice.

'Aitch?' She tried again, louder. 'Stop messing around.'

She lowered her torch to point the way and that was when she saw it: a small circle of light, like a train in a tunnel, moving towards her and getting bigger. The light shifted up, illuminating Aitch's face from below. Distance was hard to gauge in the dark, and she was much closer than Rena had thought, only a dozen or so steps away.

'Rena! This is incredible! You've gotta see.' In the weird torch-light, Aitch's teeth flashed in a broad smile.

'Diamonds?' Rena moved forward with confidence now, knowing Aitch had already traversed this ground.

'Nup. Better. Well, suppose that depends on your point of view but… Stop!'

Aitch pointed her torch at the ground between them. Blackness pooled like the doormat at hell's gates—a hole, a natural shaft in the floor of the cave.

'Shit.' Rena clapped a hand to her chest, feeling her heart going at double its normal speed. 'How about a bit more warning next time?'

'Sorry. I assumed you were looking where you were going.'

'Arsehole.'

'Dickhead.'

In the light of their torches, both women grinned at each other.

'How deep?' Rena set the metal detector on the ground behind her then laid down on her stomach, commando crawling toward the edge. Opposite her, Aitch also laid down.

'Not sure, but there's water in the bottom of it.' Aitch dropped a stone into the void. They heard a few clatters then a long silence before, far off, the plonk as solid hit liquid.

'Underground spring or stream.'

'Yeah.'

'Given I didn't find diamonds in the main cave and that the initial push of water from outside could easily have had enough force to wash the tin down this way, maybe Marty's stones are down there.'

'I know!' Aitch's voice was filled with excitement. Hell, she was almost crowing.

Rena flicked the beam of her torch in Aitch's direction, lighting up her face and the huge shit-eating grin on it.

'What the hell are you so chipper about?' she asked.

'Well, it's a beautiful day in the Kimberley, we're all alive, and we've had the opportunity to see this awesome place!'

'Okay, that's mildly heart-warming, but there is the small matter of losing two million bucks' worth of Argyle diamonds.'

'Shit, Rena. What were the odds of finding them? Look, I've figured out you're both an optimist and a woman who does whatever the hell she wants because you have no fucks to give, but even you must've thought that with the murders and general crazy shit, someone else has already got those rocks and is probably miles away.'

Rena sighed. 'Yeah, but even when you're old, there's still that little kid inside who dreams of finding treasure.'

'Dream on, baby girl!' Aitch pointed her torch over the lip of the hole, lighting up a space directly below her.

Rena could see a rocky outcrop, a sedimentary conglomerate of some type, judging by its mottled colour. It jutted out from the side of the shaft, forming a natural ledge. To Aitch's left it was worn smooth, but on the other it was irregular, according to the nature of its different compositional rocks. And there, caught amongst the embedded pebbles and cobbles was a can, torchlight winking from its silver surface.

'Bullshit,' said Rena. 'You put that there, didn't you? Very funny.'

'Swear to God, that's how I found it.' Aitch sounded serious.

'What, you stumbled down here in the pitch black, managed not to fall into the bloody great hole, and then what? Had a look and there it was?'

'Well, when you put it like that, I can understand why you might call bullshit.'

Rena grunted.

'But what if I tell you that I already knew about the hole because I was told about it? Because—do you feel the cool air coming up?—this thing is like a natural fridge. You can put stuff on the rocky shelf or lower a bundle on a line.'

'You knew this was here?'

'Not until today. Not until I spoke with the Aunties. Although I have to say I was bloody surprised to actually see that tin stuck there.'

'Can't be deliberate.'

'Nup. The floods swept it down here and somehow it was thrown onto the ledge rather than into the abyss.'

They fell silent, both staring down at the small tin can wedged in the rocks.

Rena inched a bit farther forward, feeling the cold breath of the earth whispering against her skin. She stretched out a hand, her fingers straining, but coming nowhere near their prize.

'Can you reach it?' she asked, retreating.

Aitch leaned forward, bending the top half of her chest into the hole.

'Be careful, for Chrissake!'

'Just get ready to grab my belt if I go over.' Aitch's voice seemed to fall away, her words dropping, following a scattering of loose earth down to the water below.

Rena angled her torch, giving Aitch the light she needed. 'Should I come over your side and sit on your legs?'

'Rena love, I like you but not that much. I'm good.' Her hand encircled the can.

'Don't bloody drop it.'

Aitch raised her head slightly, twisting her neck to look at Rena. 'You want to do this?'

'Sorry. Carry on!'

Aitch grunted. 'It's stuck.'

'Stuck, stuck? Or just sort of safely wedged?'

'Mate, I'll chuck that thing down the bloody hole myself in a minute!'

'I'll shut up then.'

'You do that. And try not to breathe in a judgemental way.'

'I—'

'Just don't.'

Rena was tempted to whistle a tune, just to be annoying, but decided not to risk the diamonds. She watched as Aitch tugged at the tin, changed her grip and pulled again. It shifted, metal scraping against rock.

Aitch let out a hiss of breath. Rena kept her trap shut.

As Rena watched, Aitch twisted the tin back and forth, each movement easing it a fraction further out of its rock cradle.

'Nearly.' Aitch paused, letting go of the tin and giving her hand a brisk shake before wrapping her fingers around the smooth surface again. 'This time,' she said, glancing up at Rena.

Rena watched Aitch's hand—the ridge of taut knuckles, the prominent tendons—on the tin within Aitch's grasp. She held her breath.

'What the hell are you two playing at?' Fletcher didn't shout, but he may as well have.

Rena had been so focused on the action in the shaft, that she hadn't heard him come up behind her.

And neither had Aitch.

'Fuck!' She jumped, jolting the tin free, even as the shock made her fingers reflexively splay.

The tin seemed to hover in midair, a horrible parody of a cartoon moment that seemed to last an eternity. Then it was in Aitch's hand again, and she was worming her way back from the edge, laughing and swearing at the same time.

'Nice entrance, Detective. They teach you that in cop school?' Aitch rolled over, lying on her back in the dirt and dark, the tin clutched tightly to her chest with both hands.

Rena shuffled about until she could sit up. 'We're doing what we came here to do.' She favoured Fletcher with what she considered her *Terminator* face, a combination of lip curl and jutted chin. Then she realised he couldn't see it in the gloom, and all his attention was on Aitch, who was getting to her feet, and the tin in her hand.

'Is that what I think it is?' He gestured with his torch.

'Haven't opened it yet,' said Rena.

Aitch edged past the hole, her back against the wall of the cave, and then she was standing next to Fletcher.

'Better give me that.' Fletcher gestured to the tin in Aitch's hand. 'Chain of evidence, that sort of thing. Ordinarily, I'd take photos of where you found it, but without proper illumination, there's no point.'

'Aitch and I can provide statements if you need them,' said Rena.

'Count on it.'

By the light of their combined torches, Rena saw Fletcher pull a latex glove from his hip pocket. He snapped it on then accepted the offered tin, weighing it in his hand. Then he gave it a shake.

It rattled like hail on an iron roof, and as the echoes receded, Rena heard him blow out a long breath. She wanted to make some sort of glib comment, or crack a joke, but she had nothing. Much as she'd hoped for it, assessed the geology and the characteristics of the site with optimism and the thrill of the hunt bubbling through her veins, the fact they'd actually found Marty's diamonds had surprised her.

'You coming?' Aitch asked, extending her now-free hand. Rena allowed herself to be hauled upright.

'Ta.'

'You ladies right? We haven't got all bloody day. Let's get out in the light and see what two million dollars' worth of Argyle pinks looks like.' Fletcher was already walking ahead.

'You do know they're not going to be all polished and pretty, right?' Rena called after him.

'As long as they look like two million bucks to someone.'

Aitch shrugged and fell into step with Rena. The two of them walked side by side, following the rapidly receding, shadowy shape of Bob Fletcher as he headed towards the faint glimmer at the cave's mouth.

THIRTY-TWO

By the time Rena and Aitch stepped into the light, Fletcher had already disappeared, not even the clatter of stones to alert them to his progress through the landscape.

Rena stood, waiting for her eyes to adjust, feeling the dry, warm air on her face.

'Have you been here before?' she asked.

'Don't think so. Not that I remember anyway. But maybe when I was a kid.' Aitch shrugged then moved slowly, not towards the return path, but deeper into the cleft. 'Might have a bit of a look while we're here. Maybe Tyse... Don't know when I'll get back this way.'

'Want company?'

'Nah, mate. I'll only be a few minutes.' Aitch craned her neck, staring up at the point where the blue sky lay like a lid on the red cliffs.

Rena wouldn't have minded a bit of exploring, but the pull of the diamonds was stronger. She nodded. 'Right-o. See you back there.'

She watched as Aitch began to pick her way around a fallen boulder, then turned. Fletcher would only wait so long before opening the tin and she wanted to be there to see the sunlight strike the stones for the first time in years.

Rena made good progress, the terrain feeling familiar beneath her boots, her knee offering only the occasional twinge. She was just slowing down to pick her way around the cairn of stones when she heard Fletcher yelling. She couldn't make out his words, but the tone was unmistakable. It was the authoritative shout of a police officer, commanding. But to Rena, there was also a note of something else.

Fear.

'Bob!' she bellowed, then threw herself across the scree, feet slipping, stumbling over the scattered rocks. Rena fell on her bad knee, but was up again immediately, ignoring the pain.

Then the sound of a gunshot cracked through the air.

'Shit.'

She was out of the fissure, barnstorming down the slope, trying not to fall, not wanting to check her pace. Then she could see the police Land Cruiser and, slumped against the driver's door—no, sliding down it—was Bob Fletcher, left hand clutched to his abdomen, blood staining the shirt beneath.

For a moment Rena froze as her brain tried to process what she was seeing.

She took a step and a chunk of rock near her feet exploded, followed half a second later by the sound of a shot. Rena looked down, expecting to see blood pumping from a bullet hole, expecting to feel pain, relieved to see nothing and to find herself unscathed.

Her head snapped up. Rena looked at Bob again, unmoving. There was no one else out there on the flat; the shooter had cover. Damned if she was going to cower here when Bob needed help.

She took off running across the open ground. Another shot and she flinched but didn't break stride. She reached Bob just in time to stop him falling. Grabbing his shoulders, she lowered him gently to the ground.

'Rena,' he grunted her name through clenched teeth.

'I've got you, Bob. What happened?' He was like a rag doll as she arranged his legs in front of him and made sure his back was against the wheel.

'Shot.'

She crouched next to him and gently moved his bloodied hand to check the damage.

Bad. The shocking pink of torn flesh, blood still flowing. She replaced his hand, pushing it, eliciting a hiss of pain.

'Keep pressure on it. I'll get some bandages, and we'll get you back to the Crossing. They'll sort it there.'

Rena went looking for his bag with the first aid kit, finding it already stowed in the back of the Land Cruiser. She half-crawled into the vehicle, feeling the vulnerability of her exposed back, the target she presented, not giving a fuck.

Rena dragged the kit out, ripped open Velcro tabs and zips, finding stuff she could use, but not what Fletcher really needed: suture material, surgical instruments, and a doctor who knew how to use them. This meagre supply would do. It had to. She slung the bag over her shoulder.

'I'm coming, Bob!' As she turned from the rear door of the Land Cruiser, Rena caught a flash of movement from the corner of her eye. She looked.

A man was standing about fifty metres away, feet braced wide. And he had a handgun trained on Rena.

'Jesus Christ.' Rena locked eyes with the shooter, unable to make sense of what she was seeing.

Then she remembered Bob.

'You wouldn't—'

The gunman pulled the trigger.

THIRTY-THREE

In the split second before the shot was fired, Rena registered a narrowing of the gunman's eyes and she threw herself sideways, her shoulder slamming into the ground. Her leg was suddenly on fire, but she kept moving, crawling away, around the side of the Land Cruiser, out of range.

She stopped, checked her left leg. Nothing like a bullet wound to take the focus off a strained knee. It hurt like a bitch and was bleeding profusely, but not pumping, so maybe not too bad. Nothing compared to Bob. Rena looked along the side of the vehicle to where he sat. Bob was staring back at her, eyes wide, and for a moment she thought he was dead. Then he blinked.

'I'm okay, I'm okay,' she whispered.

He nodded.

Where was the shooter? Was he coming to finish the job?

Rena didn't dwell on it. She crawled towards Bob, shoulders tense, expecting to feel the bite of a bullet, wondering if she'd hear the sound of the gun before she was face down in the dirt.

Then she was kneeling beside him. He was pale, a fine sheen of sweat visible on his lip. She gave him what she hoped was a reassuring smile then got to work, packing gauze on the wound, wrapping a bandage around him to try to hold everything in place.

'We'll get you into the car in a minute. You're doing great. The only pain relief I could find in your kit was aspirin; you want some?'

Bob shook his head. His eyes were screwed shut and his breath was juddering.

Rena yanked a cotton sling from the first aid kit and checked her bleeding leg. A chunk of flesh was missing at about mid-thigh level, but it looked like the bullet had missed everything important. She tied the fabric around her leg, as tightly as she could.

Where the hell was Aitch? Surely the sound of the shots would have reached her, even in the rock fissure. And even if she hadn't heard anything, shouldn't she be back by now?

'Bob? Let's get you into the back seat. Sure you don't want drugs?'

He grunted. Opened his eyes, gripped her bicep with his free hand. 'Diamonds,' he said.

'Fuck the diamonds. Come on.' Rena clambered to her feet, finding her injured leg weak and painful but functional. As carefully as she could, Rena helped Bob to stand. He slumped into her, heavy, doing his best to stay upright.

It was only a couple of steps from where he'd been to the back door of the Land Cruiser, but each one was agonisingly slow, and each one cost him dearly, despite Rena holding as much of his weight as possible. His bum hit the seat and his head rolled back, giving her a moment of panic before he fought off the wave of unconsciousness.

'Legs,' she said, lifting his feet into the cab. Somehow between them they managed it, got his entire frame into the Land Cruiser and in a position where he could lie down on the back seat. Then she lifted his free hand and held it in hers.

'Deep breaths,' she said. Rena waited until he complied, then gently closed the door.

'Mate!' Aitch was strolling out of the scrub, a smile on her face.

'Get in, you're driving.'

'What happened to your leg, Rena? You cut yourself or something?'

'It's nothing, just hurry. I'll tell you everything once we're moving.'

Aitch frowned but didn't argue, jogging down to the Land Cruiser, stopping abruptly when she saw the blood smeared down the front fender. 'What the fuck? Where's Fletcher?'

'Back seat. He's hurt bad. Now are you going to drive?'

'Shit.'

They piled in. Aitch took one look at Bob in the back seat, swore again, then brought the engine to life. 'Sorry, Detective, I'll go as gently as I can, but I'm going for speed not comfort.'

As the four-wheel drive began moving, Rena punched Ito's number into the police-issue satellite phone. She sat sideways in her seat as she talked, one hand reaching through to rest on Fletcher's leg. Her own thigh was throbbing, but Rena ignored it, a minor distraction in a major shitstorm.

They bumped through a shallow wash and Fletcher cried out.

'Sorry, sorry,' Aitch winced as though the pain was hers.

Rena was still talking but she increased the pressure of her hand and twisted her torso right around, so she could look Bob in the eye and offer him a nod of reassurance. It felt weak, useless, but he met her gaze and held it. Maybe for now that was enough.

Rena didn't bother with niceties or the bigger story. She just told Ito that her partner had been shot, it was bad, and he needed urgent medical help. Triple-O was the standard emergency number, but Rena figured Ito would have the necessary pull to scramble more resources faster and she was right, although in the Kimberley, isolation and distance meant rapid medical attention could mean hours. She stayed on the line, listening to Ito shout instructions and finally, to inform Rena of the plan. The call ended abruptly, and Rena leaned closer to Aitch.

'Fast as you can,' she murmured.

Aitch didn't reply, she just hunched over the steering wheel, focussing on the ground in front of the bullbar. Rena felt the speed increase slightly.

'Right, we're set.' Rena raised her voice, speaking to both Aitch and Bob. 'Ito's on it. Flying Doc is going to meet us at the highway.'

'When you say meet us...' Aitch twisted the steering wheel to the right then back again, skirting a termite mound.

'Ito knows where we're going to come out of the rough, so she's closing it off. They're going to land the plane on the highway.'

Aitch nodded. 'Good to know.'

'Hear that, Bob? Help is on the way.'

'Rena,' he said.

She watched as he mustered strength.

'If I don't make it—'

'None of that,' she said. 'You're not going to die on me. Or Aitch. For one thing, how would I explain it to Ito? The two of you have been suspecting me of all sorts of things, so if you bloody go and die on me now, how will it look?'

She was rewarded with a choked laugh that became a grimace of pain.

'You've got a lot to live for, Bob.'

He closed his eyes, then seemed to force them open, his brows arching with the effort. 'Before I loop out then,' he whispered.

Rena wanted to tell him to shut up and save his energy, but she knew it would be pointless, and he'd only waste more of his strength arguing with her.

'Okay.'

'He was waiting. For the diamonds. I didn't... He...' He shut his eyes again, but only for a second. 'He took them. So sorry. But how did he know we were there? Tell Ito. Tell her there's a leak.'

'The stones are nothing. I know it would've made a splash, good PR and all that, but in the scheme of things, they're nothing. Just carbon.'

'Two million dollars' worth of carbon,' said Aitch.

'Not helping, mate.'

'Just saying what I bet Detective Fletcher is thinking.'

Fletcher grunted, presumably in assent.

'How about you shut up and drive?' Rena said it with a smile. The more they could lighten the mood now, the better.

'Just make sure Ito knows there's a rat at the station.' Fletcher's voice was sounding softer and there were longer gaps between his words. 'How else would he know?' He sucked in a deep, shuddering breath.

'I'll tell you how else, but you're not going to like it,' said Rena.

He frowned at her, eyes glazing as he fought to hold on to consciousness.

'I saw him. The bloke who shot you.' Rena shook her head, dragged a hand across her eyes. 'Shit.'

'Jesus, Rena, what?' Aitch risked a quick head turn.

'It was Marty fucking Kinnane.'

THIRTY-FOUR

Back in that moment, when Rena had been rifling through the medical supplies, she'd been thinking only of the severity of Bob's injury and what she was going to do to keep him alive until they could get him proper help. Tom had died on her despite everything, and she was damned if she was going to let it happen again. Especially when she was the reason Detective Bob Fletcher was out here; he'd got shot on her watch. Of course, he wouldn't see it that way, but that was irrelevant. Rena could've talked him out of coming, or kept her trap shut and then simply done it herself. She'd pushed the self-recriminations away, focusing on the immediate issue: minimise blood loss, reduce pain, try to keep Bob conscious.

Then she'd emerged from the back of the Land Cruiser and seen the gunman. In the shock and panic of Bob's injury, she'd ignored the possibility that the shooter might still be around. Might, in fact, be lying in wait ready to ambush and kill them all.

Time had seemed to slow, but her senses heightened. She could see the gun—not the one she'd fought over with the Minister for Defence, but a pistol—was pointed at her chest. Then she'd registered the figure behind the gun: male, tallish, camo pants, dirty white T-shirt, sweat stains at the neck and armpits, bush hat pulled down low throwing the wearer's face into deep shadow. Something about him struck a dissonant chord of memory.

As she stared down the barrel of the gun, Rena had only one thought: 'Fuck this. Bob needs my help. I don't have time for this arsehole.'

The man moved slightly and as the sun caught his face, Rena's dissonant chord had become a shrieking alarm. She'd stared, realisation dawning, and saw recognition flood Marty Kinnane's face: a widening of the eyes, a slackening of the jaw.

Then Marty's expression had shifted, he fired the gun, and Rena was in the dirt.

'Isn't he the car-fire barbecue dude?' Aitch asked, breaking into Rena's thoughts.

'That's what we thought, but apparently not,' said Rena.

They were making better time now, driving on the tracks left by Rena and the cops when they'd followed the trail Marty had made from the Great Northern Highway to his base camp in front of the ridge.

'Ya sure?' Bob's voice was so soft Rena barely caught the words.

She slid her seatbelt off her torso and leaned between the front seats so she could look at him better. His face was waxy and pale, and she could see him shaking slightly. 'Am I sure it was him? Yes. Haven't seen him for years, but it was Kinnane all right. And he recognised me. Probably why he didn't kill me. Either that or he thinks I'm past it.'

Bob struggled, trying to sit up, but fell back with a grunt. 'Ito,' he said.

'I've already told her.'

He nodded, eyes closed.

'Bob, are you cold?'

He didn't respond, but there was a thick jacket stuffed in the rear footwell, and Rena grabbed it, draping it across his upper body.

'Not long now,' she said.

'That's right, should be back at the highway in twenty minutes tops,' Aitch's voice was loud with forced optimism. She caught Rena's eye, asking a silent question with a jerk of her head and raised brows.

Rena tapped the dashboard clock in response. Time was running out.

'Look.' Aitch pointed her chin at the sky, visible through the windscreen. Far in front of them, a small plane was tracking in from the west.

'You think that's the Flying Doc?'

Aitch nodded. 'Their base is at Broome. No commercial flights into the Crossing today, and if it was a sightseeing plane, they'd be over Country, not following the highway.'

'Thank Christ.'

'Rena,' said Aitch.

'Yeah, mate.' Rena was splitting her attention between Bob in the back seat and the plane, trying to do sums she didn't really want to contemplate.

'You're certain it was the bloke who was supposed to be dead, this Marty Kinnane, who took the diamonds and shot the detective?'

'Hundred percent.'

'So, who was the body behind the wheel?'

Rena sat back in her seat with a thump. 'Christ.'

'I doubt that, but I understand the sentiment.'

THIRTY-FIVE

A patrol car was waiting for them just shy of the highway; Rena could see the black line of asphalt up ahead. Several hundred metres to the left, a police four-wheel drive was parked across the lanes, lights flashing, a line of vehicles slowly gathering behind it. Looking right, she saw a mirror image: highway blocked, flashing lights, the incongruous sight of traffic banking up in a place where traffic generally meant six cars in half an hour.

Ito came out of the patrol car faster than Rena had ever seen her move, looking decidedly more rumpled too. She was at Rena's door before Aitch had time to get the hand brake on, peering in, looking for something in Rena's face then moving past, opening the rear passenger door. Heat flooded in, together with sound: engines idling, the dry rustle of the wind in nearby shrubs, and above it all, the drone of an aeroplane.

'Fletch,' she said.

Rena heard a whisper from Bob.

'You didn't fuck up.' Ito's tone was firm but there was a quiver of distress in there too.

Aitch and Rena exchanged a glance, and Rena was just about to speak when the noise of the plane rose to a crescendo. A small

Pilatus jet, marked with the distinctive blue and red livery of the Royal Flying Doctor Service, touched down on the highway in front of them.

'They made good time,' Ito spoke loudly enough to include all of them, then fixed her attention on Aitch. 'Soon as the pilot gives us the okay, you go, drive right up, close as you can.'

'No worries. I know how it works.' Aitch rested a hand on the gear stick.

With a final word to Bob, Ito closed the door and jogged back to the police vehicle in front of their own.

As Rena watched the plane complete its taxiing along the highway and begin to turn, she felt a wave of relief wash over her, followed by a burst of panic. *What if it was still too little, too late? What if Bob—* She turned to look at him again, but it wasn't a reassuring sight.

The pitch of the plane's engines changed, and at the same moment, Ito stuck her arm out of the car window, waving them forward.

Aitch was ready, dropping the Land Cruiser into gear and rolling onto the highway, pulling up within metres of the plane just as the door was released. Then the medical team was around their vehicle, moving in from both sides, lifting the burden of responsibility for Bob's care from their shoulders.

Rena felt like shit. She stepped out onto the hot road, wobbled slightly as her leg objected, then stood firm. She didn't want to crowd the people working on Bob, but she was desperate to hear what they were saying, to see the looks they gave each other, to attach meaning to their phrases and intonation. Aitch appeared at her side.

'He'll be okay, mate,' she said.

Rena didn't respond. She'd heard those empty words before and refused to fall for them again.

'I didn't know you got scared.' Aitch draped an arm around her shoulder. 'You drive around in that Ranger of yours, woman on her own, sleep on the roof. Most women travelling on their own have an RV with lockable doors and never stray off the main roads. You're fearless.'

'I used to think I was, until Tom got cancer. Locks can be broken; at least when I sleep on the roof, I'm perfectly placed to kick intruders in the face.'

'I bet you usually pack a good kick too.'

'Believe it, mate.' Rena drew in a long breath. 'But nothing is scarier than not being in control. You know, I thought about trading the Ranger for an RV? My son thought I should for exactly the same reasons. But Tom and I fitted out that Ranger together, we planned our trip around it, and I had an image in my head of how it would be, of the two of us, you know?'

Aitch nodded.

'The Ranger is who I am, who we were. Sometimes it's like he's still here, sitting in the passenger seat. And that's another thing I'm scared of: losing that. I'm not scared of dying, only of living a shadow life.'

Aitch pulled her in closer, and Rena let herself be embraced.

They watched the medical team move back and forth, smooth and efficient. Rena wanted to tell them to hurry up, even though she could see they weren't wasting a second.

Bob was still in the back seat of his police vehicle, and for a while it was impossible to tell exactly what was happening. Then someone raised a bag of fluid into the air, holding it high to get the flow going, and a man in RFDS uniform moved in close with an arrangement of gear, including a backboard and stretcher. They were ready to move Bob from vehicle to plane. Rena scanned their faces: serious, but not grim.

'Rena, Rena!' Aitch gave her arm a gentle squeeze. 'Nurse wants you.'

A woman stood in front of her, blue disposable gloves and gown, stethoscope draped around her neck, medical bag at her feet. She offered Rena a professional smile.

'Right, we're almost set to move him now, but while I have a moment, I want to check that.' She motioned to Rena's leg.

Rena looked down. The wound had bled much more than she'd realised, staining the white fabric wrapped around her thigh a deep red. With that knowledge came an awareness of the pain. She welcomed it, a tiny atonement for what she'd brought upon Bob Fletcher.

'It's just a scratch.'

The nurse arched an eyebrow. 'Right. Someone was shooting at you, but you just what—scratched yourself on a branch? How about you let me be the judge?'

Rena tried to untie her makeshift bandage, but the fibres had swollen, tightening the knot. Before she had a chance to think about it, the nurse was crouched in front of her, scissors in hand. She eased it off, then sat back on her heels, probing the edges of the wound with a professional touch.

'Bloody hell, that must sting.' Aitch had moved so she could also examine the damage.

'Just flesh.' The nurse continued to prod. 'No major vessels, no bone. Straight across the side of your thigh. You want to come with us? We have a spare seat and that really should be properly cleaned and dressed. Maybe a stitch or two. It's going to leave an almighty scar, though.'

Rena shook her head. 'Thanks, but it's not as though I had Tina Turner's legs to begin with. I'll get it sorted at Fitzroy Crossing. My only concern is Detective Fletcher. Please look after him.'

'You're sure?'

She nodded.

The nurse rummaged in her bag and handed Rena a thick gauze pad.

'Liz!' The call came from the doctor, standing next to the open back door of Bob's police Land Cruiser.

'Right, that's me. You will get that taken care of?' She gave Rena a stern look, but didn't wait for her to respond before hurrying away.

Less than five minutes later, they had Bob out of the car, sliding him onto the stretcher with practised ease, arranging monitors around him. When she thought the moment was right, Rena stepped forward, wanting to see him again before they loaded him into the plane. Wanting to remind him not to fucking die. Wanting to say sorry.

Her injured leg almost gave way under her, but she did it, finding a place next to the stretcher as it was wheeled the few metres to the plane. His eyes were open above the oxygen mask covering his nose and mouth, staring straight up as though he was afraid it might be the last time he ever saw the infinite blue of a Kimberley sky.

After a nod of permission from Nurse Liz, Rena eased into Bob's line of vision. He blinked at her, tears forming in the corners of his eyes, and everything Rena had been going to say vanished from her thoughts. On the other side of the stretcher, the nurse noticed and leaned in with a soothing hand on Bob's brow and comforting, reassuring words. But after all she and Tom had been through, Rena knew tears. Bob wasn't frightened. Those were angry, frustrated tears: He was hurting, but he was also seriously pissed off. He was still looking at Rena as they readied the stretcher to move it into the plane and so, although she didn't say anything, she made a silent promise to him. And in that last beat before he was lost to her view, Rena gave him the thumbs-up.

Then the plane door was closed, the engines were powering up and those left on the ground were scrambling to get out of the way. Rena climbed into the Land Cruiser again, slightly surprised to find Aitch back behind the wheel, grateful for the wide-open windows that let the hot wind blow through, driving the metallic scent of blood out and away.

Aitch gunned the engine as soon as Rena closed the door, swinging around the police blockade on the highway, making for Fitzroy Crossing. Rena reached through the open window, angling the side mirror so she could watch the plane take off, winging its way in the opposite direction, climbing fast.

'Where will they take him?' she asked.

'Perth or Darwin, probably Perth.'

They were both silent, the kilometres falling away beneath their wheels, the buffeting wind whipping their hair and clothes. With Bob safe and receiving proper care, Rena turned her mind to Marty. Now that he had the diamonds, could they find him? He'd shot a cop, so they'd throw everything at locating the bastard, but he'd already managed to hide in the outback, and he must have a car or a dirt bike or something. Rena figured the chances of catching him were slim to none. Except two million dollars' worth of diamonds was actually worth fuck all if you couldn't get them to a buyer. Rena's good leg jiggled as her mind churned.

When they reached the outskirts of town, Aitch let the speed drop away.

'I'll take you to the hospital then return this,' she said, slapping the steering wheel.

'No time for hospital.'

'Rena.'

'Look, I'm up-to-date with my tetanus, I'm not gushing blood, and I don't give a fuck if I end up with a scar.'

'Still...'

'We've got shit to do. Aitch, you asked me something back there when we were bush-bashing our way back to the road.'

'Yeah.'

Rena looked across at the woman next to her, seeing the tension in her jaw, the clenched hands on the steering wheel.

'You think it was Tyse, don't you? In the car fire.'

Aitch nodded, swallowing hard.

'Which means—although that crazy fuck Eric had those sneakers—that it's pretty bloody likely Marty killed Tyse too.'

'Why?' It came out as a broken whisper.

'Don't know that yet. But someone might. Every thief needs a fence, a person to sell to.'

'Chuck.'

'Let's ditch the police car, then see if we can find him, shall we?'

THIRTY-SIX

They'd only just parked outside the police station when Ito pulled in behind them. She met them on the hard-packed gravel between the two vehicles, and Rena looked from Ito to Aitch, gauging emotions. The detective wore the expression of a woman still in shock, but wrestling to regain the upper hand: slightly glazed eyes, a jerkiness to her movements as though there was a fractional disconnect between thought and action. Aitch on the other hand had mustered her feelings, corralled off some of the trauma and sadness, and now seemed ready to let anger drive her. Her hands were on her hips, feet planted wide, and the rise and fall of her chest told Rena that Aitch had plenty to say.

Rena positioned herself a fraction in front of Aitch. She didn't think Aitch would have a crack at the detective—it wasn't her style. But a bit of a buffer never hurt anyone, and there was no time to waste on accusations and recriminations. No time for guilt. They could all beat themselves up later about the things they wished they'd done.

'Any update on Bob?' Rena asked.

Ito shook her head. 'They were taking him to Perth, so we won't know anything until they've seen him there. He lost a lot of blood, but he was stable when they left. The crew was, and I quote, cautiously optimistic.'

'Will you let me know when you know?'

Ito nodded. 'When you called in, you said the shooter was Kinnane.'

'It was. No doubt.'

'Fuck. It was a presumptive ID, but fuck. Dental and DNA are still weeks away. If he was lying low, why show himself now?'

'To get the diamonds. He shot Fletcher, then I appeared. Guess he didn't expect it to be me, someone who'd recognise him. He took a shot at me, but I can't quite work out why he didn't follow through and kill me. I mean, now we know he's alive, you'll be hunting him with everything you've got.'

'Damn right.'

'More effort and resources than you people put into Tyse's disappearance,' said Aitch. There was heat in her tone, but Aitch's hands had dropped to her sides. She met Ito's eyes with an unblinking gaze. 'I know it wasn't your case, and I've sure as hell heard all the excuses, but now might be a good time to take that a bit more seriously. Maybe send a DNA sample down to the lab, see who was really in that car.'

'Aitch, I—' Ito began, but Aitch cut the flow of her words with a raised hand.

'Don't need to hear it, because if that is Tyse, and if that prick killed him and nearly took out Detective Fletcher as well, I'll be damned if he not only gets away with murder but gets the diamonds as well.'

'Two,' said Rena.

'What do you mean, two?'

'Not one murder, two. I think he killed Wally as well; he wanted Wally's metal detector to look for the tin of diamonds. Wally often did that stuff and kept quiet about it, and maybe Kinnane was getting desperate. He took a chance, but Wally said no. Then Wally started putting two and two together. He heard that Marty—his client—was the one who died in the fire, which meant whatever was hidden out there was up for grabs. Wally figured it must be worth something and decided to go after the stash for himself.'

'But how would Kinnane know that?'

Rena shrugged. 'Maybe something Wally said in a voicemail when he was trying to make contact. Or maybe something he said to someone else in Fitzroy Crossing, someone connected to Marty Kinnane and the plan to move the diamonds.'

'Chuck.' Aitch spat the name out.

'Chuck? Stewart Rothwell?' said Ito.

Rena explained their thinking. 'So, we—you—need to find Chuck, fast. Maybe you could even find out where he was planning to meet Marty to collect the diamonds.'

'How about you both come inside and we can talk about all this properly? Get you a sandwich, some water. You look as though you need something.'

Rena frowned. 'With all due respect, Detective, what the hell?'

Ito shrugged. 'It's a great theory, except for one thing. We scooped Chuck up not long after the three of you left this morning.'

'But that's great! You can squeeze the little prick until he tells you where the meet is, then be in position when Marty Kinnane shows.' Aitch smacked a fist into the palm of her other hand.

'Yeah, about that. Mr Rothwell wasn't very forthcoming at first. Quick to lawyer up and shut up. At least now I know why he had that smirk on his face when I told him we were looking at him for Kinnane's murder.'

'Can't you cut a deal? Lesser charges or a good word with the judge in exchange for information.'

Ito held out her hands, palms up, and shrugged. 'Not this time.'

'Why not?'

'Because when you called after Bob...when you called'—Ito nodded at Rena—'and told me who had shot him, I went back to Rothwell. I told him we had Kinnane and that not only was Kinnane talking, he was pinning the car-fire death squarely on Chuck Rothwell. Then I told him I was also going to do him for shooting Wally.'

'And?' Rena couldn't keep the frustration from her voice. She didn't want explanations; she wanted to move.

'And that's one thing about some crims; they have standards. Theft, smuggling, cheating, blackmail...all just a way to make a quid. But they don't stretch to physical violence and murder. Chuck was affronted that I'd suggest such a thing, then when I drove the point home and he realised there was a fair chance he'd cop a murder charge, he turned chatty. Told me everything.'

Ito paused. Rena wanted to grab the woman's shirt and give her a shake. Then Ito sighed and shook her head.

'He said he had nothing to do with Kinnane personally, but he'd heard the rumour about Marty's stash and hoped he could get in on it.'

'Bullshit,' said Aitch.

'He was counting on Rena to do the hard work, then he was going to swoop in and nick the stuff. Chuck also has an alibi for the car fire—which we were able to verify easily. At the moment he's still in the lockup, but I honestly don't think he knows anything about Kinnane's plans.'

'So we're fucked. Marty Kinnane has his diamonds, he knows the country, and presumably he has a way to smuggle them out. He'll go to ground out there and quietly return to civilisation in some other town days or weeks from now. Fucking murderer gets away with it. Shit.' Aitch turned, raking both hands through her hair.

Aitch's words shook an errant thought loose in Rena's brain. Back there, looking at Marty with the gun trained on her, Rena was sure she was about to die. And she didn't care. In fact, Rena felt a flash of gratitude: The decision was out of her hands; she wouldn't have to go on without Tom anymore.

So she turned her back, expecting a bullet that never came. Why hadn't Marty shot her, the one person who could ID him? Part of her was still pissed off to be alive, so the question had niggled away, and now she thought she had the answer.

'That's it!' she said, slapping the back of her hand against Aitch's bicep.

'What?'

'I know why he didn't shoot me.'

'How does that help?'

'He didn't shoot me because it doesn't matter anymore if I, you, the police, the whole damn Kimberley know Marty Kinnane is alive.'

'Why not?'

'Because he's not going to ground. He's not going to hide out. Marty fucking Kinnane has a plan to get the diamonds and himself out of the country really quickly, probably within the next twelve to twenty-four hours.'

Ito and Aitch exchanged a look, raised eyebrows, a mouth shrug from Ito. It was an expression Rena read as, *The old broad might be right.*

'Okay, I'll bite,' said Aitch. 'How?'

'No idea.'

'So we're still fucked.'

'Possibly. But I'm going to phone a friend.'

THIRTY-SEVEN

'Rena! Margot and I were just talking about you. How are you? Where have you been?' Les sounded much better than the last time they'd spoken, but Rena didn't have time for bonhomie.

'Nowhere really, Les.'

'There's a lot of nowhere out there in the Kimberley, Rena. Can you be more specific? I'd like to look it up on the map. Doing a lot of my living vicariously these days.'

There was no way Rena would get what she wanted without making this conversational concession.

'I'm in the crossing now, but I've been on the Gibb River Road. Checked out a few places up that way, then swung back down here. I know you'll want me to give you chapter and verse, so you and Margot better invite me over when I'm back in town.' She took a quick breath and ploughed on before Les could get a word in.

'Thanks for that message you sent me. Very helpful, but I do have one question.'

'Shoot.'

Rena winced. She was still outside the police station, pacing—albeit with a slight limp—up and down as she talked. Aitch and Ito were supposed to be going inside to deal with some admin and rustle up food and coffee, but she could see them hovering, standing just to one side of the door. They were making a bad job of feigning conversation; both of them kept glancing her way.

She batted a hand at them then turned her back.

'You mentioned all the ingenious ways people managed to get diamonds out of Australia.'

Les laughed. 'You wouldn't believe some of the ideas they dreamed up and got away with.'

'Try me.'

'Well, I don't know about now, but when Argyle was in full swing, it was a criminal offence to sell or distribute rough diamonds in the whole of Western Australia. They brought in a lot of special laws with the Argyle Legislation and amendments to the Crimes Act. Easy enough to get them out of the state, but out of the country was another thing entirely. Of course, because diamonds from any given region have their own characteristics, a specialist diamond merchant could easily recognise an Argyle pink, so anything turning up outside the usual channels would raise a red flag. That meant a thief didn't just have to smuggle diamonds out of Australia; he also needed contacts overseas: a cutter in Antwerp, a dealer in London with a veneer of respectability. Someone who could magic up a backstory and provenance for the stones.'

'Sure, sure. But tell me how they got them to Antwerp or wherever.' Rena tried to keep the impatience from her voice, but that was the problem with getting your information from a consummate storyteller. Any attempt to interfere with the rhythm of the narrative caused problems.

'Is there more to the Marty Kinnane story? Has his fabled cache turned up?' Les's tone was sharp and Rena could picture the glint of bifocals, the lines on his wrinkled brow deepening as bushy eyebrows arched.

'Les. Mate. I can't tell you much just yet—I'm here with the police—but I'll give you the whole story as soon as I can. For now, I need your word that this goes no further.'

Rena heard a sharp inhalation and knew she had Les on side.

'The diamonds have turned up, but the cops think they're heading out of the country. Soon. I told them you'd know how it was done in the past, which at least gives them a starting point for now.'

'So the game's afoot!' Les actually cackled. 'In that case... There's body cavities and swallowing packages, just like the drug smugglers do. But then there was also a network of airline cabin crew with diamonds in tubes of pink toothpaste, bottles of pink shampoo, and jars of high-end face cream. All carried in their personal luggage, of course. Word is they got somewhere between thirty and fifty million dollars' worth of stones out that way.'

Rena whistled. 'Any recovered?'

'Hardly a one.'

Rena was silent. If Marty had a setup like that, their chances of intercepting the stones were virtually none. She'd pass the info on to Ito, but short of watching for Marty or, hypothetically, rummaging through the sponge bag of every person flying out of Perth International, there was nothing much they could do.

'Any stories about people who didn't have a network of crooked cronies? Greedy, paranoid bastards? Whatever you've got, Les, however tenuous. Anything about how a lone operator could get diamonds out quickly and quietly?'

Rena could hear Les's wheezy breathing over the line, Margot murmuring in the background. She looked over at the police station. Ito and Aitch had given up all pretence and were now gesticulating at her—big, questioning shrugs from Ito and some watch tapping and miming of a crank handle by Aitch, the unmistakable sign to wind things up.

'Well, there was something. A bit fanciful and still more than one person but maybe only one or two more, and a far more covert setup. It was only rumour and innuendo, though, you know, a friend of a friend overheard something somewhere. So more than likely just a story, the sort of legend that grows around diamond heists. Although, now I think of it, perhaps the fact it seems so unbelievable is actually the mark of a slick operation.'

'Cut to the chase, Les.'

'Sorry, Rena, sorry. They moved the diamonds out of the country at Horizontal Falls.'

'Come again?'

'It's the place where all the cruise boats come in, or you can fly in on a tour from Broome or Derby. You get off your boat or seaplane and get on a small boat to go through the falls when the tide is running.'

'Right.'

'So a diamond thief—let's call him Kinnane—flies in on a day tour. Kinnane gets on a tour boat for the run through the falls and at some point passes the stones to a cruise passenger who's joined the same boat. Tour ends, Kinnane goes, and the cruise passenger gets back on their ship, sails out of Talbot Bay and that's it.'

'Why there?'

'Traffic. Lots of day tours, some overnight tours, and most of all, lots of bigger cruises coming and going. And it's bloody remote.'

'What about private boats? Could you sail a small boat into Talbot Bay?'

'Definitely.'

'Thanks, Les. I've got to go.'

'You'll let me know what happens?' Les's voice quavered with excitement.

'You'll be the first. Love to Margot.' Rena tapped the screen of her phone, ending the call.

She turned to Ito and Aitch, who were already heading her way.

'I've got another sight to see. And to think I thought solo travel was going to be boring.'

THIRTY-EIGHT

Ito didn't like it. She'd already got her team to issue a bulletin with Kinnane's description and orders to approach with caution. It would be circulated to all Australian international airports because that, she told Rena, was the way small-time crims got out of the country. Only gangsters like Tony Mokbel had the wherewithal to escape in a private yacht. Besides, on the off-chance Kinnane was planning to abscond by boat, the obvious places to get out were Fremantle or Darwin. Derby or Broome at the very least. Hauling your arse to somewhere remote like Talbot Bay only added layers of complexity.

But, as Rena pointed out, just west of Talbot Bay were the islands of the Buccaneer Archipelago; shifty bastards had plied those remote waters for centuries. If someone was pursuing you, where better to disappear? If they weren't close on your tail, how would they even know you'd gone, let alone where? Remote meant few witnesses.

'But how is he going to get there?' asked Aitch.

They'd moved inside, set themselves up in a meeting room with coffee, tea, and sandwiches. Halloran and a couple of other uniforms were propping up the corners of the room, taking notes, ducking in and out to variously check on or update things.

'He has a vehicle or dirt bike,' said Rena.

'Yeah, nah. That gets him out of whatever remote corner he's been holed up in, but there's no way to get to Talbot Bay and the Horizontal Falls except seaplane or boat.'

'Right, but how close could he get? Could he actually get himself there or not? Close enough to send up a drone, make a drop? Or nowhere remotely in the neighbourhood?'

'There are no roads into that area. At all.' Ito was biting off her words.

'We're not talking about roads, mate...Detective.'

'I'm telling you there's nothing. No access.'

'Show me. Where's your map?'

Glances were exchanged, and Ito nodded to a young policewoman at the back of the room, who had short blond hair and an eager face.

'Find us a detailed map, would you please, Constable?'

'Ma'am.' She dipped her head and hurried from the room. Rena remembered being that enthusiastic about work. Fitzroy Crossing probably wasn't the easiest of postings, but this would certainly represent a break from the ordinary.

'There has to be some way to get up there. I know it seems implausible, but the more I think about it, the more I'm sure that Marty Kinnane is planning on leaving with his diamonds from somewhere near Horizontal Falls.'

'It's not implausible; it's fucking crazy,' said Ito.

'Only if it doesn't work.' Rena drummed the fingers of her left hand on the table. She'd applied Betadine and a fresh bandage to her bullet wound then downed two Panamax, and now the paracetamol was doing its job, the pain in her leg reduced to a dull throb.

'Look, maybe the reason Kinnane didn't finish me off was he thought I was already dead. Maybe he thought I was injured enough to not be a problem, or maybe the prick recognised me and had a pang of remorse.'

Someone snorted.

'No, I'm not buying that one either. But the other alternative is, time was a factor. If he's meeting a cruise boat or a yacht, it's only going to be there—wherever there is—for a prescribed period of time. Miss it and the whole plan is fucked.'

'But surely it would've only taken a minute to hunt you down and shoot you again?' Aitch put a sarcastic spin on her words.

'Unless he thought Fletcher or I might be waiting to ambush him, or he knew you'd be along shortly and that would mean more trouble. Maybe it gave the sick bastard a thrill to know he'd been recognised, that his clever plan had a witness; I don't know. But he's a thief and a murderer, and I reckon he's planning on getting out of the country. So can we concentrate on that rather than your confusion over my continued existence?'

Ito sighed. 'Coast guards have been alerted, but they can't be everywhere at once.'

'Which is why I'm going.' Rena slapped the palm of her hand on the table. 'I'll get on the next tourist flight from wherever I can—Derby, Broome, Kununurra—get down there and…'

'And what?

'Look for Marty, look for his contact and the boat they're probably going to escape on, then let you know.'

'Rena, if you want to see the Horizontal Falls, fine. But come on—this is crazy! There are dozens of easier ways to skip the country with a small parcel of stones. Why not head for Darwin and a fishing trawler?'

Rena was about to answer when the constable reappeared. She handed a map to Ito, who unfolded it on the table between them, then stretched across and jammed a finger onto it.

'This is where you encountered Kinnane.' Ito dragged her finger across the paper, moving northwest. 'And here is Talbot Bay and Horizontal Falls. This bit'—her finger ran a manic circle around a section of coast—'includes the Dambimangari Indigenous Protected Area, a military area, and a nature reserve.'

Ito sat down so heavily her chair rocked back and she threw her hands into the air. 'It's a fairy story. And we've talked about this enough. I've got more important things to do, realistic leads to follow.' She began to gather her things.

Rena stood, leaning over the map. It was recent, detailed, and confirmed everything Ito was saying. Between the Gibb River Road and Talbot Bay, there was a vast swathe of open country, much of it shaded red, restricted. She'd been a fool. Letting Les's wild stories grab hold of her imagination.

'Detective Ito, I—' she began, forming an apology as she spoke.

'No, I said enough.' Ito was already moving towards the door, her officers falling in behind her.

Rena started to straighten up, when a notation on the map caught her eye. She bent closer. The word was hard to read, buried beneath the red. 'Ito!'

'Leave it, Rena. That ship has sailed,' said Aitch. Her voice was gentle, but she was on her feet too. 'Come on.'

'But this is it! This explains how Marty Kinnane can get to Talbot Bay.' Rena tapped an urgent finger on the map.

'Mate.'

'Look! Right there. Oobagooma.'

'It's military. Let it go.'

'It's a fucking uranium mine. It's someone else's, but Verne Industries also has a mine in that area!'

'How is that possible?' Aitch moved forward to peer at the map.

'It happens. A mining company gets consent from the Commonwealth and the Department of Defence—maybe pays compensation—and hey, presto, a mine on restricted military land. Anyway, look. There's an access track on that land leading from Meda on the Gibb River Road running all the way up to here.'

As she spoke, Rena traced the line on the map. 'Then it's not far to Talbot Bay.'

'But…'

'Marty Kinnane was working for Verne. Even if he isn't actually supposed to have access to that mine site, how hard do you think it would be for someone like him to steal or fake some other worker's permissions?'

'Well, shit.'

'Yeah. And if he's been driving since we parted company, he's got a bloody good head start.'

'Not if we're flying in.'

'We?'

'That prick killed Tyse. You'd better fucking believe it's we.'

THIRTY-NINE

They didn't waste any more time.

While Aitch went to look for Ito to tell her about Rena's discovery, Rena got busy searching for last-minute spots on a Horizontal Falls tour. The Wi-Fi connection in the Fitzroy Crossing police station was fast and reliable, and after a few minutes surfing the net on her phone, Rena found what they needed. Then she put in a call. It wasn't that she was averse to booking things online, but given the short notice, she wanted the certainty of talking to an actual person.

With no idea how quickly Marty would get to Talbot Bay, Rena played it safe and booked the overnight package: flight from Derby, numerous boat trips both through the falls and in the surrounding waters, and overnight accommodation on a houseboat in a premium cabin.

'Guest names?' The booker asked, his tone perfunctory.

'Rena and Hepzibah.'

There was a momentary silence.

'I'm sorry, I didn't quite catch that.'

'Rena.'

'Yes.'

'And Hepzibah. H-E-P-Z...'

'Very good. I'm ready for your credit card number when you are.' The man's tone was bright.

Rena rattled it off from memory, unconcerned about the cost.

After a bit of back-and-forth confirming details, Rena ended the call. It was only a two-and-a-half-hour drive to Derby, a trip they could realistically make at dawn tomorrow and still be in time for the flight. But Rena wanted to move, to feel like she was closing the distance. She made for the door, almost crashing into Aitch, who was hurrying back in. They stopped either side of the threshold.

'Ito's already gone. Apparently, they're setting up a task force in Broome. And pretty much anyone they could spare from here, Halls Creek, and Kununurra is out looking.'

'So it's just us?'

Aitch shrugged. 'I've asked them to pass along the message, and I know it'll get done; it's really a question of whether Ito is prepared to listen. I mean, if someone says, *Ma'am, there's an urgent message for you here from a Rena Novak. It's about Horizontal Falls*, well...'

'Fair point. We'll hope for the best. Meanwhile I have us booked on the overnight trip, leaving Derby tomorrow morning. Oh, and we're sharing.'

'Fine by me. Probably going to be the talk of the Kimberley within a day, though.' Aitch flashed a quick smile.

'What say we head down to Derby tonight?'

'Nup. Time we got you to the hospital and got your bloody leg seen to.'

Rena shook her head. 'Not necessary. I'll go to the chemist, grab an extra packet of painkillers and some antiseptic. That'll do.'

'We have a few hours up our sleeve, and you need treatment,' said Aitch.

'It's just a big bloody gouge. They'll flush it, tut a bit, and we will have wasted everybody's time. They've got actual sick people to look after.'

'If I didn't know better, I'd say you were afraid, Rena.'

Rena looked down, fiddling with her phone.

'Seriously, is that it?' Aitch's voice was gentle, a semitone lower.

'I'm not afraid. It's just… I just…' She looked up, then turned away, blinking hard. 'Since my husband… I haven't been in a hospital since Tom died, and when I think of setting foot there, smelling those smells, hearing those machines, the squeak of rubber shoes and wheels on lino, the rattle of a curtain pulled around a bed… I don't know if I'll be able to keep my shit together.'

Aitch was watching her, head to one side, eyes full of sympathy, and Rena braced herself for commiseration and cajoling. But then Aitch put a hand on her shoulder.

'No sweat, I hear you, mate. But this is Fitzroy Crossing. It's nothing like your big-city hospitals; there are only twenty-six beds. Besides, your leg needs attention, and more importantly, this is the perfect excuse for me to visit a certain nurse. I mean, no offence, but in this situation you're the perfect wingwoman. I get to look compassionate and reliable, and your job is to talk me up while he sutures or bandages or whatever. So, forget you, this is really about me.' Aitch smiled.

'You're going to make eyes at each other and bond over my bloody thigh?'

'Baby steps, mate. Baby steps.'

'Well, I suppose it's more romantic than waiting till my injury turns septic.'

'That's the spirit. Let's go.' Aitch increased the pressure on Rena's shoulder, and Rena reached up, patting Aitch's hand with her own.

'You're a dickhead, you know that, right?' Rena broke the contact and moved into the hall.

'Yeah, but I'm a dickhead who cares.'

'You want me to feign a heart attack? Give you a chance to impress your nurse with a bit of CPR.' Rena spoke over her shoulder as they made their way out of the police station.

'Nah, mate. I may be caring, but if there's any mouth-to-mouth happening, you're not part of the picture.'

'Right. I'll keep it to a few yelps of pain then.'

'Good woman.'

It was still dark when they left the next morning in Aitch's ute, Rena in the passenger seat with a clean bandage on her leg and Aitch behind the wheel, a broad smile plastered across her face.

They'd exchanged hello grunts and collected coffees from the servo, then Rena asked, 'How'd you sleep? I was out like a light on those painkillers.'

'Sleep?' said Aitch, her smile getting even wider.

After that, Rena abandoned the small talk. There had been no word from Ito, despite Rena leaving messages on her mobile, and the hospital in Perth wasn't releasing any details about Bob Fletcher's condition, except through official police channels. In lieu of conversation, Rena fiddled with the aged radio until she found a reasonable signal. Music and talk eventually gave way to news, and suddenly Ito's voice was filling the ute's cab.

Detective Fletcher has undergone surgery and is currently in a serious but stable condition.

Aitch leaned over, no longer smiling, and turned up the volume.

The suspect is currently at large, but we are closing in and expect to be making an arrest soon.

'Bullshit,' murmured Rena.

Police and border force have been mobilised across the state, and indeed, the country. As this is an ongoing investigation...

The audio switched to a reporter, who gave a detailed description of Marty then finished with:

Police warn Martin Kinnane is armed and dangerous. If you see a man matching his description, do not approach, but phone triple-O immediately.

Rena punched the On/Off button, silencing the radio. 'Maybe we should call triple-O and report a sighting of Marty at Talbot Bay.'

Aitch grimaced. 'Either they'd send someone, there'd be no sign of the fucker and we'd have wasted police time and be in the shit. Or—and this is more likely—all tips are reported up the chain, Ito would get it, dismiss it out of hand, and you'd still be in the shit.'

'Or they might send someone and nab him with the stones.'

'Mate, I hear you. I'm in this car, about to catch a plane and share a damn cabin with you because I reckon you might be right. But if you were Ito, if you had finite people and resources to deploy, what would you do?'

'I'd tell me to piss off.'

'Right.'

Rena sighed. 'Well, if I'm wrong, at least I'll be wrong in one of the most spectacular environments in the world.'

'Remind me to take a selfie of us.'

'Shut up and drive.'

FORTY

The plane was small, a twelve-seat Cessna Caravan capable of landing on water or a runway. In the terminal, Rena hung back until she'd had a chance to suss out their fellow passengers. She didn't expect to see Marty on this or any other flight, but she checked anyway, and once she was sure she was among strangers, she gave each of them the once-over. If Marty were passing the stones to someone, then at this point, everyone was a suspect. Well, except for the five children accompanying two sets of parents. Rena had heard of computer whiz kids pulling off major crimes like hacking into databases and scamming money, but she figured it was safe to assume none of the under fifteens on the flight were part of an international diamond smuggling syndicate. She said as much to Aitch, who raised a sceptical eyebrow.

'Mate, don't you know the first rule of conspiracy theorists everywhere is trust no one? What if it's one of the parents using their kid for cover? Haven't you heard of people shoplifting and hiding the loot in the pram under the baby's blanket? Or trying to smuggle shit out of the country in the lap of a wheelchair patient?' Aitch kept her voice low, flicking her eyes sideways to a man currently holding a pink, glittery unicorn backpack and nursing a takeaway coffee while his curly-haired daughter ran amok.

They were sitting on the uncomfortable chairs ubiquitous to airports everywhere, a view of the tarmac and their plane to the left, and a counter to the right where staff were currently preparing to weigh each passenger before embarkation.

'Fair call,' said Rena. ' So if we can't trust anyone, even the toddlers, what say we just look for Kinnane?'

'The moment you point him out, I'm ready. Which reminds me, in case I see him first...'

'Yeah?'

'What does Marty Kinnane actually look like?'

'You're kidding.' Rena twisted in her seat, pulling away from Aitch and favouring her with a look of incredulity.

'Nup. I mean, up until yesterday we thought he was dead and before that he wasn't even on my radar, except for what you told me about the crap that was going down with the violet diamonds. Not relevant, mate. Not relevant. But now we know he's not only alive and kicking but a shitheel as well; it matters.'

Ever since the moment the officer had told her the corpse in the burnt-out car was presumed to be Marty Kinnane, Rena had held an image of the man in her mind, but it was the Marty she had known decades ago, a man she'd not seen for more than twenty years. Back then, Marty had been a cocky bastard, confident of his own abilities in everything and not afraid to tell you about it. Easy enough to see why he'd stolen the diamonds and probably part of the reason he'd gotten away with it. Marty was the sort to breeze past security checks, joking with guards, offering bags and pockets for inspection and secretly laughing his arse off because he had the stolen diamonds somewhere else. He had a certain magnetism, until you saw through him. Yet looks-wise Marty Kinnane was best described as average: average height, average weight, slightly square-jawed but otherwise unremarkable face except for his eyes. His eyes were an unusually light shade of yellow-brown and they seemed small, until you realised Marty always had them partly closed as he sized up whatever situation he was in.

Rena hadn't worked closely with him for very long, but it had been long enough to see through the matey facade to the snake beneath. Over time, her own experiences were given weight by the stories of others. And on the one occasion—a work Christmas function—when Tom had met Marty Kinnane, he'd come back to Rena shaking his head. 'Keep away from him, Reenie. He'd tuck you in, say good night, then murder you in your sleep that one,' he'd said.

Rena had forgotten all about Tom's assessment until she'd seen Marty yesterday, pointing a gun at her. Then it had come flooding back.

The image of Marty standing there was crystal clear in Rena's mind, and she painted the picture for Aitch. Kinnane was essentially the same man he'd been all those years ago, but now he sported the beginnings of a paunch, and the face beneath the hat had more lines, crow's-feet emphasising the narrowed, calculating eyes. Rena had also registered that Marty Kinnane had some sort of tattoo wrapping around the bicep of his right arm, the one holding the gun.

'What sort of ink and how big? Lots of colours?' asked Aitch.

'One dark colour—black or dark blue. I was too far away to make out what it was, although to be honest, I wasn't exactly worried about his tattoo; it sure as hell wasn't a peace symbol.' Rena glanced quickly around the small terminal, aware that the volume of her voice had risen as she relived the moment.

No one was looking their way, in fact, everyone else was now lining up at the counter and taking their turn on the scales. She refocussed on Aitch.

'If you pushed me to describe the tattoo, I'd say it was like a mountain range.'

Aitch nodded slowly. 'Weird eyes, tat, got it. I'll keep a lookout.'

They both stood, joining the line for the weigh-in. Rena watched the people ahead of them. A woman at the front was arguing about the reading on the scales, but otherwise everyone was relaxed, ready for a day trip or an overnight adventure. As soon as they were processed, people drifted over to the door opening out to the tarmac. There was no security screen, no baggage x-ray or metal detector; presumably there was no need.

Rena leaned forward, closer to Aitch, who stood just ahead of her. 'Hey,' she murmured.

Aitch turned her head, eyebrows raised.

'Just remember if you see that tat or those eyes, there's a gun involved.' Rena kept her voice to a whisper.

Aitch nodded, and they both looked over at the little girl holding one of her dad's hands, the other clutching the unicorn backpack.

For the first time, Rena hoped she was wrong about Marty Kinnane and Horizontal Falls.

FORTY-ONE

The plane took off to the west then immediately banked, bearing almost due north. There was enough engine noise to make talking difficult, but Rena didn't care. She was pressed up against the large window, watching the country unfold beneath them. They crossed Stokes Bay, leaving behind the characteristic mudflats and mangroves of the Fitzroy floodplain for the sandstone of the Kimberley foreland. It was harsh, remote, and utterly spectacular. The aerial view gave Rena a different perspective on the geology, but she really wanted to be down amongst it. Was that where Marty was, thousands of feet below, also making his way to Talbot Bay?

With some effort, Rena pushed thoughts of Marty Kinnane aside; there was nothing to do right now but enjoy the flight. As she leaned her forehead against the Plexiglas, Rena could almost hear Tom's hearty laugh; he'd never lost his joy in life and would have been as excited and delighted as a child to be in this small amphibious plane, flying in perfect weather over red earth and cerulean sea.

Rena blinked hard but still had to pull off her sunglasses and scrub a hand across her eyes. She kept her back to the other passengers, face to the view, and hoped no one noticed. *Shit, Tom.*

The pilot was tracking up the coast now, making sure everyone had a chance to see as much as possible. Rugged islands, coral reefs in brilliant turquoise waters, soaring sea cliffs, and craggy headlands, most of it made up of rocks deposited in the Kimberley Basin over 1.7 billion years ago.

The plane swung over the Buccaneer Archipelago, where rocks had been buckled into large folds and broken along fault lines by ancient movements of the earth. The same folding had produced the Horizontal Falls, tilting rocks up until they were nearly vertical before the sea breached a sandstone weakness, eroding its way along a join or crack to create a narrow gap, then hollowing out a wider inlet in the mudstone and shale that lay further inland.

As the plane began its final descent, Rena started to worry about Marty again. There were a number of boats dotted about in the water below, ranging from small private yachts to a cruise ship big enough to carry a couple of hundred passengers. Any of those watercraft could be part of Marty's plan, which just brought home to Rena how crazy this whole thing was. Short of clapping eyes on the man, there was no way for Aitch and her to do this. She hoped Ito had at least sent Marty's description to the people who worked here and to the captains of the larger vessels.

The plane dropped further, skimming the surface of Talbot Bay, then they were down, taxiing through calm waters to a pontoon and large houseboat. Around her, people were laughing at the novelty, thrilled to be in this incredible location. All Rena felt was grim determination.

She remembered the sharp, hot pain of the bullet ripping the flesh of her leg, an annoyance, an insult, but ultimately nothing. Then she thought of Bob, sitting in the dirt, in an ever-widening pool of his own blood.

For most people, seeing the Horizontal Falls was a once-in-a-lifetime experience, a bucket list thing. If Marty Kinnane turned up here—with or without a gun, Rena didn't care—she'd do whatever it took to nail the bastard. Rena would see the Horizontal Falls knowing lifetimes were finite, buckets ultimately kicked.

FORTY-TWO

'So what now?' Aitch was waiting for her on the pontoon dock as Rena stepped from the plane. They'd been separated during the flight, the pilot allocating seats to achieve the best weight distribution.

'Hang on.'

They handed in their life jackets and edged away from a cluster of selfie-taking fellow travellers. The tour company ran a slick operation, governed by the eleven-metre tides, and there was already a crew member beckoning to them, hurrying them upstairs to where morning tea waited.

'Twenty minutes!' the man called, pointing out cabins, answering questions and somehow keeping everyone flowing in the right direction.

'So, I repeat, what now?' said Aitch, as they leaned against the railing.

Rena tugged off her baseball cap. 'Damned if I know. I got us this far; I was hoping you'd have something to offer by now.'

Aitch snorted. 'I reckon we start by asking these people about the other boats around here, see who's new, who's been hanging around without actually looking at the falls, that sort of thing.

Maybe the staff out here party with blow-ins, or maybe they push out a tinny in the evenings to go fishing and they see things.'

'Sounds like a plan. What reason do we give for asking?'

'How about you're thinking of buying a boat and doing the grey nomad thing by sea, tracing the coast? You want to know if many people do that and come here, what the camaraderie is like, all that sort of stuff.'

'But if anyone asks me a boat question, I have no idea what I'm talking about.'

'Mate, you've already proven you're a bullshit artist. You can come up with something.'

'And where are you in all this?'

'I'm your good friend.'

'So we're planning to sail the high seas together?'

'Bloody hell.'

They dumped their backpacks in their cabin, then Aitch led the way out onto the lower deck and around to starboard where boats were docked, ready to run the Horizontal Falls. Rena could see a uniformed employee bent over one of the boat engines and was about to call out when the man straightened up and spotted them. He stepped to the edge of the boat, frowning; then his face lit up.

'Aitch! As I live and bloody breathe! What the hell are you doing here?'

'Cam?' said Aitch. Rena could hear shock and disbelief in her voice.

The man—Cam, apparently—jumped onto the dock and hurried toward them. Rena stepped aside, allowing him to come face-to-face with Aitch. For a moment, they stared at each other, then he wrapped bear-like arms around Aitch, pulling her into a massive hug. Aitch, surprise still evident in her slightly wide eyes, returned the gesture.

Cam looked to be about Aitch's age, with a nuggety build: the strong legs of a man used to balancing on a boat's deck, calloused hands, trim, dark-brown beard, and blue eyes framed by a sunglasses-shaped tan and wrinkles, the sort acquired by staring out over vast distances and squinting into the sun.

Rena took a couple of steps away and turned so she was half-looking out over the water while still observing the two. She waited through a second, smaller hug and a fist bump.

'So. What the hell *are* you doing here?' asked Cam.

By way of answer, Aitch gestured to Rena. 'Before I answer that, I want you to meet a friend of mine. Cameron, this is Rena. Rena, Cam. Cam and I were at school together in Broome. Haven't seen each other in what? Ten, fifteen years?'

Rena stuck out her hand, and Cam gripped it firmly, giving it a hearty shake.

'Nice office,' said Rena.

Cam laughed. 'I know, right? I think part of the reason Aitch here looks like she's seen a ghost is that last time she saw me, I was heading for law school in Melbourne. You here for the day or overnight?'

Rena shot Aitch a questioning look and got a small nod in return: Aitch trusted this bloke.

'We're here for the night—'

'Sweet! We can catch up later, but more importantly, you're gunna be blown away by the falls—eighth wonder of the world!'

'The thing is,' said Rena, 'we're looking for someone.'

'Here? One of our people?'

'No,' Aitch jumped in. 'Well maybe someone meeting one of your people. But probably not.'

'You're not making much sense right now, Aitch.' Cam screwed up his face, an exaggerated parody of confusion.

Rena leant close to Cam, lowering her voice. 'Long story short. We think a bloke who stole Argyle diamonds and killed a couple of people might try to get out of the country from here. We reckon he's still on his way, but he might have a contact here, either with a private boat or on something like that'—she gestured at the cruise ship—'to help him.'

'You're pulling my leg.' Cam smiled.

'I wish.'

'Because the boss had a call from the WA Police asking about any unusual activity or the like. We all had a good laugh. But you're dead serious?'

'I know it sounds crazy, but yeah, we are. The police are keeping tabs on all the conventional routes, and chances are they'll pick him up somewhere, but...'

'I mean, I guess it could be done. There are boats in and out of here all the time; cruise companies large and small, private things; we don't keep tabs.'

'Talk to any of them?'

'Hardly ever. Some of the private people, maybe, when they're out in their dinghies. But mostly that's just a hello, a wave and make sure they're out of our way.' Cam shrugged. 'But, Christ! Are you saying this bloke might come overland? That's impossible! The whole region is locked up tighter than a fish's bum.'

'When he's not stealing and murdering, the man in question is a field geologist who works for mining companies. I—we—think he's probably got access and a dirt bike.'

'Fuck.' Cam turned and spat in the water. 'Those fucking mining companies and the goddamn government. If it's not uranium, it's copper, and do you know there are a couple of mining tenements less than three Ks away? And they're active? They've got this'—he threw his arms wide, taking in the entirety of Talbot Bay and the McLarty Range behind them—'one of the most amazing places on the planet, a pristine environment—and they're going to screw it up.'

Cam looked like he was only getting started, but Aitch put a hand on his shoulder. 'Mate. Agree. And I'm sure the Dambimangari people agree. But right now, the point is we reckon this fucker can get here, and if he does we need to stop him from leaving.'

Cam's hands had curled into tight fists, but after few more muttered profanities, he blew out a heavy breath. 'Okay. I'm in. What do you need me to do?'

'Don't ask me; talk to the boss.' She gestured to Rena.

Rena looked at Aitch and Cam, then out across the water of Talbot Bay to the twenty-metre-wide breach in the nearest ridge of the McLarty Range, the outermost of the two gaps that made up the Horizontal Falls. At the moment, the water was comparatively calm. She let her gaze roam over the sandstone strata, the colours marking the tide height: black at the bottom, then white, then shading into red. Through the gap Rena could see the second ridge, about three hundred metres farther back.

'Do you go through the second gap?' she asked.

'No, never,' said Cam. 'The Traditional Owners call the falls Garaanngaddim, and it's an important place. They ask that no one goes through that gap, so we don't. But if you're asking me if I could go through, navigate it, yes, when the tide wasn't running. It's only about seven metres wide, so it's dangerous when the water's really flowing. I wouldn't do it alone, and I'd certainly never risk it with passengers.'

'I doubt Marty would give a stuff for the wishes of the Traditional Owners, but that's good to know.' Rena turned around and rested her hips against the railing. 'I think all we can do is watch and wait. And have a fast boat ready in case we need it. That's your job, Cam. How powerful is your boat?'

'Nine hundred horsepower.'

'That sounds impressive.'

'When we run the falls in about an hour or so, you'll see for yourself how she goes against the water.' He jerked his head towards the boat behind him with its four large motors.

'Ah, that brings me to the next point. Show me your tide chart.'

'Why?'

'There are two possibilities here. Either Marty has a small craft stashed somewhere up a gorge or even back beyond the second set of falls, in which case he has to come out when the water is calm, like now.'

As one, they all turned to look at the water flowing through the nearest gap. To Rena's eye, it already looked a bit more active, with a little bit more chop and ripple. She could hear the faint drone of a plane on a scenic flight, the volume rising as it neared.

'What's the second?' asked Aitch.

'Someone out here—or who will soon arrive out here—goes back through both gaps and picks him up. They have to look like tourists, but they also have to get through the second gap without attracting too much attention.'

'So, what are you thinking?'

'You could go through the first gap at any time then tour the embayment, fiddle around back there for as long as you needed, except for one thing.'

'What?'

Rena pointed skywards, where a small plane was now visible, tracing a graceful curve high above them. 'Scenic flights, helicopters, seaplanes. All full of people looking and taking photos. With pilots who might raise an alarm if they saw something unusual.'

'Which means...' Aitch's eyes widened.

'Yep. I reckon Marty is going to try to get through the Horizontal Falls at night.'

FORTY-THREE

That afternoon, they joined some tourists, and Cam took them through the falls on the inbound tide. The calendar had just ticked over into September, and with the change of seasons came the spring tides; today it would peak at 10.3 metres, tonight at 10.56 and in between, it would drop by more than nine metres. These huge tidal shifts created the Horizontal Falls—the change so rapid, the water level rose or fell out in Talbot Bay too quickly for the level in the embayment and beyond to keep pace, causing water to build up against the narrow gaps. Rena found it hard to get her head around the idea that at its peak, water was flowing at about one million litres per second.

As Cam swung the boat through the gap and into the embayment, Rena could actually see a difference in the water level before the boat powered through in a cloud of spray. To either side of them, vicious currents swirled close to the rocks, sometimes even sucking their powerful boat sideways for a metre or so before releasing them into the general turbulence, white water, and small whirlpools that whispered of ferocity beneath the surface.

Rena had chosen to sit in the back so she could watch Cam work as well as appreciate the land and sea. When he had the boat in calm waters, she leaned close.

'What's the force of the current like in the middle of the gap right now? What would happen if you fell in?' she asked, raising her voice over the boat's engines.

Cam's face was impassive behind mirrored sunglasses. 'Don't fall in.'

'Asking for a friend,' Rena shouted, making a joke of it for anyone who might be listening.

'Later.'

Cam took the boat past the gap a couple of times, and Rena could see him assessing the current, picking a line. Then he pulled the boat away, swung it in a tight arc, and powered them into the heart of the maelstrom. Just when Rena thought they were going straight through, Cam made another adjustment and the boat sat there, right in the centre, holding its place like the eye of a storm. Rena watched as he held the wheel steady, his hands twitching and tweaking as the currents tried to pull them in all directions. It looked like Cam was hardly doing anything, evidence of his skill as a skipper. Then he gunned the engines, and they roared into Talbot Bay.

Another boat was out there, its skipper waiting at a safe distance for a run at the falls. The passengers, in that strange, universal manner of travelling camaraderie, began waving and calling hellos to the passengers on Rena's boat.

Rena hated that sort of shit and was happy to leave the reciprocal bonhomie to others. But she turned to look at the other boat, interested to see a transit through the falls from this perspective.

And her stomach dropped.

'Shit,' she muttered, sliding down in her seat. Aitch was leaning forward and hadn't noticed, but her position provided cover, blocking Rena from view.

Rena could feel her heart beating, hard and fast, and not because of the white-water ride. Sitting in the other boat, looking for all the world like innocent tourists, were Adam and Mike.

What were the odds? Rena thought back over their interactions. The men had seemed...normal. Like regular people, only with a big, expensive motor home. Very expensive. She'd always considered herself a good judge of character, but Rena was the first to admit she'd not been herself since losing Tom. Even so, could she really be so wrong about Adam and Mike? Were they here to rendezvous with Marty Kinnane?

'Double shit.'

'You okay, Rena?' Cam was watching her.

'Yeah. Fill you in when we get back.' Rena gave him a thumbs-up.

'Sure?'

Rena nodded, but didn't bother with a reply because Cam was looking away, attention on the twenty-metre-wide passage through the rock, and had opened the throttle once more.

Back on the houseboat, Rena and Aitch settled in for a drink on the deck. They chose a spot away from the rest of the overnight tourists that gave them a good view of the falls on their right, as well as the broad expanse of Talbot Bay. To the west, the sun was getting close to the horizon, colouring the sky pink and orange, chasing the ocean with gold.

Rena wanted to explain her earlier behaviour, but Cam had been bailed up by a couple of chatty guests who seemed determined to relate every boating story they had, despite the evident strain in his customer service smile. When he finally managed to extricate himself, Rena and Aitch were ready. Hauling themselves up from the low divan, they went to meet Cam as he stepped onto the dock.

'Where does that other boat belong, the one that was out there at the same time as us?' Rena could hear the tension in her own voice.

'It's one of ours,' said Cam. 'As well as this baby'—he slapped the railing he was leaning against—'the company has a small ultra-luxe houseboat complete with a gourmet chef and, of course, a boat of its own. It's moored up Cyclone Creek. You can see the mouth of the creek there.' He gestured to the southeast, where the darkening waters disappeared into another submerged valley.

'So it's another group of people staying overnight, like us?' Rena ran a hand around the back of her neck.

'Well, they're paying more for the five-star experience, but yeah. Why?' Cam frowned.

'I'll get to that. Where does Cyclone Creek go?'

'I've never pushed right up there. I mean, some of us that live and work out here in the season go crabbing up that way, but never right up the creek. It twists and turns its way back into the McLarty Range.'

'So maybe someone could follow the creek the other way? Use it as a path through the ranges and down to Talbot Bay?'

'Geez, I dunno. I guess. Where's all this coming from all of a sudden?'

'I saw two people on that boat that I know. Or rather, two people I met in Fitzroy Crossing, who told me they were travelling, just like me.' She shrugged.

'Holy shit,' said Aitch, turning to look across the bay at the entrance to Cyclone Creek. 'You think they're in on it?'

'I—' Rena shook her head. 'I have no idea. It's probably nothing. Just gave me a turn to see them here after everything.'

'I bet it did. Did they see you?'

'Don't think so. If they did, they pretended not to.'

'So now what? Should I tell the boss, bring the other crew members in on this whole thing?' asked Cam.

They were still standing next to his boat, trying to look relaxed, like they were talking about nothing.

Rena considered Cam's suggestion. It was tempting, but she knew how those things went. She gestured to one of the uniformed crew, currently cleaning a boat, then pointed to another tidying the lounge area and setting out jugs of water and juice.

'How well do you know all these people?' she asked. 'Do you trust them?'

'Some really well, worked with them for years. Others, it's their first season and...' Cam held out a hand, palm down, and rocked it from side to side.

'If it's just a coincidence Mike and Adam are here, if there is even the slightest chance that Marty's contact is one of the crew, we can't risk it. A heads-up from the cops is one thing, but if you make noise, we give away the fact that Aitch and I are here.'

'What about if I just tell the boss, or one or two people? Extra eyes, extra muscle, extra security?'

Rena shook her head. 'When I used to work in remote locations with groups of people, telling one person something basically meant sticking a poster on the notice board. Human nature. You're all living in close proximity. If you tell one of your mates, he'll tell one of his, and everyone will know within the hour. If we clue your boss in, he may feel it's his responsibility to tell the whole crew.'

Cam didn't say anything, but his face spoke volumes.

'Look, Cam, we didn't mean to drag you into this; hell, this isn't even your fight. But the man killed a friend of Aitch's plus one of mine. And then he tried to murder a third person, another friend.' As Rena said it, she realised it was true. She didn't just feel responsible for Bob Fletcher, for drawing him out to that remote place on her quest to find the diamonds; she actually considered him a friend.

Aitch slapped Cam on the shoulder. 'Chances are he won't turn up here.'

'You need me. I can keep an eye out and be ready to cast off if anything happens.' Cam stuck his jaw out. 'Even if he's all the way out here in the middle of Talbot Bay in a little dinghy and there's fuck-all swell, do either of you know how to pilot a boat?'

Rena and Aitch exchanged a glance.

'Right. So, what, he'd cruise past while you yelled *Stop, thief* at him? Then phone the cops, who'd notify water police or the coast guard, who'd scramble a boat or a chopper, which would get here an hour or so later at the earliest—assuming it was available—by which time—'

'He'd be gone, and we'd be up shit creek.' Rena finished the sentence.

FORTY-FOUR

In the end, Cam volunteered to sleep on his boat, leaving Rena and Aitch to keep watch. It meant he was at the precarious mid-point between being actively involved and just happening to be in the right place at the right time should they need a fast boat. They also agreed that Cam should alert one of his colleagues working on the luxe houseboat, just in case.

'After all,' said Aitch, 'Kinnane is such a slippery bastard. What if he passes the stones to them then pisses off back into the bush? They'll leave, and we'll be none the wiser.'

Rena knew it was the right decision, but it also felt like both relinquishing control and possibly screwing things up entirely. In the end, Aitch suggested they spin a yarn, tell Cam's mate that Adam and Mike had been overheard talking about borrowing a boat and taking off with a couple of bottles of booze for a night trip. It was enough of a story to ensure the men would be observed closely and prevented from straying more than a dozen steps from their cabin, but also—as Cam pointed out—not the stupidest thing a tourist had tried to do around here. Which made it entirely plausible.

Rena hoped she was wrong about the men. Not only had she liked Mike and Adam; if they were involved, there was a good chance Marty would simply vanish back into the Kimberley, and Rena would never see the diamonds, let alone have the satisfaction of making Marty fucking Kinnane pay.

Out to the west, the massive, orange orb of the sun sank into the ocean, setting on the day, and on their uneasy, half-arsed plan.

The moon wasn't quite full, but it was large enough to provide a good deal of ambient light, reflecting off the water and bathing the rising coastal cliffs in a ghostly bluish glow.

Dinner had been eaten several hours ago, the wild-caught barramundi tasting like nothing to Rena, her water glass repeatedly drained and refilled, more as a result of preoccupation than any desire to keep hydrated. Some of their fellow guests were still taking advantage of the mild spring evening to sit on the deck and revel in their night on a houseboat in the Kimberley, a night never to be repeated, never to be forgotten.

Rena sat at the back—or what would constitute the stern should this floating edifice ever be cast loose from its moorings—and gazed out across the still water. She didn't focus exclusively on the darker space between the rock faces but tried to take in the fuller picture. The lights of other vessels dotted the bay. On some there was only a single lamp to mark the boat's location; in others multiple lights shone, laughter and voices travelling across the rippling water to Rena, mocking her solitude.

At least such sailing parties could be discounted: It was the quiet boats Rena suspected, the places from which someone might embark to rendezvous with Marty. She wasn't stupid; she knew another boat could slip into the bay under the cloak of darkness, eschewing running lights in favour of stealth. But she could hear no engines, no soft put-put of an outboard, no plop of an oar.

The cruise ship was still there, a scattering of lights glowing on deck and from its myriad windows and portholes. The irregular array looked to Rena like a patch of starry night sliced from above and dropped into the water. She felt sorry for the people on board. No doubt they were enjoying themselves, but they were cocooned within the ship and the cruise itself, unable to see what lay beyond their floating universe.

Rena inhaled, drawing in the scents of ocean and land. Here the brine was the predominant smell—salt, ozone, the piscine tang of seaweed and fish. Above that, the lingering top note of eucalyptus and dry earth, faint but pervasive.

Aitch was on the other side of the houseboat, tucked in a corner where she could see some of the water, but all access to the crew quarters. If someone stepped out at night, Aitch would know about it.

Rena was hoping if anything happened, Aitch would be too far away. She had been glad of the company and—when the shit hit the fan—of Aitch's cool, capable response. But that was before they knew Marty was alive, before Bob was shot. She didn't know why she was so certain Marty would come this way, but she was. If not tonight, then tomorrow or the next, but Rena knew eventually he'd turn up, and when he did, she didn't want anyone else in the line of fire.

Unlike the others, Rena had nothing to lose.

Marty's continued existence and the possibility of him getting away with murder filled her with rage. Why did people like that get to live when jewels like Tom, who never hurt a fly, who did so much good, who loved and was loved in return, were taken?

Rena would stop Marty or die trying.

FORTY-FIVE

He came with the dawn.

Rena had given up and was thinking about a second night on the houseboat, when out on the water, something moved. According to the charts Cam had shown her, low tide had occurred about three and a half hours ago, which meant the time of slack water had passed, and the outgoing flow was pushing back into Talbot Bay, already creating pressure in the first gap, building on itself minute by minute.

She'd spent the night alternating between quietly prowling the deck and sitting in a hard plastic chair, which at least helped to keep her awake. The chair was tucked against a wall, and Rena had been leaning back, resting her head against the cool surface, when she felt the hairs on her arms stand up. Hunching forward in her seat, Rena looked out across the water towards the gap in the range, only discernible because it was slightly less black than its surrounds.

She strained her hearing, listening for whatever it was that had caught her attention. Maybe nothing more than a croc surfacing. All around her silence pressed down, then gradually, she recognised again the noises that had been the soundtrack to her night: the gentle bump of boat against the dock, the lap of rippling water, the susurrating flow moving from embayment to bay as the turning tide began to gain momentum.

Rena could hear nothing anomalous.

Quietly, she stood and moved to the end of the dock. She kept low, worried about standing out against the whiteness of the houseboat, its faint lights not enough to capture her in full, but possibly enough to throw her shadowy form into stark relief.

She waited, watching.

There! Again no sound, but a small piece of moving night, a darker shape on the scintillating water. Too big for a crocodile and travelling in the wrong direction to be one of the passengers of a private boat, out for a spot of fishing or to catch the majesty of the dawning sun from outside the Horizontal Falls.

Rena couldn't call Aitch without waking everybody, and there was no way she was going to waste time tracking her down, only to possibly put her in danger. If she could've left Cam out of it as well, she would have, but it was true what the skipper had said: Rena could sit here while Marty—assuming it was Marty out there—went past, or when the moment presented itself, she could quietly rouse Cam and set off in pursuit.

Now all Rena had to do was wait a little longer and see what actually emerged from the gloom.

Finally she heard it, barely more than the soft splash of a fish rising, flipping and descending again, but once she had it, the sound became clear to her. A slow, rhythmic disturbance of the water. The sound of a paddle dipping in, out. In, out.

This was it.

Rena felt suddenly alive, buzzing as though electricity was coursing through her system. Marty was taking it slow, presumably trying for stealth over speed. Where was he heading? She could wait a bit longer, see where he went and hopefully expose his local contacts, running the risk of losing Marty all together. Or Rena could act now. Intercept him, let the collaborators get off scot-free, but recover the diamonds and nab Kinnane. The murdering prick.

It wasn't a difficult decision.

FORTY-SIX

Rena slowly eased her way along the dock to Cam's boat.

Around her, the day was growing lighter minute by minute. Rena fought the urge to hurry, to shout. She raised her head over the edge of the boat.

Cam was awake, already at the helm, staring straight at Rena.

'You hear it?' he hissed.

Rena nodded. She stepped onto the boat and moved down to join Cam.

'You reckon it's him?' Cam was staring out across the water now, neck turtled forward as though the extra couple of inches would render Marty visible.

'Who else?' Rena murmured. 'He must've had a portable kayak with him. Pretty ballsy.'

'Ballsy's right. No word from Cyclone Creek, which means he came through the falls.'

They fell silent, and Rena thought about Marty's plan, which was both clever and audacious, and how satisfying it was going to be if they could fuck it up for him.

Their boat rocked slightly, and then Aitch was standing beside them.

'Waiting for me?' Her voice was low, but the rhythmic plop of Marty's oar abruptly ceased.

A bird took off from somewhere on the nearest rocky ridge with a loud fluttering of wings, and in the quiet that followed, Rena became aware of another sound. Moving water.

Marty had timed his pass through the falls well, but now the tide had really turned, surging back into Talbot Bay and the water beyond.

Somewhere in front of them, Marty resumed paddling.

'What's the plan?' Cam's words were barely a sigh.

'You got a spotlight on this thing?'

'Jumbo torch is the best I can do.' Cam reached down, fumbled for a moment then pressed a large marine torch into Rena's hand. 'It's bright and throws light a good four hundred metres or so.'

'Let's go get him then,' said Aitch.

'Wait. What exactly are we going to do? Do you really think he's going to chuck in the towel now?' Rena ran her hand over the torch, feeling for the on-off switch, then looked at the sky. In a few minutes, it would be light enough to reveal Marty's position, but the spotlight was vital. They needed to see him clearly: Rena had been shot at once. This time she wanted plenty of warning if Marty pulled a gun. Rena planned to light him up like a Christmas tree and watch his hands at all times.

'We didn't get to this point to just sit on our arses.' Aitch shrugged. 'And he's on his way to somewhere.'

'The moment I start this, the whole houseboat will be awake. Not to mention half the people on other boats in the bay. If he's dangerous, once we go, we have to go fast,' said Cam.

'Right. This is all I've got, so feel free to make your own suggestions or ad lib. Aitch casts off, I get ready with the light, and Cam fangs it out into the bay. Get in front of him, cut him off from wherever the fuck he's going.'

'And then what?' Aitch's voice was slightly louder now, but they'd passed the point of caution.

'Damned if I know.'

'Maybe if he doesn't see the pair of you, he won't suspect anything.' Cam flipped a couple of switches on the console in front of him. 'Hunker down, and I'll try the polite approach.'

Rena looked at Aitch.

'Worth a try. At least that way we might get close,' said Aitch.

Rena sighed. 'Do it. Just watch for a gun.'

FORTY-SEVEN

Rena and Aitch sat on opposite sides of the deck, slumped down as low as possible, and Cam got the boat underway. Other than feeling the movement as they slid through the water, Rena had absolutely no idea what was happening.

It was driving her nuts.

She looked back at Cam, head and torso visible at the helm, and at the same moment, heard the engines throttle down.

'G'day, mate!' Cam was looking to his right, and in the dawning light, Rena could see he had a smile on his face. To Rena it looked pretty tense, but Cam's voice sounded steady.

Rena strained her ears, listening for a response.

A masculine mutter, the words indecipherable.

'Haven't seen you hereabouts. Which boat are you on?' Cam was doing his best.

'Over there.' This time Rena heard the answer clear as day.

'Which one?'

Careful, Rena thought.

'Only it's still early and the sun's barely up. Would you like me to escort you back? Just to be safe.'

'I'm fine.' There was an angry bite to the words.

'Sure? These waters—'

'Just piss off and leave me alone!' Marty's voice was loud; while they were talking, Cam must've brought the boat really close. It sounded as though Marty was right alongside, just beyond the hull where Rena was currently hiding.

And now Rena could hear something else, a low droning sound that seemed to come from somewhere inland, rapidly getting louder.

The noise resolved into a clear rotor slap, just as a helicopter appeared, flying low over the nearest ridge. For a second Rena was puzzled; it was too early for scenic flights. It altered course slightly, heading straight for them, and now she could see the word *Police* written across the nose of the chopper.

From across the boat, Aitch caught her eye, a deep, puzzled frown creasing her brow. 'Ito?' she mouthed.

Rena shrugged in response.

Cam was leaning sideways, trying to look up at the helicopter as it slowed its forward movement, hovering overhead. From where she sat, Rena could see people looking down at them. She grabbed at her baseball cap, feeling the downdraft and the increased rocking of their boat.

'Martin Kinnane!' An anonymous voice boomed from above.

For a moment nothing happened, then the boat rocked violently, and Marty was there, hauling himself over the side a few metres away from where Rena was now scrambling to get to her feet.

They locked eyes, and Rena saw surprise bloom across the man's face, but before she could do anything, Marty had the gun in his hand. Perhaps it had always been there.

'Shit,' Rena swore. She'd been distracted by the police helicopter—they all had. Except for Marty fucking Kinnane.

'Put down the weapon!' Ito's voice, distorted by the chopper's loud-hailer.

Without looking away from the people in the boat, Marty raised the gun above his head and fired in the general direction of the police chopper, before lowering his arm and sweeping it from Cam to Aitch to Rena. The helicopter tilted away like an old man with slow reflexes then found a new position, a little higher, a bit further removed, still hovering.

From the corner of her eye, Rena could see people appearing on the houseboat, stumbling from cabins and holding up mobile phones to record whatever the hell they were about to witness.

'Marty,' she said.

'I thought you were dead.' The gun was still pointed at Rena, the hand that held it rock steady.

'There's a bit of that going around.'

'What the fuck were you even doing out there? Out here?'

'Holiday.'

Rena studied Marty's face. He looked haggard, sunburned, bearded, sunken-cheeked, but his eyes blazed with the fever of desperation, of the prospect of seeing millions slip away at the final hurdle. A narrow, padded strap was visible over his left shoulder, a messenger bag or backpack hanging out of sight, its contents presumably worth millions.

'What say you call it quits, hey?' Rena took a small, cautious step forward.

'Fuck that.' The gun rose slightly, and Rena stopped. She tried to keep her posture loose and relaxed. Mrs Unthreatening, just a pensioner.

'Mate. There's a bloody helicopter full of police literally over your head and probably a boatload on the way. And in case you haven't noticed, there's no easy road out of here. Come on.'

Marty jerked the barrel of the gun, flicking between Rena and Aitch then across to Cam. 'Move over there, both of you. Go and stand behind him.'

Aitch gave Marty a hard stare. 'Why'd you kill Tyse?'

Rena could hear the fury in her voice.

'Who?'

Aitch's face twisted, and she looked like she was about to launch herself across the boat. Rena stepped in front of her and put a hand on her chest, keeping it there until she felt an easing of tensed muscles. Aitch pulled in a breath.

'Tyse. The young man behind the wheel of your car.'

'Oh, him. Found him snooping barefoot around my camp. He told me he'd watched me digging and wanted to know what I was doing.' Marty shrugged. 'Didn't know what he'd seen or who he might tell. Plus it gave me a chance to disappear without Verne coming looking.'

'You prick.'

'Yeah, a prick with a gun. Now move.'

Rena had her back half to Marty, and now she gave Aitch a look—eyes wide, lips pressed—which she hoped conveyed a message of *Cool it; just wait*. The exchange between Aitch and Marty had acted as a distraction, and while it was going on, Rena also noticed the vibration of the boat increase a fraction. Cam had powered the engines up slightly, the change covered by the noise of the hovering helicopter. They were no longer holding their place in the bay. Instead, the boat was moving slowly towards the falls, gently pushing back against the outgoing tide.

Rena followed Aitch to the helm, raising her eyebrows at Cam as she moved past.

'Be ready to drop,' muttered Cam, his lips barely moving.

'Listen, Marty,' Rena raised her voice. 'I don't know where you were going in that kayak, but—'

'But now I have a decent boat that can get me out of here.'

'Not enough fuel to get very far,' said Cam.

'Don't need to go far. Just out of the bay.' Marty glanced at his watch. 'There's a seaplane coming to meet me.'

Rena laughed, hoping it didn't sound too forced. 'What? You don't think the police have closed this airspace?' She circled a hand over her head.

For the first time, Marty's expression wavered, a small crease appearing between his brows then vanishing, replaced by a sneer and a lip curl.

Rena was facing the falls, which were getting closer with every second. Although it wasn't yet anywhere near the strength it had been yesterday when Cam had run them through, Rena could see the water foaming and the current racing close to one rocky wall. She could still hear the chopper, but it sounded just a bit fainter now, perhaps unable to follow them close to the cliffs.

Hidden behind the console, she felt the pressure of Cam standing gently but firmly on her foot. Whatever the skipper was planning, Rena needed to hold Marty's attention.

'How about you put the gun down?' Rena stretched out a hand.

'How about you shut up?' Marty swung his arm to the side and fired a shot into the water.

Then the stern of the boat swung abruptly, caught by the stronger current near the gap. At the same moment Cam opened the throttle.

'Now!' yelled Cam, already twisting the wheel.

Rena shoved Aitch and they hit the deck together. Marty, still on his feet, was thrown off balance by the abrupt change and staggered backwards, his thighs hitting the boat's handrails. He was there for a moment, arms windmilling, bag and gun already gone, as he tried to maintain his equilibrium. Then Cam adjusted for the current, the boat shifted again, and Marty lost the battle.

Rena lunged forward, making a desperate grab for anything. Her hand closed around Marty's ankle but the force of the water was immense, dragging her toward the rail. Tom's face flashed into her mind, and she smiled.

Someone seized the waistband of her shorts. 'Let it go!' Aitch shouted in her ear.

She hung on a moment longer, fighting the drag, then Marty's ankle was ripped from her grasp and he was gone. Rena and Aitch fell to the deck.

Rena lay there for a moment, catching her breath. feeling the boat settle as they motored away from the current's force. Then she pushed herself to her knees and turned to Cam. 'Where's he likely to come up?' she shouted.

Aitch had hauled herself into a seat and was scanning the water racing through to Talbot Bay, but Cam just shook his head. He swung the boat through a broad, gentle curve.

'He probably won't. The current's sucked him under and the pressure… He's already dead.'

'He can't just ride it out?' Rena clambered to her feet, chest still heaving.

Cam laughed, a grim, humourless sound. 'Not only will he be crushed by the water pressure, there's a fair chance we'll never even find a body.'

'Crocs? Sharks?'

Cam shook his head again. 'Nup. It's about forty metres deep, and there are caves down there, nooks and crannies eroded by that.' He gestured towards the white water surging through the gap. 'Sucks you in there—or rather your lifeless, crushed corpse—and that's that. No time for crocs.'

'Shit.' Rena dropped heavily into the seat next to Aitch.

'Hang on,' called Cam, and the nose of the boat lifted as he took them back to the blue waters and sunshine of Talbot Bay.

FORTY-EIGHT

Ito pulled up a chair. She'd positioned herself on the other side of the table from Rena and Aitch, but there was no formality to it. They were on a border force patrol boat, which had arrived in Talbot Bay not long after their final trip through the falls. Outside on the water, two ABF tenders, together with numerous private boats, were still sweeping the waters on both sides of the falls where Marty had gone in.

So far, as Cam predicted, there had been no sign.

'What changed your mind about Marty coming here?' Rena had her hands wrapped around a thick white coffee mug.

Ito sighed. 'I still can't believe he tried it. But to answer your question, after we'd put out the BOLO for Kinnane, we got a call from a pilot. He runs a seaplane charter and he had a booking that set off alarm bells.'

'Marty?'

'Pick up in Talbot Bay and drop off at a boat anchored somewhere near Cockatoo Island.'

'Cockatoo Island? Iron ore mining.' Rena nodded.

'Actually, there's also a resort for rich folk on the other side of the island. Alan Bond built it.' Ito raised her own mug and took a sip.

'You're kidding.' Aitch had her chair pushed back from the table and was sprawled, legs extended, hands folded on her stomach. She looked exhausted.

'Sadly not. But that was what tipped the pilot off. Resort's closed. No reason to go there. He was smart enough to tally his bad feeling with our search for Marty Kinnane and so...' Ito gestured, taking in their surroundings.

'He said he killed Tyse to keep him from talking,' said Aitch.

Ito's mug clattered against the table. 'We found Eric and his story checks out. He said he'd been with Tyse, that Tyse would often take off his shoes to feel the earth. They split up, and then all Eric could find was the shoes.'

Aitch's head dropped forward and her shoulders shuddered.

'I'm so, so sorry, Aitch,' Rena said.

They waited, giving Aitch the time she needed. After a few minutes her breathing settled and she sat up, dragged a hand across her face and pulled her chair closer to the table.

'Sorry,' she said.

'There's no apology for grieving.' Rena reached out and wrapped an arm around Aitch's shoulders.

'What now?' asked Aitch.

'Fletcher's on the mend, and there'll be an inquiry into the shooting when he's up to it. Plus formal reports and inquests for Tyse and Wally, and of course for—'

'Yeah, don't say his name. I'm sick of hearing it, and frankly it shouldn't be spoken.'

Ito nodded.

'Are you arresting anyone else?'

'Investigations are ongoing.' Ito gave them a wry smile. 'But I doubt it. Chuck doesn't appear to be directly involved, and although we haven't gotten to the boat out at Cockatoo Island yet, that looks like a charter.'

Rena thought of Mike and Adam. She was sorry she'd doubted them, but she pushed the guilt aside with a mental shrug. Life was too short for energy-sapping emotions.

'And what about—'

There was a sharp knock on the door and a man dressed in a navy-blue jumpsuit came in and bent close to Ito, murmuring something in her ear. Ito looked up, eyes wide.

'It appears that one of the search boats has found something.'

'Marty?'

'A messenger bag.'

The officer retreated, closing the door quietly in his wake. For a moment the only sound in the room was the faint buzz of the ceiling light. Then Ito cleared her throat.

'There's a tin. Could you...? We need to verify the contents.'

Rena pushed back her chair and stood, a spasm of pain suddenly reminding her of her injured leg. She leaned on the table, feeling old but somehow, not as old as she'd felt last week.

'Sounds like you need a geologist. Let me show you what two million dollars' worth of pink diamonds looks like.'

EPILOGUE

Rena hadn't seen Aitch for two days. They'd arrived back in the Crossing, exhausted, and parted on a long, silent hug. Rena wanted to think, and she knew Aitch needed space to breathe. It had been one thing to suspect Tyse was dead, but Rena knew when faced with the loss of someone you loved, the heart always held hope. Then reality grabbed you by the throat and screamed the truth in your face.

It was time for Rena to move on. She'd sent Aitch a text, but in the absence of a response she had gone about her preparations, checking tyres and restocking the Ranger. She had said goodbye to Jo at the bakery—coming away with bags of biscuits and a couple of doorstop-sized sandwiches Jo had pressed on her *for the drive*—and squared things with Ito. Now, in the relative cool of a Kimberley morning, she was sitting behind the wheel, windows down, engine off, phone in hand, staring at Aitch's number.

She hadn't wanted to phone Aitch, hadn't want to intrude on her grief and time with Tyse's family and friends, but Rena could feel the horizon beckoning her forward: She needed to leave. Her thumb hovered over the Call button.

The passenger door opened, and Aitch slid in beside her.

'Thought I might have missed you,' she said.

'Nah, too disorganised.' Rena studied Aitch's face, seeing facets and planes that hadn't been there before, carved by both wisdom and loss.

'Bull.' Aitch smiled.

'How are you doing?'

'I'll get there.' Aitch shrugged. 'Besides, there are others who…'

'Yeah, I know.'

They sat in silence, staring through the dusty windscreen at the road ahead.

Finally, Aitch turned her body to face Rena. 'So. What now? What are your plans?'

'I was thinking about Ningaloo, swimming with the whale sharks. It was something Tom always wanted to do.'

'Then you should definitely do that.'

Rena nodded. Last week just the thought of ticking off Tom's bucket list would have overwhelmed her, but…something had changed inside her. She didn't know what exactly—that remained intangible—but she felt lighter. It was enough for now.

'You want to come?' she asked.

Aitch shook her head.

'Another time then.'

'Another time.'

'After Ningaloo, I'm heading straight down the coast to Perth. Bob Fletcher is on the mend, but he's got a way to go. I want to tell him what happened and let him know he's not as alone as he thinks he is.'

'Alone? He's probably sweet-talking every nurse and female doctor in the place!'

'Well, you know I'm not too shabby as a wingwoman.'

Aitch tried and failed to hide a broad grin. 'Go on then; you've got a long drive ahead of you.'

'And all the time in the world.'

Rena leaned across the centre console and embraced Aitch in a tight hug, feeling the other woman's arms come around her too.

They sat that way for a moment, until Aitch finally pulled away and dashed a finger under each eye.

'Will I see you again?' she asked.

'You have my number and if you call, I'll always answer. I won't necessarily be just around the corner, but you and I have travelled a distance together, so I reckon you can never get rid of me now. Not really. Oh, and besides, you need to look after this for me.'

Rena pulled something from the pocket of her shirt and dropped it into Aitch's waiting hand.

Aitch looked, and the tiny diamond flashed violet in the sunlight.

'Rena…'

'Just remember. That's what intense pressure does; it makes diamonds.'

Aitch nodded, closed her fist around the stone then bent close and kissed Rena on the cheek. 'See you,' she said. 'Safe travel.'

She was out of the Ranger before Rena could reply.

Rena watched Aitch in the rearview mirror until she was gone, then started the engine and pulled away.

For the first time since she began to travel, she was excited, anticipating the possibilities, eager for what lay ahead. But for now, there was only Rena and the road.

It felt…right.

ACKNOWLEDGMENTS

If there is one person I can never thank enough, it's my wonderful agent, Grace Heifetz at a4 Literary: hand-holder, voice of reason, cheer squad, and friend. Thank you for embracing my grey nomad with such gusto, and for everything you do each day to keep this show on the road. You are a powerhouse!

Thank you also to Diane DiBiase, Beth Deveny, and all the team at Sourcebooks. It is always such a delight working with you (even when we're trying to translate odd Australian terms into something that makes sense at your end). I feel so lucky to be part of the Sourcebooks family.

I would've been lost without the generous assistance of Grant Pearson, materials scientist and gemologist. Grant answered all my questions about diamond colour and formation in great detail and with unflagging enthusiasm. Thank you so much, Grant. Any errors are mine!

Finally, a huge thank-you to all the people, locals and travellers alike, who I met and talked to in the Kimberley. Your knowledge, passion for the land, and the stories you shared were a gift. You helped me to see the country in ways I never could have imagined.

ABOUT THE AUTHOR

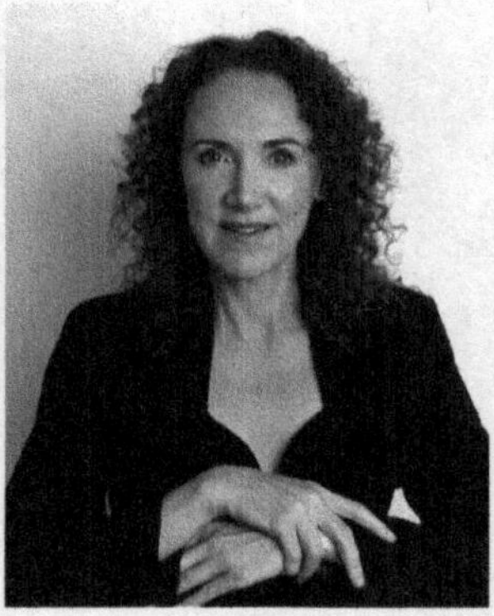

© Rebecca Taylor Photography

Katherine Kovacic lives with her dogs in Melbourne, Australia, and is the author of many books and short stories. Her 2023 thriller, *Seven Sisters/Kill Yours, Kill Mine,* was shortlisted for an Australian Crime Writers Association Award for Best Crime Fiction and is currently being translated into several other languages.

You can connect with Katherine on Instagram or find out more at katherinekovacic.com.